Miki's Mad

ALSO BY GEORGE TANABE

NON-FICTION

Japanese Buddhist Temples in Hawaii: An
Illustrated Guide (2012)
with Willa Jane Tanabe

Sources of Japanese Tradition, Volume One:
From Earliest Times to 1600, Second Edition
(2001)
with Wm. Theodore de Bary, Donald Keene,
and Paul Varley

Religions of Japan in Practice (1999)

Practically Religious: Worldly Benefits and the
Common Religion of Japan
with Ian Reader (1998)

Myoe the Dreamkeeper (1992)

The Lotus Sutra in Japanese Culture (1989)
with Willa Jane Tanabe

Miki's Mad

GEORGE TANABE

DEUXMERS

Published by Deuxmers, LLC
PO Box 437305, Kamuela, HI 96743
deuxmers.com

Printed in the United States of America.
ISBN: 978-1-944521-21-9 (Softcover)
ISBN: 978-1-944521-22-6 (Ebook)
First edition, March 2024

CONTENTS

BLACK KARMA

A GRAY AND WHITE CAT ARCHED ITS BACK, PUSHED ITS front paws forward and dropped from the open porch to the gravel path by the pond ringed with ice slivers already moistured by the morning sun. It shook its fur, puffing it out, walked through the open gate to the hardpack road and headed to Bungo Bridge leading into the ancient bamboo grove. Neighbors would ordinarily have been out, sweeping the street and setting up stands to sell sandals, umbrellas and pickled vegetables to travelers on their way to Kyoto, but on that cold January morning of 1868, rumors had emptied the street and the cat trotted quickly across the bridge before the children could run out, grab it by its neck and scold it for trying to enter the Forever Forest.

The cat walked past the only stalk allowed to grow in the middle of the road, revered for the divine *kami* living in its thick hollow, coated on the outside with a fine powder no one dared to dust off unless they were stupid enough to touch the untouchable. Even the cat chose to rub itself on a lesser sapling, then stopped, sniffed the air and moved forward with half-steps. It stopped again, adjusted its sight to the lacey shadows and saw a pair of eyes staring out from under a pile of dried leaves. The cat sniffed its way closer, meowing a few feet away from the stranger, a fourteen-year-old samurai attendant, who tried to shoo the cat away by glaring at it. *Chikusho*! *Stupid cat*! The forward scout had just returned moments earlier, nearly stumbling over the boy and reported in a whisper that the advancing enemy soldiers, only twenty minutes away, still did not suspect an ambush. The cat meowed louder and stepped closer to the boy, who looked at Master Yoshida crouching behind a large boulder and saw him draw his index finger slowly across his neck. The boy pushed his sword under the leaves in front of him, turned its cutting edge up, let the cat come within range, then jerked the sword upward and sliced off its head, dropping it to the ground with barely an audible gurgle. Master Yoshida's disciple had scored a perfect, truly elegant, first kill.

An icy breeze swept through, knocking the bamboo stalks together in an unordered clacking of hollow sounds. Gombei Taga released his sword and shoved his hands under his stomach, then put his head down to ease the pain in his shoulders and neck. In the privacy of the frozen earth, he gave in to silent tears and stretched tightly to keep his shivering from becoming a panic rising from the blood draining from his head, down and out, seemingly through his feet. He wiped his eyes, trying to erase the image of his father, himself a fencing master in the service of the ruler of Iwakuni on the western coast of the Inland Sea.

A swordsman gains honor by killing enemy warriors, Father had said, but should he take innocent life, then he must die. Gombei reached out and gripped his sword, still coated with the blood of the cat, surely an enemy cat, whose innocence had been compromised, no, obliterated, by its threat of exposing his hidden position. Damn cat! Gombei had done what he had to do, what he was meant to do, what Master Yoshida had ordered. He shoved his sword under some leaves again and prayed that the burning from his stomach rising to his throat would not be followed by the remains of his morning meal of boiled barley and pickled plums.

When the thirty warriors from Iwakuni had been taking up their positions in the grove, Master Yoshida himself had covered Gombei with dried leaves and spoke reassuring words. "Trust your training and you'll be all right. This is your first battle, so stay close to me. Remember that we fight for Emperor Meiji and we will destroy the shogun's guards. Miserable traitors." Master Yoshida commanded the combined force of traditional samurai and modern infantry armed with muzzle loading rifles and revolving pistols. Knowing that the shogun's guards likewise mixed the old with the new, he had positioned his men according to whether they fought with blades or bullets.

Gombei rested his neck again, then forced himself to look out over the ground—how else would he see the enemy, soon to arrive at any moment? Master Yoshida was a specialist in the art of reconnaissance, a new term for what used to be called spying, and was an expert in detecting enemy scouts. It would not be hard to spot them since anyone approaching the grove had to pass through the small settlement of families, then cross Bungo Bridge before entering the grove. Gombei and Master Yoshida were closest to the bridge, hiding so that the enemy would rush past them before they jumped out to seal any attempt to escape by retreat. Gombei struggled to remember his training.

Their eyes, Master Yoshida had said repeatedly, watch their eyes. They can mask everything else, but not their eyes. Gombei cleared away some leaves, pressed one ear to the exposed earth, forcing himself to bear the cold; all the better, Master Yoshida had said, to hear footsteps when the ground is frozen solid. They're coming! Oh, yes, they're coming! A dozen, no, fifty, maybe a thousand soldiers all marching in step to the beatings of a racing heart. One of them will come running up to me and stop, plant his feet in a challenge, sword angled toward my head. His eyes, Master Yoshida had said, when you face your opponent, watch his eyes … and lips. He will stare at you, sword at ready and when his eyes widen ever so slightly, he will fix his glare and tighten his lips and that is when you know he will strike. You must never give yourself away; keep your own face blank by emptying your mind of all thoughts. When fish escape, they dodge and dart, they do not think. When the *mamushi* snake is ready to attack, it coils itself like a spring and does not think. Thinking slows your action, betrays your strategy across your face. Do not think. Do not think. So much to remember! So little time! They're coming, a million angry boots stomping the frozen ground. Oh yes, stance, almost forgot, right foot forward, knee bent but not too much, back straight, firm grip but not tight and do not think, do not think. Wait. Did the cat just open its eyes? Is that head still alive? Gombei blinked to clear his tears, then saw the little girl walking toward him, calling for her lost cat.

She was five or six years old, her brown and yellow striped kimono tied loosely with a hemp cord, a white cotton pouch hanging around her neck. "Bungo Bridge" was written in black ink on the face of the pouch; "Miki," her name, below it. In her innocence, she looked brave, walking into a grove full of warriors coiled like springs. Miki spotted her cat, stopped and leaned forward to get a better look as she tried to comprehend the bloody separation of the head from its body. Gombei glared, *Go back! Go back!* but she kept coming closer and Master Yoshida signaled Gombei again, drawing his finger across his neck.

Gombei shook his head. *But she's just a child, a baby sister!* She stopped, covered her mouth with her tiny hands, just as a grown woman would in horror and Gombei looked at Master Yoshida, who was slicing his finger furiously back and forth across his neck. He glared at Gombei, mouthed a silent curse, then drew out his sword and shifted his gaze to the girl.

Gombei jumped from his cover and snatched the startled child. She started to scream, but he covered her mouth with his hand and ran to the aged camphor tree off to one side. "Shh, Miki, don't cry, you'll be all right," he whispered to the disbelieving girl. He heard Master Yoshida clicking his tongue like a bush cricket to signal the approach of the first enemy scout. Miki struggled and Gombei pressed his hand harder over her mouth and was surprised at how she kicked wildly in anger, not fear.

Thwack! The archer crouching next to Gombei behind the

large tree hit his mark, dead center in the throat of the unsuspecting scout, a perfect to-the-spine shot. The silence of the arrow still had a tactical advantage over the giveaway noise and flash of firearms. They waited for the rest. A minute … was it five? The enemy soldiers clattered over the bridge, saw their dead scout still gripping the feathered shaft with both hands and realized too late that they should not have entered the grove, which erupted in gunfire and warriors bursting out of their concealments. Gombei let go of Miki and ran back to his sword lying in the leaves. The Iwakuni infantrymen fired in volleys, taking turns to reload, shoving powder packets and bullets down muzzles as fast as they could. After the first two or three rounds, their orderly maneuver fell into a fire-at-will confusion and in the strugglings at close quarters, the swordsmen and lancers proved their worth equal to the modern gunners. The cries of the afflicted were all the same, lead slugs or steel blades making no difference in the sounds of wounding and killing. Master Yoshida rushed two reloading riflemen, taking away their advantage of distance and Gombei followed him with his sword, finally able to perform his duty of protecting his Master's back.

Holding his sword in his right hand, Gombei turned to his left just in time to see an enemy soldier staggering toward him, his chest shattered in a tangle of flesh and fabric. The falling rifleman's outstretched arm caught Gombei in the face, knocking him down. Gombei managed to shove the dead man off and thrashed the thick layer of leaves, trying to find his dropped sword. Master Yoshida pursued two guards fumbling to reload their time consuming rifles as they retreated backwards, bouncing their backs off bamboo and brush, not daring to take their eyes off Yoshida's upheld blade. One of them spun around and broke into a run, while the other veered to one side, threw his spent rifle on the ground, picked up a spear, circled around Yoshida and charged him from the back. Gombei screamed, apologizing for allowing the man to get between him and the Master and grabbed a cocked rifle from a dead enemy soldier, aimed it at the back of his master's assailant and pulled the trigger. The roaring kickback knocked Gombei flat and when he shook off his daze and picked himself up, he saw his victim writhing on the ground close to Master Yoshida lying still.

Gombei screamed again and ran up to the two bodies. The dying guard held his slimy guts in his hands, reasonably trying to stuff them back into the jagged hole torn open by the exiting slug. Master Yoshida was lying on his back, shot through his chest, a small hole spurting blood in slowing pulses. Like the girl trying to understand the separation of the cat from its head, Gombei tried to figure out what had happened. Had the fleeing rifleman managed to reload, turn around and shoot the Master? That was impossible since Gombei remembered seeing Master Yoshida wheel around to face his rear attacker just at the moment Gombei pulled the trigger. He looked down at the two bodies and saw the lineup: the bullet had gone right through the guard's back, tore out his belly and hit the Master in his heart. Gombei fell forward, his own weight suddenly unsupported by consciousness and when he came to, smeared with heavings of boiled barley and pickled plums, the battle was over.

It was a quick rout, as would be the rest of the short civil war. The Emperor's warriors would beat the shogun's guards in other battles, allowing Emperor Meiji to take back his power from the useless shogun. For over 250 years, the Tokugawa shoguns had ruled Japan in the name of their emperors, but in the age of American black ships powered by steam and armed with cannons, they proved to be pitiful weaklings unable to keep the western bastards out. Pressured to resign and give back his power to the Emperor, the shogun refused to admit failure and called the supporters of the Emperor rebels, and the rebels, calling themselves loyalists, had no choice but to overthrow the insurgent shogun by force. They would call it the Meiji Restoration and Japan would be a new nation, convinced of the wonders of western technology as the means to eastern supremacy.

The Iwakuni fighters leafed through the grove by Bungo Bridge and picked up the bodies of their comrades. Gombei wrapped Master Yoshida in a canvas cloth and helped place him on a wagon for the journey back to Iwakuni. He found his sword and finally had a chance to scrape off the drying blood of the cat.

On orders from Takamori Saigo, commander-in-chief of the forces fighting for the Emperor, the Iwakuni contingent assembled by Bungo Bridge. Saigo amply filled out his reputation as a strongman — tall, barrel chest, thick neck, mean eyes, booming voice. "I'm proud to tell you," he said to the twenty survivors," that the Emperor has officially named our coalition his Imperial Army. You fought with valor and deserve His Majesty's blessings." He walked past every soldier and thanked each one personally. He stopped in front of Gombei, considered the smell of vomit and asked, "Young man, who is your master?"

"Yoshida ... Master Yoshida."

"Ah yes, our best spy." He scanned the line for him.

"He was killed," Gombei explained, looking at his feet, wiping his eyes.

Saigo placed a fatherly hand on the boy's shoulder. "How?"

"Bullet ... bullet from ... an enemy rifle." Gombei spoke softly but he did not lie.

"And you, your name?"

"Taga..."

Saigo looked up at the rest of the soldiers and issued a command. "See to it that the Taga boy is cared for, that he returns home safely."

As they walked slowly out of the grove and passed the camphor tree, Gombei saw Miki lying unscathed and serene, staring forever into a sky unseen.

◆

Gombei's mother took one look at her son entering the garden gate and burst out crying. She saw the distance in his eyes, his fear of focusing. She dropped to her knees and welcomed him back but heard nothing in return. If only she could embrace him as a child, but he was returning as a samurai hardened by horrors he would not tell. She respected his reserve, his inner retreat and she guided him to a bench, made him sit and bent down to remove his sandals. "Welcome back," she said again, daring to rub his feet lightly, but he stared at things only he could see.

"Ah," said his father, appearing in the doorway, "welcome back! Glad to see you are alive. Iwakuni is proud of you, all of you, for the glorious victory you have brought home. Come in, come in. We have many matters to discuss, so many changes taking place. What a fine warrior you've become!"

Gombei followed his father into the family room and waited his turn to offer incense at the altar to their ancestors. He removed his sheathed sword from his sash and laid it next to his cushion. His father asked to inspect it, pulled the sword out from its scabbard slowly and raised the hilt to his forehead. Turning the cutting edge against the light, he read its signs of use, passing his master swordsman's thumb lightly against its sharpness.

He smiled. "I see that you struck … at least once." He noticed a spot of dried blood on the back edge and scrapped it off with his fingernail, unbothered that Gombei had missed it in his cleaning.

Gombei leaned forward a fraction and his father bowed deeply, the first time ever to his son in recognition of the daring of one so young. Gombei sat quietly as his father got up, left the room, then returned with a narrow brocade bag. He removed the bag and unsheathed the sword from its black and gold lacquered scabbard, exposing the wave pattern running the length of its cutting edge and the Buddhist deity Aizen engraved within a flaming halo at the hilt. With a metal chopstick, he punched out a small bamboo peg from the shark skinned handle, gave a sharp tap at its base to jar the blade loose and pulled the handle free. Incised on the unpolished tang was the name of the maker, Kiyomasa, and Chinese characters for "three bodies," certifying the number of stacked cadavers the sword had cut clean through in a single test swoop.

"This was used by my father and before that, his father and before that … your … great … great-grandfather. This is the Taga sword, passed down to each son after his first battle." He reassembled the sword, sheathed and bagged it, tying the silk straps in a neat ribbon and held it out horizontally with both hands. Gombei had no choice but to receive his legacy.

"Father … I struck with my sword, yes, but I … I should tell you … I must explain…"

"No," his father interrupted, stern once again. "A samurai never discloses the details of his kill. It is between you and your opponent and it must be kept that way. Speak of it and you dishonor the warrior, shaming him by telling others how he lost his life. Nothing can be more private between two men." He slipped Gombei's own sword back into its scabbard and returned it to him. "Two swords," he said proudly. "You have earned them both." Gombei looked down at the floor.

"*Oi!*" his father called out. "Sake! Bring some sake!"

Gombei's mother brought sake on a red lacquered tray, handed her husband a small cup and filled it to its golden brim. She turned to Gombei, being certain to block her husband's view and carefully dripped one drop into his cup. Gombei stared gratefully at his nearly empty cup and for the first time since his return, looked into his mother's face. Her eyes widened, ever so slightly and her lips, pressed together, spread in a faint smile. She filled her own cup, moved back and joined her husband in toasting their son.

"And now," she said, even before his father had lowered his cup, "it is time for Gombei to bathe and rest." She stood up, bent over to touch Gombei lightly on his elbow and led him out of the room, leaving his two swords by the cushion in front of the altar to the ancestors.

They walked down the long hallway and turned a corner. "Thank you …" Gombei said quietly, "thank you."

◆

"Mother?"

Gombei pulled the futon higher around his neck and listened to the cold clacking of the bamboo in the garden, the swishing curtains. She moved toward the sliding doors, which she should shut and would, for sure. Mother had that way of anticipating what needed to be done before he had to ask, even now, ten years later at twenty-four, he was a warrior but still her son.

"Mother?"

She sat on the threshold in the opening between the sliding doors. Against the sheen of the veranda polished by the moon, she was just an outline of crumpled kimono.

"Shut the doors. It's cold. Do I have to ask?"

She hummed a cat song.

Gombei jerked the covers over his head. Her humming moved closer, right next to his head. He pressed his palms together and pleaded. Please, please, you don't understand. It was a mistake. I told him you were just a baby sister. Really, I did. Go back to Bungo Bridge, go back to sleep. Under the camphor tree. It happened so long ago, enough time to forget.

But she reached under the futon anyway and pressed her small hand over his mouth, filling his lungs with the smell of camphor.

◆

Though the New Japan disbanded the samurai and replaced them with everyman soldiers armed with cheating weapons that roared with the pull of any unskilled finger, the Taga Academy of Fencing did well. Gombei's father had transformed the lethal tactics into an art of movement promoting comportment and mental discipline beneficial for students, businessmen, government officials and even women. Gombei maintained the equipment, repairing the breast plates, cleaning the webbed visors, polishing the wooden staves curved gently as swords but thick enough to withstand practice blows. The latest saying borrowed from English summed up his feelings about the school, soon to be passed on to him by his aging father: a *double-edged sword* keeping him busy in the present on one hand, but never letting him forget the past on the other. If you take an innocent life, then you must take your own. Time had erased the details of Bungo Bridge but fed his feelings about Miki and her cat.

Late one afternoon, Gombei walked to a rocky ledge rising straight up from the ocean. He watched the waves surge against the overhang, felt the sea spray against his face and decided it was the right spot. He took out the two swords, the three-body heirloom and his own cat killer, crossed his ankles and lowered himself into a sitting position, back straight. He placed the swords in front of him and slipped his arms out of his sleeves, pushing his cotton robe down his waist to expose his belly. Holding the swords in his lap, he inched forward until his knees jutted over the edge. Passing his left hand slowly across his navel, as if to swab his flesh clean, he leaned forward and looked down into the waves. Yes, the water was deep enough. He thought of Master Yoshida, the shogun's guard, the cat, and Miki, and he apologized to each of his victims individually. He begged forgiveness from his father and the rest of his ancestors. Gombei held the swords straight out in front of him and dropped them into the ocean.

He looked across the wrinkling water and watched the clouded sun sink into the sea. Every night the water puts the fire out, but the fire can never dry out the water during the day. I have had enough of swords forged in fire and now it is time for me to wash off my bad karma in the ocean and be reborn a new man, someone Miki will not recognize, even if she meets me. I will become a fisherman.

Gombei stripped down to his loincloth, pinched his nose, leaned forward and let himself tumble into the whitewashing sea.

11

DEATH BY FUGU

B Y 1880, WHEN HIS SON SHUZO WAS BORN, GOMBEI HAD
been blessed by the gift of forgetting. Not completely,
of course, but Miki visited less frequently and when
she did appear, most often at night or when he rested, which
is why he kept busy, she did not stay for long. She too was a
child of time, only hers was fixed and that was the reason
why she always tried to take him back to Bungo Bridge.

With a boat and dozens of shrimp traps, Gombei made a
comfortable living, enough to plan on having more children,
preferably sons. Shrimp made it possible to have a larger
family and more sons would mean more shrimp. He had his
own cornucopia and it was a much better means of making
a living than the way of killing men. Whenever he sailed by
the rocky ledge, he thought of his swords, by then nothing
but honorable rust. He tried not to think about his victims,
especially Miki, how she had struggled, unusually strong for
her age, defiant. Already he had convinced himself that he
had covered only her mouth, certainly not her nose, that she
had been able to breathe and was just sleeping, suspended
in an enchantment that would continue for as long as the
bamboo clacked softly in the wind, that she'd never awaken
from her life of slumber, because if she did, she would be
mad.

As for the others, they were dead souls, ghosts circling
somewhere in the heavens. He had killed them out of
righteous duty, even when it was by mistake, but the temple
priest said that killing, even of the honorable kind, brings

black karma and Gombei was sure that was why he and his wife Sumiko could not have more children. Gombei himself had been an only son, the lack of siblings a family curse, retribution against a line of warriors trained to kill in the name of honor. Gombei took this as a sign, a warning that a man with only one son ran the risk of running out of descendants and he raised the boy with the care of a gambler down to his last throw of the dice.

Except for one man in the village, an eccentric old-timer, no one fished for the poisonous *fugu* blowfish, even though the waters off Iwakuni were good grounds for it. It was an ugly fish with small, pursed lips and a plump body resembling a satchel. When it sensed danger, it blew itself up like a balloon, making itself larger than the mouths of predators could handle. Its head was rounded with eyes pushed forward and away from its sides toward the middle to make a face eerily like a child's. If it had feet, it would resemble a porcupine with dozens of sharp spines sticking straight out, ready to sting enemies with a lethal toxin. While fugu were plentiful, the market was small, limited to specialty cooks who knew how to separate the flesh from its eleven deadly parts, especially its easily punctured liver.

No one knew the old man's real name, so everyone called him Kawa-san, "Mr. Leather." Tanned by salt and sun, Kawa-san lived by himself in a shack pieced together with packing crate boards and tattered sails. Young boys brave enough to believe they were risking their lives carefully picked out rocks large enough to do some damage but light enough to throw and crawled toward his shack to heave their shots from distances they dared not shorten. If he saw the boys, Kawa-san cursed them in a spray of spittle over his mangled beard and threw rocks back at his assailants, who ran in evasive patterns and gathered again at a safe spot to trade harrowing accounts of their escape from death.

Gombei was Kawa-san's only friendly visitor, the only person who sometimes envied his reclusion. Catching more fugu than he could sell at market, Kawa-san gave his surplus to Gombei for shrimp bait, charging only the price of needy conversation.

"Need more shrimp bait? Can give you more if you wish."

"Thank you, but I have enough."

"Stay awhile. Don't go. Let's see … your boat … ah … your boat. Sailing all right?"

"Yes, it is sturdy and reliable. Oversized tiller, you know, for strength."

"And … ah … your son. What's his name? Yes, your boy, he good?"

"Shuzo's fine. I can't wait for him to grow up and help me fish."

"Shuzo … yes … good boy. Doesn't throw rocks at me. And wait … don't leave, not yet. Shall I … ah … shall I show you how to clean the poison out of fugu?"

Kawa-san demonstrated the proper technique for cutting the flesh safely, but Gombei never took any of it home. Sumiko said she would never touch that fish and worried about Gombei's use of it as bait. Kawa-san lured Gombei to stay even longer by building a fire on the beach to roast the cleaned out fugu.

"Why do you spend so much time with him?" Sumiko asked, truly baffled about her husband's friendship with the village outcast. "He scares me. How can you trust him to make the fugu safe to eat?"

"Kawa-san is harmless, misunderstood by everyone. He's a gentle soul and knows everything about fugu. Besides, there's something exciting about eating poisonous fish."

"Useless daring," Sumiko muttered. "Of interest only to men."

The youngest of nine children, Sumiko had learned to defend herself by asking baffling questions. Like a Judo master, she exploited her opponents' slightest imbalance and threw them what they least expected. When an older brother had ordered her to clean his muddy clogs, she asked him if the mud came from the streets or the farm. "What difference does it make?" he snapped. "A lot," she said. "Street mud is mixed with dog shit, but the stuff from the farm is from chickens and pigs. Do you really think they are the same?"

"Hmm," he said, pondering the difference long enough for her to excuse herself, saying that Mother needed her help.

◆

The translucent flesh of the fugu had a slight sweetness that still did not make up for its bland taste. It was on the dry side, especially when broiled and had no aroma. Gombei's favorite was mackerel, laden with oil, flavor and smell. As for fugu, its main attraction was the taste of death.

"How about some *tessa*?" asked Kawa-san.

"*Tessa*? What's that?"

"Fugu sashimi. Fresh, chewy."

"Why is it called tessa?"

"You don't know?" Kawa-san was surprised he knew a word Gombei didn't. "*Teppō* sashimi, teppō is the firearm. Too long to say, so tes-sa. Get it?"

"Yeah, but why teppō?"

"Because both can kill you."

Gombei walked away from the fire, its occasional crackling now sounding like rifle shots. The guard had just sat there on the ground, puzzled, desperate, trying to push his guts back in. And Master Yoshida, so still under a painless sky. Like Miki. They were all right, Gombei assured himself, weren't they? Gombei walked quickly, started to run, then sprinted on the sand, faster, farther, vowing to stop only when his misery ran out. No rest, no rest, until I am clean, exhausted of my killing karma, purged of my poisons. Just keep going forward, one more step and another, burn it all up. He rounded a curve in the beach, stumbled and fell onto the soft, warm sand and dropped his forehead onto his arm and let the tears drain what little self-respect was left in him. He turned his head, laying his ear gently on the sand and listened for the marching, but heard only small waves lapping and washing, lapping and washing. Slowly he pulled himself onto his hands and knees and looked down the beach all the way to the rocky ledge jutting out into the deep water. That's where he had killed himself and was reborn a fisherman. It's over. The warrior I had been is dead. Remember? I am a fisherman, simple and naive like Kawa-san. Innocent. Remember? Of course. He got up and walked back to Mr. Leather.

"Ah, Gombei, there you are." Kawa-san was slicing some tessa, arranging it fan-like on a plate. It never occurred to him to ask Gombei why he had run off. People did strange things, he never knew why, like the boys throwing stones at him. It was normal not to understand. "Have some tessa."

"No thanks, Kawa-san. It's kind of you. Very pretty, laid out so neatly like that. But I must be getting home."

◆

"*Gomen kudasai*! Is anyone home?"

At ten years of age, Shuzo was allowed to open the front door to see who was calling. A middle-aged Japanese man wearing a western style suit apologized profusely for his intrusion. He took off his black brimmed hat and ran his hand once through his middle-parted hair.

"Is this the home of Gombei Taga?"

"Yes, but my father is not in."

"I was told he knows someone who catches fugu."

"Well, yes, he does. He's at the dock right now. I can take you to him if you wish."

Shuzo slipped on his clogs, straightened his back and led briskly. The man complimented the boy on his quickness and explained that he was a fish agent from Shimonoseki seeking to purchase dried fugu. Shuzo saw his father cleaning the boat and ran ahead to explain. After exchanging greetings with the agent, Gombei took him to meet Kawa-san and was astounded to hear him offer to buy at a generous price all the fugu Kawa-san could supply. The agent said he would pay five yen per kilogram, two more than what Gombei got for his shrimp. Seven yen for the prized tiger fugu.

"Well?" said the agent, waiting for an answer.

Kawa-san looked at Gombei. "I … I … don't know.

16

Gombei … what do you … I mean … I don't know." He held his arm out, hand limp at the wrist and motioned feebly to Gombei.

"Your offer is kind," Gombei said to the agent. He looked at Kawa-san."But Kawa-san is not sure. He lives a simple life and this would be a business arrangement, an obligation." Kawa-san nodded in agreement, relieved. "I'm sorry," said Gombei, reading the old man's face, "but Kawa-san cannot help you."

"And you? What about you?"

"Me? Oh, no!" Gombei laughed apologetically. "I don't know how to catch fugu."

"Well, that's too bad." The agent spat on the sand, pulled out his gold chain watch and turned his back to shade its crystal glass face from the sun. No time to waste on these peasants, too poor and stupid to know what's good for them. This Gombei seems to have had some training, but still he's a fisherman, no different from that old man, dried out and smelling like rotting fish. What's wrong with these people? "Which way's fastest back to town?"

"My son will take you," Gombei offered. "Shuzo, show this gentleman the way back."

Shuzo looked at the agent, then at his father and said, "No. I want him to stay."

He did not laugh out loud, but Kawa-san was amused by the boy's remark, one of those silly things kids say. It's what made them so delightful, asking for the moon and the chance to catch the rabbit curled up in its light. Gombei flushed and didn't know if he should ignore his son's comment or scold him for disobedience. The agent snapped the cover of his watch shut, slipped it back into his pocket, walked up to the boy and put his hand on his head. "So, you want me to stay?"

"Yes, because we can give you all the fugu you want."

"Shuzo! That's enough! Now show the man the way back."

Shuzo put both of his hands over the agent's hand still planted on his head and declared with the conviction of a schoolboy singing the new national anthem, "Kawa-san cannot do it by himself, Father, but we can help him."

It was so simple, the obvious manifested in the words of the young boy. Shuzo felt the agent press his fingertips on his skull, massaging approval and a sudden respect. Gombei started a reprimand again but was stopped by his own intriguing confusion about whether they could do this together. Kawa-san mumbled softly, as if he didn't need to point out what was apparent, what changed his mind, but finally said clearly, "Why, yes, I can show you, Taga-san … how you can help me."

The agent slipped his hand free from Shuzo's head and held out his fingers. "Five yen per kilogram, gentlemen, five yen. Seven for the tiger."

Gombei grunted.

"Good!" said the agent. "We have a deal. I'll be back next month. Perhaps, now, the boy can show me the way back to the village?"

◆

Two hundred feet of seine line with hooks dangling from branches every ten feet, twenty chances to catch fugu, but of those hungry enough to bite, half would chew right through the lines with their parrot-sharp beaks. Sometimes they caught fugu with two or three hooks still in their mouths. "So you see," Gombei said, "some might have escaped in the past, but eventually they all get caught." He stored his shrimp traps and made his own seine line with Kawa-san's help and together they ran two boats, two lines, hauling in half a dozen fugu every half an hour with each baiting — mussels were best — and from sunrise to noon, they filled their wooden tubs with red eye, spotted and the occasional premium tiger. When he was not in school, Shuzo sailed with Kawa-san and bailed his leaky boat. Back on shore, the men cleaned their combined catches and Shuzo laid out the filets on straw mats in the sun.

The fancy agent came every Saturday, flashing his gold watch and twirling a cane unneeded for walking. He weighed the dried fugu on a brass balance scale and packed them into a woven rattan suitcase carried by a porter. After paying for the lot, he joined the fishermen in their fugu roast. The young porter refused to risk his life, even though Shuzo guaranteed his safety with demonstrations of eating tessa. When the agent and his porter left, Gombei gave half of the money to Kawa-san, who was able to make a deposit on a new boat, promising the builder to pay the balance in regular installments over the next year. Gombei vouched for Kawa-san's reliability.

"Can you supply me with fresh fugu?" the agent asked Gombei one Saturday. "I'll pay you double."

Shuzo would later point out that since five dried fish equaled the weight of one alive, they increased their profits tenfold. It makes no sense, thought Gombei, to be paid more for fewer fish, but Shuzo was good in math.

"But how will you take the live fish back to Shimonoseki?" Gombei asked.

The agent looked at Gombei's boat with its oversized tiller and stout mast. "That," he said, pointing to the boat, "is how *you* will take the fish to Shimonoseki for me."

Gombei nodded, sealing the arrangement.

◆

About a hundred and twenty-five miles around the coast from Iwakuni, Shimonoseki was a major port on the tip of western Honshu, the main island in the archipelago. Ships flying flags Gombei could not identify lined the wharves of the crowded harbor. Gombei docked close to the fish market with its strange tribe of people shouting words he did not understand: *flick pocket, hand's weight, two by nine, ten over six*. They had their own slang and customs and were it not for the agent, an insider himself, Gombei would have been shunned as a dumb foreigner. In addition to payment for the fish, Gombei received a shipping fee, which he did not have to share with Kawa-san. He always spent a night or two at an inn near the market before returning home to Iwakuni and the proprietor soon treated him as a regular.

The agent introduced Gombei to the owners of the finest fugu restaurants in the city. Gombei sold the best tiger fugu to them directly, bypassing the middlemen and their mark-up. Shimonoseki fugu is the best, they told Gombei, but your Iwakuni tigers are almost as good, so good that most of our customers cannot tell the difference, as long as it's cooked. But as tessa, we only serve the finest from Shimonoseki.

"You must come with me to the restaurant tonight," the agent said to Gombei. "There will be a special event in the private room in the back. Be there at seven."

On his way over, Gombei passed a haberdashery, a brand-new store. He gazed through the window, walked in and came out with a bowler hat, perfect for that evening. It was the first time he had been invited to any social event of standing and he knew it was for special people. At the gathering in the back room, the agent introduced him as Japan's finest fisher of fugu, avoiding the lowly word for fisherman. This fugu fisher, he told everyone, uses secret techniques and what he practices is an art. "An art, my friends, that only he has mastered." The restaurant owner explained that while fugu from Shimonoseki was the best tasting, the ones from Iwakuni were more toxic. "Tonight," the owner announced, "we are serving Iwakuni fugu caught by this artist." The agent whispered to Gombei, who then tipped his bowler hat and bowed. Everyone nodded slowly in return and clapped politely.

"Gentlemen, you have been invited for a very special reason." Dressed in chef whites with a cleanly starched apron and cap, the owner stood at the head of two rows of low tables long enough for sitting a dozen men on straw mats. Exuding the confidence of his stocky frame and thick, steady hands, he explained the reason for the special gathering. "As our best customers, you have heard many tales about fugu and its dangers and we all share an interest — for some it is an obsession — in eating fugu, knowing it can kill us. Of course, it is perfectly safe at our restaurant, but you know it's possible to prepare the fish seasoned with its own poison. All of you here, at one time or another, have asked me to serve you a preparation with a hint—just a hint—of danger, but I have steadfastly refused ... until tonight." He smiled and nodded at each person.

Every man sat stiffly, condemned by their past requests. Didn't the owner know they had just been joking? What is he saying about tonight's meal? Would it be different? No one dared to show his fear by asking. The waitresses brought out the preliminary dishes, a range of delicacies to go with the outpouring of beer and sake. The tension made the alcohol work faster, or at least increased the amount taken in and their apprehensions quickly flared into brave declarations.

"Tonight, we will all die! What an honor to end my life in your good company!"

"*Kampai!*"

Someone recited their favorite poem.

*Last night I ate fugu with him and today I carry
his coffin.
Any man can die by slitting his belly, but only a
man who understands the irony of life can die by
slitting the belly of a fish!*

"What does 'irony' mean?" Gombei whispered to the agent, but the agent did not answer.

The party went on for an hour before the owner stood up again. "Gentlemen, the time has come."

Everyone fell silent, but no one sat still.

"I have prepared the fugu myself, using a recipe I learned from my master. After removing the liver, I carefully slit it open and took out an exact amount that can kill a man, but not unto death. It has to be just right—enough to kill you, but not enough to make it impossible for you to survive. A living death."

No one asked for clarification.

"Now, you all know Sasaki-san, a serious connoisseur of fugu if I ever saw one. Sasaki-san has repeatedly asked for the poisoned dish and I finally decided to grant him—and only him—his request."

The sighs of relief were audible and one man got on all

fours and bowed to the victim who had agreed to die on behalf of everyone else's curiosity. Bald though still in his forties, Sasaki returned the bow, showing his shiny pate and stood up to go to a side room. He reemerged wearing a pure white kimono, the color of sacrifice. A short, thin man, he lifted the hems of the oversized garment as he walked to the place of his final designation and looked at each person, slowly in turn, meeting their eyes in farewell, just in case. He sat rigidly in meditation, and everyone shifted into the formal position of sitting on folded knees. No one had ever seen a roomful of drunken men sobered by respect.

"Sasaki-san knows the terms of this meal and you are all witnesses. He understands that I have prepared this to the best of my ability. He also knows I cannot guarantee anything." Sasaki nodded.

A waitress brought out a single dish and placed it carefully on the low table in front of Sasaki. He bowed to the fish, then picked up his chopsticks smoothly without hesitation. He finished the small serving in three or four bites, then turned to the owner and thanked him.

"It is exquisite, unlike any other I have had. The flavor is different, unique, indescribable … slightly bitter perhaps. Thank you."

He sat motionless for ten minutes, then started to rub his hands together. They say the tingling destroys all feeling, beginning with the extremities, arrests the lungs, but leaves the mind clear. Sasaki grasped his chest, closed his eyes and leaned slowly to one side. The owner helped him stretch out into a comfortable position on his back, his limp hands folded across his heart.

One man fainted but was quickly revived. The waitresses sitting in one corner of the room started to weep, holding each others' hands. One woman covered her eyes; several others pressed their fingers over their mouths. The owner sat stoically, a Zen master presiding over life and death, trying to project confidence. Someone muttered a chant, *namanda, namanda, namanda.*

Gombei was stricken; it was, after all, *his* fish. "I'm sorry," he whispered to himself. "I'm sorry, Sasaki-san." One of the men was a physician who sat next to Sasaki and held his wrist for a pulse. Like everyone else, the doctor knew there was no cure for fugu poisoning.

Fifteen, twenty, then thirty minutes went by, more slowly than the half moon creeping across the black sky. Sasaki turned white, drained of the color of life. For five, ten, then fifteen more minutes, he remained inert, dead as far as anyone could see. One of the waitresses got up and left the room crying. Gombei scuttled to the physician's side. "I'm sorry, Sasaki-san. Please, please…"

Sasaki opened his eyes, pounded his chest in self-respiration, kicking wildly to push himself up to break some surface into fresh air; then, fell back, still. Unable even to gasp, he bit his lips, flooding it red and Gombei pulled out his shirt tail and pressed it over Sasaki's mouth. "I'm sorry, I'm sorry," he kept repeating, as if his remorse made for a good antidote. He lifted the shirt cloth, but the blood kept flowing and he pressed down again, harder. Sasaki opened his eyes, filled with fright, and Gombei was struck by how different had been the little girl's demon eyes, furious, rejecting, accusing. Gombei turned his head from side to side, trying to stop the shiver rising up his own neck. The window shutters rattled, clacking like bamboo, like metal clips against a mast. Gombei dared not close his eyes for fear he'd see her. But he saw her still and he pressed his hand harder over Sasaki's mouth.

"*Shh*, Miki, you'll be all right. Be quiet. Everything will be all right. How did you find me here? *Shh*, Miki, don't cry." The physician stared at Gombei for a moment, startled by his senseless muttering, then grabbed Gombei's hand and pulled it away, allowing Sasaki to bleed and breathe.

"*Argh! Argh!*" Sasaki rolled over, braced himself on his elbows and threw up. The waitresses screamed, the men shouted. "He's alive! He's alive!" The owner rushed to Sasaki's side and Gombei looked around the room, searching for Miki.

"Are you all right? How do you feel?" Everyone crowded

around Sasaki. He coughed and gaggled some more, then asked for water. He sat up, the waitresses started to wipe up the mess and the owner asked everyone to move back. Several waitresses fanned him, and he finally caught his breath. Many would later say that they had seen a glow around his head.

The owner helped him up and took him to the side room to clean up and change his clothes. Everyone else returned to their seats and resumed the party with a vigor unleashed by relief. Everyone said they had never seen anything like it. Some said it was a miracle, others said it was the owner's skill. When Sasaki and the owner came back, everyone shouted and cheered. Gombei tucked his blood-stained shirt back into his trousers, looked for Miki but she was gone, and he easily fell into the riotous celebration. The toasting was loquacious, and no one ran out of expressions of cheap adulation. They raised their glasses to their hero, the bravest man in Japan, the immortal, the man who survived death! Then they turned to the greatest chef, the amazing master, the wizard, the discoverer of eternal life. They even hailed the greatest fisher of fugu, the artist, the ocean man in the bowler hat. They went on endlessly, trying to top what had already been said and then they hailed each other, fellow witnesses of medical history made that night.

The waitresses brought out clean fugu and everyone took their turn falling over, lying still—though they could reenact death for only a few seconds—and then woke up, jubilantly declaring their return to life, a new occasion for another round.

"Sasaki-san, tell us, what was it like? What was death like?"

"Surely death is the greatest experience of life."

"If you can live to tell about it! *Hah*!"

"Tell us!"

Sasaki was calm and did his best to recall his experience. "Well, it was like ... like death."

"Well, of course. That goes without saying. But what was it like?"

Sasaki kept trying. "It was like … like … nothing. I mean, I felt nothing."

"Didn't you see anything? Any lights? Hear any sounds?"

"No. Nothing."

"The greatest experience anyone could have and it was *nothing*?"

"Yes. Nothing."

It was two or three in the morning when enough of them decided that being overly drunk was like unto death, a sign that it was time to go home. They drifted away slowly, though some passed out and stayed till the morning, Gombei and the agent among them. When they finally got up, they were served a fine — and free — breakfast. The restaurant owner personally escorted Gombei out to bid him farewell and as the fisher of fugu, the ocean artist, passed several of the night's guests, they bowed deeply to him and Gombei remembered to tip his bowler hat, grateful that their drunken compliments survived as sober respect.

As he approached the dock, he pulled the hat low over his eyes and turned around to see if he was being followed. She had appeared next to Sasaki-san, but having confirmed that he was now alone, Gombei started to run until he tripped over his realization that upon releasing his hand from Sasaki's bleeding lips, what he had heard as her whimpering was actually a dragon cat hissing out wisps of camphor.

WOODEN CLOGS

MIKI LEFT HIM ALONE FOR MONTHS AND GOMBEI BEGAN to wear his growing familiarity with Shimonoseki as proudly he did his hat. Big city knowledge, that's what he had. He lost track of the number of times he had been there, and he knew its streets and alleys as well as the coastal winds and tides. He usually left the Iwakuni dock early in the morning and pulled in for the night at the town of Hoju, his halfway point. He slept on the boat, protecting his precious fish kept alive in wooden tubs, filled and refilled with fresh sea water. After rubbing the amulet tacked to the mast for protection against meandering spirits, he would set out again well before sunrise and arrive at Shimonoseki in the afternoon to deliver his toxic catch before the market closed. The rest of the night was his.

Gombei befriended another regular guest at the inn, a merchant named Yamada, who shipped lacquerware to Europe and America. Yamada explained that foreigners like bright colors, which is why his most popular line was Ouchi lacquer made in his hometown of Yamaguchi. He had a hand in the entire process from milling the lumber to loading the ships at Shimonoseki, and he increased the frequency of his visits to twice a week because of the mounting volume of his exports. Finding themselves together at the inn several times a month, they became eating and drinking partners.

"Hoju? You make a stopover in Hoju?"

"I could sail from Iwakuni through the night, but I much prefer to sleep. Hoju is a nice place to rest."

"You should visit me in Yamaguchi sometime. It's a short distance above Hoju. Maybe on your return trip, when you do not have to mother your fugu."

Gombei accepted Yamada's invitation and visited him in Yamaguchi. Yamada took him to his shop, where Gombei was fascinated by the turners foot-pumping their lathes and shaping spinning blocks of wood with razored chisels into thin-walled bowls and platters. They made the wood seem like clay, malleable to their wills. Their preferred wood was zelkova, a native species of elm, which, when turned with skill, became almost translucent. The thinned zelkova allowed lacquer to soak through its pores and the inner and outer coatings seeped into each other to form an interlocking bond. Gombei marveled at the smoothness of the lacquered surfaces, how the craftsmen could make wood feel like glass. He envied the painters and their magical hands brushing on colors to make grasses sway, rabbits jump, birds fly, chrysanthemums bloom in glorious colors. Like the gods, they could make nature do their bidding. Gombei pressed his palms together and felt himself to be a smelly fisherman in the presence of real artists.

"Such waste," Yamada complained. "Look at all the scrap wood we throw away. This is such an exacting art that only the best lumber can be used. The cut-offs are still fine wood, but not for lacquer."

The wasted pieces ranged from a few inches to several feet in length. All were thick, since the bowls were shaped from single blocks. Gombei picked up a chunk and admired its grain. The bold, swirling pattern reminded him of his father's favorite *geta*, the clogs made of zelkova that he used only for special occasions.

That's it! Geta! This is perfect wood for geta—high-end geta at that. Geta are also made from thick chunks of wood.

They quickly arrived at a deal and Yamada happily sold Gombei the scraps at a cut-off price. He had them tied in bundles and arranged for delivery to Hoju. Though he knew he was not an artist, Gombei realized that he had just become a merchant, another rebirth, a higher escape from his past, a cut above a fisherman, even one elevated to a fisher of fugu. Yamada proposed a dinner to celebrate their new arrangement and took Gombei to his home to show him his prized collection of lacquer before going to the restaurant. "My finest piece," he boasted, "has 150 coats of lacquer and each coat takes three days to dry."

Yamada had a large family. Besides his wife and parents, he had five children, lovely, well-mannered, properly schooled, poised for their ages. Recently built, his house was large and filled with light passing unfiltered through panes of clear glass in sliding doors formerly papered. His attractive wife showed no signs of privilege, though her greatest privilege was being able to take it for granted. Gombei was envious — the dealer was about his age — and once again he thought of the curse of Bungo Bridge, where his deeds had produced black karma limiting him only to one son. As they left Yamada's home for the restaurant, the entire family gathered at the door to see them off and Gombei noticed the daughter who was about the same age as Shuzo.

"You're a lucky man," Gombei said as they arrived at the restaurant. "Such a fine family. Your daughter, what's her name?

"Which one?"

"The one standing in front."

"Ah, Hasumi. The most talented of them all." He dropped his voice and whispered, "My favorite child."

The proprietor greeted his neighborhood customer and showed him to his usual table. A waitress appeared with a large bottle of his preferred brand of beer and two glasses. She poured and they toasted each other.

"Hasumi," said Gombei. "I assume you write it with characters meaning lotus viewing. A pretty name for a pretty girl."

"And you, Gombei, you never told me how many children you have."

"Just one. A son. We would like more children, but my karma will not allow it. I … ah … used to be a samurai."

28

"Samurai? Bad karma? Then you…?"

Gombei acknowledged his past. He trusted Yamada, strange to say, this stranger, now a quick friend. Besides, he might become a relative through marriage someday. There in Yamaguchi, halfway to Shimonoseki, city of the world, he felt different, sophisticated, respected and he understood, when the agent had finally explained it to him, what irony meant. Come to think of it, in Iwakuni I have no friends, the kind I can really talk to, except Kawa-san, but Yamada here is an international businessman, knowing and articulate. He would understand and so Gombei told him about Bungo Bridge and admitted that, yes, he had done what all samurai did, but he left out the details of life taking, then told him about the rocky ledge, the swords in the ocean, the ending of his life as a samurai and his rebirth as a fisherman. A new man.

"What a remarkable past!" Yamada lifted his glass and bowed his head. "I would never have guessed you had such a, well, such a … I mean, it's not that it seems unlikely, I mean, well … here's to the new Gombei!" He tipped his head back, emptying his cup with a single swallow. "Well, now you are a merchant like me. But I have always been a merchant, while you have been in every station in life. You just need to be a farmer to have been everything."

"Or emperor. But I think merchant is best."

◆

Gombei met the delivery man at the Hoju dock and supervised the loading of thirty bundles of beautiful scrap hardwood. He had never transported this much weight before and he carefully balanced the load on his boat. He hoisted the sail and set out for Iwakuni, one foot on the tiller, one hand controlling the sail rope and the other hand holding a bamboo ladle for periodic dipping into a casket of sake. He was riding high.

At Iwakuni, he called for a large cart and had the wood delivered to his home, where he stacked them in the garden. Sumiko came out, uncertain about what she was witnessing. Shuzo ran excitedly around and over the bundles.

"Look at this!" Gombei stood proudly with his son in the middle of his wood pile.

"You're drunk," she said.

"No … well … yes, you're right, but call it happiness."

"Do we need that much wood for heating the bath?"

"No! No! This is not firewood. My goodness, no. Geta!" Gombei stretched out his hand and waved it over the wood, sprinkling his imagined magic for transforming the scraps into fine footwear. He could see it. "How many pairs do you think we have here? Hundreds? Thousands? And if we sold each pair for … fifty yen…" He laughed with delight and Sumiko could not help but smile.

"You must be hungry. Come in, dinner is ready."

◆

When Gombei told him the price of the zelkova wood, the geta-maker did not believe him. It was so cheap that he suspected the wood to be damaged by rot or insects. After inspecting the wood in Gombei's yard, the geta-maker offered to buy everything he had.

"Fantastic zelkova—extraordinary grain—and I can sell it as high grade geta at regular prices, a bargain for my customers. Well, maybe slightly higher than what I normally charge, but—and maybe I should not tell you this—your zelkova is cheaper than the paulownia I normally buy. I will take it all, but there is one problem."

"Payment?"

"Yes. I cannot pay you all at once, so would it be possible for me to pay you in installments?"

"Well, in that case I will have to charge you interest, a small amount of, say, five percent."

The geta-maker made a quick calculation. "That will be fine."

"Can you do it in ten payments?"

"Yes, I can handle that. I appreciate your cooperation. Thank you." He bowed.

"My pleasure." Total ecstasy, actually. But Gombei relied

on his old samurai discipline to mask his feelings. Besides, all he had secured was a verbal agreement.

"Let me go back to my shop and I will come back with the first payment."

Business. Ah, the love of transactions. He could assert himself in yet another new life and making deals was a quiet thrill, certainly much easier than chasing the wily fugu. Fish are smart and many were the days when he had come back with nothing. But this wood business was so easy, even though the geta-maker must be smarter than fish. He hurried into the house to tell Sumiko the good news.

Gombei thrived with his new routine. It took two or three days to catch enough fugu to fill his tubs, two days to make the trip to Shimonseki, a day to stop on the way back at Hoju and go to Yamaguchi to pick up wood and another day to get home. He was a fisherman, a shipper and a merchant, all of whom made profits. Once a week, he went to the bank, where the manager greeted him personally and Gombei did not bother to take off his hat.

A new man, freed at last from Bungo Bridge, forgetting the past by keeping busy.

◆

By 1894, Gombei had three bowler hats — one for fishing, one for the wood business and the finest for funerals and other ceremonial events. Shuzo was fourteen years old, learning every aspect of his father's business, except for the visits to the bank. Gombei became the richest man in the village, but his samurai frugality limited his public displays to his hats.

WAR WITH CHINA! The newspaper headlines sent people scurrying about in the hot summer streets. Japan, the deadly fugu, puffed itself up with bristling teppō rifles, not to defend itself against western barbarians but to drive the Chinese, barbarians all the same, out of Korea. Asians against Asians, old neighbors at that, they fought not for honor but pride — and territory. Poor Korea! The only question for the Land of Morning Calm was whether it would be overrun by the

Middle Kingdom to the north or the Rising Sun from the southern sea. Good thing Commodore Perry had not forced himself onto the Koreans! The irony — that word again — of Perry intruding on the Japanese, who secretly thanked him for waking them up to the wonders of technology and conquest. His Majesty's cruisers blasted the Chinese junks with ease and by June, the Imperial Army occupied the Royal Palace in Seoul. It was so easy, like selling scrap wood.

The manipulators in Tokyo pulled strings stretching all the way to Seoul and the new Korean government moved its hinged mouth to ask Japan for a favor: *Please, elder brother, expel the evil Chinese troops from our country*. Now it was a friendly and legal obligation, an inescapable moral responsibility, an act of compassion and the Japanese, ever gracious, did not stop with the last Chinese soldier retreating across the Yalu River border and marched into the Chinese town of Lushun, known by westerners as Port Arthur, where they slaughtered 18,000 civilians, leaving only 36 to dig their graves. The Imperial Navy completed its destruction of the Chinese fleet and the Army advanced into Manchuria, flourishing flags and banners eyed by peasants wishing for more than tatters. It was wonderfully easy, so much fun and by spring of 1895, a delegation from China made their sorry way to Shimonoseki to beg for peace.

Gombei watched the rusting Chinese ship drift sadly into its slip. The crowd waving hundreds of Rising Suns was kept a respectable distance away so that the Chinese delegates, defeated foes, could pretend to be honored guests. They were greeted by Japanese officials and a distinguished American, John W. Foster, formerly the Secretary of State, who served the Chinese as legal advisor. Gombei thought he looked like a goat with his profusion of white hair drooping from his cheeks. On April 17, the Treaty of Shimonoseki was signed, and Japan became a colonial power.

"Did you hear," said the fugu agent when they met for dinner, "that we got parts of China and all of Formosa? Can you believe that?"

"Japan is the most powerful nation in Asia," said Gombei. "China is so huge — all the more pitiful. What weaklings! For fugu, big fish are the easiest to sting."

"Speaking of fugu," said the agent, "the price for your fish has dropped, you know, the government's austerity policy. Fugu is on the list of luxury foods — can you believe that? I will need only half of your normal delivery. At half the price."

"No problem," said Gombei, still flushed with national pride and the wisdom of having diversified into the business of wood. "Kawa-san and I will cut back.."

◆

"No!" said Shuzo with all of his teenaged stubbornness and schooling. "Never!"

"But why?" Gombei was surprised. "We're equal partners with Kawa-san."

Shuzo was acting like a child, or was he learning to be a capitalist? That is what the newspaper called them, men greedy for maximum profits, decency be damned.

"If we must cut our supply in half and get half the price," Shuzo argued, "then Kawa-san's half has to go. Clean and simple. Nothing from us." The teenager clenched his fists, tightened his lips. He drew his sleeved arm across the perspiration dampening the light growth over his lip. He was frightened by his own audacity, jumping off a cliff on a dare he made to himself, but mostly he felt the excitement of certainty, the pleasure of opposing his father. He spoke on impulse but with reason, like a better businessman than his father was, calculating gain and loss. "Kawa-san must go."

Gombei felt the shiver and saw it happen again in a tempo slowed by remorse, the rifle slug entering the man's back, ripping out his guts, killing Master Yoshida. He had been fourteen, Shuzo was fifteen, but it was the same, sudden loss of youth. Gombei looked at his hand, the one that had covered Miki's mouth. Shuzo was guiltless by comparison, an innocent youth asserting his will as a privilege, a modern choice, but it was still ugly, his willingness to sacrifice a person. Gombei saw Miki, serene in the dappled light across her face. Suddenly she opened her angry eyes. Gombei jerked back, then pretended that he had just lost his balance for a moment.

"Well?" said Shuzo, pushing into his father's silence. Shuzo cleared his throat and repeated his demand, more deeply modulated. "Well?" He almost said, you weakling.

"You … you will ruin Kawa-san."

"It will be unfortunate, yes…"

"This may kill him. How can you be so … cruel?"

"It's a family matter. It's our duty. It's more important than feelings. That's what we learned in school."

Gombei felt his stomach burn. She's just a child, a little sister, but Master Yoshida glared and cursed, drawing his finger across his neck. Duty. He did it anyway, despite himself. That's what he had learned.

"All right," he conceded and tried to salvage his seniority by saying, "But let me tell him. It's my duty."

◆

"I … I … I don't understand." Too old to cry, but Kawa-san felt as if another child, thought to be a friend, had just taken away a toy from him for no reason. "No more fugu to sell? You too?"

"Well, not exactly," said Gombei. "But the market has changed, and the agent is cutting back. Severely."

Kawa-san stared at the sand and came to the realization Gombei feared. "My boat. How will I pay for it? No one wants my fugu. Not even you. No shrimp bait."

"I'll try to help you, but it won't be much. Or better yet, I'll give you my shrimp traps."

"I … I don't understand," said Kawa-san. "You will still sell your fugu?"

"Well, yes, but just a bit, a little bit. Not like before."

The old man stroked his beard and stared across the water. He sat down on the sand.

"I'm sorry, Kawa-san. But things have changed. It's the

34

New Japan." Gombei placed one hand on the old man's shoulder, but he shrugged it off, leaning to one side.

"Can't be helped, huh," he mumbled and waved Gombei away. "You cheat."

"No, no, don't say that, please, don't say that. I'm so sorry, Kawa-san. I hope you understand."

The old man got up and walked away.

◆

Afraid of telling his son about his kindness, Gombei took secret guilt offerings to Kawa-san — a little cash, a tin of rice, pickled radishes — but Kawa-san threw rocks at him whenever he approached. Gombei didn't know how the old man managed to survive, but somehow he did, constantly repairing his old boat, slapping more crate boards onto his shack. As indifference slowly replaced his shame, Gombei stopped trying to help after a while and he thought less and less of the village outcast, even when the fish agent increased his orders again.

But time worked differently for Kawa-san and as the days passed into years, he thought more and more about Gombei … and his son, that boy who had never thrown a rock at him. Kawa-san refused to let his hatred for Gombei spill over to Shuzo, a good boy who used to bail his boat. What a splendid young man! But Gombei, well, Gombei can just go straight to hell.

SHIPWRECK

W HEN HE TURNED EIGHTEEN IN 1898, SHUZO HAD TO register for the military draft and become eligible for free travel abroad to protect His Majesty's colonies from its native residents — slimy ingrates all, enemies who would destroy the Japanese civilizers if they could, even when there was no war. Though proud of their country, young Japanese men registered according to the law but sometimes against their will. They were not afraid of the enemy, but of the Imperial officers and their ruthless discipline. Everyone knew someone — a son, neighbor, nephew, cousin — who told conscription tales of mistreatment. But the system of pride and fear worked and the modern Japanese soldier, trained in advanced weaponry and strategy, disciplined by glorified suffering, fueled by crackling ideology, easily surpassed the best of the old samurai in their enhanced capacity to kill.

Schools were run on the same system and Shuzo loved the martial nature of education. Teachers commanded, students obeyed and therefore learned to read, write and compute with speed and accuracy. Shuzo hungered for the written word and devoured everything he could find. His favorites were newspapers and magazines, windows to the world Japan was destined to rule. He graduated at the top of his class and planned on becoming an Imperial Army officer, disciplined so that he could discipline others.

Gombei worried more about his ancestors than the nation. He feared that his lineage, unbroken since the beginning of time, would end with Shuzo. If his son were sent off to battle in some distant land, he might not return. If he did survive, he would be cursed by the same bad karma of killing that had denied Gombei more children. The loss of a childless son would be the end of his line and generations of Taga ancestors would perish in their afterlife with no descendants to care for them. Who would make offerings of food and drink at their graves? Like children—only worse since there were endless numbers of them—the ancestors were dependent on having descendants to feed them. It was bad enough that Gombei had killed others, but the prospect of murdering his ancestors, the givers of his own flesh and blood, scared him into thinking again like a miserable coward.

At least Shuzo only had to register for the draft and had not yet been called up. So many of Shuzo's classmates were already in camps, sacrificing their personal desires on the altar of the New Japan. There must be a way out, to do his duty but not really suffer, to keep his honor and his life. Yet they kept blaring slogans about dying for the nation, but a dead soldier is useless to his family. Like the shogun's guard. What a waste.

◆

Three men from the Iwakuni Association of Lumber Dealers visited Gombei to tell him that only members of the Association had the right to sell wood. They had tolerated him long enough and the time to act had arrived. Gombei apologized for his oversight and said he would be glad to join their group.

"That will be difficult," said Bunzo Nozaki, the head of the Association.

"I will be happy to pay the back dues for the time I was not a member."

"It's not that. It's a matter of qualification."

"What does it take to qualify?"

"Only families in the business for generations can be members."

"Then are you saying there is no way for me to join?"

They looked at him blankly.

"Then the only thing I can do is…"

They nodded without respect and left.

Gombei was worried, but Shuzo was excited by the challenge. Gombei thought his son too aggressive, was in need of humility, of conforming sense. Shuzo had been so hard on Kawa-san and was emboldened by an easy uncaring. The lumber dealers came back again and Gombei, making as if he had a choice, allowed Shuzo to confront them. They were shocked by the young man's insolent rejection of their demand and told Gombei he was a terrible father who had raised an offensive son. Gombei made excuses as he accompanied them out to the garden gate and when Shuzo was out of hearing range, he told the men that he would think about what they had said. "Think fast," Nozaki replied, pointing to the setting sun. "This is your last chance to quit our business. We will not come back again."

"If we continue," Shuzo said to his father after they left, "what can they do to us?"

"They are prominent citizens," said Sumiko. "Nozaki-san serves on the local conscription board."

"So what?" Shuzo replied. We're not breaking any law by selling wood."

"And Nozaki-san would not be breaking any law by sending you immediately into the army."

Gombei saw no way out. "They are upset about our cheap prices."

Shuzo sat down. "Then let's raise them."

"And lose our customers? Nozaki is already putting pressure on the geta-makers to stop buying from us. We have no choice. On my next trip back from Shimonoseki, I will go to Yamaguchi and tell the lacquer dealer it will be our last load of wood." There, he took a stand and felt good about being decisive, even as he wiped his brow.

"But why?" Shuzo stood up and faced his father. "We are doing nothing wrong. Besides I am not afraid of being sent into the army."

"We are going against the Association's tradition."

"But, Father, you keep saying that in the New Japan we can abandon old traditions."

"Apparently not," replied Gombei. "Some customs keep growing like bamboo."

"That's just…" Shuzo paused and considered the prospect of insulting his father. Sumiko cut in and asked, "Think about that, Shuzo, what your father said about bamboo. Which is more resilient, bamboo or zelkova? Not which is stronger, but which is more *resilient*?" Shuzo understood the implications. Which was more resilient, the Association's customs or the Taga wood business? Of course, it was bamboo, if resilience is the question. But why resilience? Why should resilience be the point of the decision?

"Which is more resilient?" she repeated. "Quick, quick."

"Bamboo."

Sumiko softly tapped her palms together. "Good. Now that's settled and we can have dinner. And you know the rule about discussing business over meals."

◆

"Paradise, I tell you, Hawai'i is paradise on earth. The skies are always blue, the ocean is a warm bath, lots of fish to catch, vegetables grow all year round. But the best part is the pay. You can earn two, three, five times what you make here. Just go for a few years, make bags of money and come back a rich man. They don't call it the *heavenly country* for nothing."

The recruiter was from Hiroshima, a few miles away from Iwakuni. He worked for a private company and knew a lot about Hawai'i. Many villagers attended the meeting, especially since government spending on factories and weaponry left little for the people's welfare. Unemployment in the countryside was high and prices were rising faster than weeds. Everyone knew Japan was growing more powerful as people fell into more poverty. More truthfully, the nation was poor *because* it was powerful. They listened intently and asked about conditions in the Pacific.

"I heard that workers in Hawai'i are treated like slaves."

"No, no, that's not true, not anymore. The first groups suffered a lot, yes, but that was thirty years ago. Our government sent officials to Hawai'i to make sure our people were treated right, and they signed agreements with the Hawaiian government. Then the Americans overthrew the Queen of Hawai'i, but they still honored the labor agreements. Just last month, the American Congress annexed Hawai'i, so now it's a territory of the United States. To go to Hawai'i is to go to America."

"I'd like to go but can't afford the fare."

"No problem. This is where my company comes in. We'll pay for your passage, and you can pay us back later."

"What about women?"

"Hawai'i has lots of women. It's a paradise for men. You'll like the women." He lowered his voice, as if only men could hear in a lower register. "And the women are loose, very easy. *Heh*."

Everyone laughed, except the women and the man who had asked the question.

"Of course, I know that," the man said indignantly. "But you misunderstood me. I was asking if our women can go too. I am thinking of sending my daughter."

"Ah! Forgive me. Yes, women can work on the plantations too. There are more men, of course and…"

"So, what about … well, you know … intimate relations?" Another man, also trying not to be misunderstood, wanted to hear more about the *heavenly* women.

"Well, I don't know about intimate relations." He lowered his voice again. "But I can tell you about sex. In Honolulu, the main city, there is a place called Chinatown and eighty-five percent of the whores are Japanese. And almost all of the pimps are Japanese men. I know these numbers because the man who started the company I work for was a pimp in Hawai'i. He's good at recruitment."

"How much money can we make?"

"A lot. I know a guy who paid us back in ten months and still had enough to support himself *and* send back 130 yen to his family here. Now think of it, a 60 kilo bag of rice costs 3 yen, so that's the equivalent of 43 bags of rice! In only ten months!"

Gombei stood up. "What about the draft? Can a man be drafted if he goes to Hawai'i?"

The recruiter looked around as if he could sweep the room clean of government agents with his gaze. He spoke in a whisper. "This is the best part of it. If you go to Hawai'i, our military cannot touch you."

"But you said there are Japanese officials there."

"Their job is to make sure workers are treated fairly. If they started to round up young men and send them back to serve in the army, the government in Hawai'i would deport our officials."

That settles it. Shuzo must go. For the money and to escape the draft, to live and marry and bless the Taga family with lots of children who will care for our ancestors … and me. As he left the meeting, Gombei felt decisive.

But Shuzo was even more determined. He refused to go to Hawai'i, saying that he would gladly do his duty for the Emperor. "What good will it be to run away and survive as a coward? Do you want a coward for a son? Everyone must make sacrifices and if I die in the service of Japan, then the entire nation from the Emperor on down will honor me … and our ancestors. Which is worse, death or shame?"

Gombei knew his own preference, but realized he could not persuade his rock-headed son. There was no point in trying, not when it was time to go out and catch fugu.

◆

The trip to Shimonoseki was unusually smooth with moderate winds and temperate tides. Although he knew he would make the run many more times to deliver fugu, Gombei could only think about how this would be the last involving zelkova. If the lacquer dealer would be at the inn, then Gombei would not have to make the trip to Yamaguchi to tell him about the end of the wood deal.

As he docked his boat, he saw an American battleship, the largest of the warships in port. They stopped frequently for supplies and rest from their war with Spain, oddly being fought in the Philippines. It had started in Cuba when the *U.S.S. Maine* mysteriously blew up. At the time, it seemed so far way and unrelated to Japan, except for the widely reported deaths of seven Japanese citizens who went down with the *Maine*.

"Did you hear about the Japanese men who died in Cuba?" The fugu agent feared that the American warships in port were signs of impending Japanese involvement in the Philippines.

"What were Japanese doing on board an American ship?" asked Gombei.

"Even though they were not American citizens, they were serving in their Navy."

"Were they drafted?"

"I don't think so. They must have volunteered. I heard that some of them were cooks."

The Spanish-American War did not last long. In May of that year, 1898, George Dewey, another Commodore, destroyed the Spanish fleet in Manila Bay and by December, a peace treaty was signed in Paris. "America is following in our footsteps," said the agent. "They scored a quick victory over the Spanish, just as we did over the Chinese. They are collecting colonies, just like us. Copycats."

Mr. Yamada, the lacquer dealer, was staying at the inn and Gombei told him about the lumber association's threat. Initially, Yamada told him to ignore them, but then came to understand Gombei's greater worry about Nozaki's power to draft Shuzo and threaten the lives of the ancestors. "Maybe," he said, "we can resume our arrangement once Shuzo is safe in Hawai'i." They shook hands and Gombei asked about his family, especially his daughter Hasumi.

On the return trip, Gombei sailed past Hoju and raised his sake ladle in salute. No more wood, he thought, at least for now. He thought of pulling in for the night, but could not bear to be in Hoju. Perhaps further down the coast. The winds were good and he considered making a straight run to Iwakuni, but he was tired and saw no reason to take chances. Better to play it safe. He pulled into a small fishing village and spent the night on his boat.

Gombei waited for the mists and winds to rise in the morning and calculated an arrival home in the early afternoon. Offshore, he picked up a good breeze, but by mid-morning it turned wild, forcing him to trim back. Waves slammed his boat, sending sprays that puddled and sloshed against his feet. He held on to the sail rope with both hands, but as the tiller kept slipping out from under his foot, he lashed his foot to it. Bursts of wind jerked him upwards, stretching him on a torture rack of sail and rudder. He was relieved to see the rocky ledge marking the last few miles from home and he remembered to give it wide berth, especially in rough weather. Waves crashed against the cliff and reversed themselves into a surging rip tide forcing him even further out, so he took down the whiplashing sail and untied his foot so that he could grab the flailing tiller with both hands. He leaned his body into it, fighting the ocean itself and felt the tiller give way with a loud, clean snap. He fell to the floorboards and quickly got up to take control of the tiller, then realized he was holding it in his hands.

How could the oversized tiller break? It had handled worse conditions before. And how could it have given way ... so cleanly? Except for a few protruding splinters, the broken face was smooth and flat, as if ... but it couldn't be ... as if someone had sawn it three-quarters through. A narrow kerf, hard to see, cut from the underside. Nozaki, that bastard! Couldn't wait to learn I'd quit.

Gombei took hold of the remaining stub and tried to tame its gyrations. The splinters tore his hands and he fell back, unable to hold anything but his bleeding hands together, stinging from the salt. Wind and water shoved the boat past his village, which he could barely make out in the receding distance. The shoreline disappeared and the mountains slowly sank into the ocean. Please, please let me not lose sight of land. He bled heavily from his hands, but it was the chill descending from his head to feet that scared him, as it had under a pile of leaves by Bungo Bridge. Please, please…

She sat defiantly on the prow, hands folded neatly on her lap. She got up, straightened the collar of her brown and yellow kimono and held her white pouch as she walked toward Gombei huddled against the transom. She stood in front of him, waiting for him to look at her, but he shut his eyes and covered his ears with his bloodied hands, blocking out the sound of the manila rope, stiffened by years of salt and sun, banging its rusty cinch clips against the mast like clattering bamboo. Miki sat down beside him. He opened his eyes, blinking quickly to clear the salty water, but she was still there and he pressed his hands together, offering her a bloody gesture for mercy. "Please … please, stop following me," he begged. She looked puzzled, as if to say that her presence was not of her doing but his. "Forgive me," he said. "Believe me. I meant no harm. I tried to save you. Master Yoshida … he…" Miki looked at the sawn tiller, beheaded like her cat. "I'm sorry about your cat. I had to. Master Yoshida … he…" She was now older, her body taking shape, clear eyes strangely dry, a perfect nose, rose-brown lips that started a smile, then pressed together as she narrowed her eyes. "Please, Miki, don't be mad at me. You kicked and screamed and that is why I had to…" Gombei stopped and took a quick breath just before she placed her hand over his mouth.

◆

"Gombei, Gombei."

Ah, Sumiko. So good to hear you calling as I slip away. Sasaki said he heard nothing and saw nothing. But this is a better way to go. The sound of your voice. Is Shuzo here? I wish he would call me too. When will Mother call me from the other shore? Maybe she will see me as I get closer. I will soon be with her. And all the rest of the family. Well, Father too, but it can't be helped. This is not so bad. I wonder why we fear it? This is why Shuzo must live and have children—to care for the ancestors … and me, now that I will become one of them. This is why I want him to go to that Pacific paradise and live. I am going to a different one.

"Look, he's opening his eyes."

Shuzo? Is … it … you, Shuzo? So good to hear your voice. I found a girl for you in Yamaguchi. Good family, pretty too. Take her to Hawai'i. Run away, Shuzo. Death is worse than shame. If you stay, Nozaki will send you into the army, to become a warrior, but I broke our family's curse, threw away the swords, nothing left to give you but your life. Hawai'i, Shuzo, Hawai'i. Her name is Hasumi.

Gombei opened his eyes and stared at the ceiling. He was in his own bedding, at home, with his wife and son.

"Are you all right?" she asked.

He raised his hands to wipe his eyes and felt the heavy bandages.

It had taken a few days for the fishermen who found him on the beach some ten miles from Iwakuni to identify him and contact Sumiko. The boat had been crushed, but had held together enough to raft him to shore. A very lucky man, they said, for having such bad luck. But to Gombei, it had not been an accident.

Sawn from the underside. Damn Nozaki!

With nothing to do but rest all day, Gombei let one thought spiral into another. He damned Nozaki repeatedly but came to realize that it was all his fault. Nozaki was just a puppet acting out the drama of his own bad karma, but karma also had its mysterious ways.

It was not entirely wrong for me to have killed enemy warriors, since they were killers themselves, but I still had to suffer the black karma leading to no more children and the shipwreck. And yet I survived, and that blessing, like everything else, must have a reason. Death is the price of taking innocent life, and had I killed Miki, my retribution should have been my drowning in the sea. But here I am at home with my family, and this means that ... Miki did not die! That's it, if she had died, I too should be dead.   She was just lying under the camphor tree, serene, sleeping, dreaming of her cat. Why of course, that's it! It has to be. She's alive, otherwise I'd be dead. The law of karma makes no exception. As long as she sleeps, I'll be fine. But when she wakes, she visits me. I saw her when Sasaki kicked for his life, when I grabbed the broken tiller sawn by Nozaki. But what about that rifleman — I didn't even see his face — and Master Yoshida? They were different, warriors are meant to die, like Father said, and their honorable souls are floating in the heavens. But Miki walks on earth, following me, growing older with each passing year, a teenager by now. She will still be around long after I go. Then what? She will turn on Shuzo. But why should she wait until I'm gone? She will go after him now. Shuzo must get away, go to Hawai'i, where he can be safe. She'll never find him there, she won't even know. That's why he has to go. Makes perfect sense. A logical conclusion. That settles it. Now I can sleep.

◆

The geta-maker came to get his wood, but Sumiko told him about the wreck. "Just can't trust the weather," he said and walked away empty-handed. The weather, thought Gombei, is more trustworthy than Nozaki. Now I have no boat, no wood and no more fugu.

"What are we going to do?" Sumiko waited a week until Gombei was well enough to be asked. "Do we have enough money for another boat?"

"A row boat, at most, but not large enough for fugu ... or wood."

"Well," she smiled, "I'm just glad that you're alive. A boat is a boat."

"I should have been more careful."

"It was a terrible storm."

"The ocean is full of tricks. Never take it for granted." He did not tell her about the sawn tiller. No point in getting her upset by telling her Nozaki and his gang are nothing but thugs posing as prominent citizens. Difficult as it was to admit defeat to his hard-headed son, he decided to tell Shuzo about the tiller so that he would never be fooled by a man like Nozaki.

He called Shuzo into the family room and sat in front of the *butsudan* altar holding the memorial tablets of his deceased parents and grandparents. He lightly tapped the thin brass bowl set on a small, embroidered cushion, setting off a clear plaintive note, hanging on pins of air. He struck a match, touched it to a candle and lit three sticks of incense. After placing the incense in the censer filled with ashes, he slipped a sandalwood rosary over his hands, pressed them together and said a silent prayer to the ancestors. He moved aside and let Shuzo repeat what he had just done, as they both had thousands of times before.

"Never forget the ancestors," he said to Shuzo. "It is a great responsibility and after I am gone, you will be the only one left. Had I lost my life at sea, you would be in my place, and you would have to do everything to survive and have children." He turned to the altar and fanned his hand rapidly over the candle flame, putting it out. "If you blow a candle out, you will suffer from bad luck, so always use your hand. Bad luck. We are having bad luck right now. But the boat accident, Shuzo, was not caused by bad luck, but by Nozaki." Gombei explained how the tiller had been partially sawn.

Shuzo looked away, in the opposite direction from the ancestors. "We must get even with Nozaki. I can arrange for him to have an accident too. Doesn't he like to eat fugu?"

Gombei clapped his hands, sharply, once. "It's easy to talk of revenge, but I have already been on the path of ki … taking life. I never told you before, but you should know that when I was a samurai, before I became a fisherman, I killed several men. And now I am paying for my bad karma. Besides, I'm 44 years old right now and 4, *shi*, is a — how do you say — another word for death. It was my misfortune to have been born a warrior and my age and my past are catching up with me." Gombei confessed the reasons for his bad karma but did not say anything about Miki. He did not have to explain her, since she was, after all, alive out there somewhere, ready to follow him again. But she must never get to Shuzo.

Shuzo stared at his father, trying to see the warrior in him. A sturdy fisherman, a weak merchant, but a warrior? Who had killed men? A samurai fears no one, least of all a slime-snake like Nozaki. Why is Father afraid? He's a failure by every martial standard of his training. But none of his father's shortcomings could revoke his birthright. A failed warrior was a warrior still. And if his father had been born a warrior, then so was he.

Shuzo straightened his posture. "Nozaki deserves to be punished," Shuzo said firmly. "It is my duty to correct this great injustice and it would be wrong for me to let Nozaki get away with what he has done to you."

Nozaki ruined our family, but there might be something good in all of this. Mother's favorite story was about the farmer in ancient China who was too poor to own a horse. He lamented his misfortune until the day when a fine horse trotted into his yard. What great luck! No one claimed the horse, so he used it on his farm, tripling his yields for half the effort. Blessed was the day when the horse appeared! His son loved to ride the horse, but one day it threw him, breaking both of his legs. The farmer cursed the horse and his bad luck. Then war broke out and the local magistrate rounded up all the young men, except for his crippled son and sent the others to their deaths in battle. The farmer rejoiced in his good fortune and thanked the horse.

So, you see, no one can know when good luck will turn bad, or bad into good. That's it. Bad Nozaki. Thank goodness for Nozaki.

"If you go to Hawai'i—just for three years, one term of the contract—you will make enough money for us to start over again. That's the best way to get back at Nozaki. I know you want to join the army, to serve the Emperor but you can help Japan by helping your family. Do it, Shuzo, for our family and our nation. That is what Samuel Smiles says. Government cannot make a nation great, only people can."

"Samuel Smiles, hah. They made us read his book in school. *Self-Help*. We don't need our government to have translated that book so that an Englishman could tell us what we already know. Work hard, persevere, don't give up, be cheerful. No wonder he was called Smiles. But there's more to it than hard work. We worked hard but prices fell and that is why we had to cut off Kawa-san. We worked hard and still lost our boat because of Nozaki. Hard work didn't keep Nozaki away. What we need is money and power."

"You're right," said Gombei. "Money and power. Now I realize my mistake with the wood."

"Mistake? What do you mean? Things were going well."

"Things were better with the fugu. You see, the lesson I learned was this: sell before you buy. Every fugu we pulled into the boat was already sold, even the ones we could have caught but didn't. Now that is a good business."

"But we sold all of our wood."

"Only by chance, by good luck. I took a big risk in buying the wood *before* it was sold. What if no one had bought it? So this is what I mean by sell before you buy. It's safer that way. Sell before you buy."

"But in business you must take risks."

"Only if you're not good at it. Better to build a fortune on guarantees. And Hawai'i is guaranteed by contract. No risk. Already sold. Money in our pockets. And that means power."

Shuzo stood up and walked slowly about the room. Three years, only three years. Could his father be right, for once? He stopped in front of Gombei. "All right," he said, "three years, no more." He left the room.

Gombei struck the brass bell and pressed his palms together to thank the ancestors … and Nozaki, the accidental bad horse that brought him good luck, the reason for Shuzo to go to Hawai'i.

"Thank you, Nozaki-san. My son hates you so much he'll go to Hawai'i where he'll be safe from you and the draft … and from Miki."

Gombei rang the bell again and prayed to Miki. I'm ready for you now. Visit me anytime, stay as long as you like. Just never go to Hawai'i. Never.

UMBILICAL CORD

S UMIKO STITCHED HER GRIEF INTO THE JACKET SHE MADE
for her son. She thought of sewing some money into
the lining but decided on a Buddhist good luck amulet
instead. When he put on the completed jacket, Shuzo noticed
his name embroidered inside the neckline. The black silk
threads spoke what she could not say. Besides, speech
dissolves into air, but embroidery lasts.

Sumiko cried at the train station. Certain she'd never see
her son again, she pressed a small paper packet into his palm
and closed his fingers around it. She touched his cheek with
her fingertips and felt every feature of his face with her gaze.
Shuzo saw the brown of her eyes up close for the first time.
The whistle shattered their last moment into shards falling
onto the hard platform. Gombei looked down at his feet, his
best bowler hat in hand, as if in mourning. He picked up the
woven willow suitcase and handed it to Shuzo. "Time to go."

The train groaned and banged its way out of the station
and Shuzo leaned out as far as he could. "Sayonara! Sayonara!
Take care of yourselves!" Gombei waved bravely; Sumiko
did the best she could. Everything, anything for the sake of
the children ... and the ancestors.

Shuzo dropped into his window seat and felt a warm
fatigue spread over him like a blanket. He'd never experienced
such speed before, gliding on steel rails to the smell of black
smoke and clickety-clacking sounds going faster and faster
until they steadied into the syncopation of time marking miles

as minutes. The rhythm of the incredible machine excited him but lulled his mind into his weariness and he struggled to stay awake. He wanted to see everything, but sleep overcame his curiosity. When he opened his eyes, a strange countryside was moving across his window—rice paddies becoming villages, then potato fields, paddies again, bamboo groves, hills, the sudden blackout of a tunnel. In the darkness he remembered the paper packet in his hand, gripped with sweat and as the train rushed back out into the sunlight, he carefully unwrapped his mother's gift. It was a hard piece of sinew. Dried cuttlefish. Now why would she give me a piece of cuttlefish?

"Umbilical cord."

Shuzo looked up at the man sitting across from him. The seats faced each other in their cubicle and the slightly older man could not help but notice Shuzo's bewilderment about what he held in his hand.

"Dried umbilical cord," the man repeated. "Not as long as usual. Must have been cut in half."

"Umbilical cord?"

"Yeah, haven't you seen one before?"

"No, never have. What is it?"

The man shook his head slowly. "Connected you to your mother when you were a baby in her … uh, stomach. When you were born, it was cut to separate you from her—that is what you're holding in your hand. Except that your mother must have cut it and kept the other half. Old custom."

"So, this is my mother?"

"And you as well." The man smiled at Shuzo's naiveté and offered him some dried cuttlefish he had been eating. Shuzo could smell it—maybe that was why he had thought of it. "Put your umbilical cord away so you don't confuse it with the cuttlefish. It would be disgusting, if you…" He laughed and Shuzo relaxed for the first time that day.

"Makoto," he said, nodding a bow, "but you can call me Mako." On his way to Hawai'i as well, Mako was in his late twenties, was married and had a young daughter. A vegetable farmer from the countryside, he barely made enough to provide for his family, especially with the rising prices, so his wife and daughter went back to live with her parents while he sought, as Shuzo did, a quick fortune in paradise. His hands were leather tough — Kawa-san, whatever happened to him — and even his fingernails were thick enough for clawing earth. Clean shaven and groomed, he still had a smell Shuzo could not place, pickled radishes perhaps, or clothing pulled out from storage.

"Which plantation?" Mako asked.

"Hana. On the island of Maui. What does your contract say?"

"Mine is also for Hana."

"How lucky! We'll be together. Except for my umbilical cord, we might have traveled in silence and never gotten to know each other. Now we're connected..."

Mako laughed again and offered Shuzo more cuttlefish. Shuzo took out a paper box from his shoulder bag and with it a book fell onto the floor. Shuzo picked it up, the Japanese translation of Samuel Smiles' *Self-Help*. "Oh, Father," he said and put the book back. He unwrapped the paper box, another gift from his father and held it out toward Mako. "Try some fugu. Dried."

"Is it safe?" Mako was genuinely worried.

"Eat this and you will *never* die."

"You mean, if I eat it and die, I will go to the Pure Land and live forever."

"Think of it as you wish, but do not pass up this delicacy. Here, let's eat it at the same time. If we die, we will go to paradise together. If we live, we'll still go to paradise ... in the Pacific."

They stared at each other as they chewed, swallowed and waited. "How long does it take?"

Shuzo kept looking at Mako, whose eyes were also brown and felt something like what he felt for his mother. "Instantly," he said, snapping his fingers, "fugu kills in an instant. If you are not dead by now ... then you are already living forever!"

◆

53

Yokohama smelled like a back alley of restaurants from around the world. The docks were covered with cargo dust, grains, beans, powders and spilled liquids, making rich pickings for the fat pigeons and sparrows. But the dominant smell came from paint being splashed onto iron hulls by men dangling precariously over the sides. With gigantic brushes dwarfed by the vast areas they had to cover, they worked hurriedly, dripping as much as they applied, turning the water beneath them into overlapping circles of kaleidoscopic color. The engine oil slicks had their own palette of refracted light, more purple than the greens of the alkyd paint.

"Look at those monkeys," said Shuzo.

"Yeah," said Mako, watching the painters. "I hope they don't fall into the water."

"No, I mean over there." Shuzo pointed to a group of Okinawans waiting ahead of them in the Hawai'i line.

"Monkeys? Why do you call them monkeys?"

"Look at how hairy they are. That guy in the white shirt has so much hair on his arms. I bet his chest is like a rice field. Not like us pure Japanese."

"Aren't they Japanese—like us?"

"No, no, they're different. Darker, more hair, clannish. And they hate us since Emperor Meiji abolished their kingdom and made it a province of Japan."

"You're right. They're speaking something like Japanese, but different. Tough looking."

"See the girl with them? Different, exotic, shiny black hair. That long bag she's carrying. Must be a *shamisen*. I bet she can sing and dance and, well, gamble and drink and..."

The girl turned around and scanned the long line behind her.

"Did you see that?" Mako brushed the front of his shirt. "She smiled at me."

"Don't be silly. You don't have enough hair on your chest!"

When they finally reached the official's table, Shuzo and Mako presented copies of their family registries and passports secured by the recruitment company. The official waved them to the next table. A nurse gave them a sheet of instructions and a plain piece of rough paper. Shuzo started to read the instructions but was told by the nurse to move out of the way for the next person.

"Well," said Shuzo, "I don't feel like it yet."

"Feel like what?"

"Like following the instructions. How about you? Do you feel like it?"

Mako was completely puzzled. He looked at the printed sheet, holding it upside down.

"Oh, I see. Can't read, can you?"

"Never went to school. Too poor."

"Well, it says that you have to give them a fecal sample … I mean, some shit … so that they can check for worms. When you feel like it, go off to some corner and take a shit on the piece of paper they gave you … the rough one, not the printed sheet. Wrap it and give it to the nurse. For me, I'm not ready yet."

"No wonder," said Mako. "That's the other smell."

One of the Okinawan men went running to the nurse. The girl was lying on the floor, overcome by paint fumes. The nurse rushed over and held a vial by her nose until the girl snapped her head to one side and opened her eyes. The men fanned her and she recovered enough to realize she had fallen on her shamisen bag. She frantically opened the bag, pulled out the instrument and wailed at the torn snake skin covering. She cried out, strangely in ordinary Japanese so that everyone could understand, that the spirit of Okinawa itself was ruined, but the men reassured her that it was just a musical instrument that could easily be repaired.

"So melodramatic," muttered Shuzo. "Disgusting. Not like real Japanese women."

"Attention, everyone, attention." A short man in a uniform ordered everyone to draw closer to him. "My name is Yamamoto, and I am Chief of the Yokohama Overseas Office. On behalf of His Majesty, I commend all of you for going to Hawai'i, where, I am sure, you will work hard and be able to send money back home. You will not only be helping your families, but our nation as well. A great nation is built by ordinary people like you, not by the government."

The Okinawan woman was still crying, and the men paid more attention to consoling her than they did to Yamamoto, who tried to ignore them.

"This is an important time in our history," Yamamoto continued. "We are building the New Japan and we will take our rightful place among other nations — western nations — as an equal. You will be representatives of Japan, of His Majesty the Emperor, and you must be on your best behavior. We have received reports from Hawai'i and San Francisco that some Japanese have been drunkards, gamblers and prostitutes and this does not help our national image. But we have also heard that the Chinese are even worse and it will be important for all of you to show the Americans that we Japanese are different. They think all Orientals are alike and you must show them that we're different — strong, smart, hard-working, law-abiding, cheerful. We are not like the Chinese or the Koreans."

Or the Okinawans, he could have added.

"So remember who you are, where you come from. You are doing this for your families, your nation and, above all, your Emperor. I wish you well. Have a safe journey."

"There," said one of the Okinawan men to the girl. "I fixed it. Just a little sticky rice and some paper. It'll hold until we can do a better job of repairing it. Try it."

The girl tuned the three strings of the shamisen and strummed a set of notes. She smiled with satisfaction, sat down, gathered her thoughts and started to play a simple harvest song. The men clapped and sang, moving their hands, dancing in place. She speeded up, sliding her fingers on the thin, smooth neck to make rising and falling sounds run into each other as if each note had no discrete tone of its own. The song itself shifted away from the rice fields and became waves rolling onto a beach and back out again. Everyone listened; even the officials stopped their work. She drew them all into her tide of silken strings plucked over snakeskin and with every stroke she brushed colors of the heart, as variegated as the shimmering hues of the paint slicks in the harbor. Mako wiped his eyes.

"Ugh, I can't stand it. So melodramatic, too emotional. And twangy. It's irritating." Shuzo walked out onto the dock and sat at the edge, dangling his legs over the water. Mako went out and joined him.

"Look at the colors on the water," said Shuzo, "orange, green, yellow, red. If you jump in the water and climb back out again, you'd look like a rainbow." Shuzo threw a pebble in and rippled the colors.

"I like red. My wife's favorite color. The only lacquer bowl she has is red. So special she never uses it. Upper class, she says, red is the color of the rich."

"Losers," countered Shuzo. "Red is the color of the Taira, who were defeated at Shimonoseki by Minamoto warriors."

Mako was quiet. "Well," he said after a while, "I still like red. It's the color of my wife. And if it's the color of losers, then I guess that's what I am. Why are you going?"

"Me?" said Shuzo. I guess it's for my family. For myself, I'd rather be in the army, getting ready to ship out to China, sword in hand, men with guns under my command. We'll march through the cities, the countryside and plant groves of the Rising Sun fluttering in the breeze. Sergeant, take a squad and scour the village for rice and cloth. Arrest anyone who resists and bring them to me. We must teach them to obey our Emperor. Ah, the army! Surely there's a recruiting station here in Yokohama.

"Taga! Mr. Shuzo Taga!"

"Yes, Sir!"

Mako laughed. "It's just the nurse calling you. Why'd you call her Sir?"

"Shuzo Taga! We still do not have your sample. Please get it to us as soon as possible."

"Your shit," said Mako. "Didn't you give her your shit yet? Remember, use the rough paper, not the one with writing."

Shuzo spat in the water. "If shit is what she wants, then shit's what she'll get. That's what I'm going to give Nozaki — right up his ass — when I get back. From Hawai'i."

Mako leaned away from Shuzo. "Who is Nozaki? And why do you hate him so much?"

Shuzo told Mako about the Lumber Dealers Association and the sawn tiller. "That's why I'm going to Hawai'i. And my color's not red."

"To get revenge?"

"Well, not directly, though I wouldn't mind it if something bad happened to Nozaki. But I'm not a gangster. I'll get back at him in a civilized way. With money. Buy him out. Undersell him. Outsell him. Ruin him."

"Nah," said Mako. "No such thing as civilized revenge. Besides, you won't be able to do anything about this Nozaki unless you give the nurse your shit."

"Got to force it," said Shuzo as he walked toward a stack of crates. "Don't they have a shit house around here?"

Mako went back into the holding area inside. The shamisen player walked toward him, headed for the open dock to get fresh air. Instrument in hand, she smiled.

"Beautiful song," said Mako. "Kind of sad."

She stopped, halting him as well. "I'm glad you liked it. People like sad songs. It makes them feel good."

Mako looked up at her and she lifted her free hand to close the edges of her loose kimono over her breasts. She was tall, hardly had any hips and had braided a long red ribbon into her pony tail. Mako wanted to tell her how becoming it looked, but he could not think of the right words. He was a farmer, married, but he had to say something. "Mako," he blurted, "my name is Mako." He had never introduced himself by his first name before. Not to a woman.

"For Makoto? Truthful and sincere?" Her Japanese was smooth and correct.

"Yes, for Makoto."

"And your friend, the rude one, what's his name?"

"You've already noticed?"

"Well," she said. "It's not like he's subtle."

"Shuzo. His name is Shuzo."

"Hmm," she said, "I wonder what that means. Well, I guess I'll be seeing more of you on the boat. Maybe in Hawai'i too." She walked out to the edge of the dock and fanned herself with her hand as if she could make the paint fumes go away. Mako followed her, wondering about her name.

"Don't stand so close to edge," he said. "If you faint again, you'll fall in the water."

She stepped back a few steps. "You're right. I think I'll go back in." She walked back to the crowd, leaving Mako standing on the edge.

"Hah," said Shuzo, returning from the nurse's station. "You have your eye on the Okinawan bitch."

"She wanted to know your name."

"She did? Why?"

"Have no idea," replied Mako. "Maybe you should ask her."

A buzzer sounded and Chief Yamamoto ordered everyone to line up for boarding. The gangplank was in place and a dock hand opened the gate. The passengers at the head of the line suddenly screamed, pushing everyone back as three black rats appeared from beneath the grating and scampered on board ahead of everyone else. The men laughed, followed by the women and everyone exclaimed how startled they were, sharing their excitement with total strangers, telling each other where they were from, making friendly wagers about whether the ship, departing on a cold December day of 1899, would make it to sunny Hawai'i before the entire 19th century would come to an end. Or not.

STOWAWAY

WO SHORE HANDS UNTIED THE LAST ROPE LASHING THE *America Maru* to Japan and dropped it trailing in the slick-stained water until a sailor reeled it on board. "The umbilical cord is cut," muttered Mako, as he leaned on the thickly painted iron railing. The ship shuddered and moved slowly, a marvel that so much steel could float and move at all and yet it departed too quickly for Mako. Passengers stood on deck for a long time, watching Japan recede to the West—like the sun retreating into an endless night—for one last time. Many wept and stood and watched until they finally walked back to their cabins when there was nothing but a wake to see.

The *America Maru*, pride of the Oriental Steamship Company, had the sharply angled bow of a sailing vessel. It even had two masts that could be rigged with sails, but they were thin sticks separated by two fat stacks, angled smartly aft, discharging gritty smoke from live fires beneath the decks. Whoever designed the ship had hedged his trust of technology by making it possible for the captain to capture the cool winds in old-fashioned canvas should the fiery mechanics of steam and pistons fail. It was modern, like America, but still a *maru*, a ship afraid to let go of its sails.

The steerage section was a large room packed with double-decker bunks, enough for 200 people. Unplanned for privacy, the large single space made no concession for age or gender and only the young men could relax in the comfort of their numbers and callousness. Each bunk had a thin straw mat and those who had enough money could rent the luxury of pillows and wool blankets. Shuzo nested his things under his bottom bunk next to the obvious belongings of a woman and then went back on deck to breathe fresh air.

Mako was already there, hunched over, elbows on the rail, hands folded in prayer around a cotton headband embroidered with red threads.

"Miss your wife?"

"And my daughter." He let his tears drop into the swift water.

"Aw, c'mon, Mako. It'll only be for a short time. You'll soon be able to go back a rich man."

"Soon is not soon enough. Already it's been too long."

"Well, if you can't get your mind off home, then tell me, what's your wife look like?"

"You won't believe that a stupid man like me has a beautiful wife, but she is very attractive. Always was the best-looking girl in the village … and smart too. We grew up together, played the same games. Even when she went to school — her parents could afford it — we still did things together. But when she was 12 or 13 years old, she had her first bleeding and her father ordered her not to see me."

"Her first bleeding? Did she get hurt?"

Mako laughed. "For an educated man, you don't know much, do you? A girl becomes a woman when she bleeds from … you know … down there, between her legs."

"She does?"

"It means she can have babies. You know about making babies?"

It was Shuzo's turn to laugh, hard as it was, at himself. "Of course … I don't."

Mako explained the details. Shuzo tried to hide his surprise and fascination. "Really?" "No wonder." "You must be joking!" He connected experiences of his own body with the greater miracle of creation and asked detailed questions, which Mako answered with graphic clarity and hand motions when necessary.

"So, back to your wife. How did you manage to marry her?"

"Her father wanted her to marry someone else, but she objected. He was angry and for months we talked about suicide. She told me stories about lovers who took their own lives rather than be separated by their parents."

"I can't imagine dying for a woman. For the Emperor, of course, but a woman? It's not right."

"If you're lucky, Shuzo, you will find a woman to die for. If you're lucky."

"So, what happened then? You're still alive."

"My father solved our problem. Quiet man, work, work, work, but he wanted to help me. He went to my wife's father and promised him half of everything he grew on his farm if he would agree to our marriage. Too good for my father-in-law to pass up—after all, the woman's family is supposed to provide a dowry, which is what he would have had to give to the other man's family."

"Mako! What an idiot! You let your father sacrifice himself, make a fool of himself. It's as if he became a servant, no, a slave, all because of your ... love. You should have made a sacrifice for him, not him for you."

"I am, Shuzo, I am. That's why I'm leaving my wife and daughter to work in Hawai'i—to buy my father's freedom. Made an agreement with my father-in-law and we set a price, thousand yen. That will make him a rich man, just like that, and my father will be free."

"I guess," Shuzo said after a long moment, "I guess I'm going to Hawai'i for my father as well. Someday, somehow, I will get even with that Nozaki. He tried to kill my father— that bastard. I'm going to Hawai'i to make enough money for another boat and to destroy Nozaki."

Mako straightened up. "There you go again. Revenge and hate. That's why you're going to Hawai'i? Because you hate Nozaki?"

"I hate Nozaki because I love my father. What's the difference? Don't you hate your father-in-law? He's taking advantage of your family."

"It's not love or hate for me. Just an arrangement, you know, an agreement. And it'll work out in the end. Just have to make money in Hawai'i. Quite simple. What would you do if you were me?"

Shuzo stared at nothing. "I would," he finally said, "not love a woman. I would … just marry one. If I had to."

"Ah, you, you pumpkin head. And I thought you were a modern man. I would pity you, but my stomach is growling. It's getting late. We'll miss supper if we don't hurry."

The mess galley was crowded, and they stood in line for their rice and miso soup flavored with dried shrimp. The only seats open were next to the Okinawans, who nearly depleted the communal platter of pickled cabbage. Shuzo picked up the platter, scraped half of what was left into his rice bowl and passed the remainder to Mako.

"Pigs don't believe in sharing."

The Okinawan man sitting next to him set his rice bowl down very slowly and turned to Shuzo. "Did'ja call us pigs?"

Shuzo stuffed his mouth with rice and glared back.

"Look'it'im!" the Okinawan said. "Don't *he* look like a pig?" The others laughed. The shamisen player poked her chopsticks at Shuzo's face.

Mako grabbed Shuzo's arm and pulled him from the table. Shuzo let him prevail, but as they left the room, he turned back to say, "Pigs," but loud enough only for Mako to hear.

"What's wrong with you?" Mako was a father again. "Why hate them so much? They've done nothing to you."

"What is wrong with *you*?" Shuzo was incredulous. "Can't you see? They're Okinawans!"

"You hate Nozaki, I see that, but the Okinawans? What've they done to you? Hate, hate, hate. You hate too much. I'm going to bed. You should too."

◆

Luminescent plankton twinkled in the water, but only near the lights from the hull. Beyond that, the ocean stretched into a blackness without borders all the way to the heavens and surely to the hells as well. Shuzo remembered the Buddhist priest saying that in hell men and women with bad karma sank in a river of shit up to their necks, and giant chickens landed on their foreheads and plucked their eyes out, bit by bloody bit. Then there was the hell of unending diarrhea. Obviously, shit is so important in hell. That nurse was collecting everybody's shit. Maybe she was the angel of hell, testing the piles for the worms of bad karma. How did the stinking Okinawans pass the test? Stop. Mako is right. I should not hate them, not because they are as good as we are, but because hate produces bad karma. I do not want to fall into hell, full of fire and shit.

After dozing in a pile of fat ropes coiled on deck, Shuzo got up, stretched and saw a spot of fire slowly moving toward him. A man, drawing deeply on his cigarette, approached. Once he reached the range of the lights, Shuzo saw that he was covered with soot, a fire-sucking demon burned black. Shuzo started to move away but was captured by the man's greeting.

"Beautiful night, isn't it?" He spoke as if he were reciting poetry — measured, clear, rhythmic.

"Ah … yes, it is. But it's late."

"All the better to come on deck. Actually, I didn't expect to see anyone up here at this hour. I try to come when no one is around. Some people look at me as if I were a ghost from hell."

"You work on the ship?"

"More like *in* the ship. Way down deep in the engine room. I'm an engineer, if you can believe that, but the captain makes me work the coal pile as well. It's a dirty job."

"So, you run the steam engines?"

"And make electricity too. Aren't the lights marvelous? What power! My friend touched some bare wires once and was killed instantly."

"We need that kind of power—if we are to rule the world."

"Rule the world? We might be building the New Japan with steam and electricity, but it all comes from the west. We can never beat America and Europe."

"We must have something they don't have."

"Well, come to think of it, we do. Bamboo! Without bamboo from Kyoto, Thomas Edison—now there's a god I worship—would not have been able to sell his light bulbs."

The engineer told the story of how Edison had trouble with filaments in his light bulbs, how they burned out so quickly. Not by force of genius but by the sweat of trial and error—isn't that what Samuel Smiles preached—Edison happened to pick up a Japanese fan and discovered that carbonized bamboo slivers outlasted all of the other fibers he had tried. He sent assistants all over the world to find the best bamboo and ended his search at the Hachiman Shrine, not far from Bungo Bridge, where the thick green bamboo yielded strong sticky slivers.

"Japanese bamboo! Can you imagine that? Our bamboo made it possible for Edison to develop the light bulb commercially and thousands of them gave light to the world."

"The burning lights of Hachiman," said Shuzo, intrigued by the connections. "Hachiman, our god of war, is in every house, hiding in glass bulbs and one day he will burst out all over the world!"

The engineer coughed out smoked laughter. "Too late for that! Edison no longer uses bamboo. Everything is changing so quickly. Even the steam engines. First it had a single cylinder, then two and now three. Triple chamber, it's called— that's what this ship has. But it's already obsolete. Someone in England built a ship powered by a steam turbine—a great big fan, screaming like hungry ghosts, spinning giant propellers pushing ships across oceans. Our shipyards are already working on these turbine liners. We already have a small turbine below to turn the generators for electricity. Steam— hot wind from fire and water—amazing, isn't it?"

The twin stacks let out thick clouds so dark they could be seen in contrast against the starry sky. Shuzo felt the deep shuddering of the entire ship, quiet proof felt through his feet of the endless repetitions of the triple chambers. The engineer lit another cigarette with a match that illuminated a thick bronze plaque mounted on the wall.

SWAN & HUNTER LTD.

NEWCASTLE-UPON-TYNE

1897

It was a new ship, already in the service of the New Japan. Though he did not know how he would do it, Shuzo saw his future in steam. The engineer must have seen the same for Shuzo and even if he was moved by no other reason than being polite, his offer was perfect.

"Would you like to see the engine room?"

◆

So much steel in motion, groaning, hissing but without the shattering roar he expected. They spoke in loud voices without shouting, their increased volume requiring slower enunciation and repetition. The engineer's explanations swept Shuzo into a torrent above which he tried to stay afloat. Tall and heavy boned, the engineer enjoyed an easy confidence in his worldly knowledge and passed his sturdy fingers through his thick, greasy hair parted in the middle, in a way that Shuzo admired. He was not as old as his father, but Shuzo looked up to him with recognition of his authority, rooted not in age or status, but a mastery of science.

"Behind this wall is the coal, tons of it. This conveyor belt feeds the coal to the burners, but I have to walk into the bin and stoke the pile to keep the nuggets flowing smoothly. I have an assistant—he's in there now—but I have to relieve him often. That's how I get so dirty."

"You don't have to defend your appearance."

"I know, but I like being clean. Now look at this furnace—

filled with tubes that get super-hot to turn water into steam instantly. The latest technology producing tremendous pressure. And it's just fire and water. Wait here a second."

The engineer disappeared behind a maze of pipes and chambers and came back with a long eggplant. He placed the eggplant in a wire basket with a wooden handle and held it in front of a valved nozzle and cracked it open slowly. The steam hissed around the eggplant, which swelled up immediately and in a few minutes was cooked.

"Instant cooking," he declared proudly, "and better than boiling."

They went to a corner of the engine room where a low barrel served as a table surrounded by four wooden stools. He disappeared again and came back with plates, chopsticks, soy sauce and bottles of beer, ice cold. After a toast to steam, the engineer explained the wonders of refrigeration accomplished by compressing liquid ammonia into a rapidly expanding vapor sucking heat out of an enclosed area. They feasted; the noise, hot air and cold beer produced by mechanical power added exhilaration to their simple meal. Having adjusted his eyes to the cramped lighting, Shuzo saw more than he had previously and was impressed by how such massive complexity could produce the simple act of motion. They took turns steaming more eggplants and kept opening more bottles for each other. It was a celebration of the engineer's knowledge and Shuzo's awakening.

"Have you been to Hawai'i before?" Shuzo asked.

"Several times. But first time with this ship."

"Will you spend some time there?"

"Sailors always do. In Chinatown."

From engineer to sailor, his self-demotion was unexpectedly sudden. The man held up a fist with his little finger erect. "*Onna*, women. Nothin' sweeter than a young girl. Have you tasted'em yet?"

Ignoring the fleeting repulsion he felt for this sailor, Shuzo let himself be taken by his boast about another kind of secret knowledge. Mako had told him about umbilical cords, bleeding and babies, but did not mention sweet pleasure. Shuzo wanted to learn about it from this teacher of heat and cold, but the big man's eyes were red and he slurred in a menacing tone. He stuck his little finger into his mouth, dropped his head and sucked hard.

"It's very late. It was already late when we came down. I wonder what time it is?" Shuzo got up to leave. "Thank you for inviting me here. I've learned a lot. Perhaps I can come back again. With my friend."

The engineer removed his finger from his mouth, then raised his hand to wave goodbye, flapping it slowly at his wrist. He jerked his head up, squinted at Shuzo till he remembered his guest and managed to ask, "Know the way out?"

"Yes. I know the way back."

Shuzo reached the other end of the boiler room before he realized he had missed the narrow metal stairway leading to the deck. Maybe there was a toilet somewhere; the beer had generated its own kind of pressure. There, a door. He rushed in, feeling the urgency, shut the door and felt the walls for a light switch.

"*Ah.*"

Her voice was high, without alarm. It was an announcement of her presence, a warning issued too late to prevent him from being surprised, an apology for her being there. Shuzo jumped back, hit his head against the door and slumped to the floor. He thought he came to in a few moments, but he could not tell if the darkness was in the room or in his head. He groped about and landed his hand on the front of her cotton blouse.

"Ex … excuse me," he stammered, jerking his hand back, "but I didn't know…"

She said nothing, but he could tell she was sitting on the floor as well. He tried to stand, but the head pain weighed him down. She placed her hand on his knee, persuading him not to move. He waited for his eyes to get used to the dark, but still saw nothing. She withdrew her hand and he started

68

to reach out again, but pulled back before he could reconfirm her blouse. And then he remembered — and felt — the pressing reason for his entry. It moved him to confess.

"I thought this was a toilet … and I must find one … quickly. Is there a toilet around here?"

She muffled her giggle, girlish and fresh. "Out and to the left." Her voice almost made him forget.

He found the door latch, pushed it open as he pulled himself up and stepped out. They looked at each other in the dim light seeping into the room through the open door and her direct gaze drained him of his will to seal her back in her cell. But he remembered again, shut the door, turned around and hurried to the left.

FIRE AND WATER

SHUZO MISSED BREAKFAST AND BARELY MADE IT FOR LUNCH. His hangover lodged itself in the swollen lump on the back of his head, but the pain dissipated in his memory of the dark encounter, the feel of her breasts, the frozen moment of her gaze. She was huddled as if she were cold, but that was not possible in the steam engine room.

"Nasty bump. How'd you get it?" Mako stopped Shuzo from rubbing his head and examined his wound. "Good thing you didn't slice your scalp open—heads bleed a lot."

Shuzo told him about the engineer and the mechanics of steam and how he had slipped and hit his head on the grated stairway. The girl was too much of a secret, even for Mako. It was for him alone—alone?—surely the engineer knew.

"We can go down there tonight. I told him I would bring you along. When you stand in the engine room, Mako, you can see the future. It's unlike anything we've known before."

The afternoon stretched out to the horizon. No matter how many times he asked, the answers kept receding. Who was she? But mostly he was baffled about himself. Taste the sweetness of a young girl? Maybe Mako could help him understand, but only if he disclosed his secret. And yet he knew he could never tell anyone and *that* is what bewildered him the most. Why should he keep it to himself? He went in to take a nap, but the bunk boards pressed through the thin mat and finally made him sit up on the edge of his bed. He rubbed his head with his fingertips, going easy on the bump and saw the shamisen player walking toward him.

"Been sleeping all day, you lazy shit?" She knelt at his feet and reached under his bunk for one of her bundles, letting her hair brush against his knees. She untied the large *furoshiki* cloth and took out a small box. "Cosmetics," she replied without being asked. Slipping out of her geta, she stepped on his bunk, hoisted herself onto the wool blanket covering the platform above his, sat cross-legged and started to powder her cheeks, a sweet-sour smell sifting down to Shuzo's bed. She spoke into her mirror. "Do you know you snore at night?"

"Me? Snore? Lots of people snore around here. How do you know it's me?"

"Because you stop when I pinch your nose."

"You ... you ... touch ... me ... in the middle of the night?"

"How else can I get some sleep? Besides, I do it very lightly. Shall I show you?"

Shuzo stood up, his eyes level with her bed, her thighs showing from under her gathered kimono. "You've made enough fun of me. You shouldn't pinch other people at night, or poke your chopsticks in someone's face. Have you no manners?"

"Manners!" she howled. "Pigs have no manners! Like people who call other people pigs."

She surmised the words forming in his mind—stinking Okinawan bitch. "Manners," she said, wagging her finger as she leaned toward him. "You should remember your lovely manners." She turned his own strategy against him and Shuzo recognized a skilled opponent—an Okinawan woman at that.

Bad horse, good horse. Maybe she can be useful and I can ask her what I cannot raise with Mako. To this kind of woman I can say things I dare not mention to decent folks. She's a sorcerer, enticing men into their own yearnings while she watches with delight. She did it with her shamisen on the docks in Yokohama and she can still do it with the instrument of her lips playing out scales from charm to insult. Manners, she said. This she-devil deals with secrets about men, keeping and divulging them as she wishes. She knows how a single gaze, crafted for effect, can unravel a lifetime of manners, how a touch can burn. Maybe I could ask her. But first, manners.

"I'm sorry. It was rude of me to call you pigs. I was hungry and angry, but still I have no excuse. Please forgive me."

"I can forgive your hunger, but what about your hatred?"

"My friend already scolded me about that. I don't know. What can I do about it?" The question, his request for her help, slipped out before he could stop it.

"Nothing, really. It will disappear—if you're lucky. It may be happening right now."

Luck. Mako said I will be lucky to love and now she is telling me the same about hate. There is nothing I can do about luck.

"Well, I do not want to talk about love or hate or luck. But I would like to ask you about … well, women." He did not wait for her response. "Let me be blunt. Why are women so full of fire, burning confusion into men?"

"Fire? Women filled with fire? You have it backward—the fire is in men … like you. Women are water. And when *your* fire burns *you* into confusion, water can put the flames out. That is what women do—they drench your fires with water."

Shuzo squinted.

"You'll see," she added, "if you're lucky." Then she dabbed some powder playfully on his face and Shuzo felt no insult.

◆

"What's wrong?" asked Mako. "Did the food upset you?"

"Dinner was fine. I've just been thinking … about things … things I still don't understand."

"Like what?"

"Well, like fire and water … I mean, steam power and Japan."

"You read too much, Shuzo, get carried away into the clouds. Keep your feet on the ground and worry about things you can see and touch, you know, family and jobs and growing vegetables."

"And you read too little. Here grab this railing and feel

the vibrations. That is power generated by clouds of steam. Look at this ship. Tons of steel floating on water. Would it have occurred to you that iron can float? No, only a dreamer, a reader of books, can dare to think about … clouds … and turn it into something … into transportation!"

"And what cloud will you ride?"

"I don't know, Mako. But here comes the man who might show us the way."

The engineer was bath fresh, clean and sober, smoking his usual cigarette. He turned his face seaward and blew out a series of brief smoke rings. "Just like a locomotive," he announced, "on its way to Paris or London or New York. So is this your friend who will join us tonight?"

"This is Mako … uh, I never got your last name."

"Toki."

Taga and Toki. Shuzo understood for the first time the alphabetical reason for their assignment to the same plantation on Maui.

"Pleasure to meet you," said the engineer. "And you, I never asked your name, even though we partied last night."

"Taga. Shuzo Taga."

"Kato. Hiroshi Kato. And I have a surprise for you tonight."

"You're not covered with coal dust." Shuzo mentioned the obvious.

"Unlike you poor fools in steerage, I can take a bath anytime I like. Lots of hot water down where I'm at." He blew out more smoke rings. "Come, let's descend into the belly of this sea dragon."

At the table in the corner of the engine room, the engineer repeated the eggplant offering of the previous night and with sobered eloquence, explained again the wonders of steam and refrigeration. "We make heat and manufacture cold. Feel that beer!" They steamed everything—vegetables, dried fish and even a can of beans.

"Food in tin cans," the engineer pointed out, "another great invention. Heat food, kill the germs, seal it and no spoilage. The French invented canning, it was Napoleon's greatest military secret. But the British learned it in time for Waterloo. Now armies march to the rattle of tin cans. To your health! *Kampai!*"

"See, Mako," said Shuzo, wiping the foam from his lips, "he knows all about technology."

"But some things never change," the engineer said through a mouthful of beans. He clapped his hands and the girl came out with a tray of cold beer. Her hair was braided down her back, stylish in an unplanned way. She was trim and had high, firm breasts that her loose cotton blouse could not obscure. Her coal black hair, the thin lines of her dense eyebrows and her dark eyes made her skin seem as white as any western woman, but smoother, especially with the moisture in the room. Her blouse was tucked into indigo-dyed cotton trousers worn by field laborers.

"Well, aren't you going to say hello to my guests?"

"Good evening." She looked at Mako, avoiding Shuzo.

"What … ah … is this your daughter?" Mako asked.

The engineer laughed, hissing above the steam. "Spoken like a father. Do you have a daughter?"

"Yes," Mako replied, declining her offer of beer.

"If she were my daughter," said the engineer, "I wouldn't be able to do it to her." He took another bottle of beer and drank nearly half of it in one gurgling swig. "But here's my surprise for you. You can have her tonight. For free."

Mako got up. "Time to go." He looked at Shuzo. "I said time to go."

Shuzo stared at the bottle in his hands. "Well, then, good night, Mako, if you must leave us. Sleep well."

"It's time to go." Mako used the stern father's voice.

"Then go. No one is stopping you."

"It's hot as hell in here," Mako said and left.

"Sit, sit," Kato said to the girl, "and pour for your guest."

"But we have no cups."

"Then hold the bottle to his lips! I'll make a proper whore outta you yet!" He finished his bottle and turned to Shuzo,

74

wiping his lips with his arm. "Hav'te train'er by the time we get to Hawai'i or she'll never be 'cepted by the Boss in Chinatown. At least, tha's the deal I have with 'im. So you see, tonight's part of her training. Do *her* the favor. Tha's why she's free."

All I know is what Mako told me. I should have asked the shamisen player for details. How would I start? Does this girl know? Will she teach me?

"Use the room with the bedding and lights," he said to her, "so you can see what you're doing. Remember what I showed you. And, you, lucky boy, gimme a report in the mornin', or I'll make you pay like a regular jerk."

"How much would that be?"

"Very expensive. Young, white as snow and, as you can see for yourself, very beautiful. In Hawai'i, she would cost ten dollars."

"And what part of that does she get?"

"Put it this way. She gets what you make on the plantation —sixty, seventy cents a day. That's good money."

"And how much does the Boss pay you?"

"Twenty-five dollars for every girl I deliver."

Shuzo got up, put an eggplant in the wire basket and walked over to the steam valve. He steamed the purple eggplant till the skin wrinkled brown and walked back to the table.

"I'll double your take," Shuzo said, "fifty dollars."

"What? What're talking 'bout? You don't have fifty dollars."

"How long will you be in port?"

"A week at least."

"Give me five days and I'll pay you fifty dollars. For her."

The engineer did quick calculations, then burst out, "You clever bastard! You sneaky little rat! I see what you're up to. But you're no dummy. Aw'right, deal."

They shook hands, just like the Americans did. The engineer picked up a full bottle of beer and walked off to his room.

Shuzo looked at the girl, who smiled and lifted a bottle to his lips. She did not let it down until it was emptied, all over his face and chest, giving her reason to unbutton and remove his shirt. "But not here," she said softly and led him to the room with the bedding and lights.

What he did that night taught her more about love than the engineer had shown her about positions, more than her mother had said about perseverance and duty and certainly more than her father had displayed when he wept, finally, as he took the cash and counted it to confirm the worth of her body. Shuzo was different and she couldn't believe how lucky she was to feel love so suddenly for a man to live for, to die for, though she could not explain exactly why she'd do that, except that he was so clever, so daring, so quick to take her away from the engineer with a promise instead of cash. He was the first person ever to touch her, deep down, right into her heart. Shuzo, Shuzo … whoever you are, shooting your clever tipped arrows into my soul and into Kato's ass.

Sell before you buy, Father had said. Shuzo put his hands on her shoulders and ran his fingertips slowly down her arms. She was his. He had just bought some water, his first, and it was already sold to men on fire.

BUBONIC BURNINGS

AH MOOK WAS BURNING AND NO ONE COULD PUT HIS fire out. He turned pink with fever, then red from fissured veins and finally black from festering under his skin. He shook violently, threw up, ached in every joint and watched the ceiling of his Chinatown grocery store spin out of control. No one would go near him, and someone finally called the Health Department in downtown Honolulu.

The American doctor hurried through the noisy streets of Chinatown, following the fingers pointing to Ah Mook's grocery store. He entered the back room, took one look at the splitting pus-swellings and stepped back with one word.

"Buboes."

"Bu ... boes?" Ah Mook repeated.

"Your swellings, the rings around your rosies, are called buboes. As in bubonic plague."

"Bu ... bonic ...?"

"Black Death."

Ah Mook closed his eyes and blood oozed from split pores. The doctor left quickly, muttering something about ashes, ashes, all falling down.

The public health authorities blamed each other for not having the courage to shut the harbor down completely. Once again, they went down to the docks to inspect the latest arrival and observed the dead rats falling off the pallets of rice being unloaded from the *America Maru*. Several men swept up dead rats into piles, beat the few still staggering about and shoveled them into the harbor. The health officer ordered an immediate stop to the work and sealed off the gangplank.

"Thank goodness the passengers are on Quarantine Island," he said to his assistant. "Send word that they should be kept there until I clear them. We've got to stop this. Already this is the seventh infected ship in as many weeks."

◆

After entering the channel to the harbor, the *America Maru* had stopped at the end of the long pier built from the edge of the channel to Quarantine Island, where agents examined the passengers' bodies and passports. The narrow walkway had been built over half a mile of the shallow reef and newcomers always pointed excitedly to the fish and crabs in the clear, coral waters. From the tiny island they could look at the city across the harbor and were anxious to get on with the business of remaking their lives. Normally, arrivals were quartered in several buildings for eight days, but the plague had extended their stay. Mako had looked for Shuzo but had not been able not find him.

The engineer had been afraid that Shuzo might abscond with the girl if he let them go ashore to earn fifty dollars in five days, so he had kept Shuzo's passport as security for payment. The more serious problem with passports was that the girl did not have one and would have to be smuggled off the ship. They hid below and watched the steam engine idle as they listened to the footsteps of the passengers disembarking overhead. An hour passed before the pistons resumed their hissing strokes as the ship left the pier at Quarantine Island and continued up the channel to the wharf at the bottom of Nu'uanu Avenue. At the captain's signal, Kato had shut the engine down and the ship drifted perfectly to a stop alongside a pier. The *America Maru* had been secured with thick ropes behind the *Pacific Star* and the unloading of the rice — and rats — had started. An hour later, the health official had ordered a halt to the work and sealed off the gangplank, ruining Shuzo's plan to pose as a worker and carry the girl off in a rice bag.

◆

"How long will we be in quarantine?" he asked Kato.

"I don't know. We ran into the plague in Shanghai, but they didn't place us in quarantine. But surely it will be longer than the five days you have to pay me."

"We'll sneak off tonight," said Shuzo.

"It won't be so easy. They've posted an armed guard at the gangplank."

"What's the English word for doctor?"

It was one of the few words of English the engineer had mastered.

◆

The guard worried more about rats than men. He scanned the dock in the dim evening light, ready to bayonet anything that moved.

Shuzo crawled halfway down the gangplank on his stomach under cover of the squeaking and groaning of the hull rubbing the timber wharf.

"Doc-ta."

The guard did not respond, so Shuzo raised his voice of hushed distress. "Doc-ta!"

"Who goes?" The guard spun around and chambered a round in his rifle.

"Dooc-taa!"

"Oh my god!" The guard moved toward Shuzo, then stopped. Shuzo spread his arms out and went limp on the gangplank. "Oh my god. He's got the plague!"

"Doc…"

"Don't move! Stay right there. I'll get some help." He backed away, then turned and ran.

She sprinted onto the gangplank with their willow suitcases. Shuzo jumped up, took his case and led the way through stacked cargo on the dock until they emerged on Nu'uanu Avenue, which conveniently ran straight from the harbor into the city and on toward the mountains. For several blocks, their geta made the only sounds on the sidewalk planking, but as they entered the downtown area, people were milling about in the evening trade illuminated by brand new electric-arc street lights. They stopped under a large tree with branches spreading as wide as it was tall and from their cover they watched, cautious about their undocumented presence.

Japanese, Chinese, Hawaiian, Portuguese and white men mingled leisurely, listening to the Japanese pimps pitching their wares. Their common language was a Japanese-Hawaiian-Chinese but mostly English pidgin punctuated by hand gestures and quick smiles, or frowns. Negotiations were simple and decisions led to entry into one of the houses. Shuzo counted sixteen of them. Further up on the left side of Nu'uanu Avenue, he read the Japanese signs for Horisho Restaurant, Susumago Photo Studio and Hoshino Watchmaker.

"Strange," he whispered to her, "that a man would want his photo taken or know the time in an area like this. But food makes sense."

They picked a path of shadows leading to the back of the restaurant. Shuzo walked into the kitchen and went up to one of the men.

"Horisho-san."

Horisho stopped, stared and tried to place a name with the face.

"You don't know me. I'm new here, but I've already heard about your restaurant, best Japanese food in Honolulu. In truth —and forgive me for being so bold—I am looking for work and I wonder if you could use some help." Looking toward the girl, Shuzo added, "And my sister as well. We're willing to do anything just for meals."

Horisho turned toward her, swiping the greasy sweat from his forehead and let his eyes linger on the powder whiteness of her face etched by carefree strands of black. He wiped his hands on a dirty apron, strings wrapped around his thin waist and tied in front. Anything? Just for a meal?

"All right. The dishes there. Wash them. Both of you."

"Thank you, Horisho-san, we shall not forget your kindness."

The boiling pots—miso soup, water, tempura sauce—and bubbling oil from crusted cast iron skillets added stickiness

80

to an already humid night. Shuzo ladled hot water into a dishpan, rubbed a pure white Ivory soap onto a piece of burlap and scrubbed the dirty dishes. The girl rinsed, dried and stacked the mismatched earthenware on the open wooden shelf. After Horisho had called out for more clean bowls, Shuzo stopped grabbing whatever happened to be at the top of the dirty pile and washed according to the shortage on the shelf. At 10 o'clock, every stool around the seven pine tables was taken and Horisho reassigned the girl to help the middle-aged, pregnant waitress.

At midnight, Horisho forced the last lingering customer out and locked the door. It took another hour of cleaning and putting away before the waitress set out the leftovers on the largest of the tables.

"How can the three of you do all the work?" asked Shuzo, aware that the five of them had been barely able to keep up with cooking and serving. Horisho held a bowl up to his mouth and shoveled in rice with his chopsticks.

"Do what we have to do," said the waitress, reaching for the fried mullet. "So you're new in town? Couldn't have come at a worst time, what with this plague. Wish we'd stayed in Kumamoto, but my husband wanted to get rich. Me, the only thing I got so far is pregnant." She looked at her cook husband, who found his food more interesting.

"In Honolulu, yes, we're new," said Shuzo, "but we've been in San Francisco for a year. We came in on the *Pacific Star*." The girl looked only at her plate as she ate.

"Good thing you didn't arrive on the *America Maru*," said the husband-cook, taking a break between bites. "We hear she was loaded with the plague and her passengers will be stuck on Quarantine Island for some time."

"It'll be hard for the sugar plantations," said the waitress. "No workers coming in. Now that Hawai'i is American, Chinese no longer welcome. But in the old days, they came in plenty. The long pier at Quarantine Island? Still called the China Walk. Kind of rickety. I almost fell in the water, what with lugging the suitcase. The heavier one. I wish we could move out of this rat hole and live on a plantation. Or go home."

"Well," said Shuzo, "we went through immigration in San Francisco, so we didn't have to do it again here. But we don't have jobs, so we are grateful to Horisho-san. Thank you, Horisho-san."

Horisho grunted.

"He no talk much," said the waitress. "Talking to customers is my job. Horisho-san takes the money, my husband cooks. But not at home."

"You're married?"

"I said my husband, didn't I? We came over together, one of the few. Most are unmarried men." She looked at the girl. "Too delicate for the fields. She'll fry in the sun like this mullet. I mean it, the Hawaiian sun is like fire. Going to work on a plantation, aren't you?"

"Maybe," said Shuzo, "but coming from San Francisco, we're not under contract, my sister and me. Well, it's getting late. And tomorrow ... Horisho-san, could you use us again tomorrow?"

"As long as they don't burn us down," said Horisho, picking his teeth.

"Burn you down?"

"The Health Department," explained the waitress. "They're running the city right now, have more power than the president or governor or whatever he's called. They've been burning buildings suspected of the plague and this area is always mentioned. I think it's just an excuse to get rid of the whore houses, but who knows what the haoles are thinking."

"Hau-lays?"

"White people. It's Hawaiian for whites." She looked at the girl. "Haole skin, she has. You sure you born in Japan? Not San Francisco? " She laughed, all by herself.

"Thank you, Horisho-san. You're so kind. I hate to keep asking you for favors, but could my sister and I spend the night here?"

Horisho shook his head, then looked at the girl. "No good

here. Better you stay my place. Not much, but cleaner than the restaurant floor. Too dirty … for her."

◆

Two futons covered most of the single room floor in the shack on the edge of Chinatown and Shuzo quickly took the middle position. The small house was built on four-by-four posts two feet high, allowing the breeze to pass underneath, cooling the floor. She moved close to Shuzo, sharing the blanket. He remembered what the engineer had said about sweetness and he could not let Horisho get near her. Shuzo used his fingers to keep his eyes open and let himself fall asleep only when he heard Horisho snoring.

Shuzo was wakened by so many birds cooing and warbling at dawn. "Breakfast at the restaurant," Horisho explained as he went to the toilet. "Get your sister up." She opened her eyes.

"Thank you for taking care of me," she said quietly. "You're so good at … arranging things. Last night, how did you know he was the owner?"

"He had the most worried look on his face."

"But why did you tell him we came from San Francisco?"

"Ah, San Francisco. Remember what a good time we had there? You do remember, don't you? If you can't remember, then just pretend, because if you don't, we'll be in trouble. But come on, now, we have a lot to do and I don't have everything figured out yet. This is the first of the five days. Do you see the worried look on my face?"

When they arrived at the restaurant, the police and firemen had already cordoned off the area around it. They passed out flyers and even though Horisho could not read English, he knew what it said. They wanted to burn before the winds came up. The steam pumper was racking hot and the firemen hosed down the photo studio and the clock shop. They fanned out with pitch torches and set fire to the sixteen brothels and the Horisho Restaurant. The flames climbed the wooden structures and roared into the morning blue sky, then backed down into the char. The firemen watered the ashes down, packed their hoses and left.

"How can they do this to you? Will they pay you for your loss?" Shuzo waved his hand at the smoke.

"They say they'll pay us. It's not their fault. It's because of the plague. It's in our interest too. Don't want to catch the black death. Better poor than dead."

"But you lost your restaurant. Why didn't they give you time to take your things out."

"The things are contaminated too. Everything had to be burned."

"What are you going to do?"

"Don't know. Hard to find a location like this. So many people at night. And it takes a lot of money to buy plates and pans."

"Horisho-san, you have been kind to us and I will try to help you."

"What? You're penniless. Washing dishes for meals. How can you help me?"

"I can't do anything right now, but give me a few days and I'll return the favor. In the meantime, I still need your help. Could I use your place in the evenings up to, say, 11 o'clock. Without you."

"Without me? What ... do you plan ... on doing?"

"Ah ... how shall I put this? Shall we say ... a little bit of the evening trade?"

Horisho could not believe the implication. "You mean ... you mean ... with your sister?"

"Just don't come back till eleven. And don't worry. Everything will be all right."

◆

The famous Hawaiian sunset bathed everything in soft orange. Not like Iwakuni, where the color of evening was gray. Shuzo went alone to the burned out brothels, where the men themselves looked ashen. Some turned and walked away; others lingered. They are the ones still burning. The

84

shamisen player was right after all. You can see it in their eyes. Shuzo went up to a well-dressed haole man—he can pay a good price—and motioned for him to follow. The man understood right away. Shuzo flashed ten fingers, the man shook his head and spread out one hand. Shuzo responded with nine fingers, but the man shook his head and agreed to eight. "But I have to see the girl first," he said, "to see if she's worth it." Shuzo shrugged and continued to lead the way.

The girl stood up when they entered Horisho's house. She wore a plain kimono tied with a narrow red sash. She looked to one side and the man stared, surprised by what he saw. He stepped forward, but Shuzo stopped him and pointed to his shoes. He took them off and moved toward her. Shuzo placed his hand on the man's arm, halting him again and nodded to the girl, who untied her kimono, letting the front edges part. The man took off his hat and started to remove his coat, but Shuzo stepped in front of him and showed him ten fingers. The man fumbled for his wallet and gave Shuzo ten dollars.

In the dark fresh air smelling of ginger, Shuzo sat on the outside steps, pleased with what was going on inside. Father was right—sell before you buy. And I am only doing this for Father. Water puts out fire. This is a good place, Hawai'i is, and soon I'll be able to send some money home. But first I must pay the engineer and get my passport back. But wait. It's of no use. I'm here illegally, unprocessed, unregistered even with my own consulate, but I'm here. We didn't do the China Walk to Quarantine Island, where immigration papers are completed. Hah! Kato is holding my passport as if it were valuable to me, but it's worthless! Why would I show anyone my unstamped passport and prove my illegal entry? Hah! I don't have to pay Kato. I'll take the girl and he can keep my passport. But, no, that would be wrong. I am doing this for Father's sake, for justice, for what is right. To get even with Nozaki. My word is better than my passport and I will pay him. I wonder how Mother is doing? What is today anyway? December thirty-first? How could I have missed it? It's New

Year's Eve. Don't they celebrate it here as we do in Japan? Horisho must have been too involved with his loss to have paid any attention. And what about the American with the girl? What do single young men care anyway ... about New Year's Eve? It's just another night of the same old fire. Or maybe it's his way of celebrating. Stunning, so milky white, her skin stranded by her hair ... she was incredible ... when she untied her sash. Was that a shooting star?

When the man came down the steps, he adjusted his cuffs and held out his hand. Shuzo clasped it and shook a foreigner's hand for the first time. Her first foreigner too. In this business, English was not required — bodies speak.

Shuzo rushed up the stairs and into the room, waving the ten dollars, but stopped when he saw her sitting on the floor caressing her arms with lingering strokes, weaving an unseen screen to shelter behind a place for herself and herself alone.

Shuzo dared to intrude. "Are you all right? How did it go?"

She continued her self-caress.

"Did it go all right?"

She stopped, but did not look at Shuzo. "Yes," she finally replied. "He was gentle. Not like the engineer."

"Look. We made ten dollars. In fifteen minutes ... or less."

She glanced at him, barely a sign that she was all right. It was not the first money she had ever earned, but she did not know what she had fetched for her father, who had taken the envelope and pushed her forward to the engineer on the dock by the great steamship. She had cried out for her mother, but her father walked quickly away, back to the fishing village on the Yokohama coast, where he could use the money to pay for a doctor to treat his sick wife. On the way to the harbor, he had said that it was for her mother's sake and for her younger brothers and sisters too, that they had no alternative, that she was making a sacrifice for the family, that they would never forget what she was doing, that it was breaking his heart, that ... and she had reached out to grasp his cracked leather jacket, knowing he was trying to console himself.

The engineer had wasted no time in starting her training at the bottom deck of the ship, in a room blazing with electric lights, showing her positions and how to insert soft pads to keep from getting pregnant. As he spread her legs apart and forced himself in, she crossed her arms over her breasts, keeping them there as he quickly tensed, then lowered his chest onto her as if she were meant to soften his sleep. She struggled to breathe against his snoring weight, but she refused to cry and silently chanted her mantra: *For my mother, my father, my brothers and sisters.* The sound of those words dulled her senses and as long as she kept saying them, more forcefully as the pain had increased, she found something, a little more than forbearance. It was, she hated to admit, something like pleasure and that is what made it so disgusting.

She could do this, she could do this, she had to and now, as she looked at Shuzo holding up the ten dollar bill, a fortune she could multiply, she realized that part of the money was hers, her own and she saw a measure of her worth. She couldn't do it by herself, she needed him, her sudden partner whom she had no choice but to trust. Besides, she knew he cared. Which was why she loved him.

In the brightly lit room, she had discovered a love seed bursting into full flower, skipping the growth in between because for sixteen dormant years she had nurtured it with vague hopes and certain dreams.

"You," Shuzo had said to her, stroking her arm again, "mean everything to me. You will make my trip to Hawai'i worth my sacrifice. You will make it possible for me to return home and ruin Nozaki. I'll make him pay—heh, that's the word—for destroying my father."

Shuzo's face had reddened from alcohol, just like the engineer's, but this man was saving his abuse for someone else. He ranted words she had not heard before and she did not understand what he meant, except that those words seethed with passion, a furious resolve, a reckless willingness to do anything to reclaim whatever it was that this Nozaki, whoever-he-is, had taken away from his father. He had stroked her arm in the steel cage of a room, nothing more had happened, and she had felt his feeling for her, the first time anyone had felt her like that, and it couldn't have been more different from the groping of the engineer. Shuzo cared by not taking advantage. He had drawn her into his obsession and she felt embraced, warm, protected by his need for revenge, his love for his father, extended now to her.

So that's what this is, love. I'm part of your family now, I'm your sister, you said it yourself, though I'd rather be your wife and I can do this, Shuzo, for you, only for you. If I could speak like you, my warrior, then I'd tell you a very long story…

Shuzo folded the ten dollar bill, aligning its corners perfectly and put it in his pocket. He laid his hands on her shoulder, stroked her arms and like morning glory first touched by the sun, she reached out and spread her fingers over his chest.

"Happy New Year," she said softly.

"New Year? Oh, yes, of course! How could I forget? Yes, yes, Happy New Year. It's the last night of the century, all of one hundred years!—can you imagine that?—and tomorrow is a brand new era! Happy New Year, ah…" He looked at her, she who belonged to him, but he still did not know her name.

"Miki," she said, answering before he could ask. "My name is Miki."

THE ANGEL

O N THE FIRST DAY OF THE TWENTIETH CENTURY, HORISHO
showed his guests around town. Every business was
closed for the holiday, so there was no point in looking
for a new site for a restaurant. Horisho took Shuzo and Miki
up the slopes of Punchbowl, the dormant crater that
sandwiched the city between itself and the harbor.

"From here you can see the whole city. See that building
there? Iolani Palace. Used to be for the Hawaiian kings and
queens, but now it's the capitol building of the Territory. Look
at the ships in the harbor. Over there, Naval Row, where the
American warships are at anchor. And there, out in the middle
of the harbor, the China Walk to Quarantine Island. See the
long walkway sticking up out of the water over the reef?"
Freed from his restaurant on a holiday, Horisho was almost
loquacious.

"Look, more smoke," said Shuzo. They must be burning
another section in Chinatown. Even on New Year's Day."

"Rats and the plague don't have holidays," said Horisho.

"The Boss must be looking for new places as well," said
Shuzo. "I wonder where the girls will do business?"

"Speaking of the Boss, how did it go last night?" Horisho
spoke to Shuzo but looked at Miki.

"Very well," replied Shuzo. "The man paid us a good
sum. We'll be able to help you with your new restaurant,
Horisho-san. In fact, why bother with a restaurant? Why don't
you just join us in the night trade?"

"Not sure about that. The Boss is a good customer and I

don't want to compete. Besides, the restaurant's good. Lots of friends. No need to turn the Boss into an enemy."

From Punchbowl, they walked back to Nuʻuanu Avenue and hired a horse cab for a trip into the valley up its slope to the summit of the pass to the windward side of the island. As the vegetation changed from dry grasses to koa trees surrounded by wild ginger smelling sweet even without their summer blossoms, Shuzo imagined that they were entering a fairyland, enchanted but different from anything he had read in travel accounts and story books. A light rain fell, warm, sliding off in beads from giant, heart-shaped leaves and when the drizzle stopped, the moisture remained in the humid air, the soggy barks of trees, and the moss-soaked ground. At the crest, they walked to the Pali Lookout and stepped back from the edge of a thousand foot drop scooping ocean winds into a howling rush. "Watch this," said Horisho, as he picked up a pebble and threw it over the edge, where the upward blast blew it back over their heads. "Good place to jump off, if you're not sure about committing suicide," he said. Miki pushed her face into the updraft, covered her ears and looked over the howling edge.

◆

The first evening of the new century—their second day in Hawaiʻi—was better than the last night of the old era. The same gentleman brought a friend, who readily paid Shuzo's price. They took turns, each one waiting outside Horisho's house, giving Shuzo the chance to practice his list of English words. When they were ready to leave, they all shook hands and one man kept pointing to the ground and nodding his head. He pointed to the burnt brothel area and shook his head. Shuzo understood: it was good here, better than there. They left and Shuzo had twenty more dollars.

It was so easy for him, but when Shuzo went into the house, Miki was crying. "What's wrong, Miki? Did they hurt you? What's the matter?" He picked up her cotton *yukata* and wrapped it around her. She sat with her arms folded around herself and Shuzo knelt behind her and held her by her shoulders. "It's all right, Miki, everything will be all right. Don't cry." He tried to wrap his arms around her, but couldn't find a comfortable position.

"I can't do it," she said at last. "I thought I could, for you, but..."

"But what? Does it hurt?"

She shook her head.

"Are you afraid of them?"

Miki turned around and looked at Shuzo, shaking her head. She pointed at her nose.

"You? What about you?"

"I ... I'm ..." She cinched her yukata tightly. "I get scared when they're doing it."

"Oh, Miki. Is that it? But there's nothing to be afraid of. They won't hurt you. I won't let them, you know that. Just call me and I'll be there."

"No, no," she said. "Not them. Myself."

"Scared of yourself? Now, Miki, how can you be afraid of yourself?"

"It's like going to that windy cliff," she replied. "I go up, up and then at the top, so confusing, I want to jump."

Shuzo was even more confused. What is she talking about? The men drive her up a cliff and she feels like jumping? Into the wind that could blow her right back? Because she's afraid of herself? Afraid of enjoying sex with gentle strangers? It scares her because she likes it so much? Well, whatever the reason, it would be terrible if she refuses to do it. But we all have to do what we have to do. If you put your mind to it, you can do anything. That's what Samuel Smiles says. Then there's the old samurai trick, something Father always talked about even though he didn't have the courage to put it into practice. When you are afraid of doing something, pretend you are someone else doing it. Better yet to be something other than a human being, like a kami, a buddha, a spirit, and then *they* will do what you have to do. If she's afraid of herself, all she has to do is not be herself by being someone else.

"Try," he said. "You could be Kannon, the goddess of mercy. Or, how about Amaterasu, the heavenly shining one? Or, let's see, well, really you should pick someone yourself. Who would you like to be?"

Miki thought about it and Shuzo was relieved. It's working. She's not thinking about whether the idea was good or not, but about which person to be. "Anyone," he urged, "you can be anyone you wish."

"I could be," she started, "I could be—a ghost."

"If you wish. It'll work. Trust me."

◆

The next evening, Shuzo waited on the steps. Two men appeared, well-dressed, haole. Shuzo had not seen them before, but they already knew the price. The first man paid ten easy dollars and walked up the steps. Shuzo was as nervous as the second man was impatient. "Good god," he said after a while, "why is Harry taking so damn long?" When Harry finally came out the door, he lit a cigarette and sat on the top stair. His friend paid Shuzo and walked quickly up the stairs.

"Hey, Frank, slow down, I gotta tell you something," said Harry. Frank stopped. "She's something else, I tell you, never had one like her."

"Like what?" asked Frank.

"Well, she ain't like them wrassling whores. You know, the fat ones falling all over you, acting silly as if they're funny. Moaning and farting. But in there"—he pointed his thumb over his shoulder—"she's something else. You won't believe it. She's like … an angel … yeah, an angel, that's what I say."

"An angel?"

"Yep, you can put gold on that." He sucked slowly on his cigarette as Frank hurried in.

Frank took an even longer time and when he finally came out, he sat next to Harry, who offered him a cigarette. Every breath of smoke was a chance to clarify. Frank made up his mind and declared, "You're right, Harry. I don't know how else to say it. She's an angel, by god. But, hey, did she do to you what she did to me at the end?"

"You mean…"

"Yeah, the little sighs and the pulling, like she really likes it. Made me feel…"

"Like you were fucking an angel."

◆

Word of the angel spread and Shuzo, still worried about Miki, set a limit of two men a night. When they were doing it to her, she pretended to be a ghost or a spirit or a kami, anything but herself. It gave her a strange serenity the men thought angelic and she learned to hold on to her pretense, but as they hurried to their conclusions, she could not help but to return to herself and pull them into her pleasure. Their stale moaning repulsed her back from the edge and they rolled off, looking as if they had fallen from a great height. The men boasted to their friends as if they were sharing a secret: Ever fucked an angel? Tell you where you can do it. You'll never go back to the fucking whores again.

By the fifth day, Shuzo had ninety dollars, six months' worth of plantation pay. In ten days, he could take in a whole year's worth of weeding the fields! On the morning of the sixth day, he went to pay the engineer, but the *America Maru* was still in quarantine and no one could get on or off.

As he walked back to Horisho's place, he saw the smoke of more fires, set with hopes of burning the plague out of Honolulu. Armed guards set up ropes across entry points to Chinatown and allowed only designated groups to leave for their mandatory stripping and scrubbing with Castile soap and water in temporary bath enclosures, open at the top so that the authorities, so many of them, could peer in, especially at the women. After their baths, they were given new clothing and taken to shelters posted with guards carrying rifles.

One fire raged outside the roped off area. The firemen controlled it, keeping the flames confined to one house, Horisho's place. Shuzo ran the rest of the way.

"What's ... going ... on?" He barely got the words out.

"Can't you see?" replied Horisho, holding a single suitcase. "They're burning my home. First my restaurant, now this."

"Miki, where's Miki?"

"I thought she was with you."

"No, no, she wasn't with me. I went down to the harbor by myself."

"The firemen always check. Clear everybody out before they burn." Horisho tried to get an explanation from one of the firemen, but they could not understand each other.

"Horisho-san." A well dressed Japanese man wearing a bowler hat approached.

"Ah, Fujita-san." Horisho bowed.

"Too bad about your house," Fujita said.

"I don't understand why they're burning it. It's not in the infected area."

"But it's a whore house, Horisho-san, a whore house. The Boss found out what was going on here and told the police that a brand new whore from the *America Maru* and its cargo of rat shit was working there."

"*America Maru*?" Horisho turned to Shuzo. "I thought you came on the *Pacific Star*?"

"The Boss is mistaken," said Shuzo. "We came in from San Francisco."

Fujita dropped his cigarette and mashed it into the ground. "Horisho-san, tell your friend here that this is a small town and everybody knows everything. There are no secrets. Especially among the Japanese."

"Where's Miki?" Shuzo asked.

"You mean the new whore? I don't know," replied Fujita.

"I thought you said everybody knew everything."

"Well," said Fujita, "some people know nothing. But I saw the Boss talking to the health officer, who went in the house and brought her out. So young, so white, wearing only a kimono with a red sash. The Boss took her away. You know — well, I shouldn't tell you this, but everyone knows — he likes to try every new girl out. So that he can set the price. Maybe fifteen dollars for her. What did you get for her? Don't tell me. I know. Ten dollars. Too cheap, from the haoles. The first guy, foreman at the Iron Works. He told all his friends. The Boss was pissed, but he envied you. Rich haoles never come to see his girls, only poor sailors. Your girl, she's special." He spat on the ground and walked away.

Horisho kicked a stone. "Shuzo, I won't be able to help you anymore. Fujita works for the Boss, knows everything and I can't be associated with you. I should have known better than to let you use my place."

"I'm sorry, Horisho-san. I understand. But I will pay you something for your trouble."

"No, no. I don't want any money from you. Besides, the health officer promised compensation for my loss." Horisho started to walk away. "Be careful, Shuzo," he called back, "be careful with the Boss."

Insiders. It was Nozaki's game all over again. But an army officer does not run. Fujita was right. There were no secrets. It would not be hard to find the Boss.

◆

"Welcome to Hawai'i!" The Boss did not stand up from the small table on the wide veranda surrounded by red canna lilies. Shuzo walked up the front steps and did not miss the meaning of his gray *hakama* skirt and a black *haori* jacket, just what the trade bosses wear. "So you're the new pimp—or are you a boss yourself? And the girl—very attractive, yes, very nice, so pale, very skillful. You trained her well. Top dollar. Ah, but I am being rude. Let me introduce myself. I am Morita. Please, sit down." Boss Morita poured a cup of sake and pushed it toward Shuzo.

"Taga. Shuzo Taga. Glad to meet you." Morita was so friendly Shuzo felt nervous. He was tall, heavy-boned, large for a Japanese. The Boss wore a wide brimmed straw hat and spoke like an educated man. In the New Japan, Shuzo's high school teacher had said, reason is more important than etiquette. Every problem must be examined thoroughly, critically dissected without regard for personal feelings. Sentiment gets in the way and must be pushed to the side. Even the old samurai were decisive, doing what they had to do, not what they wanted. Shuzo decided to be direct.

"Where is my girl?"

"She's fine, just fine," said Boss Morita. "Now show me some manners and drink your sake. Don't worry about her. She'll be treated well, just as I am treating you as an honored guest. Act like one."

"But I have come to get her. She works for me."

"Really? I asked her about her papers and she said she had none. Perhaps you have them?"

Shuzo stiffened.

"Well?"

"I don't have them with me at the moment."

"But you do have papers for her, right? Her passport?"

"Of course, but let me explain…"

"Taga-san, allow me to give you a little advice. When you tell a lie, you must be convincing. You're a terrible liar. You don't have papers for her. Illegal. That's what she is. And that means anyone can own her, or the police will. Let's not waste your time or mine. I control the women in Chinatown and if you'd like to work for me, we can talk. But you do not work for yourself. Understand?"

There's something terrifying about him. He frightens me and I envy him. He would make a good army officer. Concentrate. He is more direct than I and I cannot match him. Manners, yes, manners.

"Morita-san, please forgive me. I am new here and I do not know how things are done. Like everyone else, I am just trying to make a living for myself and my family back in Japan. I ask your forgiveness … and your help. As a fellow Japanese."

Morita was amused. "Taga-san, you're a slow learner. You have no skill in being sincere. I would forgive you if your apology were genuine, but a cheap 'I'm sorry' doesn't work."

Shuzo wiped his forehead with an open hand. He had been caught, exposed in his naked deference and suddenly he felt comfortable, at ease with returning to confrontation, not to run and hide like his father, that weakling. Honesty, ice-solid candor—that is what Samuel Smiles required for the building of a great nation.

"Morita-san, when you greeted me and said welcome to Hawai'i, were you sincere? Do you really welcome me here? No, you wish I had never arrived here and that is because I am more than you can handle." Shuzo lifted his sake cup toward Morita ever so slightly, held it out for a moment and dribbled the sake on the floor. A body guard unfolded his fat arms, dropped them to his sides and started toward Shuzo, but Morita waved him away. Shuzo put the cup down on the floor. They had passed the point of sheathing what they had quickly—much to their mutual surprise—drawn and crossed.

Morita lifted the large sake bottle and pointed its neck to Shuzo in the typical offer of another drink, inviting him to submit to his kindness, but Shuzo did not pick up his cup. Morita waited for a few moments, then reached across the table and emptied the bottle onto Shuzo's lap. The fat guard howled. "What a waste of good sake! I wouldn't lick the stuff from the floor, but it'd be great to do it off his balls!" Morita grimaced, pretending to be offended by his assistant's crude remarks.

Shuzo got up and started to walk toward the steps. The assistant shouted, "Look at him! Pissed his pants!"

As Shuzo stepped down, Morita called out, "Taga-san! Wait! You have guts all right and I respect that. I have one more thing to say to you."

Shuzo turned around.

"Welcome to Hawai'i!"

◆

The burnings and bathings ordered by the Health Department reduced the number of new cases of the plague and the authorities lifted the quarantine on the *America Maru*. Shuzo went to settle his obligation to the engineer and retrieve his passport for no other reason than to have it.

"I came after five days," he explained, "as promised, but the quarantine was still in effect."

"I understand," Kato replied, "but I was not worried since I have your passport. In doing business, it's good to have guarantees."

Shuzo did not take the time to explain the value of his word over his useless passport, but he told him about the haole customers, how Boss Morita envied him. Anxious to get back to Chinatown, he paid the engineer fifty dollars and thanked him for his trust.

"Trust? I had your passport. Don't you know how security deposits work?"

Shuzo shook his head. "Have you heard anything about when the passengers will be released from Quarantine Island?"

"The captain just told me they should be allowed to enter the city in a few days." Kato recounted his money. "Imagine. You've been in Honolulu for only a few days and have already made a fortune. How is the girl? Never got her name."

"I had her for five days myself, but then lost her to Boss Morita. Do you know him?"

"He's the one who buys my girls. How much did he pay you?"

"Nothing. He knows she entered illegally and will turn her in if I insisted on payment or tried to get her back."

Kato thumped his finger against Shuzo's head. "Think, Taga-san, think. Who can take her away from the Boss? Not you, not me."

◆

The Honolulu Iron Works produced as much noise as it did railings and gates for the growing city. The banging of thick plates and girders, the scraping and grinding, the chatter of the chain hoists, the hissing of pleated bellows, the pounding of iron against iron—even people speaking the same language could barely understand each other against the loud commotions of steel.

"What?" shouted the foreman, holding an open hand to one ear. "What did you say?"

"Prease … talk … you." Shuzo had memorized a list of twenty words translated at his request by Horisho's cook, who knew at least a hundred in English. Shuzo pressed his fingertips together against his lips, then turned them toward the foreman, opening and closing them rapidly.

The foreman understood, especially since he recognized the pimp of the angel. He wiped his blackened hands on a dirty towel, took off his canvas cap and ran open fingers through his blond hair, as if he needed to be presentable to the man who had the girl whose fairness matched any American woman's. He remembered how firm and supple she had been, how she had moved with him, neither leading nor following, how she had been his first Oriental girl. He had had Hawaiian women before and haoles as well, but a non-white with white skin was too exotic, unexpected in his imagination of possibilities. He could still feel her rhythmic pressing and withdrawal, like small waves spreading on night sand, disappearing through its loose grains, playing out and coming back again, coming, coming. He had been seduced into a swirl of emotions he had never experienced before and, seeing Shuzo, he wanted her again.

"Let's get outta here and find a quiet place to talk." He opened and closed his fingers as Shuzo had done and pointed to a lauhala tree outside. He took out a pack of cigarettes, held one out for Shuzo, who refused.

"So," he said, blowing out smoke like a breath of fresh air, "how is that girl of yours?"

Girl. That was on Shuzo's list. "Gir … gir … ga-lu. Boss tay-ku ga-lu."

"Took her? Bet he did, aw'right. Told my boss 'bout her and he liked her too. A whooole lot. Said she was an angel." He pointed to someone in the Iron Works, then flapped his arms as wings.

Shuzo didn't understand, but he knew that the foreman

hadn't either. He shook his head. "No, no. Boss … Morita … tay-ku." He jabbed a finger toward Chinatown.

"Boss Morita? I know him, everyone does. Boss Morita took … ah … take … girl?"

Shuzo nodded, bouncing from the waist up. He pointed to his nose, the equivalent of an American pointing to his chest to indicate himself, then held out both hands, swiveling his wrists to signify he didn't have her. He reached into his pocket, pulled out a ten dollar bill and offered it to the foreman. "You … findu ga-lu. Gi-vu me." He acted it out, trotting toward Chinatown, making a grabbing motion and coming back.

The foreman took a long draw, the better to think. Boss Morita was not one to cross. There was that sailor who tried to sneak away without paying for the extras and he never made it back in time to catch his ship. The foreman studied the burning tip of his cigarette, divining its wisps, remembering. He passed his hand through his hair again.

"All right," he said, taking the ten dollars. "I'll do it. But I gotta think of a plan." He tapped a finger to his head.

"T'ank you, t'ank you." Shuzo bowed to the man he had to trust and gave him a piece of paper on which he had written in block letters, KOBAYASHI HOTEL. "Maybe," Shuzo started the sentence he had practiced, "maybe you say, rat bite ga-lu get sick." He tapped his own head.

◆

Jerome Stewart had left Idaho City in 1898 after the gold rush had panned out, as they said, leaving his blacksmith shop to his older brother Peter. White miners had sold their cheapened claims to Chinese willing to extract less for more work, but business was still good for Stewart Bros., the Chinese miners needing their tools and services no less than had their white predecessors. What worried Peter was books and Jerome's love for them. He drank words like the Chinese smoked opium and would sit for hours, intoxicated by stories of strange places. Peter tried to hide *The Principles of Nature*,

100

Her Divine Revelations and a Voice to Mankind, a frightening title proving that the clairvoyant author was crazy, but Jerome demanded it back and Peter gave in, being afraid simply to throw it into the garbage heap. Jerome's other favorites were more acceptable, the adventure tales by the respected Robert Louis Stevenson and Isabella Bird's rapturous accounts of her travels to the Orient and the Sandwich Isles. More than the living spirits of the dead summoned by clairvoyants, it was his own exotic fever that afflicted Jerome, and in a town of people working the earth, he dreamed of the ocean, small boats of reckless men sticking harpoons into gigantic whales, schools of squid swarming clear lagoons, smoked ducks dripping oil from racks in noisy Chinese markets, Japanese kimonos and chopsticks. He yearned to follow Isabella's tracks and Peter would have tried to prevent him from leaving if he had been convinced that he could reason obsession out of his brother.

Jerome's own doubt about the reasonableness of his fascination kept him from leaving and in order to settle the issue in his mind, he went to see a Shoshoni fortune teller, whose antiquated cooking pot he had once fixed by forging a strip of metal over the crack. Jerome told him the long story of his interest in the tropics and the Orient and brought it all to a single point: should he make the trip or not? The old man did not pray or chant or perform a ritual, but told Jerome that he would find his answer in the howling of wolves since animals could capture people's hearts. Come back, he said, on the night of the next new moon.

On the appointed night, Jerome went back and they walked out to a grassy knoll, sat and waited. The wolves started to howl, as they did on most nights and the fortune teller listened to their conversation, their moaning stories traded back and forth. He heard for the first time their modulations and changing pitches, the range of lower and higher notes, the varying number of barks before the drawn out wailing. For the fortune teller, every shrill was a word, a message, and he sorted through their meanings and came to their conclusion.

"Mr. Jerome," he said with distilled clarity, "the howlings say go." Jerome was delighted and thanked him profusely and never noticed that the wise man did not say whether the howlings were of the wolves or Jerome's own heart. For him, the wolves had solved his problem and they had a natural wisdom surpassing human intelligence. When he told his brother about the reasons for his decision, Peter sighed in exasperation and offered his good wishes and fifty dollars to help with the trip to Seattle and a steamer for the Orient.

From the deck of the *Nevada* approaching the Sandwich Isles, Jerome had watched the dark tip of Haleakalā poke through the clouds over Maui, loom larger, turn blue, then green with patches of brown, as Moloka'i floated into view, up out of the ocean. The steamer cut through the channel, O'ahu on the right, and rounded Diamond Head to the lee in the late afternoon sun, a wash of orange bleeding into red. As they approached the harbor's mouth, he glanced down at Isabella's book, opened to a dog-eared page.

> The nights are glorious and so absolutely still, that even the feathery foliage of the algaroba is at rest. The stars seem to hang among the trees like lamps and the crescent moon gives more light than the full moon at home. The evening of the day we landed, parties of officers and ladies mounted at the door and with much mirth disappeared on moonlight rides and the white robes of flower-crowned girls gleamed among the trees, as groups of natives went by speaking a language which sounded more like the rippling of water than human speech.

The *Nevada* took on the channel pilot from his small sailboat, eased into the narrows, passed the China Walk elevated over the reef to Quarantine Island and tied up at the wharf at the bottom of Nu'uanu Avenue. Jerome walked the gangplank, jumped off, headed to Chinatown, smelled the ducks dripping from racks and went all the way to the deserted beach at Waikiki, where no one saw him take off his clothes and dive into the ocean of his dreams. Jolted by the initial cold of the water, he was delighted by how quickly it felt warm, the amniotic sea of birth inviting him to a new life, forever. In the confluence of water, air and fading sun, he floated, his toes bobbing along the coral earth. Everything he wanted was here and he would let the *Nevada* leave without him. Easily.

Already a master smith at twenty-six, Jerome had been hired as a foreman at the Honolulu Iron Works and the ease with which he was blessed with a job caused him to write excited letters to Peter. After a year that blurred with new experiences, his employer extended a loan for him to purchase a small house on Makiki Street on the lower slopes of Punchbowl, and Idaho City disappeared from his sense of home. He wrote to Peter, regaling him with true stories, urging him to come, but Peter was doing well, was ready to marry and start a home where he belonged. "And what about a wife?" Peter had written back. "Are there enough women of our kind in Honolulu?" Jerome wanted to tell Peter about the white Japanese girl, but decided to leave her out of his reply. She had been, after all, a commercial transaction, a passing moment in a night of stars shimmering like lamps hanging in the algaroba trees.

Jerome left his Makiki house early in the morning to give himself enough time to stop by the Kobayashi Hotel and return the ten dollars to the Japanese pimp. What had he been thinking of when he agreed to rescue the girl from Boss Morita? It was insane, not only because Morita was a dangerous man, but because her allure had faded like stars in a morning sky. A passing fling not even worth mentioning to his brother. The memory of the night with her had been recent when the pimp had made his bold request, but after a few days of hammering at the Iron Works, of receiving the letter from Peter with his domestic question, of thinking about turning his Makiki house into a home with a good wife followed by children, Jerome was ready to give up the girls in the night trade.

From Makiki Street, he walked to Nu'uanu and saw the smoke of another Health Department ordered burning in Chinatown. The morning paper had announced that Block 15, the area surrounding Kaumakapili Church, would be burned. Despite the systematic fires, the plague still claimed its victims and a group of doctors, some very prominent in town, had expressed doubts that fire could burn the *pestis* out of Honolulu. But he trusted the Health Department and, truth be told, the burnings had increased business for the Iron Works. Already he had received orders for fabricating fences and gates for the camps being built for residents burned out of their homes.

Jerome came up to the side lane where Morita had relocated his brothel to a large, two-story house with a wide veranda. The street was empty and quiet, returned to normal from the frenetic transactions of the previous night. The orange canna lilies screening the veranda were morning fresh, ready to hold firm till noon, when they would yield to the afternoon heat by drooping their petals. It was a rusty squeak that caught his attention, then the sway of the chains attached to the porch swing from the ceiling. Back and forth, coming and going, slowly. He stopped and saw her sitting in the swing, even fairer in the sunlight.

A morning greeting, nothing wrong with that in the proper light of day. Jerome turned into the lane, walked up to the closed gate at the picket fence and tipped his hat. "Good morning. Beautiful day, isn't it?" She looked back blankly, not recognizing him or the words he spoke. The swing moved forward, taking her into the full sun, then back again into the shade of the eave. Sun and shade, sun and shade. He turned to leave, then looked at her again. The changing light did not affect her expression, a mask that could not hide her sadness, or was it the visible tip of an iceberg of anger? Jerome turned to leave again, but he opened the gate and entered the yard instead.

"Are you all right?" he asked, walking up the three steps to the porch. She planted both feet on the floor, stopping the swing. She did not respond to his request to sit next to her, so he stood, remembering what she looked like underneath her large sleeved blouse, her blue cotton skirt hemmed below her knees. "Are you all right?" he asked again, now more certain that something was wrong, that he might have had something to do with her sadness, for he was the one who had bragged about his find and sent his boss and friends to her. They all talked about her, friends sending more friends and though she was a recent addition to Boss Morita's stable, she was in great demand, even as her price quickly ran up to an exorbitant twenty dollars. They had paid well, a fair exchange, one that favored her, if anything, so she had no reason to be troubled, really. She pushed the swing into motion once more, sun and shade, and looked straight out into the yard. The silence on her face declared an indictment, though he was uncertain of her exact complaint, but Jerome felt responsible and apologized anyway, quietly asking forgiveness for whatever, if anything, he might have done. The bells of Kaumakapili Church in Chinatown struck, nine times.

He started down the stairs and sensed that she might be following him, but he dared not turn around and look at her face. Halfway across the lawn to the gate, she touched his sleeve, reached for his hand and came up beside him. They kept walking across the yard, his hand in hers and she opened the gate, for him, he thought, but she stepped onto the gravel sidewalk first and pulled him toward her.

"*Oi*! Son-a-bitch! Wat da hell!" Fujita burst through the door, jumped the steps and ran across the yard, repeating the expletives of his waterfront English. "Son-a-bitch! Wat you doin?" He grabbed Miki and pulled her away from Jerome.

"Nothing," said Jerome, straightening his sleeves, answering Fujita's question. Miki looked at Jerome, directly, for the first time. "Well … uh … nothing except for … the rats. I mean, I was just carrying out my orders from the Health Department."

"Healt' Depa'tment? You not docta, you fo'eman at da Iron Works."

"That's my regular job. But I've been deputized—you know what deputized means?—by the Health Department, ah, to bring in persons suspected of the plague. They need to be disinfected and put in the holding camps. This girl came in on ... on a ship with rats and was bitten. Rat bite ga-lu get sick. Plague. Understand? Bu-bo-nic plague."

Fujita let go of Miki and stepped back.

"You can keep her if you like," said Jerome, feigning nonchalance, "but if I were you, I'd let her go to the shelter. And ... I'd burn her bedding and belongings." He glanced up at the second story bedrooms, pointed to the smoke in Chinatown, reached into his pocket and pulled out several sheets of folded paper. "Let's see," he said, as he looked for the Health Department's order for five new iron gates for the quarantine camps. "Here it is." He showed Fujita the official seal of the Health Department printed on the purchase order. Not able to read English, but recognizing something official in the seal, Fujita was convinced of Jerome's authority and stated mission and backed away a few steps.

"Excuse me," Jerome said officiously, reaching for his pen, "but since she was living in your house, you will need to sign the bottom of this order to authorize her release ... you know ... to let her go."

"Okay, okay," Fujita muttered and took the pen from Jerome. He scribbled his name in Japanese. Jerome blew on the wet ink and squinted at the characters he could not read. "Let's see, your name is...?"

"Fujita."

"Ah yes, Mr. Fujita, thank you so much. I shall report that you were most cooperative." He held out his hand. Fujita stepped forward, by now grateful for the thoroughness of the Health Department, offered his hand in return, then decided against touching the man next to the infected girl. He smoothly transitioned his hand motion into a wave goodbye, walked quickly back into the house and shouted out orders in Japanese, something about beds and burning.

Jerome looked at Miki, taken into his unplanned care so quickly, all because of an innocent greeting on a fine morning. He hadn't meant to and remembered that he had been on his way to tell the Japanese pimp that he wouldn't retrieve the girl. Her skin was fresh and clear like the water he had splashed in and the morning sun showed her flawless.

"Well..." he said, realizing that he had nothing to say, that even if he did, she could not understand him. "Well..." He started down the graveled side of the road, stopped and turned around. She was standing in the same spot. "Well, c'mon. You were the one who came after me." She didn't move and he went back to her. "Maybe you'd like to go back to Fujita?" His name made her glance up at Jerome and she pointed to her feet. "Oh, I see. No shoes." She took a step gingerly, trying to find a spot of least discomfort, wobbled and regained her balance. "Here," he said, offering his arm, expecting her to take it like a lady, but she was concentrating on her next step. "Shit," he said, no longer the gentleman, "let's go back and get your shoes." He started back toward the gate, but she grabbed his arm and looked up at the second story bedrooms. Fujita and the girls were laughing, mouths wide open, fingers pointing, their cackling unheard but seen through the windows. "Aw, shit!" he said, swearing resolve, which she mistook for anger and he picked her up into his arms, his frontier gallantry returned. She fell into position naturally, wrapped her arms around his neck and laid her head on his broad shoulders. She's so light, he thought, and started down the road. She looked back at the house. Fujita was still laughing, but the girls were darkened by envy.

He felt her breath against his neck as they walked toward Kaumakapili Church and he could not stop himself from thinking about the sacrament called matrimony. Had he not known her like a wife? But there had been others as well, so why should she make him think of marriage? She was just a whore, like all the rest, and he had retrieved her from one pimp to take to another.

A sudden gust of wind wobbled his balance and he set

Miki down to get out his handkerchief to wipe his dust-filled eyes. He blinked to draw out tears and carefully worked the dust grains to the inside corners of his eyes, where he carefully dabbed them out. He looked up, blinked several times to confirm the sight of the flames at the top of the twin steeples burning their way down to the sanctuary of Kaumakapili Church wrapped in smoke from fires in areas far beyond Block 15.

"People have two eyes the better to see with, two ears the better to hear with and the church needs two steeples the closer to God to be with." With that famous royal opinion, King David Kalākaua had convinced the architect to design something more ambitious than his original flat gabled church hugging the ground. Honolulu already had grandeur in Kawaiaha'o Church, exquisitely rendered in white coral, not far from Iolani Palace. Kaumakapili was on the northern edge of Chinatown and was to be for the ordinary people, green-grocers, butchers, laborers and the poor. As its twin steeples had risen, plank by fir plank, capping the high brick towers, people saw the King's point and felt themselves lifted in spirit and pride they had not felt before. And now, only twelve years after their completion, the spires were coming down, lower and lower as the flames shot higher.

Jerome ran all the way with Miki in his arms to Beretania Street, just as the burning steeples crashed onto Engine No. 1, Honolulu's state-of-the-art pumper. The firemen had pushed the steam engine to its limits, but the King's spires were closer to God than the streams of water could reach. A sudden wind had blown embers over the watered down buildings serving as fire breaks around the church and up around the steeples and from that lofty source, sparks gusted over a wide area. The fire front widened and jumped the streets — Beretania, Pauahi, Hotel, King and Queen — and marched south toward the waterfront. The fire chief ordered the remaining engines to retreat toward the Iron Works, where they would make their last stand with the help of fire boats spraying down the dock area. Still carrying Miki and too tired to run, Jerome walked quickly toward the Iron Works, a block away from the wharves.

"Here," said Jerome, stopping at a pile of belongings abandoned on the street, "put these on and run to the Palace. There should be an aid station somewhere. They'll feed you there. I've got to get down to the Iron Works." He set Miki down and grabbed a pair of leather sandals. Miki put them on and looked back toward Kaumakapili Church.

"No," said Jerome. "The other way." He turned Miki toward the Palace and pushed her. "That way. Run!"

Miki turned around and headed back toward the church. "No! No!" Jerome shouted and started after her, but he stopped, knowing he had to get down to the Iron Works quickly. Miki ran back up Nu'uanu Avenue and turned onto Beretania and stood in front of the smoldering brick shell of the church, the front façade with its stone pointed gable, the square twin towers missing their wooden spires. On either side of the church, the wooden buildings, once soaked with water, crackled as dry tinder and Miki stepped back into Block 10, which had been burned clear a week earlier. She saw what she had come back for in the nave of the right tower and ran into its protected hollow, huddled against the bricks, feeling their surprisingly cool surfaces.

"You'll be all right," she said to the cat, which she had seen from Jerome's shoulder. She tore a strip off the lower edge of her blouse and wrapped the cat's injured leg. Rocking back and forth slowly, she cradled the black cat with white spots and hummed quietly until it purred. She turned the hem of her skirt over the cat, covering its ears to keep out the sounds of dynamite set off by firemen desperately trying to blast fire breaks.

"You'll be all right," she said and whispered a song about the rabbit in the moon.

ANNA

Dear Father and Mother:

Happy New Year! It must be cold in Iwakuni, but I hope you are well. I arrived in Honolulu just at the end of the last century and welcomed the new era on this tropical island. The trip over was smooth, uneventful, boring actually and I didn't get seasick. On the train to Yokohama, I met a man who was also coming here on the America Maru. Mako is his name. He is married and misses his family. All of us do.

I am happy to report that Hawaii is truly a land of opportunity. I have a feeling that I will do very well here and I hope to be sending you some money soon. As you might have read in the papers, Honolulu is suffering from the plague, but it is confined to Chinatown. It's not that bad, really and the controlled burnings seem to help.

Well, this is just a short note to wish you a Happy New Year and to let you know that I am ready to work hard in the cane fields, make some money and return home. Give my best to Grandpa and Grandma.

Shuzo
Kobayashi Hotel, Honolulu
January 20, 1900

There, my first letter. I'm sure I can post it with the clerk downstairs. It's risky to be carrying around so much cash. I need to open a bank account. Didn't I see a sign for the Yokohama Species Bank? I'll send a modest amount back home, not that I'm unwilling to support them, they're my parents after all, but they'd wonder about how I'm making my money if I send too much. I can hardly believe it myself. But I shouldn't get ahead of myself. If I don't get Miki back, I'll have to work on a plantation. For seventy cents a day. Chicken shit. But ten dollars in fifteen minutes! I wonder what that Iron Works foreman is doing. I've been waiting at this hotel for nearly a week. Maybe he's run off with my ten dollars. Boss Morita, that bastard, thug of a thief, making money off Miki. My Miki. Is he giving her any of it? Is that smoke I smell?

"Out! Everybody out!" A clerk ran up and down the hallway, banging on doors. "*Kaji*! *Kaji*! Everyone out!" Shuzo threw his few belongings into the willow suitcase and went out into the hallway. One man was in his underwear, stretching his arms. Shuzo walked toward the stairway and was nearly knocked over by someone bursting out his door, still in his underwear.

"Mako?"

"Shuzo! What are you doing here? Where've you been?"

"Here. I mean, I've been here in Chinatown. And you? Shouldn't you be on Maui by now?"

"The interisland steamers aren't running because of the plague. They kept us on Quarantine Island for a long time and released us to this hotel. We've been reassigned. You too. Where have you been? They called your name and I told them you were sick. We're going to a plantation on this island. Place called Waialua. You're coming, aren't you?"

Mako's room door was still open, but someone closed it from the inside. Mako put his hand on the brass knob.

"Fire! Fire! Get out!" The clerk was running through the hall on the floor above.

"You have ... a guest?"

Mako looked down.

"*Oi*, don't worry," Shuzo said, as he put his hand on Mako's shoulder. "I understand. This is Chinatown. And we're all alone in the middle of the ocean. But how'd you arrange for a whore to come to your room? And tell me, Mako, you can tell me, you're my teacher, after all, how much does she cost?"

Mako cleared his throat. "Later, I'll tell you later. Right now we'd better get out of here. Saturday. The train for Waialua leaves on Saturday. From the station by the river." Mako cracked the door open, slipped in and shut it quickly, but it was open long enough for Shuzo to hear the muted sound of a shamisen.

◆

They said it was a *controlled* burning, but it got out of hand, way up there, by the church. Didn't it used to have two tall points? Shuzo walked quickly on Queen Street toward Waikiki, but on Nuʻuanu Avenue, uniformed soldiers with bayoneted rifles and men armed with clubs stood behind a rope line.

"Get back. No one leaves the area."

Shuzo understood the language of rifles and clubs, but he set his suitcase down, rolled up his long sleeves and held his arms out, turning his hands over. "No sick, no sick," he said.

"Sure, sure, no sick," someone snickered. "But you Chinese. Stay in Chinatown."

"No Chinee. Japanee."

"Same thing. All infected."

I need to learn English, to tell these stupid bastards that we have guns and bayonets too and warships. We sank the Chinese fleet, do they know that? And colonies, we had them before America took over these islands. And the Philippines for that matter. Shuzo stepped up to one of the guards and ran his finger on the smooth leather strap crossing his chest. The soldier just stood still, then stepped back and unshouldered his rifle. A stocky man with a thick mustache tapped Shuzo's chest with the end of his hickory axe handle. "You making fun of us?" Shuzo nodded, bobbing his head. "See?" someone said. "They always apologize."

Shuzo picked up his willow case, turned up Nu'uanu Avenue and headed toward Kaumakapili Church, but two soldiers stopped him and pointed with their bayonets toward a compulsory bathing station.

◆

Jerome helped the firemen position their pumpers on the north side of the Iron Works, the west side being left for the fire boats and their incredibly powerful pumps capable of sending water streams all the way from the harbor. Satisfied that the Iron Works was safe, Jerome headed toward Kaumakapili Church to look for the girl. He found her sitting in the open nave, eyes closed, cat cradled in her lap. A strange creature, he thought, and he tried to shake off the attraction of her sadness with the reminder that she was just a common whore, even though she was available for an uncommon price. At that price? A common whore, *even* at that price. That's all she was.

"Are you all right?" he asked for the third time that day. She opened her eyes, looked at Jerome and smiled without joy or relief but an inviting recognition that awakened him. She stroked the cat and he reached out and touched her hair. "Can you get up?" he asked, looking to see if she still had on the leather sandals. He reached for her arm, helped her up and put his arm around her shoulder. Without thinking about what he was doing, he led her and the cat to his house on Makiki Street.

Jerome threw some rags into a corner of the kitchen and she placed the cat on them. He heated some water for her bath — she was covered with soot — then led her in and helped her undress. She was not shy and he looked at her, then pulled the shade down over the window. It wasn't the first time he was seeing her and besides others had gazed as well, friends he now regretted. But he had brought her to his house, where he could no longer think of her as a common whore who

113

belonged in another kind of house. She was in his home, so he helped her into the tub, gave her some soap and towels and left the bathroom, closing the door behind him.

From the kitchen cupboard he took out a bottle of bourbon, poured a shot and jerked his head back. He refilled the glass. What am I doing? Where is this going? She cannot be my companion, never. We cannot even speak with each other. And yet he thought of sleeping next to her every night, of waking to the smell of bacon frying in the morning. They could show each other what to do and it would work out in silence; no, not in silence but in *a language which sounded more like the rippling of water than human speech.* As for communication, he already felt an affection far deeper and more moving than what he had felt with women of his kind, as his brother had put it, and their endless blatherings. Surely we could try. She likes me as much as I am attracted to her. It's mutual. It happens this way, doesn't it, without reason? Between unlikely people? It's all in the stars and other powers beyond our control. Surely she would prefer a life with me rather than with that pimp putting her out night after night with strangers.

Ah, but the pimp! I'll return his ten dollars and offer him twenty more. Not that I have to. It's not like a commercial transaction. More like a dowry, a gratuity, a finder's fee. He does not own her and she can walk out on him at any time. She's free and can choose any life she wants. Can't she?

Anna. I shall call her Anna.

She came out of the bathroom wrapped in a towel too small to conceal her completely. Jerome gathered her clothes and started to wash them in the bathtub, the water still warm and soapy. She stood behind him and laughed gaily, this tall American washing her clothes. "You're not mocking me, are you?" he said smiling, knowing that even if she was amusing herself at his expense, he was pleased to have heard the rippling in her voice. He rinsed her skirt and blouse, squeezed it as much as he could and stepped out onto the porch to hang them on a line. He was hungry, went into the kitchen, picked her up from the cat's corner and carried her to his bed. She

114

took off the towel as he undressed and he lay next to her, feeling her presence, unhurried. This is how it could be, day after day. She turned on her side and touched his face. "Anna," he said, "from today on, you will be Anna." He rolled toward her and reached down between her legs, but she cast her eyes to the ceiling, remembering something, slipped out of his grasp and out of bed and went to the kitchen to talk to the cat. Strange creature, he thought, pulling the cool sheet over him and waited for her to come back to bed.

◆

"I can't go to Waialua," Shuzo said to Mako at the train station. "Not until I find Miki."

"Miki? Who's Miki?"

"You know, the girl we met in the engine room. You see, well, it's a long story that happened in a short time. I'll tell you all about her later."

"She's with you?"

"Well, no, as you can see, not right now. But, yes, she's with me." Shuzo looked at the Okinawan woman. "And *she's* with you?"

"Sort of, I guess. We got to know each other on Quarantine Island. Nothing else to do."

Shuzo stifled a smile to keep from laughing and Mako soft punched his shoulder. Were any of the other guys clever enough to work as fast?

"What about the stink … you know, her gang?"

"They had contracts at Kahuku—another mill on this island. But Chiyo—that's her name—she's going to Waialua, where we've been reassigned."

"At the hotel, the woman in your room … the shamisen … Chiyo?"

"Figure it out, Shuzo. I'll give you a hint. The woman in my hotel room didn't cost me anything. To answer your question about price. And what did Miki cost you?"

"More than you can imagine, more than I can explain right now."

"Mako, time to go," Chiyo said. "Train's leaving." She tugged Mako's arm and smiled at Shuzo. "Oh, yes," she said, resuming an old conversation. "Fire and water. Remember?"

"Look," said Mako as he picked up his bag. "I'll make excuses for you, but get yourself to Waialua as soon as you can." Chiyo kept hold of his arm and they ran to board the train.

Ah, Mako, you're married and you love your wife. Your beautiful wife. Why do you get all the beautiful women? It makes no sense, dumpy guy like you. And when we first met Miki in the engine room, you walked out in self-righteous disgust. You're a damned hypocrite, Mako. Everybody's crooked here. Is it the air? The ocean? The vast distance from our families? On the ship over, Chiyo slept on the bunk above me, dropped down to pinch my snoring nose. She powdered her face, then mine, that witch. She's cast a spell over Mako, she's a spider wrapping her victim in her web. Mako is too weak to resist her. She can get anything she wants. Not like real Japanese women, shy and passive. But why Mako? I wonder what it's like to have her put out my … I mean, his fire, but then, I'm not on fire and she can pour herself all over me and I wouldn't care. But Mako, he's drowning in her water and his poor, beautiful wife, at home with her favorite color red. Damn you, Mako, you sleazy pig, you've become one of them.

Shuzo stared after them, even after they had disappeared into the train and as the whistle blew out steam and the cars banged against each other until the engine gained a steady pull, Shuzo kept on staring and wished he was in Mako's place. Waialua, a more isolated place, a secret haven where anything can happen because nobody would find out.

◆

From Kukui Street down to Queen Street, from the river across to Nu'uanu Avenue, the fire burned 38 acres, almost all of Chinatown. The government built hasty quarters for the refugees, kept trying to scrub everyone clean and secretly hoped that the disaster was the final cure, but people still came down with the plague, though at a less than epidemic rate. The entire area looked like a war zone, torched by barbarians running wild through the streets. Everyone said, endlessly it seemed, that it was a miracle no one died, from the fire, that is.

The real miracle was the speed of the cleanup and rebuilding. The government did its best to compensate for losses, but its best was a pittance, though Shuzo was impressed that it even made the effort. Would the Japanese government have done the same? Maybe more. New lumber was piled in stacks, new structures framed and Chinatown rose like a phoenix from the ashes. The Iron Works had been saved and Jerome was busier than ever.

Jerome refused to talk with Shuzo, saying, truthfully, that he was too busy with rush orders. Shuzo kept going back, waiting for him to take a break, which never happened, and finally caught him as he was walking out at the end of the day.

"Ga-lu, my ga-lu? Morita-san no have."

"Your girl? Ah yes, forgive me for being so busy. But yes, I have your girl." Jerome pulled out his wallet and took out thirty dollars. "I'm returning your ten and paying you twenty."

Shuzo looked at the money and understood Jerome's intent. "No, no money. Ga-lu."

Jerome had not considered the possibility of Shuzo's refusal and suddenly felt trapped. If he doesn't take the money, then am I stealing the girl from him? Can I still keep her, rightfully? But he does not own her. Never did. Nobody owns her. She gets to choose. Still, he stuffed the money in Shuzo's shirt pocket.

Shuzo took it out and threw it back in Jerome's face. He cursed him in flawless profanities of his native tongue. A man of no honor, a dirty crook, stinking American, stupid bastard, slave trader, kidnapper, sexual pervert, the shame of western civilization. Even in Japanese, he finally ran out of adjectives and nouns and shifted to verbs. I'll cut your balls off, stuff them in your ass, hitch you to a wagon like a shit-horse and make you pull me around the streets of

Honolulu. I'll … I'll … and Shuzo realized the futility of what only made Jerome smile, bewildered and amused.

"I'm sorry," said Jerome, "but you don't own her and she is staying with me because she wants to. I'd take the money if I were you, but if you don't want it, then fine, it makes no difference to me." He picked up the thirty dollars and held it out, but Shuzo spat on the ground. Jerome stuffed the bills into his pocket and turned away.

Shuzo followed him, dropping back out of sight and watched him go up the stairs of his Makiki Street home. Posted above the ground, the house was painted white with green trim around the doors and windows, screened to keep the mosquitoes out. He stood in front of the house and scanned the windows for Miki, then saw her on the side porch hanging his washed shirts and trousers next to her underwear.

"Miki!" he called out, waving. "Miki!"

She turned and looked at Shuzo, then went into the kitchen and never came out. What happened, Shuzo? You were supposed to protect me, keep me by your side. But you let Morita take me away, pass me around all those men with clean suits but filthy minds, really dirty, I tell you, you won't believe what they made me do. I love you Shuzo, still do, but what happened?

Jerome picked up his new telephone and in the first call he ever made other than as a test, he contacted the Health Department and requested an armed guard to escort a Japanese pimp to a plague detainee camp surrounded by security fences recently made at the Honolulu Iron Works.

"Anna, you're free to go with him, if you wish." Jerome held the front door open and motioned the way out as the guard took Shuzo away. She sat on the sofa with her cat, its leg still bandaged and didn't move. "Well, I guess that settles it." He kept the door open for Ma Lin, his Chinese cook, who had just entered the front gate.

"Flesh mullet," she said in reasonable English, announcing the evening meal as she came up the steps, two canvas bags in hand. "And sweet potato and baked banana." The old woman favored her good leg and started toward the kitchen, then stopped when she saw Miki curled on the sofa. She glanced at Jerome, then continued on, knowing better than to ask, not for fear of embarrassing him but because she already knew.

"I wasn't able to tell you," Jerome said. "about my guest. Do you have enough food?"

"Plenty," Ma Lin replied. She reached in one of the bags and pulled out a small roll of newspapers. She was a part-time housekeeper for Rev. Frank Damon and his growing family, from whom she learned English during many years of service. Jerome thanked her for her regular gift and sat down to read *The Friend* and Damon's articles about his travels. Jerome gained a better sense of the rest of the world from *The Friend* than he did from the local newspapers and also learned about Damon's impressive work in Honolulu.

"Seems like the school on Chaplain Lane is doing well," he said to Ma Lin.

"Vely good, the school doing vely good. A hundred fo'ty students. All boys, mostly Chinee."

Damon's wife had been born and raised in China and was fluent in Chinese. Musically talented, winsome and full of energy, Mary aided her husband as ably as she had her missionary parents. Jerome was inspired by their commitment to educating Chinese and wondered if the same could be done for the Japanese. For Anna. Wouldn't it be wonderful if she could speak English and learn the ways of the west? Mary was eagerly sought in social circles, was regarded as something of a marvel, a haole woman speaking Chinese. Anna is extraordinary in her own way, I can see it in her, very bright, perceptive, she'll absorb English like water. Once she's fluent, she'll be the talk of the town, despite her past, or maybe because of it, a story of personal transcendence. Wearing a silky dress, always at my side, filling my friends with envious dreams of finding their own exotic sprite. He looked at her stroking the cat on the sofa.

"Okay. Dinna." Ma Lin finished setting the table.

"You joining us?"

"If okay."

"Fine," said Jerome. Ma Lin had an open invitation to stay for dinner and accepted irregularly. But this was good, the three of them, added a formality useful for Anna's training. Even if she was an old Chinese cook, she worked for the Damons, one of the most prominent families in town.

Miki picked up the fork and poked the fried fish gently. "Chopsticks?" Ma Lin asked. "You want chopsticks?" She got up from the table and pulled out a pair of chopsticks from her bag and laid them next to Miki's plate. Miki slowly ate half of the fish, put her chopsticks down and stared at the upside eye dulled from frying. "Best part," said Ma Lin, eating the white hardened eye from her fish. Miki got up from the table, took the rest of her fish and gave it to the cat.

"Someting wrong, Mistah Jerome," said Ma Lin, "wit dat girl, ah, *withh thhat* girl." She tapped her finger against her head.

Ma Lin did the dishes, gathered her things and said goodnight, all the while keeping an eye on Miki. She left and Jerome settled into his chair with copies of *The Friend*. He lit an oil lamp, the electric power lines having been scheduled for his neighborhood for next year. He looked for the oldest copy of the newspaper, wanting to read them in chronological order. Rev. Frank Damon was dreaming again, of new schools for Chinese, Japanese and Korean students, the Asiatic factor, he called them, destined to play a greater role once they were taught Anglo-Saxon principles and ideals. It's not a question of possibility but of opportunity and his schools offered that. Anna needs to go to one of Damon's schools to fulfill her destiny by my side. He looked at her and glanced outside. The evening was darkening too slowly and Jerome couldn't wait to go to bed. He walked over to Miki sitting by the cat on the floor and reached down to touch her shoulder, letting her know that she had been talking with the cat long enough.

She drew herself on all fours and hissed at his leg. He squatted down to her level and she pounced on him, pushing him over with her hands, curled like paws, against his chest. She bared her teeth and spat another hiss, her eyes oranged by the lamp light and lowered her head toward his exposed arm.

"What the…?" He pushed himself away from her and she crawled toward him, then stopped and stared. He cast side glances for avenues of escape, his size and strength of no advantage as his instincts told him he was prey. "Anna?" he said, trying to bring the girl back. She crawled back to her cat and curled up beside it and Jerome heard a deep purr, a rippling but not of water. He got up, walked backward into the kitchen and picked up a knife, then returned to the living room, sat in his chair and watched her sleep.

Miguel had once told him of a young girl who had turned into a dog in his village in Portugal. She had snarled and barked at her mother, who ran out to get the priest, the one who did the exorcisms. He took one look at the dog-child and shook his head, saying there was nothing he could do. Too far gone, he said, beyond the reach of prayer. She allowed only her father into her room and he entered slowly, set down her food, cleaned up her mess and left as quickly as he could.

"So what happened?" Jerome asked his apprentice, "did she ever return to normal?"

"No. After several months they sent her away and no one talk about it after that. It was like she no exist and I suppose she didn't. As a girl."

Miki got up and Jerome gripped the knife. She looked at him quizzically, brushed her dress smooth and went into the bathroom. She came out wearing her light cotton yukata and looked toward the bedroom. "You go on to bed," he said to her, waving her to the bedroom. "I'll be in later." Miki went back to her cat, stroked it a few times and went into the bedroom.

Someting wrong with her, Ma Lin had said. Jerome closed the bedroom door and placed a chair against it. He lay on the sofa, fully dressed and tucked the knife under a cushion. By his side, winsome and fluent in English, he had imagined, but now he had seen her hissing and he could not fall asleep. The cat, that's it, the cat put a hex on her. Wolves did the same to children lost in the Idaho wilderness. He'd heard stories. One rancher, following the instructions of a Shoshoni elder, cured his daughter by shooting the culprit wolf and cutting out its heart. Jerome looked at the sleeping cat and drew the knife out from under the cushion.

◆

Jerome woke up to the sound of the blocking chair scraping the floor. In the dawning, he saw Miki push the door open enough to slip through sideways and she went straight to the corner for her cat. She dropped to her knees and patted the rag, then lifted it up. She looked around the room. Jerome sat on the edge of the sofa, wishing he had kept the knife after washing it in the kitchen. He held his breath when she looked at him, but let it out upon seeing no sign of the cat in the girl. It had worked, she was Anna again, saddened, as any girl would be upon missing her cat.

"It's not here," he said of the obvious. She walked around the room to make sure, checked the corner once again, then slipped back into the bedroom.

"*Hai, hai,*" she said. Jerome was relieved to hear her speaking calmly in Japanese, but he still got up and went into the kitchen.

"He did it for your sake," said the cat. "Do not hold it against him. He cares for you. He wants you to be … well, maybe, his wife."

"I understand," said Miki. "He's been kind, such strong hands, but so gentle. I shouldn't have attacked him last night."

"It wasn't you, it was me. I felt a bit jealous. Strange for a cat to say, but he likes you too much. He wants more than you can give and I worried that you might try to please him, I mean, other than in bed. You do not know these people, but I am from here, a church cat and I will help you."

"Thank you."

122

"No, thank *you*. You saved my life. I couldn't move with my broken leg. Burning rubble all around me. Might have starved to death. Thank you."

"Did he hurt you last night?"

"It hurt. The knife did. But he kept apologizing. Kept saying, what am I doing? Upset and confused. Frightened, I think."

Miki was quiet. She got up and looked out the window. "Where did he bury you?" she asked, wiping her eyes with the wide sleeves of her yukata. "I want to give you some flowers, offer some incense."

"No, no," the cat protested. "That's for the dead. He took my heart, but not my soul. I'll always be with you. In your heart since I no longer have mine. Better this way. I love you, Miki."

"Love?"

"That's right. He loves you too, in his way. Do you love him?"

"Love?"

"That's what I said. Don't you know what love is?"

"I'm only doing this for Shuzo."

"Shuzo?"

"That's right. Wait. Where are you going? Are you leaving?"

"I'll be back. I'll never leave you, Miki. I mean, not forever."

The red ginger outside the window bobbed in the morning light, shaking off drops of dew from labial petals folded around green shoots already sprouting roots, live birth without seeds. Across the narrow stretch of grass, she saw a mound of fresh earth next to the fence. Miki left the window, went into the parlor and sat next to Jerome. He moved over stiffly, keeping his elbows on his knees, his hands placed together, head down, blond locks covering his neck.

"Anna," he said, without looking up. "I love you. It's crazy and I can't figure it out, but I love you. From the first time I saw you. Never felt like this before. But last night, I was frightened and I'm afraid—I mean, afraid—that it just won't work out. You're too … different. I realized that. I've decided to take you back to your, well, you know, the guy you were with. I'll get him out of the detention camp and have him come back to get you." He kept his head down, defeated by a glimpse of something he did not understand, though he recognized something horrible. His love was undiminished, but it did not triumph over his fear. He got up to get his coat, to leave while he was still resolved, but he stopped, just as he had at Fujita's gate to offer her an innocent greeting that morning. He turned around.

"Anna…"

Miki did not understand his words, but she knew enough by his eyes, his voice, his pressing hands, his lowered head, this kind and gentle man. She stood up, walked over, took his hand and led him toward the bedroom. He dropped his coat and felt himself being drawn back into her lack of pretense, her innocence, that irresistible potion, unspoiled by upbringing, some kind of allure underived from social cultivation. That was why their different languages had not been a barrier between them and he was certain that he was the first and only person to see directly into her soul. Certainly not that pimp blinded by greed.

I was nothing but a paying customer that first night, like all the others enchanted by this angel, but something changed in front of Fujita's house, when she wrapped her arms around my neck, and I could feel her soul, her need to be rescued, and here at my house, our home, she is walking unpaid into my bedroom and I, the one possessed, am following her freely. She will soon be speaking in English and will be dancing at my side at the Merchants' Ball, both of us oblivious to the envious stares.

But as suddenly as his hope had flared, he remembered the cat's heart still beating in his slimy hand and as he shut the bedroom door, he ended his morning reverie, determined to make this the last time, the very last time, and then he would let her go.

124

WAIALUA SUGAR

T
HE PASSENGER TRAIN LEFT THE MAIN TERMINAL BY THE
Honolulu Iron Works, passed the Iwilei Prison and
picked up speed as the Oʻahu Insane Asylum came
into view on a low hillside. The train skirted around an inlet
of Keʻehi Lagoon and traversed the Halawa plains through
cane fields, then made a sharp right turn to go around the
innermost reaches of the first two lochs of Pearl Harbor and
headed to its first stop, Waipahu Station. Hardly anyone got
off, a few travelers boarded the train, which then resumed its
journey around the third loch and stopped a short distance
away at the ʻEwa Mill, its corrugated steel buildings splattered
at their skirts with the surrounding red dirt stretching out
into fields of green cane. Out of ʻEwa, they passed close to
the base of a small volcanic cone, then ran parallel to the
roadway on the narrow flatland between the sea and the
beginnings of the Waiʻanae Mountains with its alternating
ridges and valleys. The train followed the Waiʻanae coast just
above the sandy shoreline tumbled smooth by waves rolling
in unhindered by barrier reefs. The water was immediately
blue, untinted by shallow green. It was not rough, but only
good swimmers challenged the noisy surge in and, more
seriously, its silent undertow out. Even from his window seat,
Mako could feel the scale of the Pacific, a thick and endless
ocean stretching out to a horizon so wide he could see the
curvature of the earth.

Chiyo moved to an empty seat on the right side of the
train to view the mountain ridges, the hot, dry and jagged

opposite of the sea. The barren hills, occasionally pocked by caves, were successive layers of ancient lava piled high and preserved by a scarcity of rain, an abundance of which would have eroded it into fertile soil. Drought-loving *kiawe* trees, called algaroba by the haoles, grew widely spaced apart among the grassy rocks and *panini* cactus and covered the ground with short branches of dried thorns, a wicked defense against men who still preferred bare feet. Its twisted timber was hard as coal, great for burning, so dense it did not float in water.

So much of the landscape reminded Chiyo of Okinawa, another volcanic island, but the colors were tinted by salt spray and distance, brown receding into green into blue and purple at the highest peaks. On the upland slopes, lush forests were spotted by patches of chartreuse, almost white, groves of *kukui* nut trees. Staghorn ferns quilted together *ʻōhiʻa*, *ti*, mountain apples, guavas, *koa* and variegated brush, all watered by clouds loosened of their moisture as they scraped over the mountains, leaving little for rain by the time they reached the leeward edge. But the rains, wherever they fell, filtered through the lava aquifer that was the entire island and formed a vast subterranean reservoir, pressured by the weight of the land to send up sweet water through fissured springs, even in the parched Waiʻanae plains. Between the barren ridges, farmers funneled the water through ditches to raise animals and vegetables for the leeward settlements. Where the land remained dry in large tracts, sisal plants thrust their long, pointed leaves directly out of the ground, the lack of water toughening the fiber strands valued so highly in San Francisco for making rope.

The train slowed and banged to a stop at Waiʻanae Station long enough for passengers to board with their chickens, ducks and bundles of everything. The engineer blew the whistle, opened the steam throttle and the train groaned forward a few yards before stopping with a lurch that threw Chiyo against the seat in front of her. A tall Hawaiian man, trim in his western suit and dashing mustache, stepped quickly aboard, thanking the conductor for stopping for him. "Welcome aboard, Colonel," said the conductor, snapping a salute. He must be some kind of official, Chiyo thought, a military officer in civilian clothes, or maybe a judge. The train pulled out and passed the open end of a large valley, then a smaller one and gained in elevation and leveled out on a narrow ledge blasted and shoveled out of a steep slope dropping into the sea.

"Look!" said Mako, calling Chiyo to rejoin him on the oceanside of the train. "Look at the water down there." Blue-green waves smashed onto the rocks and disintegrated into pure white sprays high into the air and as they neared Ka'ena Point, the northern tip of the island, the waves grew larger and hurled themselves with frightening abandon. The engineer stopped the train at a spot where the ledge widened amply on the ocean side of the tracks and everyone got out to watch the waves destroy themselves fifty feet below. Mako walked over to a large black boulder, touched it and declared it hot enough to fry eggs. For the moment they were sightseers on vacation, delighted with oddities, and Chiyo held Mako's arm and pressed herself against him. A huge wave hit the rocks below with an explosive roar, sending a burst of fine mist into the air, catching the sunlight as a little rainbow, colors floating, then fading into nothing with the dissipating breeze.

Mako had seen tiny rainbows in the mist hanging at the bottom of the Double Falls on a trip with Shizuka to the Sandan Gorge outside of Hiroshima, the only time they had traveled for pleasure. They had just been married and had enough money for a short trip during late fall. Brilliant in the clear blue sky, the full sun was still no match for the cold that brought out the fiery best of the mountain maples. They spotted a rainbow trapped in the mists hanging steady in the roar of the falls and they moved about until they found the angle that made the colors most intense. They stood still, freezing the rainbow with their gaze. "In classical poetry," Shizuka said softly to him, "the word for color also means passion." She composed a poem on the spot and spoke its revisions until she finally settled on a preferred version.

The colors of the misted sun,
Frozen forever,
As long as we do not move.

"Well," she said, "it's still not right. Misted sun is awkward." But Mako thought it was the most beautiful poem he had ever heard.

I wish you were here in Hawai'i, right here on this ledge, watching the rainbows come and go like silent bursts of fireworks. You would like Chiyo and you would know that what I feel for her does not change what I feel for you. Not a bit. Chiyo makes me want you more, but you are so far away and she is right here, holding my hand in this strange land. We never held hands, you and I, but she is different and I like her touch. You would understand, I know you would, wouldn't you? If you were here, I would hold your hand too. This island, it's new, it's not Japan and we can act as if we were different people. And Yuki? Is she alright? I miss you both so much.

He stood still with Chiyo, but the salt rainbows went flying away, disappearing as quickly as they came into view. What poem would she write about that? Could we seize the rainbows by running after them?

"You'd like Shizuka," he said, looking toward the ocean.

Chiyo glanced at him, but withheld her question. "Time to go," she said. "The conductor is calling us back."

As the train made the turn around Ka'ena Point, several passengers asked the conductor to stop again, this time to watch the dancing albatross. The males pranced in front of their women, squawking and bobbing their heads and tails, spreading their six-foot wings. But the conductor kept the train moving along the shoreline, and Mako saw something else new: flat reefs under shallow water clear as glass. A man dressed only in a loincloth, gave a quick jerk to his fishing pole and pulled up a fish, pure silver wiggling in the sun.

Fresh fish, shimmering and shiny from the ocean. "I'd like to do that," he said to Chiyo. "Shuzo knows how to fish. He can teach us."

"I know how to fish," she said. "Did it in Okinawa. Wouldn't you rather have me teach you rather than your ... friend?"

"You don't like Shuzo, do you."

"He disliked us first, calling us stinking pigs. What do you *naichi* people have against us Okinawans?"

"Nothing, as far as I'm concerned. But Shuzo, well, don't take him seriously, his prejudice, that is. People like him think you're different, coming from a remote island and besides you're ... you're..."

"We're what?"

"Hairy. It's a fact."

Chiyo held out her arm and pushed up her sleeve. Mako stroked it. "See, not much more, but more hair than I have. But I like it, especially your brows. Let's face it. You do look different. But look, if Shuzo could know you like I do, he'd think differently."

"Well, we did talk on the boat. Remember I had the bunk above him. He asked me about fire."

"Fire?"

"You know, what men feel for women."

Mako laughed. "He knows nothing about it. I had to explain everything to him."

"He'd be so easy to seduce. So easy." She noticed Mako's smile disappear and quickly added, "Not that I'd want to."

◆

The mountain range angled away from the tracks, leaving a widening field of rocks and grass between them and soon the ridges and deep valleys turned purple in the distance and the land was fertile soil, gently sloping up from the railroad tracks to the foothills. A few shacks and farms appeared and then the sugar cane, field upon field, swaying its sweet promise of wealth for everyone.

Resembling a cross between reeds and bamboo, the young sugar cane grew straight in orderly rows, ditched for irrigation, but as it reached twice a man's height, the juice-laden stalks could not support themselves upright and tumbled over each other in an impenetrable tangle. Men with wide machetes cut the ripe stalks one by one, unraveling the mess and stacking them in orderly piles for packers, several of them women, to haul to mule trains. In the torrid heat, they wore canvas chaps over denim pants and thick sleevings over their arms, bandanas around their necks, gloves and hats. The stifling layers were necessary for protection from the razor sharp leaves covered with a stiff fuzz capable of prickling flesh like tiny needles. The heat was murderous, an added curse to the slicing leaves, the stinging fuzz.

"That's what you'll be doing," Chiyo said to Mako.

"And you'll be hoeing weeds," said Mako, who had a hard time imagining Chiyo in the fields. "Think you can do it?"

"Of course. Women are tougher than men. But surely, Mako, we can find something else to do. Can't we?" Mako shrugged.

The train slowed down as it passed the Waialua Mill, brand new and still in the making. Everything was of iron, the girders, the corrugated roofing, the washing trays, the grinding rollers, the boiling vats, the tall stack pouring out smoke. A steam engine buried somewhere amongst beams and pipes fitted together in a confusion as tangled as the cane in the fields, hissed and puffed with steam to turn gears and pulleys. Mako thought of the engine room of the *America Maru*, the drunken engineer and his free offer of the girl, how he had left disgusted because she reminded him of his daughter and he pitied her and her father for having to sell her.

Would I have done the same? Sell Yuki? I'd never do it, that's why I'm here to work in Hawai'i. I'd never have taken advantage of the engineer's girl. But Chiyo, well, she's different, a grown woman, a free and willing companion for quenching our fires that night behind the shed on Quarantine Island. It happened so quickly, but she was the one burning and I gave in because I was so lonely for Shizuka, not that I wanted to. The nights are different here. And the air, the water, spiked with enchantment. Where was Shuzo at Quarantine Island, when everyone else had gotten off? He'd better show up here in Waialua, where he's supposed to be, but then why should I have to cover for him? But, of course, I will. Was Chiyo serious about seducing Shuzo?

The train stopped at Waialua Station in the middle of the village and Mako and Chiyo grabbed their suitcases and got off. Chiyo clutched her shamisen. A little further down the tracks, they saw a magnificent, two story building with high gables and two poles flying American flags.

"Welcome to Waialua, the best plantation on the island! Most modern mill and our system of ditches bringing the best water and plenty of it. Welcome! Welcome! That building over there is the brand new Haleiwa Hotel, where only the rich can afford to pay four dollars a day. A week's worth of wages! But what a palace! Running water, swimming pool and its own electric lights! This is Waialua—new mill, new hotel, new railroad, new life. Welcome to the heavenly country, where you will make your fortune! All plantation workers, right this way, follow me."

The young Japanese man, cleanly dressed as proof that not everyone worked in the fields, kept his arm in the air and led his group to a horse drawn wagon fitted with benches. There were about a dozen men, Chiyo the only woman and they were quiet, busily memorizing the passing details of their new home, a Chinese grocery store here, a tailor shop on a side street, a fruit stand up ahead. They saw other Japanese men walking on the side of the hard dirt street, a few Chinese, some Portuguese, several Hawaiians, an occasional haole man and a woman with, amazingly weird, hair the color of gold.

"So many different kinds of people," Mako said to himself and Chiyo nodded. So strange that these foreigners will

131

be our neighbors, after we'd grown up where everyone was the same. But why should we be surprised, we've already crossed a line of difference, Chiyo and me, Okinawan and naichi, single and married. The Japanese men on the opposite bench stared at Chiyo and glared at Mako, who looked back at them as a blurred group, defiantly but without meeting any man's eyes.

◆

"Name?"

"Toki. Makoto."

"Let's see Toki … Toki … yes, here you are. This is your identification *bango*, number 168. Don't lose it. You'll be paid by the number, not your name. No number, no pay. Got it?"

Mako picked up the tag. It had a hole for a chain. Number 168, round, brass, that's who he was.

"Name?"

"Taira. Chiyo."

"Taira? Okinawan, isn't it?"

"Could be Japanese as well." She placed her arms behind her back.

"I guess so," the Japanese clerk said, "the only Okinawans in this shipment were sent to Kahuku plantation. All men." He found her on his list. "165," he said, as he handed her the brass bango. It's a good thing you're not Okinawan, otherwise I'd have to give you a tag of a different shape. Okinawans are not the same, you know, not the same as the Japanese people. Wonder if we even have one? Chinese are hex, Portuguese square, oh well, it doesn't matter now. You're Japanese. Next!"

Chiyo clutched her bango against her chest and walked over to Mako. "Japanese. In Hawai'i, I'm Japanese." She laughed at her newly minted identity.

"No," said Mako. "In Hawai'i you're just a number, 165. That's all."

"But round. Just like you." She placed her tag over his, matching the circles in a perfect fit.

From the plantation office they walked to Mill Camp 1 and the agent showed them their quarters, the men separated from the women, but everyone would stagger their times in the common bath house. The houses were built on long lanes branching off a main road, about eight lanes with ten identical hutches each. The ridgelines of the single gables ran parallel to the lane, each roof sloped forward over an open porch and swept in a longer line toward the back over the bedrooms and kitchen. They were all painted green and roofed with black tar paper. Each had a small backyard.

"Tonight?" said Chiyo to Mako as she turned down her lane and Mako nodded.

◆

As Jerome walked with Shuzo from the plague detention camp to a nearby livery, he explained his reasons for giving Anna back—what he had read about spirits and animal possession, his concern for her state of mind, the need to send her to the O'ahu Insane Asylum, if, that is, she got out of hand. Shuzo understood nothing of his disquisition, but felt his decency, which was all he really needed to know. Despite their differences of blood and speech, Shuzo felt close to Jerome. Jerome cared and Shuzo liked him for that, as well as his tall physique, blond hair and sweaty smell that gave Shuzo a rise as he imagined bathing together with this handsome white man. What would it be like to bathe together? At the stable, Jerome helped Shuzo hire a wagon from a Portuguese man who spoke in gestures decoded by Jerome's repetitions of the essential words—horse, five dollar fee, two dollar deposit, return by anyone. From the livery to his home, Jerome gave Shuzo driving lessons and Shuzo pressed himself against his teacher, the better to learn.

"Good luck," he said, certain of Shuzo's need for it. Jerome placed Miki's new suitcase in the back, then helped her up.

"Goodbye, Anna."

Shuzo looked at the map Jerome had drawn, flicked the

reins as he had practiced and steadied Miki as the wagon jolted forward.

"Goodbye, Anna."

◆

Once past Punchbowl, Shuzo headed toward Pearl Harbor, roughly following the train route, but at the middle loch, he turned right and headed to the interior of the island on a road stretching over the central plateau between the Ko'olau and the Wai'anae Ranges, the double backbones of the island. The Ko'olau Range was nearly twice as long and its northeastern side was windward, the first to catch the trade winds and its rains. Its cliffs were nearly vertical, seriously eroded by weathering that produced rich land and thick tropical forests from the slopes to the sea. The leeward coast of the Wai'anae Range was the opposite, hot and dry. The central plateau between them was a combination of both, being leeward of the Ko'olaus and windward of the Wai'anae Mountains. Forested in spots, it was mostly an open plain of *pili* grass, useful for thatch and mattresses. The horse had only one road to follow and Shuzo folded and put away his map.

"I was worried about you," said Shuzo. "I thought I had lost you to Boss Morita and then to that American foreman. I paid him to get you out of Morita's place, but then he took you to his home. It seems that you liked it there."

Miki did not reply. Morita and Fujita seemed so long ago. How many men did she serve? And Jerome? "I only did it for you," she finally said.

"For me?"

"That American — his name is Jerome — very kind and he took care of me." She stopped and tried to formulate an explanation. "As long as I was with him, Morita could not touch me and that was better for you." Surely Shuzo would understand that she did it for him. "You do prefer Jerome rather than Morita?"

"I see. I never thought of it that way. Yes, anyone but Morita. Someday I'll get back at him too. Nozaki and Morita."

Nozaki again, the man for whom Shuzo's hate had taught her about love. He made it all so complicated and she was content to give herself over to Shuzo, the only person she could trust. Her only fear was separation. "Where we're going, we'll be safe, won't we?"

"Of course," said Shuzo, flicking the reins to hurry the horse. "I have a plan."

He always had a plan and she leaned against him, placing her hand on his thigh.

"You liked Jerome, didn't you?"

"I did it only for you," she said again, not knowing how else to explain it. "You're not upset with me, are you?"

"Upset? No, no. You did the right thing. What's important is that we're together again. Ready to do business. In Waialua. Far from the damn fool Morita."

The sun hovered above the ocean, then touched its edge just as they reached the crest of the long slope down to the north shore spread out below them. Shuzo looked at Jerome's map again and pointed at the rounded peak of the Wai'anae Mountains. "Mt. Ka'ala," he said and panned his finger along the ridgeline running to Ka'ena Point. They could see a whole section of the Wai'anae Range on the left, the new mill straight ahead, but Shuzo could not find the grand hotel in Hale'iwa. "The hotel," he said, trying to see past a gulch to his right, "it's somewhere over there, according to this map." Jerome had marked its location with some pride, having directed the fabrication of ornate hinges, door pulls and gates for the luxury hotel.

"Let's stop and watch the sunset," said Miki, but Shuzo snapped the reins and the horse bolted forward, forcing her to grab the seat to keep from falling backwards. The hotel, he had said, and she knew exactly what he had in mind. Parched by the sun even though she wore a wide brimmed hat, jostled all day by steel rims dropping hard in holes and bumping over rocks, not having had anything to eat or drink, she was tired. Her hands and arms hurt from gripping the hardwood seat and its iron handle and she could not find a comfortable sitting position no matter which way she shifted. But it was the talking that made her so weary, so much to think about and explain. She climbed into the back of the wagon, curled up on her side, placing one arm under her head, then turned on her back and saw the first stars come out, jiggling in the sky.

◆

Shuzo pulled into the front entrance of the hotel, stopping next to a fancy black carriage. The doorman came down the stairs and told him that deliveries were made at the back. Shuzo ignored him, walked into the lobby past the lanterns and lamps and went to the desk. "Room," he said to the clerk, "two man." He held up two fingers.

"Excuse me," said the clerk, "you must be mistaken. This is an expensive hotel."

Shuzo looked at the wall behind the desk, but there was no posting of the room rates. He did not know the right words, so he took out a dollar and laid it on the counter. The clerk shook his head and wagged an upright finger from side to side. Shuzo laid another dollar down.

"No, no, it's not about the money, it's ... well, I have to speak with the manager," said the clerk, turning to the bellhop. "Bobby, call the Colonel." Shuzo laid down another dollar, but the clerk pushed it all back to him.

A handsome Hawaiian man appeared, dressed impeccably in a black suit that matched his hair, eyes and mustache. His posture was straight, almost stiff, but he walked like a sprinter. Upper class, royal even, he was comfortable with the higher stations, but upon seeing Shuzo, he relaxed his shoulders, ready to be ordinary.

"Good evening," he said, offering his hand. Shuzo accepted his handshake. The Colonel turned to the clerk and asked, "What's the problem here?"

"Well, sir," said the clerk, "he looks like a plantation worker to me and it's just that we've never had one stay here before. In fact, we've never had a Japanese guest."

Colonel James Kalama recognized Shuzo's disciplined

bearing and wondered if he was a military man like himself. Having served King David Kalākaua and Queen Lili'oukalani as Protocol Officer during the days of the Kingdom, Colonel Kalama had developed a keen sense of first impressions on his extensive travels to America, Europe and the Orient. He was seldom mistaken in his judgments of character and could easily spot faults — vanity, deceit, meanness — especially when people tried to hide them, but he was even better at detecting virtues.

At the Moscow coronation of Alexander III, the Tsar had been intrigued by the Hawaiian Kingdom far away in the middle of the ocean, which, he remembered, a Russian adventurer had once tried to claim for the Romanovs. Kalama had extended an invitation for the Tsar to visit, saying that the waters of Waikiki would wash away the constraints of formality and allow him to be his true self, and the Tsar was surprised that the representative of the Hawaiian monarchy knew of his discomfort with protocol.

Ordinary people were easier to read and Kalama took Shuzo for an enterprising man whose ambition matched his brazen nerve. It was all so obvious, parking his wagon at the front entrance and laying down dollars on the counter. The clerk was right. This was the first time a Japanese man had walked in and asked for a room and the Colonel was intrigued. The man was Japanese, but his money was already American. He smiled and bowed ever so slightly, turning his head to one side as he kept his eyes on Shuzo. "Welcome to the Haleiwa Hotel." He snapped his fingers at the clerk, who helped Shuzo register, then walked with Shuzo out to the wagon and assisted Miki out from the back.

"Mrs. Taga," Colonel Kalama said, "a pleasure to meet you." He turned to Shuzo and shook his hand. "If there's anything you need, my staff will help you. My name is Kalama, James Kalama, but you can call me Kimo."

From their second story room, they looked down on the sprawling lawn, its walkways lit with torches. Shuzo studied the ladies in long dresses and cane-wielding gentlemen out strolling for no other purpose than to enjoy the night. The air smelled of the sea, seaweed to be exact, and the rhythmic washing of the waves folded easily into intervals of silence. Only the well-to-do could afford to do nothing, walking solely for pleasure. Some people are born into wealth, others work their way up, but most remain poor no matter how hard they work. How can I get rich? A few men were alone and Shuzo nodded his head. "*Yosh*," he said approvingly, "yosh."

Miki went into the bathroom and experimented with the plumbing, amused with the water gushing out of faucets and, more wondrously, draining out unseen. She bathed and came out in her cotton yukata, pulled the covers back on the double bed and ran her hands over the clean sheets. She took off her yukata, got into bed and waited for Shuzo. She wanted to tell him how splendid he had been downstairs, getting this room and she thought about the best way of saying it.

"I'll sleep on the couch," Shuzo said, still looking out the window.

Miki clutched the edge of the sheets. "Plenty of room in this bed," she said.

"I said I'll sleep on the couch." He picked up his suitcase and went into the bathroom.

Miki slipped out of bed, put on her yukata and went downstairs in her bare feet. She walked across the lobby trailing stares, and the clerk raised his hand toward her but did not know what to say. The manicured grass felt cool on her feet and she walked across the footbridge over the stream merging with the ocean fifty yards away. On the beach, she sat on the dry sand above the reach of soft lapping waves, then stretched out on her back and looked at the stars. She had never seen so many before, never noticed their different shades of white, blue and sparkles of red. Her mother used to make decisions by consulting a book of western astrology, which was superior, she had said, to the superstitious Japanese system and she'd taught Miki the names and shapes of the constellations dotting the pages. There, the Big Dipper and follow the lineup to the North Star. And Orion, huge, imposing, dagger hanging from his belt. The scorpion,

138

majestic and lethal with its tilted head, pincers, long, curving body, tail turning back on itself, hooked on the end. The scorpion was poised to strike with the deadly tip of its tail, marked so clearly with two stars set in the exact position of the eyes of a cat.

So that's where you are! I can see you every night. You said you wouldn't leave me. Weary with relief, Miki passed in and out of a light sleep, then got up when she felt a few drops of rain. She headed back to the hotel and saw Shuzo marching across the lawn toward her. She looked at the scorpion again and saw the cat's eyes dim and disappear behind a cloud. "Good night," she said, as Shuzo gripped her arm and pulled her back to the room.

◆

Shuzo emerged from the dark lobby onto the spacious veranda, where the eaves and railing framed the ocean and sky into a band of blues and greens silvered by the morning sun. The smells were new, bacon and coffee, and he walked to an empty table next to a man sitting by himself. Dressed in a white suit—even his shoes were white, a boast of his freedom from labor—the young man carefully picked up the cloth napkin from his lap, lightly dabbed his lips and set it down to resume reading, newspaper in one hand, the other resting next to his coffee cup and yolk-smeared plate. A few guests stared at Shuzo in his crumpled long sleeved shirt and heavy cotton pants, his thick hair unruly. An elderly gentleman got up from a table by the railing, walked briskly to the front desk to complain, then returned and said something to his wife, who got up and left with her husband, chin high though she looked down straight ahead. Shuzo was amused by the power of his mere presence to drive the couple away from breakfast, although, he noticed, no one else seemed to care. Curious about the small commotion, the young man in whites set down his newspaper and looked at the Japanese man sitting at the table next to him. He smiled at Shuzo, sipped his coffee and resumed his reading.

Miki stopped at the threshold to the veranda, spotted Shuzo, but continued to stand and look at everyone else. The dining area was half-filled with a dozen people, several of whom looked back at her and wondered about the young woman dressed in an indigo kimono with red stripes, a brown silk sash tied around her slender waist. More than her dress, the coconut hat on the Japanese girl intrigued and confused them, a yellow-green brimmed weaving of young fronds banded with a lei of tiny purple and white flowers. Even Shuzo was puzzled about the hat, though he remembered that she had told him about going for a walk and joining him later for breakfast. One woman seemed delighted by Miki's blended fashion and motioned her over to get a closer look, but Miki stood still, oblivious to the increasing attention directed her way. Just as Shuzo was about to go up and get her, she entered the area and made her way over. The young man, still absorbed in his newspaper, barely noticed her, but her decorated presence registered enough for him to raise his hand slightly.

"Miss," he said without looking up, "I'd like more coffee."

Miki sat down in the empty chair across from him. He put his newspaper down, looked up at Miki and jerked backwards, his knees hitting the underside of the table, rattling his empty cup. Shuzo thought of intervening, but decided, like everyone else, to watch.

"Oh!" The young man regained his posture and tried to place his sudden visitor into a knowable category. "Oh! Excuse me," he said. "Am I at the wrong table?"

The woman who had wanted a closer look at Miki burst out laughing. The young man's neck and cheeks flushed, the red more evident against the white of his suit and he was still confused, but his etiquette took over where his understanding ended. "Um, hello, er ... good morning. My name is David, I mean Harry, well, Harry David actually." He held out his hand, Miki took it and he finally recognized something familiar.

He's hooked, thought Shuzo, just like a fugu. Miki has that way about her, shameless, demure. I saw it myself that night in the engine room. But I can't let it become obvious here. The laughing lady is now looking suspicious, jealous would be good, but not in the way she is wondering about something awry. They are still holding hands and looking at each other far too long.

Shuzo got up and stood by the young man, who released Miki's hand. "Gud mo'ning," Shuzo said in his best English. "My name Taga."

"Oh! I'm sorry," he said, reddening again. "I didn't mean … I mean … please join us … well, not that we're together … ah … won't you have a seat? Oh my gosh, please forgive me, is she your wife?"

"No t'ank you." Shuzo smiled to put the young man at ease. "Afta eat, walk ovah deah?" Shuzo spoke quietly, casting a glance at the bridge over the river.

"Why, yes, of course."

Shuzo helped Miki up and together they sat at their own table. She took off the coconut hat and placed it on her lap. Shuzo wanted to ask her where she got it, but he didn't want to speak in Japanese. He ordered — eggs, bread and tea. They had their breakfast and walked over to the bridge, where the young man in the white suit was waiting.

◆

After a week of nightly visitors, who, for their own sake, were properly discreet, Shuzo was a hundred dollars richer. The single men whispered to each other and word reached not a few husbands. Is it true? Heard she's an angel. What's it really like, you know, doing it with an angel? Aided by an observant housekeeper, Colonel Kalama figured out that the young woman was not Mrs. Taga. The night clerk reported her midnight walks and once followed her out and heard her, no kidding, talking to the stars.

Kalama called on Shuzo and tried to make him understand that he would not allow the night trade in his hotel, although, truth be told, he had no control over his guests having the girl's services at a separate location, the satisfaction of their needs, after all, not being totally unrelated to his professional interest in offering the best of island hospitality. Kalama owned a vacant house in Waialua village, not far from the train station, a ten minute walk from the hotel and he offered to rent it to Shuzo. "That way," he said, "you would not be disadvantaged by not having a place to live."

Shuzo could not follow the meandering implications of his double negatives, but understood the basics of his offer—house, rent, guests, not at the hotel—and accepted his terms. He made Kalama understand that in return for sending guests to the house, he would give him a share of the profits. The Colonel refused, saying it would be wrong for him to receive payments from immoral, let alone illegal transactions, wrong for him even to make referrals. The rent was for a place for Shuzo to live, that was all, and what he did there was of no concern to him, lordy, lordy, it was none of his business, provided, of course, that he maintained the house properly. If, however, the bellhops were to make suggestions, then how could he as the hotel manager object, since he would have no knowledge, none whatsoever, no sir, of the private conversations between his staff and the guests? It was not his practice to eavesdrop, no, he would never think of doing that since he trusted his employees, honest men and women, all of them. Shuzo tried to sort Kalama's words out, was not sure that he even got the gist and simply nodded in agreement, the tone of the Kalama's voice seeming friendly enough. Frustrated with his inability to communicate, Shuzo made a request, stumbling through it until Kalama understood his desire to hire someone to teach him English.

"Josephine," Kalama replied, "she'd be perfect. I'll send her over to the house once you're settled in. Which should be, I hope, this evening."

◆

I was grateful, not just to Kalama, but to the accidental horse of chance from that Chinese story I had once dismissed as stupid. It all made perfect sense: everything happened by accident. Meeting Mako, running into Miki, coming upon Horisho's restaurant, encountering Jerome and now, Kalama's kindness, none of this had taken place according to plan. The most amazing thing is that they were all fortuitous, making me instantly rich. Hawai'i is not a land of opportunity, but of good luck. There is no reason why the gods should bless me so frequently, no explanation attributing cause. The Buddhist priest was wrong in saying that we reap what we sow, that things happen by karma, by our own deeds and misdeeds, as if life were a mathematical equation of adding and subtracting. How silly to think that two goods and two bads zeroed each other out. Is telling a lie to Boss Morita bad or good and by what magnitude, zero, three, five?

Of course—and this is a matter of common sense—no one can sit around doing nothing and expect the blessings of chance to fall into one's lap. Samuel Smiles is right, well, up to a certain point. No doubt we have to work hard, help ourselves, but Smiles placed too much importance on effort, an error he shared with the Buddhists. Work hard, they say and you will be successful, be good and get good karma. But it doesn't always work out that way. Look at the laborers in the cane fields, misguided fools, working a hundred times harder than I, and earning a hundred times less. They are oxen taking the safe path of hard work alone, afraid to take chances, finding comfort in believing that karma leaves them no choice but to suffer in the scorching sun for wages, tricking them into thinking they are not slaves. But they are slaves, to their own fears. My rule is work hard and trust chance, no, work hard and take chances. The deluded think that God or the Buddha or past lives or ghosts or ancestors determine their fate, but I know it's chance. Everyone does his best, but why do only a few get rich? Luck. The leisured guests at the hotel are lucky, that's all. My god is Chance. And Chance has touched me once again and her name is Josephine.

Josephine Kaumaka credited her life not to Buddhist karma or blind chance or the loving Protestant God of grace, but to the Catholic Church. Her grandmother Luiza had been baptized by the first French Catholic missionaries in Honolulu, but when they were expelled by the Protestant oligarchy, Luiza fled to remote Waialua and started her own parish in the foothills of Mt. Ka'ala. Father Joseph Desvault, after whom Josephine was named, had arrived in Waialua in 1840 and had built the Church of St. Michael the Archangel out of local stones and coral pounded into lime for mortar in a large clearing at the edge of the last cane field toward the mountain. The Church looked like a miniature cathedral, complete with reinforcing buttresses and a bell tower dedicated in 1853, when Josephine was three years old. She was educated at St. Michael's, which competed with Rev. John Emerson's Protestant church for the minds and souls of the people of Waialua.

Emerson and Desvault had been constant rivals, determined to prove each other's Christian religion wrong, and in the competition for converts, Father Desvault had been more successful with his free feasts, gifts of clothing and, most importantly, his dispensation of people's sins through ritual absolution instead of moral prohibition. From his church close to the seashore, Emerson railed against the Catholics in the foothills, accusing them of promoting immorality, carrying out cannibalistic rituals of eating the body of Christ and drinking his blood and worshipping idols. "They are no different from the heathens we seek to bring into the light of the Savior," he thundered. "The papists are pagans!"

Josephine had learned all of the arguments as catechism and had loved to shout out the right answers with her classmates.

"Do we come to beg your food?" the priest asked.

"No!"

"Do we beg for your money and fish?"

"No!"

"Do we sell our books?"

"No, Father, you give them out for free!"

"What do those *other* teachers do?"

"They beg what is ours and sell what is theirs!"

Their favorite part of the catechism was the Great

Confrontation, a true story, they were told, and they retold it in a reversal of roles, the children asking the questions, the priest answering. Tired of the Protestant accusations, Father Joseph led a band of followers to Emerson's church, right there on the banks of the river where the Haleiwa Hotel would be built and challenged Rev. John to a debate. At first, Rev. John did not want to come out.

"So tell us, Father, how did Father Joseph make him come out?"

"Father Joseph said in a loud voice, 'Your silence is my victory!'"

"So tell us, Father, how did Rev. John come out?"

"Meekly, very meekly."

"And what did Rev. John say?"

"He said Catholics worship idols and images."

"And what did Father Joseph do?"

"He took out a Protestant book and opened it to a picture of the Crucifixion. Rev. John looked at it and said it was just a picture."

"A picture! A picture! And what did Father Joseph say?"

"He held the Protestant picture of our Crucified Lord in front of Rev. John's face and said, 'If it's just a picture, then spit on it.'"

"Spit on it! Spit on it! What did Rev. John do?"

"He went back into his church."

"And tell us, Father, pray tell us! How did he go back in?"

"Meekly, very meekly."

By the time she was fifteen, Josephine had read every book in the school's small library. Rev. John retired that year and his successor established the Waialua Female Seminary and named the dormitory Hale'iwa, "house of the 'iwa bird." Josephine's hunger for books was stronger than her distaste for Rev. John's errant gospel, so she dared to enter Hale'iwa and persuaded the housekeeper to let her help with the cleaning in exchange for the chance to read the books in their library and that is where she came across Samuel Smiles' famous book, *Self-Help*. When she started her career as a twenty-five year old teacher in the Waialua Catholic School, she used it for inspirational readings and urged her students to use their God-given talents to the fullest. "God helps those who help themselves," she repeated, not realizing that the Protestant girls at the Seminary were being told the same thing.

Josephine never married and now at 50, was asked by Colonel Kalama, the manager of the new hotel whose name was borrowed from the Seminary dormitory, to teach English to a young Japanese man. She took an immediate liking to Shuzo, his discipline, his photographic memory, his probing questions. She used *Self-Help* as a textbook and with his own Japanese translation, he memorized long passages in English with perfect comprehension. She was delighted by his previous familiarity with Samuel Smiles and quickly agreed to begin their lessons with the story of John Hathaway, the favorite character of Shuzo's father. In five months, Shuzo acquired an impressive vocabulary and in eight months he could recite long sentences, speaking like an orator, stumbling on pronunciations but not their meanings and Josephine worked with him on enunciation.

"The valuable examples which they furnish of the power of self-help, of patient purpose, resorute — *no, no, reso-lute, lu, lu* — working and steadfast integrity, issuing in the formation of truly — *good!* — noble and manly — *excellent!* — character, exhibit in language not to be misunderstood, what it is in the powwa — *pow-er, er, er, spread your lips like you're smiling* — of each to accomprish, ah excuse me, accom-plish — *good!* — for himself; and elokently — *no, no, qu-qu-ent-ly* — illustrate the effisasy — *ka-ka, hard c, then soft c, ka-sy* — of self-respect and self-reliance in enabling men of even the hum-bel-est — *only two syllables, two sounds, hum-blest* — rank to work out for themselves an honorable competency and a solid reputation."

Josephine had tears in her eyes as she clapped her hands together softly. This was a teaching experience she had never had with the children in the Catholic School. His English was like clay in her hands and she could hardly keep up with molding it, so quickly did he do its shaping. But there was something more than language, more than memorization and pronunciation, for she had never taught a young man before, someone closer to her in age and yet a foreigner, so different in culture. But as he learned his second language, he seemed by increasing degrees no different from herself and she realized that he understood the meanings of resolute, power and efficacy exactly as she knew them. She felt close to him, an affection mixed with pleasure and because she had never felt this way before, she was afraid of what would happen if she gave him a hug. "Excellent, Shuzo, well done."

Colonel Kalama's request had been utterly novel and Josephine might have refused the chance to teach Shuzo had she not been such a secret admirer of the handsome, unmarried Hawaiian Colonel. Convinced that he and any other man, for that matter, would not find her attractive, not delicate enough—lips too thick, heavy boned frame, nose wide and flat, coarsely matted hair, wide hips and sagging breasts—she had never shown him any sign of her desperate interest and presented herself as nothing other than a dedicated old maid willing to give up her personal life for the sake of her students and her Savior. Sometimes he called her Sister Josephine and it bothered her that she could not determine if his monastic implications were prompted by banter or respect. He had called on her at home to ask about English lessons for a Japanese man and as she could not bring herself to invite him inside, she spoke with him on the porch, wishing all the while that she were younger, lighter and less gray, but she caught herself in her own delusion and remembered that she had never had to ask a priest to absolve her of any sin of the flesh. She may have agreed for the wrong reason, but she was happy to be working with Shuzo, pleased as only a teacher can be when her student excels, delights in his own learning and confirms her vocation. Still, there was that something else, something that happens when minds connect—or was it hearts?—and as she looked at her prize pupil, she wondered if this young Japanese man could possibly see her in a way the Colonel couldn't. Fifty years old, she thought. Any longer and I'll be too old.

◆

Mako worked with the *hanawai* irrigation gang, running along ditches to open or close sluice gates, hundreds of them spaced out according to some educated man's survey of the slope of the land. Water, methodically diverted from the mountains into the fields, was Waialua's blessing, the surveyors said, but for Mako, it was a curse. Chiyo was assigned to the *hoehana* women weeding the long rows that ended with the beginning of another line. She made up Japanese *holehole* songs to keep their minds in better places, singing about laying down the Portuguese foreman on his back and riding his cock, all the while the man on the horse smiled and urged on her singing, so good, he'd say, to hear them laughing and enjoying their work. Every day was the same, as were the months.

Mako and Chiyo met often after their baths and took walks along the cane field roads, but only when the moon was out to give back to the cane their faint colors stolen by the night. They had their usual places, none satisfactory, since the blankets were thin and the mosquitoes thick. I wish, Chiyo would say, we had our own house. They always walked toward the mountains, in the direction of St. Michael's away from the camp and found themselves one night peering into the empty sanctuary, unlit except for a votive candle flickering beneath the feet of a bleeding man outstretched on a cross.

"*Oi*," whispered Mako, "it's spooky here."

"That's because a god lives in there."

"Maybe," said Mako and he paused, "maybe that god can solve our problem."

"What?"

"Don't they perform marriages here? If we're married, we could get out of the single dorms and get a plantation house for ourselves."

"But you're already married."

"In Japan, yes. Sumiko's name was crossed out from her family registry and entered into my family's. That's all it takes to be married in Japan. But here it's different. I wonder if they even recognize my marriage here. And it's not like I'm crossing Sumiko out, which is how I'd divorce her. Which I wouldn't. Why in the world would I? But in Hawai'i, legally speaking, I'm not married. Anyway, it's just for the housing. While we're here."

"I don't know, Mako, I don't know, it doesn't seem right. We need to think about this. Couldn't we just leave the plantation and do something else? I hate the fields. I hate sugar cane. I hate Hawai'i."

"We have to honor our contract. We have no choice. They'd send the police after us if we didn't."

"Shuzo didn't. He didn't even show up."

"Well, they would have sent the police to find him. Breaking the contract is breaking the law. But I told them Shuzo had died. Of the plague when we arrived. They didn't care enough to check. But where the hell is he?"

They heard rustling in the bushes — mongoose or rats — and decided to head back to Mill Camp. Mornings started early — up at five, at the transport wagons by six.

"Think about it," said Mako, as Chiyo headed to the women's quarters. "See you tomorrow."

Most of the men were already in bed when Mako entered the building. He carried his shoes and walked to his bunk, where, lying on top of the covers, half asleep, was … Shuzo.

Mako sighed with relief and felt like punching him out. "*Oi!*" he said as loudly as he dared. "Where the hell have you been?"

Shuzo opened his eyes. "Mako, good to see you." He looked over at the man in the next bunk snoring. "This is not a place to talk and it's late. Where the hell have *you* been tonight? Been waiting for some time now."

"No, the question is where have *you* been? You can't just not show up after signing a contract." Mako glanced at the man in the next bunk, lowered his voice and muttered explicitly, "The only reason why you are not being hunted down is because I told them you died from the plague. Now I have to make up another story to explain why you are here."

"Tell them I died and was reborn again, just like the priests always say. But, look, don't worry about it. Listen, do you know the Haleiwa Hotel?"

"I haven't been off the plantation since I got here."

"Just follow the main road on the coast toward Kahuku. You can't miss it. This Sunday. At 10 in the morning. On the foot bridge over the river."

"Why? What are you up to now?"

Shuzo pressed a finger on his lips. "Shh, would tell you but can't talk now. Don't want to wake these losers up."

Mako cringed. Shuzo got up, walked to the door and put his shoes on. He stepped out and in a few moments, Mako heard snapping reins and a wagon rattling away.

CAT'S EYES

"HEY! SHUZO!" JEROME LEANED ON THE VERANDA RAILING and waved to Shuzo waiting at the foot bridge. He walked quickly down the steps of the hotel and crossed the lawn.

"Je-rome! Good morning."

Jerome stopped, wide-eyed. "Your English, my god, I can't believe it!"

"I been studying hard. Listen to this: The greatest slave is not he who is ruled by a teapot, ah, despot, great though that evil be, but he who is the … th-rall … of his own moral ignorance, selfishness and vice."

"I … I'm speechless. Where did you learn to talk like that?"

"Samuel and Josephine. Wonderful teachers. But why you here?"

"Why am I here? Well, Mr. Goodale, you know, the plantation manager, has big plans for the mill and needs some custom-made machinery. It's a major project and I'm handling it for the Iron Works. I'll be here for a week and will be coming often throughout, oh, at least a year, I would say. How's Anna?"

"Fine. Very busy. We have our own house."

"House? Not a, you know, *that* kind of house?"

"Yes, that kind. But for you, Jerome, free."

"No, no. No more of that for me. I put Anna on the wagon and said goodbye. And, by the way, about the wagon, the one you rented. The owner wants to know when you'll return it."

"I buy it. How much, you think? Hundred dollars okay?" Shuzo pulled out a roll of cash and peeled off a hundred dollars. "Please give to him."

"You're doing well, I see. And Anna, is she really all right?"

"Down the road, across from train station. You come any time."

Jerome looked at his watch and excused himself. "Good to see you. Give my best to Anna. And don't worry. I'll take care of the wagon."

Mako had arrived and was waiting by the bridge, astounded as much as Jerome had been about Shuzo's English. "I can't believe it, Shuzo. You spoke to that American entirely in English. How did you learn?"

"I've been working hard, Mako, but not as hard as you have been. Let's find some shade and talk."

Though it was only three miles away from Mill Camp, the Haleiwa Hotel was as far away in Mako's mind as was Maui. The hotel was not just for white haoles but for well-to-do haoles and even the Portuguese workers never gave it a thought because their plantation wages did not make them the right kind of white. To Shuzo it was a matter of manners in this new land and he had dared not risk any transgressive crossing of the line isolating the hotel from the camps and he knew himself to be a lucky exception, one who'd be wise to enjoy his luck but not press it. And so he had stayed at his liminal house, receiving guests and never went to see Mako. Besides, had he shown up in the camps, someone might have recognized him and recalled that minor irritant called a contract and force him into the fields. Months had turned into summer, then fall, if such a change in time existed in this land of identical seasons and he quietly collected his cash, storing it in a wooden trunk. As the end of the first year closed in, Shuzo was confident that no one would remember how he had entered Hawai'i, no one, that is, except Mako and Chiyo, but they were friends.

Mako spoke mostly about Chiyo, how he wanted to marry her so that they could live together, how this would not affect his feelings for his wife. He and Shizuka had agreed not to exchange letters for fear that communicating would stoke their longing for each and besides, Mako couldn't write without the help of someone else. A marriage in Hawai'i would be for just three years, the term of the contract and Chiyo would help him preserve, no, increase, really, his love for Shizuka. Chiyo understood the convenience and if the two women ever met, as he hoped they would, they would like each other. For sure. And Shizuka would express her appreciation to Chiyo. "Right, Shuzo, don't you think?"

"I would think," said Shuzo, "they'd want to kill each other if they ever met."

"That," said Mako laughing, "is exactly what *you* would think. But what do you know about women? Or men, for that matter? The only thing you understand is money. And hate."

"That," said Shuzo, "is exactly what *you* would think. But what do you know about me? But, look, this is not what I want to talk about. English has opened doors for me and there are other opportunities coming up. I need someone to run the house, you know, take care of Miki." Shuzo explained the night trade, the arrangement with the bellhops, the minimal English he would need, key words Shuzo would teach him. Handling the haoles would be easy and they pay so much, but the hard part would be to organize the Japanese men. But, and this is the good part, he had a plan. Now, none of them could afford the ten dollar fee, but if they formed groups of ten with each person contributing a dollar a week, they could each take turns, a different person every week and in the course of ten weeks, they would all get a chance with Miki, right here in Waialua. Ten men, a dollar a week per man, ten weeks, a hundred dollars. Or, they could make the long trip to Chinatown—and who had the time or money for transportation, food and lodging in addition to buying a slob-whore in Boss Morita's filthy house? But what about a girl the haoles line up for? Right here in Waialua! You know what they call Miki? An angel. Ever had sex with an angel? And sometimes I charge them twelve dollars. Shuzo thought for a moment, then recited a line from Samuel Smiles, translating it for Mako: those who have the patience to find quality at a higher price are more frugal than those who waste a penny on trash. He couldn't remember the passage exactly, but it didn't matter, it was appropriate, even with his revisions.

"You're a genius," said Mako, "kind of, well, evil, but a genius. But there is one thing you haven't considered. My contract."

Shuzo laughed. "See, you really don't understand me. I've got it all figured out. I'm going to buy out your contract. The only question is negotiating the price with the plantation, but I just met a haole friend, that guy who was just here, his name's Jerome and he knows Goodale-san, the plantation manager and he will help me, for Anna's sake. He'll show up at the house, tonight, I bet."

Mako was dazzled by Shuzo's scheme and knew better than to ask who Anna was. But he did ask about Chiyo, about buying out her contract as well. Shuzo hesitated, but agreed when Mako said he would do this only if Chiyo could be with him. All or nothing.

Shuzo laughed again. "Mako, you are beginning to think like me."

◆

Shuzo was wrong. Jerome did not show up that night. Around eight o'clock, a middle-aged haole man knocked on the door, saying that the bellhop at the hotel had sent him.

Shuzo asked him to remove his shoes before entering and collected his ten dollars. He asked the man to wait while he went back to the bedroom, where Miki was sitting on the bed. "Customer here," he said. "Ready?" She looked at Shuzo and he thought it might be better to let her rest, but, well, just one, just one for tonight.

The man entered the bedroom and Miki stood up, holding her yukata robe closed at her breasts. She let go of the edges and walked to the man to help him undress. He slipped off his wedding band and put it in his pocket. She led him to the bed and made him sit, then she stepped back and let her yukata fall to the floor. Their first pleasure, she knew, was just to look, as if she would be different for being Japanese. They always seemed to think so and he mumbled some expletives as she walked up to him and locked her arms around his neck. He wanted to press his face against her breasts, but she tightened her arms on the sides of his neck, holding his head away, then dropped to her knees and spread his legs. Her gentleness was almost a restraint, which he found immensely exotic. He grabbed her by her upper arms and tried to pull her onto the bed, but his impatience was greater than his strength, which she had stolen away from him, leaving him helpless against her manipulations. He discovered a pleasure that was greater for his being passive, giving himself to this aggressor of tenderness and he had never experienced anything like it before. "God Almighty," he murmured, referencing the divine and rested his portly body backward on the bed. Miki lifted his feet onto the bed and went to the closet to get some rope.

Shuzo was having a late dinner when Miki came out, dressed for her nightly walk. "Done?" he asked, surprised. "Is he still in there?" Miki nodded, slipped on her sandals and left the house. Shuzo went into the bedroom and found the naked man, gagged and tied, a human X, to the four corners of the bed. Angry, limp, humiliated and confused, the man was unceasing in his muffled complaints.

"What the hell?" he gasped, as Shuzo removed the handkerchief from his mouth and untied the ropes.

"Well, sir," Shuzo started, "well, sir, please don't upset. I think, hmm, I think she trying new tech ... tech ... new method. You like it?"

"Well, at first, yes, I admit, I liked it. But then she got dressed and left."

"New method," said Shuzo. "Must be patient. She plan to come back and undress again. You like see clothes come off?"

"Hmph." He thought about it. "Hmph."

"I give you money back if you like."

"Will she be coming back soon?"

"Yes, of course. Take off her clothes again. You want wait? I tie you up again?"

"No, no, heavens, no. I'm done for tonight." He got up to dress.

"I give you money back."

"Well, okay, but in all fairness, a five dollar refund will do."

◆

Miki sat on the beach and looked at the cat's eyes over Mt. Ka'ala. She grabbed a fistful of sand and let it dribble out slowly.

"Did you do it?" asked the cat.

"Yes, I tied him to the bed."

"Like I told you?"

"Exactly."

"Did he like it?"

"At first, but he was struggling when I left."

"Good."

"What shall I tell Shuzo?"

"Tell him you're tired, that you want to stop."

"I told him months ago, but he said I had to keep doing it."

"Why do you listen to him?"

"He takes care of me, he's the only one I can trust. I'll do anything for him. But he won't listen to me. I can tell him I'm tired, but he won't listen to me."

"Well, then," said the cat, "you'll just have to keep tying them up."

◆

Jerome went to see William Goodale about releasing Mako and Chiyo from their contracts. This was the second time Shuzo had asked him to be a liberating agent. He agreed to do it, of course, for Anna.

Jerome talked to Goodale about the buyout after discussing the specifications for the new boiling vats, designed to be the largest of any plantation. Goodale valued Jerome's expertise and he listened carefully. The man and woman will be working for Shuzo Taga, he explained, a man of extraordinary talent and while Jerome was not clear about the details of their plan, he was certain it would contribute to the pacification of the workers. Young, single, full of another kind of energy even after a brutal day of work, the laborers were still too eager to drink, argue and fight. How many times had Goodale been forced to call the police? How many workers had he lost to convictions of disorderly conduct, to jail time, which only made them meaner on their return. The Buddhist and Christian missionaries tried to temper their passions by filling them with guilt, prescribing self-restraint, and promising a wondrous future in eternity, which sometimes worked, but more often had a bottling effect, increasing pressures and outbursts of doing what they said they shouldn't. What they need, William, is not more whippings in the field by the feared lunas—how Christian is that—but orderly outlet and natural expression, opportunities to release their passions in private bedrooms leading to public docility. Entertainment will help too, music and drama to draw out sweeter feelings of affection and sorrow. A theater, that's what they need—art and culture—and you, William, will be the beneficiary of their contentment. Happy workers produce more. Enlightened management.

William Goodale sat quietly in his swivel chair. He got up and clomped across the wooden floor with his field boots and looked out the window toward the Kawailoa uplands, where, to the amazement of his workers, he had recently walked into the irrigation tunnel they were digging. A mile long, a record length, right through a mountain bored from opposite ends by teams expecting to meet perfectly in a center point calculated with the magic of mathematics by a young engineer. One man had been crushed by a cave-in, but Goodale went in anyway, inspecting the work, praising their progress. Enlightened management, eh? This blacksmith from the Iron Works reads too much, but maybe he has a point. He turned around and faced Jerome.

"Theater?" asked William Goodale. "These people plan to build a theater?"

"Well, not exactly, it's my idea, that's not what they have in mind, not right now at any rate. They're thinking of a brothel."

"Oh heavens," said Goodale, "you don't have to tell me everything. Orderly outlet, eh, well, as long as they keep it orderly. But I've got to see results, you know in work productivity. All right. I'll let them buy out their contracts. A hundred dollars for both. Do they have the money?"

"Mr. Taga does," replied Jerome.

A hundred dollars. Not bad. Shuzo could purchase Mako and Chiyo for the price of a horse and wagon.

◆

"Why did you tie the man to the bed?" Shuzo couldn't hide his irritation. "We lost half the fee on that one."

"Tired," Miki replied, "I'd like to stop. I still get scared, sometimes."

"You can't. Mako and Chiyo are joining us and we'll have more mouths to feed. In fact, we have to increase our business. Mako is going to organize the Japanese men."

"I'm tired." Miki didn't know how else to put it, but her downcast worried Shuzo.

"Oh, Miki, I'm sorry. I've been pushing you too hard. Maybe we should rest. Take a vacation. Would you like that?"

"I'd like to stop."

"Of course, for a short time. Where would you like to go? We can take the steamer to Maui. Or Hilo. What would you like to do?"

"Stop. I want to stop."

"Fine. We can stop right now. How about a trip to Honolulu? We could visit Horisho-san and see how he's doing. Remember how we worked in his restaurant? That'll revive your spirits. He was so kind to us. Shall we leave tomorrow?"

"No," she said, knowing the futility of persisting. She had no desire to see Horisho or go to another island.

"No? You don't want a vacation? Are you sure you don't

want to go? Really, Miki, you should take a rest. But if you don't want to go to Honolulu or see another island, well, we could continue, I guess, but I would hate to see you suffer from exhaustion. Tell you what. I'll let you continue with customers, but you must promise me that you'll let me know when you want a break. Anytime. Promise? It's all up to you."

Miki went into her bedroom and Shuzo went to the back room to get it ready for Mako and Chiyo.

That night, Miki tied up another man, who, released, demanded a total refund. Shuzo insisted that Miki take a rest, but she insisted on continuing as was her given choice and she received a customer the following night, lashing him to the bed as well. The men at the hotel whispered among themselves, the angel's gone and now there's a witch and from the third night, no one came.

◆

Shuzo told Mako about the problem with Miki. She was tired of haole men, and he urged Mako to hurry with their triple-ten plan since Miki would be comfortable, rejuvenated for sure, with Japanese men. It wouldn't be as lucrative as the haole men, ten dollars a week instead of a night, but it was still better than plantation pay and besides, the workers should be given a chance, not only because they were paid so little, but because they were fellow Japanese, and so many. It would not be right to take advantage of them. But if Mako could organize three groups of ten, or perhaps four and if Shuzo could do the same at the Kahuku Plantation, half an hour away by train, they would be back to the level of business with the Haleiwa Hotel. Samuel Smiles again: lower the price but sell more. Miki would be busier, but she can handle it—with Japanese men. "She could be herself," said Shuzo, "and not have to pretend to be a ghost, or an angel."

"Angel?" Mako asked.

"That's what I said. But it's too complicated to explain. I'm not sure I get it myself, those haole men, you know, they're weird sometimes. Who knows what's on their minds."

Mako suggested that he take Miki with him so that the men could see her and Shuzo agreed, adding that it would be another practice of fairness. Customers should be able to examine, well, not exactly — they should have the chance to see what they're buying.

Mako and Miki arrived at Mill Camp and from the shadows saw a group of men gambling under a kerosene lantern hanging from a branch of a mango tree in an empty lot. The night was turning cool, but they were hot and sweaty from a foul homebrew passed around in large brown bottles, from the heat of their laughing and shoving. Most of them had their shirts off, a few were wrapped only in loincloths, their foreheads banded by strips of threadbare towels. In the dim shadow directly below the lantern, two men squatted, facing each other and took turns slapping their best cards down on a square board — *Yosh!* — *Ha!* — as if their shouting could improve their hands. The heckling onlookers were illumined by a brighter circle of light, their eyes glassed like tiny beads, glazed with caring for nothing but winning their own wagers between themselves and when one man finally threw down the winning card — *Yah!* — the losing groans were louder than the triumphant shouts.

A man by a cooking fire said the food was ready and handed out skewers of sizzling fish and chunks of sweet potatoes baked in the ash. They sat around the betting board, eating and reliving the game card by card, the losers telling the loser how he could have won. Calmed by fish and potatoes, one man started to sing a *holehole bushi*, one song of the many they made up in the fields to distract them from cutting cane into a sweeter fantasy they imagined waiting for them after work.

Tomorrow is Sunday,
Husband gone away,
I'll be home all day,
Why not come and play?

Everyone joined in, clapping and dreaming of the hankering woman singing in their own male voices.

I read my contract
Once again today,
But even in the small print I see,
It does not say, "No adultery."

They laughed, sadly, knowing the fiction of this wonderfully cheating wife and they sang the verse over and over again, slower and softer in the dim light. Was she fading away like stars in the harsh light of morning, was she sinking deeper into their desires? Or was she stepping out of the dark into their circle of light, appearing like magic from their lyrics?

"Excuse me, gentlemen, but may I introduce Miki?" Mako spoke with excessive politeness, deliberately. Submissive in the fields under the gaze of foremen with whips and passive in the community from their social insecurity, the workers were unruly among themselves at night, trying to regain their manliness by harassing each other, vying to see who could be more mean. Politeness was a way of losing self-respect and they enjoyed its absence in their nightly sessions of reclaiming themselves, so when Mako displayed such civility, they would have delighted in humiliating him, proudly demonstrating that they most certainly were not gentlemen, except that she was so beautiful in her pink yukata tied with a red sash, the lines of her hair sweeping across her white forehead from one side over her ear into a bunch tied loosely behind her neck. Miki moved up next to Mako, more clearly into the light and leaned her head ever so lightly on his shoulder.

They were flustered at first, their rude standard of manhood suddenly called into question when they realized that this lucky bastard—wasn't he the guy who had been in the camp for some time and then left with the Okinawan witch—was polite as hell and therefore—so that's how it works!—

had a beautiful woman at his side. A few muttered a lame nice-to-meet-you and Miki smiled at them, telling herself that she could do this, go on pretending to be a ghost, a Japanese ghost, not an American angel, that maybe Shuzo was right in her need for a short break. And yet she held her breath as she looked at the half-naked men, smelly already though they had bathed and she reminded herself that she was doing this for Shuzo. The only person she loved and could trust. Besides the cat.

Mako made his pitch, answered some questions and when thirteen men said they would sign up, Mako apologized ever so politely and said that the limit was nine men, well, normally so, but in this special case, just for them, he could allow ten. One man offered to pay more than the dollar a week, but Mako said that would be unfair to take advantage of the rest. What he could do, however, was to start a waiting list, in case any of the first ten might want to drop out, as, of course, they were free to do. Mako memorized their names, scheduled their payments and visits and told them how to get to the house.

"Thank you, gentlemen," Mako concluded. "You will be pleased with our services. Miki and I look forward to seeing you and we will, I assure you, become friends. I apologize for intruding unannounced, so please excuse us." Miki bowed and the men jumped to attention, arms at their sides. They bowed in return and held their polite postures as Mako and Miki faded into the quieted night.

◆

"Well," said the cat, "so you're going to do it?"

"I guess so. Shuzo's right. He always is. The Japanese men are different. They seemed sad."

"But why can't Chiyo help? She's pretty and has nothing to do."

"Never thought of that," said Miki. "It would make it easier for me."

"Shuzo will never allow her to do that."

162

"Why not? It would mean more money."

"She means more than money to him," said the cat.

"Liar! Liar! She's just like me!"

"No, she's not."

"Go away! I hate you! I never want to see you again!"

The cat purred and Miki ran into the house crying.

◆

The triple ten system worked brilliantly, ten men, ten weeks, ten dollars rolling like waves into a hundred. Mako organized three groups and had a growing waiting list, while Shuzo succeeded in getting two groups from the Kahuku Plantation. A total of fifty men contributed a dollar a week and each man had one night with Miki during the course of ten weeks. That brought in $200 a month, of which Shuzo kept $50 for himself and Miki and gave another $50 to Mako and Chiyo. He deposited the balance of $100 into his bank account, his wooden trunk having filled up with too much cash and risk. Shuzo asked Miki to take on hotel clients again, but she refused, saying that Chiyo should do it. "On second thought," said Shuzo, "we should stick with the plantation men, as the system is working well. We really don't need the hotel." Miki went into the bedroom and buried herself in the blankets. He's protecting Chiyo. I'm doing it just for Shuzo, but is he sleeping with her?

For three cycles of ten weeks, for nearly eight months, Miki endured. She apologized to the cat and pleaded with it to come back, but the cat stayed away. She accused the cat of abandoning her, of breaking its promise never to leave, but the cat did not reply. Every night, after her client left, she looked over Mt. Ka'ala and called the cat, screeching like the wild peacocks, but the Scorpion changed its time and position and for weeks did not appear. Miki grew thinner, more remote and the men began to complain that there was no pleasure in sleeping with a live cadaver. Shuzo offered to take her on a vacation to regain her strength, but she told him that if he wanted to go somewhere for relaxation, he should take Chiyo. "As for myself," she said to Shuzo, "I will continue to do what you want me to do." Shuzo admitted that Jerome had been right, that she was at a breaking point and he stopped taking subscriptions, forcing her to rest. He made a last deposit of cash and when the teller handed back his account record, he looked at the balance and once again had to transpose the long string of dollar numbers into its equivalent in yen, his more familiar scale of prosperity.

Even with the payments to Mako and his regular contributions to his parents, Shuzo had more than enough for the rest of his life. Still, he worried about bad luck and had to insure himself with more money. He was anxious for Miki to recover, but she stayed in the house all day, hardly coming out of her bedroom. Jerome stopped by for a visit and told Shuzo that Miki seemed to be suffering from depression, which Shuzo dismissed as a western malady and insisted that all she needed was rest and, even better, an engaging distraction, perhaps a trip to someplace new. She was tired and bored, that's all, nothing wrong with something that ordinary.

Jerome shook his head and told Shuzo as bluntly as he could that Miki had gone over the edge and plain lost her mind. "Anna, my poor Anna," he lamented. "She's gone mad."

◆

Mokulē'ia, the land between Waialua and Ka'ena Point, was a fisherman's paradise. Near the village, the beach was wide and sandy and the reef stretched out a hundred yards, cutting the waves down at its outer edge to create an inner tidal lake for swimming and diving, a sea pond with schools of fish swarming in with the tide, getting out before its ebb exposed high points to the seaweed pickers. Octopus, lobsters and eels, more sedentary creatures, stayed in holes and crannies, coming out cautiously though they could be fooled into taking a baited hook. The fish came in all shapes and colors, round, flat, silver, black and every shade of yellow, green and red and roamed the reef like lazy tourists, picking and eating as they pleased.

Mako and Chiyo spent their free time fishing, going out with workers with whom, true to Mako's prediction, they had become friends. They learned the techniques for the hand line, pole, spear and traps. Mako's favorite was the throw net, woven with twine from a central point in descending rows, each with increased numbers of eyes to allow the net to flare out into a circle of twenty feet. He looked for bits of rounded scrap metal, free of sharp edges and attached them as weights to the outer perimeter. He experimented with coiling and holding the net, draping it over his elbows and shoulders and aimed his throwing style at achieving a full and perfect circle. The thrill was in the stalking, watching for hours for telltale flashes of silver bellies, scouring the small waves rolling in as advancing berms, their front faces smooth windows into the shallow reef below, but only for seconds before they crested in a whiteout. He practiced the arts of invisibility, never allowing his shadow to precede him, crouching lower as he approached, stepping silently and then, when he dared not get any closer, he waited for the one breaking wave to spread white foam over the surface as a screen to keep the fish from seeing the net flying through the air and come crashing down over them.

"Terrible day," said Mako, returning from Mokulē'ia. "Thought I had several mullet, but when I gathered my net, all I had was this damn fugu. And I didn't even see it. Brought it back for you, Shuzo, for old time's sake." He threw the spiny creature into the kitchen sink.

Chiyo held stiffened fingers by her cheeks, shaking them in disgust and told Mako to throw it away. Shuzo lifted it up by its tail and examined its puffy head. Not the same type as the ones in Iwakuni, but a fugu, deadly all the same. He'd never prepared one himself before, but he had seen Kawa-san and his father do it countless times and he knew the procedure exactly by sight.

Kawa-san had used small shears to cut the belly open,

the less likely to knick the liver, but his father had used a knife sharpened like a sword. A master of fine edges, Gombei had taught Shuzo the different angles and strokes to use on the progressively smoother water stones. Shuzo had asked him about his life as a samurai, but Gombei said that the only thing worth remembering was how to sharpen a knife. He pinched the blade between his thumb and index finger, letting the tip protrude only as much as the fugu's belly was thick and in one swift stroke, sliced it safely open, faster than Kawa-san could snip.

Kawa-san had never fished with another person in his boat before and couldn't contain his delight about having Shuzo bail the water seeping in from the cracks. In his boat, he talked constantly, sometimes to himself as was his habit, more often to the boy, just the two of them working the open sea. The old man had told him about waves and winds, the ways fish think, the techniques of snaring, snagging, hooking and scooping them up, but loved most of all to tell him, incessantly, what a good boy he was.

"Look," Kawa-san had said, pulling out a greased leather pouch from his pocket. "Show you something." He had opened the pouch and pulled out a small photograph, wrapped in waxed paper. "See," he said proudly, as he showed him the picture.

"But that's a picture of me," said Shuzo, looking at the image of himself of a few years earlier.

"Asked your father for it. My good luck charm. Works. Making more money now. You're my boy."

Kawa-san had given Shuzo money for bailing his boat, but told him never to tell his father about it. It was their own secret, sealed by companionship and it was nobody else's business. Shuzo used the money to buy magazines, *Modern Japan* was his favorite, and he dreamed of sailing on battleships, an army officer ready to disembark onto foreign lands to transform them by His Majesty's power into native soil. Shuzo read about the *Naniwa*, the most advanced cruiser in the world, protected by thick slabs of steel, 3,650 tons, 6 boilers producing the power of 7,604 horses, twin shafts from reciprocating engines. Bristling with guns like spines of a fugu, it had a ram in its bow for finishing blows. When the copycat Americans, colonies in mind, overthrew the Queen of Hawai'i, the *Naniwa* showed up in Honolulu Harbor and delivered Admiral Togo's message that all Japanese citizens were under the protection of his guns. Four years later, when the new Republic was formed, the *Naniwa* anchored at the mouth of the harbor, its guns just happening to point at 'Iolani Palace while an Imperial Navy captain delivered a courtesy message to President Dole to let him know that the Emperor of Japan did not appreciate his anti-Japanese sentiments.

Shuzo was convinced that the insular plantation owners had yet to regard the Japanese workers in their own fields as citizens of the most powerful nation in the Orient. The managers should show more respect. But what was really disgusting, inexcusable to the point of shame, was the stupid workers themselves, who groveled like servants, polite and grateful for the pittance dropped into their dirty outstretched hands. They needed to gain a healthy dose of self-respect and a different kind of discipline, one that served their interests, not the ends of their bosses. Discipline. It had not been easy to cut Kawa-san out when the orders for fugu dropped, and it was Shuzo who made the decision since his father wouldn't. It was all for the sake of the family. It was not a matter of being mean, for Shuzo had been just as hard on himself. It wasn't easy to postpone his army career, but it had to be done and that is why he did it. Discipline is so simple. It's doing what you have to do, not what you want to do.

"Watch what you're doing," said Chiyo. "Is that blood from your finger? I hope you know how to clean that fugu." She brought over a pot of water and washed Shuzo's thumb, which he had cut with the knife that should have been sharper and guided by a more attentive mind. She pulled a short ribbon from her hair and wrapped it around his wound. "Dreaming again," she said, tying the knot. "Thinking, thinking, thinking. Always thinking." She pressed her thigh against his and went to throw the bloody water out.

Shuzo arranged the translucent tessa, flesh sliced so thin they took on the color of the blue stoneware plate. Mako opened bottles of beer and offered to get Miki, but Shuzo said she was tired and wanted to rest. Chiyo brought out plates of broiled octopus, steamed fern shoots, pickled radishes, smoked *opelu* fish, soy sauce and mustard. Shuzo explained tessa, a new word to Mako and Chiyo: a combination of teppō and sashimi from the fugu, dual signifiers of instruments of death.

"I'm not having any," said Chiyo, reaching for the octopus. "I'd rather live."

"Try it," said Mako. "It's not like it'll kill you." The men laughed.

Mako ate a slice and grabbed his throat, feigning suffocation, but quickly recovered with a swig of beer. He spread his arms out and patted his chest, confirming his existence.

Shuzo picked up a piece with his chopsticks and dangled it in front of Chiyo's face. "Remember when you poked your chopsticks in my face? On the ship over?"

"You called me a stinking pig," she said.

"Look at us now," said Shuzo. "Good friends. We've changed so quickly."

Shuzo looked past the tessa into her face and remembered his impression of her as an exotic witch, a shamisen player who plucked hearts as easily as strings, the worldly woman whom he could ask questions about fire and water. She's no longer a stinking pig, that was all so silly. But how quickly we've changed? She's still what I had thought of her and that has not changed.

"Eat," Shuzo said, jiggling the tessa. "Take the chance."

She parted her lips and he slid the flesh into her mouth.

"Umm," she said, closing her eyes. "Crunchy. My first taste of death. A little bit of a thrill. You know, I'll bet…" She opened her eyes, clapped one hand over her mouth and raised her brows, as if alarmed.

"What's wrong?" asked Mako, getting up. "Are you all right?"

She dropped her hand. "I was about to say, I'll bet people would pay to have this experience."

Shuzo jumped up. "That's it!" He pointed to the plate of tessa. "How could we have been so blind! It's right before our eyes!"

Chiyo laughed so hard she rolled off to one side.

"What? What?" said Mako. "I don't get it."

"Fugu, you idiot! We'll open a fugu restaurant!"

They all started talking at once, ideas flying as freely as the beer flowed. Mako would catch the fugu, no, better yet, we'll buy them from others. Let them to do the work. We need a place, this house won't do, but Shuzo you have enough money, don't you? Recipes, we need recipes. Didn't Okinawans cook fugu too? And how about a stage? Let's build a stage as well. For song and dance and plays. Chiyo can play the shamisen and we'll hire other performers, drummers, *biwa* players, flutists, singers. Are we saying that amateurs can't perform? Will this be only for professionals? No, no, everyone is welcome. There are no professionals in Hawai'i. How many seats, Shuzo, how many seats can we have? Thirty, forty, I don't know, what do you think? I think we should charge ten cents for admission. Are you kidding? Twenty cents, easily. So what does that make? Twenty cents times … how many seats, Shuzo, how many seats?

They finally ran out of beer and questions and got tired of repeating themselves. Mako kept dozing off and finally slouched on a chair, head bent back, snoring and chortling as if deep sleep was hard work. Chiyo made a feeble attempt to clean up, stacking a few dishes. There was one last piece of tessa on the plate. Chiyo handed a pair of chopsticks to Shuzo. "Do it again, Shuzo, slip it into my mouth." She let her mouth open and he put the tessa in. She bit the chopsticks so that he couldn't pull them out and grabbed him by the waist with both hands. "Umm, the taste of death," she said, releasing the chopsticks. "Took the chance." She pulled his body to hers.

"Fire," he said softly into her ear.

"Water," she whispered.

Chiyo led him by his hand out into the cool air of the porch. In their burning consideration only for themselves, they paid no attention to Mako and did not bother to look back at the darkened bedroom, where the door had been slightly open, just wide enough for a pair of eyes to watch them all night.

DANGER AND PLEASURE

W AIALUA, "TWO RIVERS", ONE MEANDERING A LONG way from the Koʻolau Range, the other quickly coming off the Waiʻanae Mountains, both merging their mouths into Kaiaka Bay. Shuzo leased a piece of land in the delta between the two rivers, just off the new road connecting the long and short bridges. Anyone going between the mill and the village had to take that road, a perfect feeder for a restaurant. The property had an old but sturdy warehouse, large enough for a kitchen, dining area, stage and a few discrete rooms in the back. He called the restaurant *Abunai*, "Danger," in order to capture the fugu threat, but when the dining area was reconfigured as a theater for stage performances, he hung up a sign saying *Eiraku-za*, "House of Eternal Pleasure." Shuzo delighted in the suggestive combination of danger and pleasure, but the workers, too tired to care, continued to call the place by its old name, Long Bridge.

Shuzo urged the carpenters to work faster to finish his pleasure palace and he was certain that no other establishment on the entire island, Honolulu included, could offer such full services: food, music, plays and women, though he had to give the last one more thought. One of the back rooms would have a bed, the two others futon on tatami mats. If he didn't use them for the night trade, he could more honorably rent them out for lodging. As soon as the carpenters finished the restaurant-theater-brothel-hotel, he would have them start on his two-family home by the grove of Java plum trees at the edge of the property toward the bay.

The problem with running a whorehouse had to do with the new image he wanted to fashion for himself. Besides, he had no plans for using other women besides Miki and she, for the moment, was indisposed, to put it politely. He had made a fortune with her and she deserved to rest or even stop. Boss Morita was also rich, but he was a thug selling vulgar women. There was no proper standing in the business of whores and even though Miki was a *hakujincho*, a white man's nightingale, he'd lowered her down to the Japanese level, brawling laborers who couldn't pay much, which was why he had to organize them into cooperative groups. Tawdry, demeaning. Maybe it was time to quit.

Getting out of the brothel business would also solve a major problem, one that plagued him whenever he thought of home. He could never tell his parents that the money he had been sending them came from selling Miki. If Mother found out that I'm a pimp with a common prostitute, she would die from shame, a village whore being different from a classy geisha. They must never know anything about Miki. Not that I've done anything wrong by serving the demands of nature, but it's a matter of respect. That's where the restaurant theater is different, not as lucrative perhaps, but I can enjoy a moral pride and yes, I've just decided, the rooms should be for lodging and I can finally tell Mother and Father something true about the sources of my wealth.

◆

"Remarkable, truly remarkable" said Jerome, as Shuzo gave him a tour of the completed buildings at Long Bridge. "Amazing, you're just amazing. I told Mr. Goodale that you might be building a theater, but I was just guessing and had no idea it would be like this. And your house, brand new. Not as big as Mr. Goodale's, but just as nice. Is that where Anna is living now?"

"We moved in last week and she be so happy to see you. Why don't you visit her? Please, Jerome, do it for me."

The house was built in the managerial style with a hip and

gable roof, unlike the single ridgeline of the workers' quarters. It was posted three feet above the ground with wide steps leading to a large front porch. Jerome half expected to see Anna gliding back and forth on a bench swing and was relieved to see the porch empty, though he still felt as if he were repeating his innocent intrusion at Fujita's house. A courtesy call, then and now, a favor to Shuzo, beginning with an innocent greeting.

"Anna, are you in?" He knocked on the front door and peered through the fine mesh screen. "It's me, Jerome. May I come in?" He took off his shoes and entered, surmising that the room from which he had heard a noise was hers. He knocked on the solid panel door. "Anna, it's Jerome." He put his hand on the door knob but did not turn it. "I hope you're well," he called through the door. "Just thought I'd say hello, but I don't want to bother you, so I guess I'll leave you alone. Please take good care of yourself." He let go of the door knob but heard more noises and put his ear against the panel to determine if she was laughing or crying. He could hear her speaking in Japanese, short declarations, punctuated by clapping and stamping. Her voice rose and fell in a rhythmic blending with the cadence of her hands and feet. She must be dancing, he thought, as he heard her moving about the room, retreating from the door then coming back again. "Anna," he called softly, "are you alright?" He jumped back when she threw herself against the door, scratching it with her fingernails. He put one hand on the upper panel, as if to feel her through half an inch of wood and grasped the knob again. One turn, push slowly and he would be able to see the answer to his question. One turn, one push, but he let go instead and stepped back all the way to the front door and even as he put his shoes on, he kept his eyes on her door, uncertain if he wanted to see it open or not.

◆

Shuzo dedicated his new establishment in a style never seen before in Waialua. The grand opening of the Haleiwa Hotel had been more lavish, upper in class, but at Long Bridge, situated halfway between the mill and the hotel, the elite and the common mingled together, even if they did not interact across the divisions of race, language and self-esteem. Upper management and their wives grouped around Mr. and Mrs. Goodale, chatting about the new innovations at the mill, rising production tonnage, progress of the irrigation tunnels, the price of sugar.

Woodrow Davies, owner of the O'ahu Railway and the Haleiwa Hotel, arrived late with his wife in a sporty trap drawn by a chestnut horse under the reins of Davies himself, who could easily have afforded a larger carriage and a driver, but was pleased to tug the horse to a smart stop and make it back up a few steps just to show what he could make the animal do. He waved to the crowd, stepped off, sprightly for a large man, adjusted his black coat over his starched shirt and offered his hand to his wife. Unconcerned about her hair blown into tangles from their open ride, she lifted her long, plain white dress and eased herself down with her husband's help. They walked straight to Goodale, who yielded the center of attention to the entrepreneur and told the group the well-known story, in case anyone hadn't heard, of how Davies had been stranded in Hawai'i as a young seaman who had fallen off a horse and broken his leg while on a stopover in Honolulu. "When I watched the steamer leave without me," Davies said, ensuring that the moral of the tale would be correct, "I thought my world had come to an end, but it turned to be my best misfortune. Where would I be if not for that accident?"

"Well, sir," Mr. Goodale replied with the obvious. "Hawai'i would not be what it is without you. And how generous of you to have built your magnificent hotel in our town."

"That was easy," Davies said, smiling, a hint that everyone should laugh at what followed. "I had to give city people a reason to ride my train out to my hotel in my ... ah, the country." Everyone laughed, politely, gaily. Wasn't it refreshing to see a businessman honest about his greed?

Only Shuzo moved easily among the different groups.

He greeted the Chinese merchants and told the grocery owners of his plan to buy vegetables, roast duck and smoked chicken from them. The Hawaiian fishermen talked about the best times and places for catching puffer fish and Shuzo reminded them of his further need for octopus, eels, lobsters and other kinds of fish, as long as they were silver or red. Nothing green or yellow, please. Shuzo asked the Portuguese butcher if his supply of goats and pigs would be steady and the stocky man stroked his mustache with thick fingers and assured him that animals had no seasons, only cycles for mating. Shuzo walked over to the large group of Japanese workers and complimented them for wearing their best clothing. He reminded them, in case they had forgotten, that dressing up was not for the sake of pleasing their bosses but for their own sense of worth. "Remember your manners," he said flatly. "Show everyone that we are from a great nation." And to demonstrate his point, he walked up to Woodrow Davies and introduced himself.

"Ah, yes, Mr. Taga. I'm pleased to meet you. Colonel Kalama told me all about you." Davies shook Shuzo's hand. The Japanese workers stopped talking and watched.

"Thank you for coming to my party," Shuzo said. "Colonel Kalama not sure you make it, but I'm glad you're here. Welcome to Restaurant Danger and the House of Eternal Pleasure."

"Interesting names. House of Eternal Pleasure?" asked Davies. He turned his back against his wife, leaned closer to Shuzo and said in a lowered voice, "That sounds like a whorehouse."

Shuzo couldn't tell if Davies approved or not, but cautiously assumed that in a public situation, his lowered voice notwithstanding, Davies would side with virtue. Still, Davies squinted one eye, a barely recognizable wink and Shuzo was tempted to say that for you, Mr. Davies, free, but he knew better than to be so reckless. Besides, he had already made up his mind to quit the evening trade and so he leaned closer to Davies and gave him a full wink.

"I have three rooms in the back with beds and futon, but

you see, Mr. Davies, they not for men paying for women, but for guests who want to stay here in my own *little* hotel. Do you know why?"

Davies raised his brows, puzzled about the logic of the sudden question and shook his head.

"Because I want to be like you."

Davies roared, tossing his head back, slapping his large hand on Shuzo's shoulder. "I like you, Mr. Taga, you've got guts! Come, let me introduce you to my wife."

Shuzo laughed along with him, knowing that Davies had mistaken his comments for flattery, when, in fact, he had meant it seriously.

The Japanese workers stood up straighter, tucked in their shirts and matted down their hair with spittled palms. Who is this Shuzo Taga anyway, and how did he learn to speak English so well? Mistah Davies has his hand on his shoulder and Mistah Davies is more important than Mr. Goodale. Their admiration swelled and Shuzo could have ordered them to do anything, scour the village for rice and chickens, point their bayonets at the Chinese and Koreans for the glory of the Emperor.

In another show of his membership in a great nation, Shuzo interrupted Davies's story about negotiating passage rights for his railway and excused himself when he saw Jerome talking to the Portuguese blacksmith who ran the mill's small foundry. Davies in turn interrupted Shuzo's departure by saying that he wanted to talk to him about a deal he had in mind and Shuzo thanked him, replying that he looked forward to a meeting with him, later, when he had more time.

"This is incredible," said Jerome. "How did you get all these people to come? Is that Woody Davies over there?"

"Colonel Kalama got him to come. Besides we're both in the hotel business. And Mr. Goodale, well, you got Mako and Chiyo out of their contracts and he wanted to see this theater you told him about. The rest just followed. But come with me. I want to introduce you to someone."

They walked through the food area, where Mako and

Chiyo supervised a crew to keep the tables well supplied with fried fish, sashimi, roasted wild pig, baked sweet potatoes, coconut pudding, bananas, guavas and *hala kahiki*, "foreign fruit," from James Dole's new plantation right up the hill in Wahiawa. They replenished the galvanized tubs with bottles of soda water, sealed with glass balls forced against rubber gaskets inside the narrowing necks by the pressure of carbonation. Shuzo did not trust the men with alcohol, at least not for his dedication party, though he told them that the restaurant would regularly serve beer and sake. His decision was a windfall for the Spring Soda Works, Waialua's own, and the bottlers had to work overtime to fill their largest single order to date.

Shuzo led Jerome to Josephine, who was standing under a mango tree by herself. "Both of you are lovers," he said and paused to enjoy the effect his opening words had on Josephine, "… of books." He introduced them to each other and took more time to explain Josephine as the teacher responsible for his advancement in English. "She strict," he said, "like army officer." But Josephine knew he was also speaking of himself.

She also knew from the smooth skin of Jerome's face and its refusal to wrinkle as he smiled that he was at least a quarter of a century younger than she. They exchanged greetings, had no more to say and Shuzo did nothing to dispel the awkward silence. Josephine looked upon Jerome as if he were a former student, grown-up but still a young man and she, an older woman not knowing what to say to him outside of the classroom. She looked at Shuzo, who was smiling with anticipation and she wanted to correct his motives as she did his mispronunciations and glitches of grammar. A slight flush rose to her cheeks, turning them brunette, and Shuzo's eyes widened as he saw what he was looking for. She resented his satisfaction, feeling that he had tricked her into her own involuntary reaction and she pressed her lips together tightly to show some displeasure.

"Bird," said Jerome, finally. "Have you read Isabella Bird?"

"Why, yes," she replied. "I like her very much. Especially her book on Japan, less so the one on Hawai'i."

"That makes sense. You know less about Japan. I mean, you know more about Hawai'i."

Josephine smiled and relaxed. A former student would never comment on her ignorance. "And you, Mr. Stewart, which book do you like?"

"Both, equally well. Because I know nothing about Japan or Hawai'i."

And modest as well. "Come now, Mr. Stewart, I'm sure you've learned a lot about Hawai'i by now."

"Please, Miss Kaumaka, please call me Jerome."

"Only if you'll call me Josephine." She was embarrassed by her stock comment, as if she were a character in a novel she had read. She wished she could take it back but did not know how she might have put it in her own words, this being the first time she'd insisted on her first name to a man.

Shuzo broke in so that he could leave. "And I, Mr. Taga, need to see Mr. Davies again. But one question before I go. What does guts mean?"

◆

Courage, so Davies likes my courage. It's easy, once you accept chance. And he had fallen off a horse! Just like the Chinese story. He also knows about accidents and opportunity. I wonder what he wants to talk about?

"Nothing special," Davies said to Shuzo when they were off by themselves. "I just thought it might be good for both of us if you could get up a stage show suitable for my hotel guests."

"That'll be hard since I don't know anything about American music or dance or plays."

"No! No! Of course, you don't. But I want something Oriental, you know, something they haven't seen before, something exotic. Japanese, Chinese, Hawaiian. They'll love it."

"Well, let's see what I can do. I don't know if your guests will like it, but I try something."

"Of course, you will. You've got guts."

"And you too, Mr. Davies, you also a brave man."

Davies looked puzzled, but instead of trying to figure it out, he simply extended his hand, and they shook on their deal.

"Oh yes," said Davies, "one more thing. I don't care what you call your theater in Japanese, but could you change the English so that it sounds less like a whorehouse?"

Shuzo promised to talk it over with his English teacher and headed toward his house by the plum grove. The party was going well and he could escape for a moment. He entered Miki's bedroom without knocking and found her sleeping in bed.

"Wake up, Miki," he said softly. "Wake up. I want you to see something."

He pulled the blanket off and helped her get out of bed. He poured some water from a pitcher into a basin and sponged her face with a washcloth, then went to her closet. "This is perfect," he said picking out a black kimono embroidered with deep red maple leaves with hazy clouds stenciled in gold around the hem. She did not have a regular *obi*, but a white silk sash, wrapped twice around her and tied in a bow in the back had its own elegant effect. He combed her hair and wondered if he should let the strands fall loose but decided to gather it behind her and fix it with a light blue ribbon. He held both of her hands, stepped back and looked at her.

"Beautiful, Miki, just beautiful."

And she smiled, the first time in months.

"Come," he said, leading her to the porch. "Look at all those people, everyone's here, to celebrate our new restaurant and theater." He identified them all, as individuals and groups, several hundred people filling the yard.

"Look," said Shuzo, moving his outstretched hand over the crowd. "So many people, so different, but they're all together. It's like magic Miki, like magic."

The late afternoon sun put everyone in the cool shade of the plum forest, the soft trades caressed. The clouds over the Kawailoa uplands were pink, ready to start their shift toward evening red and released a light shower in veils drifting right through a double rainbow with its reversed bands of colors. This was a new palette and Japan faded like an old photograph into sepia brown and shades of gray. His guests moved slowly about, chattering in a suffusion of voices as if they were speaking a single language with specialized dialects: English for precise explanations, Chinese for hammering arguments, Japanese for useful ambiguities and Hawaiian for poetry and seduction. In fact, their verbal intercourse gave birth to a common pidgin, a bastard tongue adequate for basic information and even better for miscommunication. Two men stood close to the house, engaged in an argument or discussion, Shuzo could not tell.

"Ip I stay go wen you stay come, no stay, go."

"Watu ifu you no stay go, an' I no stay come, you go'in go?"

"Wat?"

"Oa you go'in stay?"

"Stay whe'ah?"

"Wassa mella you, you stupid o wat? I aksin' you ifu you go'in stay oa ifu you go'in go, ifu I no stay come."

"I donlru know, but I like know dis: you shuah you go'in come?"

"You dum bugga. Of cose I go'in stay come."

The two men noticed Shuzo. The Japanese bowed, while the Filipino offered a smart salute. I'm glad, thought Shuzo, we decided to serve nothing stronger than soda water. The mood was right and everyone was relaxed and having a good time. The absence of tensions was remarkable precisely for seeming so normal, for that moment, at least. It was a scene impossible in Japan, where conformity limited possibilities. Here, in this disparate gathering, Shuzo could fit each group and person into his grand scheme of suppliers and consumers and their diversity increased his chances for greater wealth. His vision was clear. Through the glassy air, he could see details sharpened by unfiltered light, his ideas taking shape into the landscape before him, right there at Long Bridge, the place between the two rivers, the only place where this strange event could happen and for the first time since he had left Japan, Shuzo felt as if he belonged to this land, if not to the people.

He put his hand around Miki's waist and when she rested her head against his shoulder, he realized that the small miracle transpiring before him was an exception to his rule and he pulled her to him, knowing that all of this had not happened entirely by chance.

"Look, Miki, look at what you've accomplished. You're the reason why this is happening. Come."

He held her hand and led her down the steps. As they approached the crowd, the people were quieted by her appearance, a girl dressed for a wedding as they used to in the Land of the Rising Sun. She absorbed their gazes and returned to them her old serenity, shameless and demure, a bridal princess in a realm of her own, possessed by something more than the man she was with, something inviting they could sense but not define. Jerome thought he knew of her possession, but now he was puzzled and questioned his diagnosis, and Josephine could not help but notice the intensity of his interest in the fragile girl. The Japanese workers swelled with desirous pride, some of them remembering what a dollar a week had purchased for them. But as she marched with Shuzo toward the Davieses and Goodales, she looked different without her sadness and the workers wondered how they had been able even to touch such beauty with their filthy hands.

"Aha!" said Woodrow Davies, breaking the spell. "Just what we need, Mr. Taga. Truly exotic! If you can make *her* sing and dance, our guests will love it, really love it. Isn't that right, Emma Louise?"

Mrs. Davies nodded, confirming for Shuzo that her husband was a man he could use. Easily.

◆

As the crowed thinned, Shuzo persuaded Jerome to cancel his stay at the Haleiwa Hotel and be the first guest at the

House of Eternal Pleasure. His room did not have the same amenities and Jerome had to walk to the outhouse at the edge of the yard. But he was pleased to be Shuzo's first guest and, as expected, his stay was free. He was also a first for the restaurant and he sat with Shuzo alone in the dining area.

"Anna was amazing. She looked like her old self." Jerome picked up his bottle of beer and toasted Shuzo on the success of the dedication.

"All she needed was rest. Everything all right. We're getting out of the evening trade."

"That's good news. For Anna especially."

"I haven't told her yet, but I think she happy. Sleeping with so many men can make any woman, you know, crazy."

"Did I ever tell you she was possessed by a cat in my house? She attacked me one night, hissing and clawing like a cat. She had a cat at that time, the one she rescued from the burning church."

"Possessed by a cat? No be silly. How you know that?"

"Because I cured her by cutting out the heart from her cat."

"Ugh, you killed a cat, cut its heart out? Disgusting."

"Made me sick to my stomach, but it worked. The next day she was calm."

"That just happen by chance. I can't believe you're so … so…"

"Superstitious?"

"Is that the word? Yes, so superstitious. But you Americans like that. You even believe a man died on a cross and then came back to life again as God. You really believe that happened?"

"I believe that, yes, I do."

"But that's absurd—Josephine taught me that word the other day—just ab-suuurd."

"Maybe. But these things happen."

"All that in past anyway," said Shuzo, "and we can forget it. We have plenty work to do. And, oh, I almost forgot. How you like Josephine?"

"Great to talk to, about books."

"Anything else?"

"You mean like falling in love? Shuzo, you're a great businessman, but a terrible matchmaker."

"You never can tell, never can tell. Didn't you just say strange things can happen? Things that no make sense? Well, I hope you sleep good tonight. See you in the morning and you tell me all about your dreams."

Miki was sitting on the porch, drinking a cup of tea. Shuzo sat next to her and told her how happy he was with the day's event. From Mr. Davies on down, people were so supportive, saying how excited they were, giving suggestions for singers and musicians, thanking him for his planned entertainments. Eventually he'd like to bring performers from Japan and maybe San Francisco as well, Chinese opera, popular American singers, a circus. "But first we start with what he have," he said realistically, "and that means Chiyo and her shamisen. Chiyo will be my first star."

Miki stood up, walked to the far side of the porch and gazed into the sky over Mt. Ka'ala. There, it's back. The Scorpion is back, pincers and head rising behind the mountain, its tail surely to follow. She walked back to Shuzo.

"Chiyo?" she said. "Your first star?"

"Oh, Miki, I didn't mean it that way. Of course, you're my first star. I told you that earlier. All of this is happening because of you. You are my first star and no one can take your place. No one. It's just that now it's time for you to rest, to stop. Remember how you asked me to stop?"

"Yes," she said. "Stop and rest. And go fishing."

"That's it, now you're getting it. It's Chiyo's time to work and you can rest and go fishing. With Mako."

"With Mako," she repeated and got up and went into her bedroom. Fishing with Mako. Alone with him on stretches of white sand, warm rocks by the sea. Sleeping on the beach on overnight trips to Ka'ena Point while Chiyo worked, playing her shamisen. But after the show, Chiyo will be with Shuzo in the back of the darkened stage, everyone gone— that's why he wants me to go fishing with Mako—and she will press her body against his. Saw them do it, Mako asleep. Shuzo only pays that kind of attention to Chiyo, no one else, not me. But I'll go fishing. Alone with Mako.

◆

"Taga-san. Are you Shuzo Taga?" The thin young man was dressed like a worker, except that his long-sleeved shirt was clean, his pants starched and ironed and he held a flat brimmed straw hat in his hand. With his leather suitcase, he was an obvious new arrival, but not one contracted for the fields. Barely twenty, if even that, he had a delicacy attributable to something other than his youth, his pale unblemished skin, his soft hands, seductive eyes, thin lips. He spoke with uncertainty, not about whether Shuzo was Taga-san or not, his question being for confirmation of what he already knew. His uncertainty was of himself, the whole of his person, beginning with how he looked on down to his innermost feelings.

Shuzo sensed his introverted weakness, but also felt the force of his beautiful eyes, a challenge awakening that old temptation to dominate a young boy. Like an army officer, that is. "Yes, I'm Shuzo Taga. What of it?"

"My name is Yukio Nozaki, from Iwakuni like you. My father is the head of the Association of Lumber Dealers."

"Nozaki? The Lumber Dealers?"

"Yes, just as I said."

Iwakuni came back in flooding color, the black rocks in the garden, the green pine boughs clipped flat, the bloody bandage tied around his father's head, the pink peonies swaying outside the bedroom veranda, the stacks of tan zelkova piled behind the flowers, the gold pin on Nozaki's lapel boasting of his membership on the conscription board. If that Nozaki is this man's father, then why is he here to see me? Shuzo did not utter a pleasantry.

"I know it's strange," the young Nozaki said in a delicate voice, "and I apologize for interfering with your work." He looked at the banners hanging in front of the House of Eternal Pleasure. "Very impressive. They told me you were very rich."

"They? Who told you about me?"

"Oh, everyone knows it. In Iwakuni. Your father does not have to work because of your support and your parents live well. Everyone knows it. It's really a small town, Iwakuni."

"So why are you here?"

"Well, Taga-san," he said, fidgeting with the brim of his hat, "I'm here to ask for your help."

If only he hadn't told me his name or said nothing about his father. He's just a young man, attractive, earnest and I should not blame him for what his father did to us. Is he asking for my help to make amends on behalf of his father? But his father, that bully clothed in feigned respectability, cannot have changed his feelings toward us, just because he's heard of my success. In fact, it has to be the opposite, jealousy and more revenge. He had the tiller sawn from the underside, thought he had ruined my father, but his scheme backfired and by chance, everything is by chance, one thing led to another and I've made a fortune. He probably wants to take the credit for my success, to mount a platform and shout, "Shuzo Taga is a rich man in Hawai'i because I ruined his father!" Absurd. Just ab-suurd. But he's not stupid enough to make that claim, he's more evil than that. He wants to ruin me, that's what he wants and he's sent his son, this innocent-looking boy, to make me fall for some trick. Or for him.

"Help? What kind of help?"

"I need a job. I came on a student visa, but I have no intention of going to school." His quick honesty took Shuzo by surprise.

"Then why didn't you stay in Japan? It's easier for you to find a job at home, I mean, Japan. Unless you have a plantation contract, it's hard to get a job here. You should go back. And stop shredding your hat apart."

Nozaki gripped the brim and looked straight into Shuzo's face. "The draft, Taga-san, I don't want to be drafted."

"But your father, he's the head of the board. Does he know you're here?"

"He's the one who told me to escape to Hawai'i."

Shuzo turned and spat on the ground. Miserable cowards! Slimy weasels! The great Nozaki, head of the conscription board, hiding his son from the army. This is a scandal! This piece of shit is running away from his duty and he expects me to help him? I'll help him, all right, I'll help him realize his duty. I'll turn him in to the Consul General. They'll send him back. He'll go to jail for evading the draft and what will Nozaki say then? "Shuzo Taga ruined my son." And I'll shove him off the speaker's platform and say, calmly, "Because *you* ruined my father." And then we'd be even. Justice, not revenge.

"Please, Taga-san, I need your help." His eyes moistened, but he kept his gaze fixed, even as he saw Shuzo unmasking his contempt.

"Shame on you, running away from your duty like this! The best help I can give you is to tell you to go home. Don't you know about our army and navy? It's in the papers here as well. Japan is becoming a great nation and you should be proud to be a part of that."

"And you, Taga-san, why are you here?"

"To make money," Shuzo snapped, barely managing to honor his insulting question with an answer. "Like everyone else. I'd much rather be in Japan, but I came here for my family's sake. Because my father's boat was *sabotaged* and he nearly lost his life. *Someone* tried to murder him." Shuzo was ready to be specific but waited to see Nozaki's response.

"I'm sorry to hear that. Sabotage? Did you ever find out who did it?"

His innocence was convincing. He doesn't know about the tiller. Why should he? Fathers never tell their sons everything, least of all their misdeeds. This young man is blameless. But, too bad, the only way to get even with Nozaki involves him, this innocent young man standing right here and all I have to do is turn him in and the Consulate will take care of the rest. Another fortuitous accident, falling into my lap. No need for violence, for beating anyone up, though I've certainly dreamed about it countless times: gagging Nozaki to silence his pleas for mercy, tying him to a rack and taking a sharp knife across his chest in a crisscrossing pattern. No, the settlement of our grievance is standing right in front of me and all I have to do is notify the authorities. Simple. Clean. Perfect. And legal. And moral too.

"Did your father tell you to come and see me?"

"No, he thinks I'm going to study English at some school, but I want to work to support myself so that I can paint and I have come to you on my own."

"Paint? But what about your duty, your military service?"

"Taga-san, look at me. Do you see a soldier?" He held out his soft hands. Thin, emaciated almost, he was not suitable material, not even for the sugar fields. "I'm not lacking in courage, but my body is weak. My father is so ashamed of me, ridicules me all the time, tells me I'm really a girl and sending me here to Hawai'i, well, he's been hiding me all my life."

"Your father is a cruel man, to others as well, and he should be put in his place."

"He's cruel, but he's my father and there is nothing I can do to change that."

Just turn him in and be done with it. Don't listen to him anymore.

The boy put on his hat. "Well, Taga-san, I'm sorry to have bothered you. I can see that you're disappointed in me too. Just like my father." He picked up his leather suitcase, which was almost too heavy for him and headed for the road to Waialua village on the other side of Long Bridge.

Good, he's gone. I'll report him the next time I'm in Honolulu. It's a matter of duty, what must be done. Easy. Nothing but a draft dodger violating his visa on top of that. And a Nozaki. Shit. What luck.

187

DRAFT DODGER

XCEPT FOR RIDING THE TRAIN, THE ONLY WAY TO KA'ENA Point from Waialua was by horse or foot. There was a wagon trail alongside the tracks, but it only went for half a mile, not far enough according to the fishermen's unassailable belief that the size of the fish was greater the closer one got to the Point. A wagon was convenient for hauling equipment and supplies, especially for an overnight trip, but only for dabblers content to stop far short of the Point and catch smaller fish. Shuzo said the fishermen were more superstitious than the Americans since they had no provable evidence for their theory. Were the fish bigger because the water was richer in nutrients closer to the Point? Deeper? Colder? Warmer? He dismissed the testimonies of so-and-so catching such-and-such at this or that location, scoffing at the fishermen's love of wishful tales. But Shuzo was not a fisherman, so no one listened to him, and besides, the man to be with was Ulua-san, Mako's fishing name.

Fishermen spoke of *ulua*, the giant trevally, with awed respect, a worthy opponent that had to be outsmarted to be caught. Since the fishermen had more stories about their misses than their catches, Shuzo regaled them with their own evidence proving, obviously, that ulua were smarter than they. The largest specimens could reach five feet in length and measure nearly two feet from their bellies to their dorsal fins to form a thick, vertical board of a fish weighing over a hundred pounds, as heavy as a sack of sugar. The white ulua fed along sandy bottoms, while the black ulua came out of their caves at night to prey along the rocky shoreline. Mako preferred the black, claiming he knew their habits better than the white, and Shuzo loved to make fun of Mako's fussy insistences of bait—live fish; hooks—Japanese made; sinkers—large bearings encased in twine; time—moonless nights; and place—Leaping Spirit Rock close to Ka'ena Point. "It's not a science, you know," said Shuzo, scrutinizing two hooks of different shapes and wondering how one could be better than the other, "but just a matter of chance. And every outing is just another occasion to be shown that fish are smarter than men."

As judged by the poor record of his catches and Shuzo's indictment, Mako had to be counted among the least intelligent of men, but he was highly sought out as a fishing partner. No one was more obsessed than Mako was with the ulua, hence his name, and in a demonstration of his ingenuity apart from comparisons with fish, Mako built a cart with wheels spaced the width of the Davies's train tracks and lined the inner rims with iron plates to keep the wheels from skittering off the rails. Instead of strapping on a bulging backpack and shouldering long poles for the ten-mile hike to the Point, Mako could easily push his cart loaded with the gear of several men, get up some speed and hop on it to ride on inertia for a dozen yards at a time. Even better was to have his companions push him all the way. If a train came up from either direction, they could lift the cart off the rails, push it safely to the side and plug their ears with their fingers as the engineer blew the whistle and waved. Ulua-san was not the best fisherman, but his cart solved the problem of transportation, especially if they had to haul, as they hoped they would, a big fish back to the village.

When Miki told Mako that she wanted to go fishing, he cancelled the arrangements he had made with two other fishing partners. They teased him about taking Miki, reminding him about women being bad luck. Her presence would change nothing, he replied, his record already being dismal in the company of men.

They set out in the afternoon with Miki riding in the shade of the canvas canopy he had rigged just for her. The load was lighter than usual and Mako could get the rickety cart up to running speed, hop on and coast a good distance while he caught his breath. They made good time over the flat terrain through the cane fields and were soon moving along the shoreline at Mokulē'ia.

"You'll like it," he promised Miki. "Especially out at Leaping Spirit Rock."

She stared ahead, brushing hair wisps out of her face.

"The Hawaiians believe that those who have lost their spirits can get them back on that rock. They also say the souls of the dead jump to the next world from that rock." He stopped and thought about what he had just said. "Hmm, never thought of it, but it doesn't make sense. You can find or lose your spirit on the same rock?"

Mako kept a steady walking pace as he studied the water and stopped at every reef shallow and small lagoon. "There," he said, pointing to the water for Miki's benefit, but she could not see what made him grab his small-eyed net. He hid behind some *naupaka* bushes, coiled the top length of the throw net into his left hand, separated the hanging skirt into thirds, one shank over his outstretched elbow, one hanging down, the last gripped in his right hand. He waited for a wave to break, then ran down the sand to the water's edge and threw his net, which popped into a full circle in the air just before it hit the water. Mako stripped down to his loincloth and waded in to gather his net into a tangled bundle of squirming fish and called out to Miki to bring down a bucket. "*Oama!*" he yelled, as he started to remove the tubular fish tinted red and green along their sides. "Ulua's favorite food." He worked quickly to get the fish into the bucket of water before they drowned in the air.

Back at the cart, he told Miki to keep an eye on the fish and to let him know when they started gasping on the surface, a sign to change the water. "You're good luck already," he said to her. "Sometimes we reach the Rock without catching any bait fish and have to chase down rock crabs. But today, oama." As he untangled and cleaned his net, Miki walked the beach picking up shells and little white flowers from the naupaka bushes.

The cliffs of Mokulēʻia slowly darkened against the lingering orange and blue sky, even though the sun had already dropped over the edge of the ocean. Anxious to get to the Rock, Mako resumed his running and riding. When the cart was slowing down to one of its stops and he got ready to jump off again, she put her hand on his shoulder and climbed down to push the cart by herself. She struggled at first, then gained some speed and almost stumbled as she tried to get back on. Mako grabbed both of her tiny hands, pulled her up and she fell into his arms. She looked at him, her face inches away from his and giggled, just like the girl she had been when they first had met in the engine room of the *America Maru*. And for the same reason why he had angrily turned down the engineer's offer of her free services for the benefit of her training, Mako held her as his daughter.

The cart rolled to a stop. He couldn't move except to tremble and he wept on her shoulder, quietly calling their names, Yuki, Shizuka, asking for their forgiveness. He was suddenly desperate, homesick for them, but what pained him physically in his chest was his inability to picture them clearly. He could conjure vague images, but as he tried to sharpen his focus, he could only see Chiyo and Miki instead. Shuzo was right, he was fooling himself. Shizuka would never accept Chiyo. How could she, as his wife? And what would Yuki think of her father, living and sleeping with another woman, claiming to love her mother as before? He put his face in his hands and Miki cradled him in her arms, swaying gently to stop his shaking, then pushed aside some boxes to make room for him to lie down and rest. She got off the cart and started to push, walking at a comfortable pace and though she had never seen Leaping Spirit Rock before, she knew it by its prominence, right off the ocean side of the tracks.

The sky was enough of a glowing mantle for her to see

her way down to the small circle of stones around the ashes of previous fires under an outcropping of the Rock. She spread a blanket in the shelter and helped Mako off the cart. He apologized, claiming he was all right and told her to carry down the box of food and water while he went to get some driftwood from a previous stash. He started a small fire for light and smoke to keep the mosquitoes away, but a cool breeze did a better job of that. Salt air and hunger made the rice balls and dried fish taste special. Mako went back to the cart, to get his fishing gear she thought, but he came back with a small bottle of sake. She declined his offer and he took a long swig straight from the bottle.

"I never thought this could happen," he said, beginning his confession, "but I'm beginning to forget Shizuka and Yuki. How can anyone forget his wife and daughter? I came to Hawai'i for their benefit and now, I just don't understand it."

He took a smaller sip of sake, mindful of making it last.

"It's Shuzo's fault. He's made it too easy for me. If I were still working in the fields, hating the heat, hating the foreman, wanting to run away, break my contract, then that would make my memories stronger, clearer, forever."

He lifted the bottle but set it down again.

"But I've been enjoying myself, that's the problem. It's hard for me to even say it. Enjoying myself! Having fun!"

He shouted his admissions of pleasure into the sloshing waves and the clacking of loose rocks in the receding water. He took a bigger swig, trying to wash away the damnation of his good fortune, his envy of suffering. House of Eternal Pleasure! I should burn it down. And then what? Ask Mr. Goodale for a contract?

"And what about Chiyo?" he found himself asking out loud. Miki had been looking at him all this time and he had confessed more to her than he had to anyone else. He could talk with others about all sorts of things but feeling bad about betraying those he loved without their knowing was not something he had ever addressed. To wrong them openly would be bad enough, but to do it in secret was unbearable.

Which was why he had hoped desperately that Shizuka and Chiyo could be friends like salve to his wounds. But now he had confessed a truth even he had not admitted until that moment. He was having fun when he was supposed to be suffering.

"It's Chiyo's fault," he said, needing again to blame. "If only she had not approached me at the Quarantine Station." He took another drink and regained his perspective. "But it's really all my fault. I can't blame anyone else. I love her, Miki. There I said it. I love Chiyo. And she loves me."

Mako sat in his guilty silence and felt a great longing for the woman whose face he could see clearly, the woman who could have chosen a younger man. He said it again. "Chiyo loves me."

"And Shuzo too?"

"What? Shuzo? Does Shuzo love me? Of course, he does. Shuzo ... oh I see, you think ... no, Miki, no, don't get me wrong. I know I dumped on him a moment ago, but I really didn't mean it. Believe me, Miki. I'm grateful to Shuzo for everything he's done for me. He's my best friend. He would never take Chiyo away from me. Besides, Miki, well, I really shouldn't say it, but Shuzo, well, he's not that kind of man."

Mako finished the bottle of sake and ate another rice ball. What a relief to have said it all, like throwing up. If only Chiyo were here. I will bring her the next time. Just the two us. But, Miki, why did I tell her everything? I know she'll never tell anyone else. Such a strange girl ... woman ... whoever she is. But I'm so glad she's here, so glad. She's a best friend too. The four of us. So much fun.

He adjusted the blanket, wrapping half of it over himself, found a comfortable position and closed his eyes.

Miki took her blanket and climbed to the top of the Rock, a flat platform, perfect for jumping up to the stars. The stars! So many, so near! She held her hand out and pinched the North Star gently between her fingers, taking care not to snuff it out. She turned around and saw the Scorpion, tail fully poised over the ocean from her new vantage point.

"Did you miss me?" asked the cat.

"Very much."

"Well, I'm back, but will have to leave again."

"I know. But you always come back."

"Wasn't it odd how he told you everything?"

"I thought we were going fishing."

"But he still doesn't know, does he, about Chiyo and Shuzo."

"Doesn't suspect a thing," said Miki. "But why is Shuzo not that kind of man? I didn't understand."

"Some men are different."

"But Shuzo loves Chiyo, did it to her on the couch."

"Just trying to prove something to himself, that's all. But never mind Shuzo. Do you know what you're going to do?"

"Yes."

Miki wrapped the blanket around herself and rested on her back.

"When will you do it?"

"I don't know."

She pulled the blanket tightly around her neck and drifted off to sleep.

◆

In the morning, the oama were dead. Miki laid out the fish in a row on top of Leaping Spirit Rock and looked out over the ocean where the cat's eyes had been in the tail of Scorpio. She hurried down to the tracks, helped Mako load the cart. They pushed it to a quick running start and she scrambled on before it went too fast. The morning ocean was flat all the way out to the bent horizon and she giggled, then burst out laughing.

"I'm going ... as fast ... as I can," Mako called out between breaths. He pulled himself up for the first coasting. Her laughter infected him and he grinned uncontrollably. So much fun! So much fun!

◆

Restaurant Danger was an immediate success. It offered fugu

as the ultimate draw, but most customers came for the mixed menu of Japanese, Chinese, Hawaiian and American dishes. Shuzo enacted his vision inspired not by racial harmony but greater profits. He had to add more cooks, dishwashers, waitresses and cleaners, and ordered more tables and chairs. As the manager, Mako had less time for fishing, but he relished his new position and shared in the rising profits.

The House of Eternal Pleasure was popular for a few months, then fell into a downturn. Shuzo had difficulty finding other performers besides Chiyo and customers soon tired of her repeated numbers. He located a woman who could play the biwa, but her lute was melancholy and soulful and the workers wanted something more exciting than music suitable for introspection. A *taiko* drumming group was a hit at first, but its aesthetic range was limited to variations of rhythm and speed for beating skinned barrels over and over and over. The best show combined them all, Chiyo's sentimental songs, the meditative biwa, the rousing drums, but it was nearly impossible to get the performers together on a regular basis. The shows were on Saturdays and Sundays, then Sundays only, then every other week.

Miki occupied herself with watching. She had her own chairs in the kitchen, dining room and one wing of the stage. She moved from one to another according to happenings and time—the afternoons in the busy kitchen, evenings in the dining room and the stage whenever there was a performance. To Shuzo's great relief, she no longer isolated herself in her room. She looked forward to dressing and grooming herself every day, getting ready for her work of watching. Though she hardly spoke to anyone, she seemed content and even Jerome remarked about her new stability.

Miki settled in her chair to watch Chiyo perform one Sunday afternoon between lunch and dinner. The audience had been dwindling over the last several weeks and only a handful of men paid the ten-cent admission to hear her play the shamisen and sing. Chiyo always started with her favorite rice planting song from her Okinawan village, though she knew Japanese tunes as well and while Shuzo tried to get her to vary the opening piece, she insisted on her choice, saying it induced her into the right mood. The men used to clap in rhythm, but on that day they sat quietly. When she sang a Japanese song about a boat pulling away from a lonely mother standing on the dock, wiping her eyes with her kimono sleeves, whispering *sayonara*, a few men leaned forward with their elbows on their knees and dropped their heads. The next selection was a children's song about walking through the fields hand in hand, a familiar favorite, but one man got up and noisily walked out. Before she finished, several other men started talking to each other, laughing quietly at their jokes. Chiyo stopped and walked off the stage.

"*Oi*! Taga-san! Mako! We want our money back!"

"Waste of time! Shit!"

Shuzo came out of the kitchen and listened to their complaints. He told them he had to go back to his office to get the money, but they didn't believe his pockets were empty and demanded their refunds immediately. They escalated their arguments with jabbing and shoving and none of them saw Miki walk out to center stage, where she looked down on them and started to laugh. It was that same laugh that had made Mako grin at Leaping Rock, and though it did not have the same effect on these men, they were silenced and looked up at her to see if they could figure out what was so funny.

She moved her arms slowly in circles and arcs, like the '*iwa* bird searching for fish. She glided toward the side of the stage, then stopped, arched the small of her back and turned her head toward the men, who watched with anticipation. Chiyo came out with her shamisen, sat on a stool and improvised according to Miki's movements. It was not a recognizable dance style, but was her own invention inspired by her watching. She crouched low and threw her net in slow motion, gathered the tangle and moved her mouth ever so subtly, gasping for air. She plucked stars from the sky and put them in a bucket, then cleaned them like fish. Chiyo revised her strumming to follow Miki's moods instead of her movements and she nearly broke the strings as she flayed out sounds to follow Miki's daring as she climbed a rock, looked up and started laughing, a chilling cry that scared the men. She calmed them by embracing herself with her arms, gently swaying to make Mako stop shaking. Then she stopped, stamped her feet, glared an accusation at Shuzo and spun around until she was behind Chiyo. She untied her own sash and let the front of her kimono open and the men leaned in all directions and moved about to catch a better glimpse of her swaying behind the shamisen player. Chiyo kept on playing though she did not know Miki's feelings at that moment and settled for a measured rhythm. Miki rested her head on Chiyo's left shoulder and brought her right hand around, slipped it into Chiyo's kimono and softly fondled her breast. Chiyo twanged a last note, looked totally confused and everyone was frozen in their astonishment for a very long moment.

One man applauded, slowly at first. "*Sugoi!*"

The rest burst out clapping. "Hah! Wild!"

"Once more, once more!"

Miki withdrew her hand, retied her kimono and walked off the stage. The men forgot about their refunds and asked Shuzo when the next performance would be. No one had ever seen anything like it and Shuzo thought her free form dance was a brilliant abstraction, incredibly modern, reminding him of what he had read about Paris. They'll be back, the workers will, to see this, they will, and so too the guests from the Haleiwa Hotel too. They will simply love it.

"Where did you learn to dance like that?" Shuzo asked Miki back at the house.

"By watching, especially you and Chiyo."

"Me and Chiyo? Don't be silly, Miki, but whatever it is, it's fantastic. Very modern, you know. Unpredictable movements on the edge of outrageous. Pure passion, unspoiled by any story. It'll appeal to everyone because they can make of it anything they want. Miki, you're brilliant."

"Someone said wild."

"Exactly. Same thing."

Mako and Chiyo came in, both of them excited.

"Chiyo, you were brilliant too," said Shuzo. "Improvising like that, right on the spot. We've got to work on this. It's just amazing."

They celebrated again, exuberant about their plan to make the theater a success. It had been a close call, but they had pulled it back from the brink and, Miki, it was all because of you, again. We're unbeatable, the four of us. What will we think of next? After months of disappointment, Chiyo was ebullient and hurried Mako into their bedroom. Shuzo was exhausted and went to his room, leaving Miki sitting by herself. She moved her hands in little arcs and circles, laughing quietly, then got up and went into her lonely room.

◆

Eager with expectations so diverse they could not all be satisfied, the men packed the theater the following Sunday. A week of rumors produced strange tales of what had happened: Miki had danced the pains of working in the fields, exactly, I tell you, she did it just like it is; the joys of swimming in the ocean, so refreshing; the freedom of birds wheeling in the air, ah, to fly; and ended by taking off all her clothes, no kidding, you should've seen it, everything, no kidding!

Chiyo came out, sat on a short bench and readied her shamisen to follow Miki's moods. "Hey, Chiyo," someone said in a normal voice that boomed in the hush, "How about you and me after the show?" Miki emerged in a plain brown kimono and moved her hand in arcs and circles while Chiyo started her accompaniment. Miki stretched herself on the gangway, ill with fever, then got up carrying a rifle in her hands and turned and ran away. She reentered the stage, skipping across the dock and ran up Nu'uanu Avenue, gazing at the new sights. She hid in the shadows, then started washing dishes, faded with exhaustion and fell down to the floor. She got up and repeated the scene, several times over, sweeping the floors, carrying out the garbage, walking slowly to Horisho's house. She dropped to the floor, got up and started another day again. She sat on the floor and waited, then stood up, still waiting, loosened her kimono, took Jerome in her arms and settled gently into bed. She spread her legs and held him and Chiyo tightened the tempo, then abruptly stopped when Miki relaxed and did not move. No one moved. They waited.

"Is she sleeping?" someone whispered.

"*Shh*! Quiet!"

Chiyo thought of resuming her playing, then realized that Miki really was asleep. There had to be an ending, so she looked at Shuzo standing in the back of the room, but he was just as bewildered as she. She walked over to Miki to make sure she was all right and was struck by her repose, disheveled, spent, at peace. Shuzo walked onto the stage and saw the same and the men followed, filing past her in a last rite filled with quiet respect to justify their leering. They returned to the floor and milled around as Chiyo placed a light blanket over her and they asked Shuzo in whispers if next Sunday would be the same. It's always different, he replied, always a surprise and you'll just have to come and see for yourself.

Which is what they did for weeks. Every performance was a different puzzle and concluded with the audience exchanging avid interpretations of what they had seen. Most were convinced she had done some kind of pantomime, though few could agree on what she had acted out and made them obsess about meaning.

I get it! A net! She's throwing a net. Don't be silly, she's throwing bags of sugar into a pile. C'mon, that's not it; she's spreading canvas out to dry. Canvas? When do we ever use canvas?

Her performances lasted a short ten minutes, long enough to spike their imaginations and extended debates, which they looked forward to as much as to her dances. Mako's staff had to ask them to step aside so they could bring in the tables to transform Pleasure into Danger and many simply stayed on for dinner. Theirs was a spirited guessing game without definitive answers, but every so often they agreed that they had no idea what a certain movement meant—they debated even a flick of her finger, an upturned face, a blinking eye—and on those occasions, which over the weeks became more frequent, they satisfied themselves by deferring to Shuzo, who insisted that what they had witnessed was a modern abstraction, just like they do it in New York and Paris and … and Barcelona! Of course, that's what it was, and they left feeling culturally advanced. For Miki, nothing was abstract and she did not have to prepare or practice the repertoire of her life.

Remembering their early failure due to excessive repetition, Shuzo limited Miki's dance to once a month and increased the admission price to forty cents, a move that resulted in longer lines for tickets. The post-performance arguments became more adamant, repeated attendance making the audience more certain in their views and they started to lay bets, though they had no way of determining winners from losers. Shuzo responded quickly and told them that he knew the true meanings of her dance. He standardized the bets at ten cents—this on top of the price of admission—had Mako collect and hold the money while he listened to all of their arbitrary opinions about a movement he selected for the wager and then, just as arbitrarily, he declared the correct analysis, matching it to someone's interpretation, selecting a different man each time to spread the pot around to make sure they would come back. After deducting thirty percent for the house, he paid the balance to the happy winner, or split it among the winners if several had come up with the same right answer. Miki's dance was as good for wagering as were cards or dice, it really didn't matter as long as the men learned the system and loved its intricacies. They took pride in their gaming invention and eagerly initiated newcomers into the finer points of dance interpretation and soon insisted on betting separate rounds on the meanings of her hands, her face and feet. Shuzo collected his repeated cuts in a businesslike manner and was careful to declare winners from among all of the men. He no longer invoked modern abstraction since every dance, including Chiyo's music, which some of the men cited to support their interpretations, had to have a definite meaning, but every so often, to keep it authentic, he told them no one had gotten it right. In that case, he returned their full bets and though he considered keeping a smaller percentage, a service fee, he decided against it. It wouldn't be right, he said, to skim a pot without a winner. As he returned their bets, he explained the elusive right answer and he was always impressed at how serious they looked, some getting the connections, others struggling to figure it out. Men like to think, especially the dimwitted, and without a mental challenge, cards, chess and every other game for that matter, would not be fun. After hard days of manual labor, the men needed a chance to make some money with their minds. He reminded himself to write this down later, lest he forget his newly discovered principle of entertainment: thinking is also a game.

How easy to use their love of betting and rumination to rig any kind of performance into a gambling event! Someday they will tire of Miki's dancing, but I will think of another wagering scheme for thirty, maybe forty, percent.

◆

A stocky bureaucrat dressed in a suit a half size too small stepped off the train at Waialua Station and hired a pony trap to Long Bridge. He told the driver to wait, stepped down stiffly and strutted into the restaurant, a leather folder under his arm. Shuzo had just arrived from the house and asked the man if he needed help.

"Taga-san? Murakami, from the Consulate. I've been assigned the case of the draft evader."

"Ah yes, I thought you might have forgotten. I reported this nearly a month ago."

"We've been busy, but I'm here to take care of it. Where is the boy?"

"He lives in the village. Works at odd jobs and spends his free time painting. A useless sort."

They squeezed onto the seat of the trap, the driver having to hang one leg out and rode slowly through the village, looking for Yukio Nozaki. After several inquiries, they located his boarding house, where the housekeeper thought he was out on Emerson Road. He's a loner, she said and nobody really knows what he does. They spotted him at the edge of the river, pondering Hale'iwa, or what remained of the old dormitory at John Emerson's abandoned seminary. The boy walked slowly to a different spot to get a better angle, held a measuring finger out and brush practiced in the air. Murakami, overly confident of his authority, shouted at him to come forward, even before they had alighted from the trap. Yukio took one look at the two men and took off running.

"Should have waited till we got closer," Shuzo muttered uselessly to Murakami and ran after the fugitive. Murakami started to run, then settled for a quick walk. Shuzo was in decent physical shape, but the one thing the skinny boy excelled at was running. Shuzo stopped, bent over with his hands on his knees for a moment, caught his breath and went back to Murakami.

Colonel Kalama helped them organize a search party, repeatedly saying that compulsory military service was just that, compulsory, in anybody's country. With the help of witnesses, they determined that the boy had not run along the river into Anahulu Valley but headed toward the Wai'anae Mountains instead. "A clever choice," said Kalama, noting that the ravines below Mt. Ka'ala were rocky and deep, easy to hide in. "On the other hand," he said, adjusting his judgment, "easy to hide in is also easy to get lost."

In either case, the boy eluded them and after five days they called off the search. Murakami posted a small reward for his capture, the Consul General himself having decided not to tolerate Nozaki's double infraction of draft evasion and visa violation. They sent runners to alert everyone to be on the lookout for the boy and as it would be impossible for him to show up in the camps or the village without being noticed, they were certain he had to be in mountains. He was pale and artistic, not the kind to survive in the wilds and as the days passed, Murakami grew more certain that the boy was lost in the mountains and was ready to declare his "whereabouts unknown," the standard euphemism for "presumed dead." After a week, he received his needed proof when two Portuguese pig hunters found his torn shirt, long sleeved and splattered with colored paints, tangled on a thorny bush on the edge of a steep ravine. They had seen something like a crumpled body at the bottom of a hundred-yard shear. Murakami closed the case.

"Thank you for your help," Murakami said to Shuzo before he boarded the train. "We'll report this to Japan and his name can be crossed off the Nozaki family registry."

"So tragic," said Shuzo, "but he did it all to himself."

◆

Dear Shuzo:

Thank you for the money you've been sending. We are grateful and proud of you. People are always complimenting us on your success. Because of your generous support, your father does not have to work, though I sometimes wish he had something to keep himself busy. He seems lost, wanders around the garden when the weather is nice and does not like to go to town. It's been a long time since he's worn his bowler hat, which is fine, I guess, since I never liked it.

Remember Nozaki-san? Something terrible happened. I am enclosing the newspaper articles about him with this note. I'll write to you again. Please take good care of yourself.

Mother

Son of Conscription Board Chairman Found Dead
Tragic Accident in Hawai'i
Sought for Draft Evasion

The Honolulu Consulate has notified the Iwakuni Records Office that Yukio Nozaki (18), son of Bunzo Nozaki, President of the Iwakuni Association of Lumber Dealers, died in an accident in Waialua on the island of O'ahu. A Consulate official had gone to arrest Nozaki for draft evasion and for violating the terms of his visa. Nozaki resisted arrest and fled into the mountains, where he fell from a cliff in a remote area. His shirt was recovered, but his body could not be retrieved because of the treacherous terrain. Bunzo Nozaki, father of the draft evader, is the Chairman of the Iwakuni Conscription Board, which oversees the military draft. He declined to comment on the death of his son.

Harsh, thought Shuzo. Someone at the newspaper does not like Nozaki. Father of the draft evader. Serves him right, however; he should be ashamed and now we're even. I did my part, did my duty.

The second clipping was dated three days later.

Head of Iwakuni Conscription Board
Commits Suicide
Son Evaded Draft

Bunzo Nozaki (61), President of the Iwakuni Association of Lumber Dealers and Chairman of the Iwakuni Conscription Board, was found dead in the Association's warehouse. An employee found him hanging from a rafter. "He was depressed," said Kakuzo Manabe, Vice President of the Association. "The news about his son's draft evasion and death was devastating. He left a letter of resignation as Chairman of the Conscription Board."

Nozaki's son died in Hawai'i after he jumped off a cliff while being pursued for draft evasion. Nozaki, a widower, is survived only by a daughter, who is married to a foreign service officer. The couple lives in Formosa. The Association will sponsor his funeral. Details will be announced soon, Manabe said.

◆

Shuzo put down the clippings and looked toward the mountains. Jumped off a cliff? Nobody said he jumped. He didn't have the guts to do that. The boy just fell. But the news of Bunzo Nozaki's suicide was a complete surprise. Shuzo read the articles over again. After years of waiting, justice had been swift, and although he wanted Nozaki to pay for what he had done to his father Gombei, he did not expect the price of retribution to be so high. He would have been satisfied with his humiliation over his cowardly son. Well, both of them were responsible for their ends and I only did my duty as a responsible citizen. And yet, two people dead for one sawed off tiller? There is no perfect math for justice and I just did my duty, had no choice, as a subject of the Emperor and son of my father.

◆

Josephine wiped the feet of the Savior and rinsed her washcloth in a bucket of water turning rusty brown. She had talked to Father Marcel about closing the doors to keep out the dusty winds from the surrounding fields of red dirt, but Father Marcel said St. Michael's was a house of God, open to anyone, always. "This is not a private club," he said. "And also, Josephine, my dear, remember, you are responsible only for the Savior." The cleaning duties were shared with other women, while the men cared for the yard and cemetery, which was growing more crowded with Catholic crosses,

Hawaiian rock mounds and Japanese Buddhist headstones. The church was open to anyone agreeing with its teachings, but in practice the parishioners were mostly Portuguese and the Hawaiian remnants of her grandmother Luiza's converts. The cemetery was a better embodiment of the inclusive ideal and families visited regularly to leave offerings of food still favored by the dead, no matter what their religion.

Josephine did her cleaning on Wednesday evenings, when Father Marcel went out for visitations. She liked the loneliness of the sanctuary and stayed on after completing chores to say prayers she couldn't in the company of nosy people attending Sunday Mass. Here, in the middle of the week, she could be by herself and speak her heart freely in the darkness. She trusted Father Marcel, but always felt awkward confessing her sins to him, only to pretend they did not share her secrets when they saw each other later. She imagined it was like having a love affair, an easy comparison for one who had never experienced anything like it, but the secret intimacy had to be similar if not entirely the same. Weren't confession and making love the most private exchange a man and woman could have? She admonished herself for having such illicit thoughts about Father Marcel and wondered if she would have to confess her fantasy as a sin. She decided she had to, since sins of the mind were no different from transgressions of the body and so she walked to the alcove of the Holy Virgin, the person who knew more secrets than Father Marcel or even the Savior himself would ever be told. As she asked for Mary's mercy, she heard the sound of glass breaking in the cemetery.

Wild dogs, she thought, knocking over a flower jar. Still, she went to the window quietly and saw a shadow move against the Japanese headstones outlined in the sheen of half a moon. It moved from stone to stone, stopping for longer at some more than at others. A wild dog or pig desecrating the food offerings left at the graves. Josephine walked slowly to the open door, stepped out and felt the ground for a rock, all the while keeping her eyes on the shadow. "Get out!" she yelled, as she threw the rock and was utterly surprised when it hit the shadow, which buckled to the ground with a dull thud.

Oh, my God. I've just killed a dog, maybe a pig. She wanted it to get up and run away and yelled at it again, but when it did not move, she went back into the sanctuary to get a votive candle. She picked her way between the Catholic crosses, skirted the Hawaiian rock mounds, approached the Japanese headstones and saw her victim, a boy, unconscious and bleeding from his head.

"Oh, my God!" she screamed. "I'm so sorry! I didn't know!" She dropped to her knees and pressed her hand against his wound, warm and slimy. She set the candle on the base of the headstone and saw the bloodied edge where he had hit his head. She grabbed the hem of her long skirt and ripped it with her teeth, tearing a long strip to wrap around his head. In the flickering light, she saw his cracked lips, his peeling, sunburned cheeks. The boy clutched a dried-out rice ball in his dirty hand and Josephine covered her mouth in horror as she saw his ghostly ribs draped by skin, blistered from exposure because he had no shirt.

She picked up the starving boy in her arms and walked back to the church by moonlight. She laid him in a front pew and lit all the candles she could find. She took heart when he started to moan and managed to make him drink some water. His eyes moved beneath his lids, but he lacked the strength to open them. The bleeding from his head had stopped and she removed the cloth strip and saw a gash embedded by bits of stone. She cleaned it as best she could, ripped a new strip and wrapped the wound again.

They said the Japanese draft dodger was dead, but Josephine pressed her finger against his neck and felt a definite pulse. They said they had found his shirt and could not retrieve his body, but Josephine used a damp cloth to clean between his blisters. As she removed the dried rice ball from his hand, she couldn't help but smile at the clever boy, who had kept himself alive on food for the dead. It was a wonder he had survived, but he wouldn't have lasted much longer. She had the fugitive there in the church, open in theory to anyone receptive to grace, but what would Father Marcel think? Surely he would nurse him back to health, but would he then turn the boy in or hide him from the authorities? Will Father Marcel stand against the Japanese government and resist its laws for the boy's sake? He will be back soon from his visitations and it will not be fair to burden him with such a decision. I must hide the boy, he is mine alone. Mother Mary understands.

She took off her dress, removed her soft cotton slip and wrapped it around the boy. She wiggled back into her dress, blew out all the candles and waited for her eyes to adjust to the half-moon outside the windows. Thankful for her size and strength, Josephine picked him up, walked out, turned right on the red dirt road and headed toward the mountains. She rested at the stream marking the end of the cane fields, then waded across its rippling shallows and went into the foothills.

As she tired and her arms began to ache, she grew more determined to make it to Uncle Hila's hut. She'd crawl if she had to, for she had found the fugitive boy, the one they said was dead and no one, by God, no one was going to take him away from her.

YUKIO REBORN

"SO, MR. TAGA, WHAT HAVE YOU PUT TOGETHER FOR ME?" Woodrow Davies greeted Shuzo with a direct question as he entered Colonel Kalama's office at the Haleiwa Hotel. Kalama's dark mahogany desk was flanked by flags of the old Hawaiian Kingdom and the new American territory and if the juxtaposition was a political contradiction, then so was the Colonel. "Have a seat," said Kalama, pointing to a Windsor chair made of native *koa* wood. "Would you like something to drink?"

Shuzo declined and answered Davies's question tangentially. "Well, Mr. Davies, I have something for you, but not possible explain, so you have to come with me to my restaurant. My carriage out in front."

On the way over, Kalama told Davies about the tragic case of the draft evader, giving the details of their failed attempts to find him. Davies was unimpressed, shrugged and said the matter could have been handled better if the fugitive had been given the chance to pay for a substitute, just as northern Union men had been able to during the Civil War. "That way," he said, "the government gets its soldiers subsidized by private funds." Kalama was quiet for the rest of the trip.

It was mid-afternoon and Shuzo had arranged for them to have the restaurant for themselves. A Japanese-Hawaiian waitress dressed in a dark blue kimono and a coconut hat, inspired by Miki, entered with a tray of beer and snacks and

Davies stopped talking to admire the girl. "Welcome to Restaurant Danger," she said in lilting English. "This pork jerky we smoke ourselves and this *opihi* shellfish."

"Now how could I have explained her back at the office?" said Shuzo. "I wanted you to see and hear for yourselves. Mariko—you can also call her Mahealani—will greet your guests."

"Very nice," said Davies, "but I thought we had talked about some kind of stage performance?"

Ah yes, Miki's dance, Shuzo explained, was wonderfully modern, stylish, abstract, just like in Paris, livened by Chiyo's shamisen music. But she was—how you say—risqué at times, and hotel guests, upstanding and proper, might feel offended. He had no control over Miki's dance and would never think of interfering with her creativity. Part of her appeal was her unpredictability—that's why the men kept coming back. And the betting was in loud Japanese and again, his hotel guests would not appreciate it, let alone understand.

"I see," said Davies. "I guess you're right. But what a unique operation. I've never heard anything like it. Betting on a dance. You're a genius, Mr. Taga. But one question. How do you know the right interpretation of her dance?"

"How I know? What you mean?"

Davies roared and nearly knocked his beer bottle over. He leaned closer to Shuzo and squinted one eye. "You've got guts all right. I wouldn't dare do something like that! Right, Colonel?"

"Ah, yes, right, Mr. Davies. You wouldn't … whatever it is."

"So, if my guests are not coming for the dance show, why should they come?"

"For a taste of death."

Davies and Kalama looked at each other. Shuzo was as unpredictable as his dancer. Shuzo clapped his hands and Mariko Mahealani brought out two dishes of cooked fish.

"Fugu," said Shuzo. "You know fugu?"

"The blowfish? Of course." Kalama turned to Davies. "You might know it as puffer fish."

"The poison fish," said Davies, "by whatever name. There should be a law against serving it."

"I serving it now," said Shuzo, pushing the dishes closer to them. "One has poison, the other does not. Take your pick. Or don't you — how do you say — have guts?"

Both men looked at each other again. They came over to talk business, not risk their lives.

"Well, now, see here..."

Shuzo laughed. "Just kidding. They both safe. Prepared them myself. Go ahead, eat. How else can you taste death and live?"

Davies went first. He cut a piece with the side of his fork, stared at it, then popped it into his mouth. "Hmm, it has a crunch ... mild ... like trout, the taste, I mean ... not the texture ... wait, now a slight aftertaste."

"Can't say exactly?" said Shuzo. "I taking bets on which one is the right answer." Davies swallowed quickly and laughed.

"What are you talking about?" asked Kalama.

"Just eat."

Kalama made the sign of the cross over his chest, picked up his fork and ate a piece. "Good," he said. "Nothing special. Tastes like fish."

"So what you think, Colonel? Think we can sell taste of death?"

"It'll go," said Kalama. "Easy. Shuzo, if you can help me make up a flyer, we can really play this one up at the hotel. We'll run a special carriage. Maybe screen off a special section in here. Mahealani will serve. Shuzo, you give them the fake challenge, you know, one is poisoned, the other not. There's only one possible problem I can think of. What if it's not prepared right and someone dies?"

"I know what I doing," said Shuzo. "I prepare all fugu myself. Learned from an old timer."

"Wait a minute," said Davies, curling his fingers to invite his plotters closer to him. "Didn't you say, Colonel," and he tried to stifle a laugh, "didn't you say that it tastes just like fish?" He paused. "Know what I mean?" He pushed back and couldn't resist saying to Shuzo that he'd take bets on his implications.

"You mean," said Kalama, "No, you're kidding, aha, *any* fish will do! Right?"

"They won't know the difference," said Davies, wagging an upheld finger. "It'll still taste like death to them, once they're told and we'll run no risk of poisoning."

Shuzo leaned back. "What closest to fugu?" he asked, turning to Kalama. "Be good to have something close to keep it, you know, real."

"'*Āweoweo*," said Kalama without hesitation. "When the 'āweoweo run in schools, it's a sign of the death of a high chief."

"Good!" said Shuzo, "I mean, the sign of death, not the chief. I have Mako get some from fishermen. Must be authentic."

Mariko Mahealani brought out grilled steaks. "Fresh from butcher," she said, "done over kiawe charcoal. More beer, Uncle Kimo?"

"Is she your niece?" asked Davies.

"Not really. But everyone's uncle or aunty."

"Not where I come from," said Davies.

"Or in Japan."

"Someday," said Kalama, "you might figure it out, what it means to be here. But I wouldn't bet on it."

"Speak of betting," said Shuzo, "you like to see Miki dance? This Sunday, at three."

◆

Uncle Hila preferred goats over people, their bleating, the goats', that is, being easy to satisfy with water or a new patch of grass. Everyone knew Uncle Hila as the man to see for a goat, a good alternative to pigs. With the stream close by, a garden, gleanings from the wild and occasional payments in fish, Uncle Hila seldom left the foothills. He did not dislike people, it's just that he was by nature reserved and could not bring himself to engage his visitors beyond the quick transactions for a goat. He didn't smile or offer pleasantries and people thought him unfriendly and someone generously dubbed him *hila*, shy, from the *hilahila* grass that closed up its ribbed leaves upon being touched and Uncle Hila is what he came to be.

Josephine had gone to see Uncle Hila to pay for a goat, which some men from the church would pick up later for the festival. He had been in the pasture huddled over the body of a nanny, pulling out a bloody kid, the last of her squirming litter. He paid no attention to Josephine as she stood over him, so she positioned herself to give him the cool of her shadow and watched him stroke the nanny's forehead, then hold his hands over her eyes as she died. He pointed to a bucket. Josephine grabbed the empty bucket, ran down to the stream and walked back as fast as she could without spilling more than she already had. He washed the three kids, bundled them in the front of his shirt and carried them back to his hut. Josephine followed with the remaining water. After nestling the kids in a corner, he came out, washed his hands and hurried back to the dead nanny with a shovel, waving it angrily over her body to chase away the disrespecting flies. Josephine picked up a stick and kept the flies off so that he could dig a shallow hole next to several small mounds of rocks. He lifted the dead nanny into his arms, looked at her face and placed her in her grave, adjusting her head and feet into comfortable positions. Josephine surmised the last step of his ritual and helped him gather rocks to pile onto its grave. With the last stone in place, they walked quickly back to the hut and as he prepared a mash for his babies, he asked her, without looking up, "Now, what did you want?"

She had explained the arrangement of her payment now with pick up later and wondered how he could ever part with his goats. She asked him how he would keep the kids alive without their mother and he looked at her for the first time, surprised by her interest. He answered her question with details of kid's food and methods of feeding and from there she asked him other questions about his animals, his garden, his pickings from vines and trees, how he lived. Answering all of her questions with unneeded details, the goat keeper did not close up like his namesake grass, even though, or perhaps because, he was touched by her presence. As she was taking her leave an hour later, he thanked her, and Josephine knew it was not just for buying a goat. She went back often in the following days and marveled at the growth of the kids, what fine animals they were becoming and who would have imagined it from their precarious beginnings.

◆

Uncle Hila recognized Josephine's voice and was startled by her coming in the middle of the night. Outside his door, he held up his kukui oil lamp over his head, peered out to the furthest reach of its light and saw Josephine struggling with the weight of someone in her arms. He reached her just as she sank to her knees, took the boy from her and followed as she led with the lamp back to his hut.

Uncle Hila worked quickly. He grabbed a jar of crushed *popolo* leaves, moistened a handful with spit and told Josephine to give him a new strip from her dress. He smeared the leaves onto the cloth and carefully removed the one around the boy's head. Centering the leaves on the cut, he tied the new compress firmly, got up and took the lamp as he ran out to the garden. In the darkness of the hut, the boy mumbled something. Josephine placed her hand gently on his warm forehead and suddenly feeling tired and scared and desperate and hopeful, she broke down and cried.

Uncle Hila returned with stalks of aloe. He peeled the skin of one to release its slimy ointment and handed it to Josephine. He did the same to another and they swathed his blisters and sunburn, dabbing gently, jerking their hands back when he flinched. "A good sign," said Uncle Hila, using his knowledge of goats on the boy, "he'll make it. Don't worry, Josephine, you did good." And Josephine broke down and cried again.

She didn't remember crying ever like this. She had wept when her grandmother died, of course, and then for her mother's passing. She never knew her father, and had her mother told stories about him, she might have had an image of him, at least as remembered by her mother and maybe that was the reason for her silence. He didn't even live on in her name, Kaumaka was Grandmother Luiza's. From grandmother to mother to her, she had no men in her life, a legacy she accepted as a curse embodied in a lack of the physical delicacy desired by men. But it was the will of God and there was nothing she could do about it. Her tears had always been for women, but now she cried for this boy because he was hers and would live, Uncle Hila would see to that and she cried for the gift of him as well. A stream of tears welling from a sudden accident; she'd never cried like this before. But Mary would understand. Hadn't she also been a virgin mother?

◆

To prolong the short program and give the men a greater sense of their money's worth, not to speak of heightening their anticipation, Shuzo had Chiyo play several numbers as a prelude to Miki's dance. The men had become attuned to her nuances of matching notes to mood and they listened carefully for clues to make them think.

Davies and Kalama sat with Shuzo in the back in order to view the entire scene. Shuzo explained what each tune was about: rice planting — her usual opening piece; a summer festival; a meeting of lovers. She stopped, retuned her shamisen and waited for Miki. After several long minutes, Chiyo went into the wings and spoke loudly to Miki, then reemerged, smiling an apology at the audience. When Miki failed to appear, Chiyo went out again, but no one could hear what they said. "Unpredictable," said Shuzo to his guests, "I told you she unpredictable." Chiyo came out playing her shamisen and Miki followed, sullen and displeased. "Is she mad?" asked Davies, but no one answered.

Miki moved her hands in small circles and arcs and ran into a cranny of the front face of the burnt-out church. She knelt down to the cat, cradled it in her skirt, then bandaged its wounded leg. She carried it to Jerome's house and settled into a domestic routine, cleaning, washing clothes, hanging them out to dry. She stretched out on the floor, a signature move, and held Jerome, night after night, then suddenly snarled and hissed and attacked his leg. She was quiet again for some time, then shuddered and whimpered, curling in contortions, as he cut the cat's heart out.

"My God," said Davies, "I've never seen anything like this. What's it all mean?" Shuzo invited him to place a bet, but he declined. The audience assumed the dance was over and started their deliberations. Mako got up to collect the bets. Chiyo left the stage, but Miki came down, took one man by his hand and led him back onto the stage. The wagering stopped.

"What the…? What're you doing?" The young man was shorter than Miki, smiled nervously, enjoyed her attention, but wondered what she was going to do with him.

"*Oi*! How did *you* get picked?"

"Lucky bastard!"

Miki stood in front of the helpless man and pulled out his loosely tucked shirt. She unbuttoned his cuffs, then the front all the way down, spun him around and removed his shirt.

The men started shouting and swearing and Mako kept pushing back the ones who surged forward. The shirtless man was emboldened by their lewd suggestions and lunged for Miki's breasts, hands and fingers outstretched, but she stepped to the side like a judo master, tripped him with one foot, sending him to the floor on his face. The crowd roared with laughter and moans from those who felt the pain of his fall. They stopped their shoving and stood in place, waiting for what would happen next.

"My God," said Davies.

Miki straddled his outstretched body, looped his shirt under his neck and held the long sleeves as reins. She tugged gently and he pushed himself up on all fours, but before he could stand up, she pressed her breasts against his bare back, leaned her head down and whispered in his ear. His eyes widened and he nodded his head and grinned with astonishment about his good fortune. She whispered to him again and he raised his hands as hooves, curling his wrists and neighed like a horse. The men held their sides in uncontrollable laughter, slapped their knees and each other and someone said that he really was the fool everyone had always thought him to be. She flicked the reins of his sleeves, the shirt still looped around his neck and he high stepped a prance, turning right or left as she directed. Davies and Kalama had tears in their eyes and laughed so hard they made no sound, except for truncated gasps for breath. Miki got off, let him stand up, came up behind him again, reached around his waist, undid his belt and pulled down his pants. The crowd didn't think they could laugh any harder, but they did, pointing excitedly as he fumbled to tighten his bulging loincloth and submitted to Miki pushing him back down on all fours. She lifted her kimono high enough to bare herself, then mounted his naked back and twisted her torso from side to side to insure a firm seating. She flicked the reins, but he, mouth wide open, could not move, so she leaned forward and whispered again. He nodded obediently, lifted one hand to move it ahead, then lost his balance and splayed out flat amidst laughter and moans, this time for his writhing from the pain in his groin.

"Oh my God," said Davies, wiping his eyes, "this is crazy, absolutely nuts. I've never seen anything like it. But you're right, Mr. Taga, I don't think my guests can handle this. Let's keep it to the taste of death."

Miki got up and let the man curl into a fetal position. She knotted the shirt sleeves loosely around his neck and slipped away. Nothing unclear about this dance, someone declared. She turned him into a horse! No, no, a horse's ass! The young man got up, untied his shirt and started to dress.

"Could you feel her when she got on your back?"

"What did she whisper in your ear?"

"Hurry up, tell us."

The young man finished buckling his belt and walked to

the edge of the stage. He bowed his curtain call. "Can't tell you," he said, proudly showing that despite their laughter, he was the one who had had the most fun. "It's a secret between Miki and me."

The men booed jealously and cursed him. Will she pick someone else for the next performance? How will she make her choice? They started to leave or stand aside to let Mako's workers move tables and chairs to set up Pleasure into Danger.

"What happened to the betting?" Kalama asked.

"Everyone forgot," said Shuzo. "Didn't you?"

Kalama shook his head about the spectacle he had just seen. He put on his hat and followed Davies out to their carriage.

Shuzo looked at the men standing about, recalling and joking. I guess they like to laugh more than think. Miki was just ... just ... what in the world will she do next? Must remember this, the second principle of entertainment. Wonder if there's a way to lay bets on laughter?

Back in her bedroom, Miki slept past dinner. She got up and sat in the dark. She never knew when the Scorpion rose or set and went out to see if it was up. Nothing over Mt. Ka'ala. She'd have to wait a few more days and then she'd tell the cat how her dance about the cutting out its heart made her ride the man like a horse. Insane, they're all nuts. They laughed like lunatics. Can you imagine that?

◆

It was days before the boy opened his eyes and Josephine was ready. "Finally," she said. "Well, now, you must be hungry." During his long rest, they woke him up long enough to try and feed him, but he could not open his eyes or get out of bed. They kept him clean and comfortable and when he did awaken and was able to see and sit up, Josephine reached for the cup of goat's milk. He grimaced with the first swallow. She thought it wonderfully normal and she lifted the cup to his cracked lips again. She dipped the tip of a spoon into a bowl of poi and he opened his mouth just wide enough for her to slip in the paste. He scrunched his face, normal again. "Go easy," said Uncle Hila. "Just a little at a time."

"You must be wondering who we are," she said, dipping the spoon into the poi again. "This is Uncle Hila and I am … Josephine." She almost said "Aunty," but she had a different relationship in mind. "Now, we know why you were in the mountains and we even know your name, everybody knows your name. You're famous, I must say. Now, here's something you don't know and I know this will sound strange, but what you don't know is that you're dead. Officially speaking. The newspaper covered the whole story and everybody's been talking about you and you're supposed to have fallen of a cliff. There was a consulate officer out here looking for you and I'm sure he's informed your parents of your death. I can imagine how terrible they must feel and I would tell them the truth, but unfortunately it is also true that you will be arrested, thrown into jail and deported if they found out you're still alive. Now if I were your mother, I'd want you officially dead but free, instead of shackled alive. But here is the best part and it's our secret: you're alive *and* free. Here below Mt. Ka'ala, at least. Only Uncle Hila and I and you, of course, now that you're awake, know that you're alive and … oh, dear, here I am telling you all of this when I should be feeding you and on top of that you don't understand a word I'm saying!" She slipped in another spoon tip of poi.

From goat's milk and poi to beans and turnips to fish and pork, Yukio Nozaki progressed back to health. The ragged edges of his head wound fused into a smooth pink and his blisters melted away in the slimy aloe, leaving small scars only where the skin had festered in lesions. His ribs disappeared from view under a thickening layer of flesh and he surpassed his old skinny weight with new muscles gained by walking the hills, carrying water and feed, chasing the runaway goats, turning the soil in the garden. When buyers came for goats, he slipped behind the brush, or sat quietly in a corner of the hut. Josephine supplied him with clothing and shoes and made him wear a wide brimmed straw hat to protect him from the sun. Still, he tanned and after a few cases of sunburn treated by aloe, his skin cured into a light herder's brown and he could go for up to a few hours without his hat. He let his mustache and beard grow and in his scraggly face and well-toned body, the previous Yukio did die and he was born anew.

Uncle Hila told him all about the animals, weather, mountains and plants and through repeated words and chores, Yukio acquired some working English and Hawaiian. Josephine, ever the schoolteacher, was more systematic with lessons she had used with Shuzo based on the Japanese translation of Samuel Smiles' *Self-Help*, which she borrowed from Shuzo, who no longer used it. From her school supplies, she provided him with paper and pencils and visited on most afternoons, often staying for an early dinner and leaving while there was still light. She hated to return to her house and said long farewells in Hawaiian, which she also used when she could not help but feel an uncontrolled welling of maternal instincts.

Uncle Hila talked all the time and when he ran out of practical information, he told stories of the old days and legends of the land, the ocean and sky. See the pile of stones on that hill? Built by the *menehune*, small but very strong men, who lived here long before the first people arrived by canoes from the southern ocean. And look at this mountain naupaka flower with its petals forming only a half circle. The naupaka flower on the seashore has the same half-shape. You see, a long time ago, a boy and a girl fell in love, she a princess and he a commoner and when her royal father found them in a tight embrace, he forced them apart and banished him to the mountains. So here he is, half a flower, waiting for his other half to come from the beach and make themselves whole someday. Yukio understood nothing the first time Uncle Hila told the story, but with each retelling, and there were many, though Uncle Hila spoke each time as if it were the first time, he understood a little more and he soon came to know the reason why Josephine sometimes called him naupaka.

It was the first flower he drew. He used the backs of his lesson papers and sharpened his Dixon pencils with a kitchen knife. Nothing escaped his graphite point and he drew every plant in the area, asking Uncle Hila for their names. When he wanted to add color to his goat sketches, Uncle Hila helped him mash berries and bark, boil stalks and leaves and thicken the natural dyes by adding the gum sap from the yellow thorn bush. From goat bristles he fashioned brushes in a range of sizes and soon asked Josephine for larger pieces of paper to mount on an easel made with straight sticks tied with twine. From the subject of goats, he moved on to the hills and struggled to scale Mt. Ka'ala down to size, but he was never satisfied with his renderings of the depth of its ravines. He went back to the spot where he had lost his shirt and painted the steep slide, the assumed site of his death, but once again he was defeated by its depth.

Josephine was a helpful critic and his exclusive collector. Uncle Hila said his pictures were nice, but Josephine saw signs of a gift from God. She urged him to try the ravine again, to master its depth. He drew a line to divide the paper horizontally in half and started painting from the bottom, which was the top of the ravine at his feet. The scrub guava and rocks closest to him he enlarged in exquisite detail with a sharpened stick he used as a pen and as he moved up the paper, that is, down into the ravine, he painted the objects increasingly smaller and blurred them and when he reached the center line, the bottom of the ravine, he used his finest goat brush to dab dozens of splotches and smears. He went up the paper to the other side of the ravine, rendering the receding distance with finer detail and ascended the slope with its miniaturized but recognizable scrub guava and rocks.

Josephine looked at the finished piece and was drawn into the ravine through the perspective of changing sizes and sharpness. Yukio thought it still needed better gradations of blurring, but Josephine declared it a masterpiece.

"I like paint you," he said to her one evening and she laughed with visions of colors splattered on her face. "Of course," she said, knowing what he had meant. And then her face did change color, as she felt the warm embarrassment of having someone study her in meticulous detail, the broad nose, the thick lips, eyes in the sheen of night. "Just my face," she said.

Yukio worked slowly. He made her sit outside the hut to catch the early evening glow on a quarter turn of her face and he saw facets of her character emerge as the light faded. Instead of doing full sketches, he did several versions of a single feature, her eyes, her nose, her chin. Uncle Hila took a great interest in Yukio's magic pencils and occasionally stood behind him and watched Josephine appear live on paper. She was dying to see the daily results, but Yukio refused to show his work to her and Uncle Hila took advantage of his singular privilege and teased her with approving smiles and faked exclamations of disaster. "What? What?" she asked anxiously. "Maybe we shouldn't do this."

For several days, he sifted through his sketches, laying them out on the floor of the hut, changing the combinations until he saw them come together as the Josephine he sought. He merged them together into a single sketch, made some adjustments and added shading, knowing his natural dyes would let the under-drawing show through. Having rendered the fine details with his pencils, he was ready to complete her mood and feeling with color. He put the portrait away for several days while he searched for the hues he wanted, boiling new kinds of bark, crushing flowers and berries, re-boiling and mixing. Josephine was glad to resume her sitting within his rapt attention and Yukio gave her color while Uncle Hila looked on, only this time in silent absorption.

"There," Yukio finally said, a month after they had started. "You like see?"

Josephine covered her face as Yukio turned the easel around and placed it in front of her. She slowly cracked her fingers open, stopping every so often to see if she could go on and dropped her hands onto her lap. She stared at herself, seeing not the face of her usual deprecation, but the woman

Yukio saw in her. Her eyes were transparent black with a hint of sadness, but they looked off into a distance of hope. Her lips were full and soft, slightly open as if to speak. A teacher, she thought at first, but no, the quiet assurance was not stern enough. The color of her cheeks — he had captured her warm embarrassment — reflected an evening light flushed with feeling, the same feeling she could no longer hold in, though she tried by covering her mouth with her hand.

"Oh, Yukio," she managed to say, wiping her eyes. She spread her arms out. "*Mea aloha, hele mai.*" He went to her and she wrapped her large arms around him and held him against her trembling body. "Oh, Yukio, your painting. You … you've captured my heart and soul." Her eyes filled with tears of love and worry, feelings she could not keep apart and she braced herself like a warrior. "Nobody," she said, daring anyone to try it, "nobody is going to take you away from me."

BADGER AND BEAR

IN FEBRUARY, 1904, THE JAPANESE DECLARED WAR ON RUSSIA and everyone thought they were crazy. Even Shuzo had doubts about the island badger's chances of winning a war against the continental bear. Taking on the Chinese a few years earlier had been one thing, but the Russians were European whites. It was all about control over Korea and the Liaodong Peninsula, which the Japanese had gained in its victory over China, but the Russians, backed by the French and Germans, white upon more whites, kept fabricating their right over that territory, especially Port Arthur, the sprawling warm water port, free of ice even in winter. The Chinese, the stinking pigs, had the nerve to lease Port Arthur to the Russians, as if it were theirs to lend, and the Russians moved in with troops and ships to defend themselves against the Japanese. Knowing they were the weaker power, the Japanese offered a compromise: the Russians could have Manchuria and the Japanese would take Korea. But the Russians ignored the bid and counted on Japan's assessment of her own weakness. The Japs, they said, know their place, and just as the Russians relaxed and settled back, the little yellow-brown men swarmed their outposts. Shuzo feared the Japanese army and navy had made a catastrophic mistake, but when he learned from the newspapers that His Majesty's forces took the sleeping bear by complete surprise by attacking the port of Chemulpo on the first day, Port Arthur on the second and issuing a formal declaration of war on the third day, he felt a greater assurance that the admirals and generals knew what they were doing.

There were international accusations of treachery and deception, but did the critics really think Japan would be so foolish to show her hand before slapping down the first card? No one, not even the westerners, played poker like that. And it worked. In a series of lightning strikes after their sneak attack, the badger was ready to kick the bear's ass, right into the sea.

Colonel Kalama went to Long Bridge to tell Shuzo about the war's effect on their plan to give hotel guests a taste of death. It had been a hit among the guests before the war, but what had been an exotic treat was now suspected of being an inscrutable plot. The fugu chef was a sneaky Jap, a little yellow-brown man, the same color as diarrhea, and could they place their white lives in his shitty hands? Short of telling them that the fish really was '*āweoweo*, Kalama did his best to reassure them it was safe, but it was difficult for them to disassociate the headlines from the national identity of the cook. Besides, the restaurant was called Danger, wasn't it?

"Not everyone is worried," said Kalama, "but about half of them are concerned enough to cancel out. Everybody's talking about the war. It's so shocking. A small nation in the Orient making war on a European giant. You think Japan has a chance?"

"We're already winning," said Shuzo, "even though we still don't have Port Arthur. But it'll fall. The foreign observers have been impressed. You've read their dispatches in your newspapers. I wish I could be there, serving under my General Nogi."

Officially America was neutral, a wise choice in the face of confusion over who to support — that is, who might win — in the unprecedented face off. It was hard not to admire the first Asian nation taking on a western power, but what if the browns beat the whites? Who would be next? It was hard not to side with the westerners, but weren't Russians just a bunch of barbaric Cossacks dressed in European civilities? The split opinion of the hotel guests matched the national mood, as some cheered the Russians on, not because they loved them but because they feared the Japanese, while others genuinely

225

hoped the Japanese would win. A few white men went to the consulate in Honolulu and tried to enlist in the Japanese Navy, but the Consul General thanked them and told them it would not be possible to sign them up.

Everyone snapped up the latest news of the mythic battle between David and Goliath fighting the first modern war of the twentieth century, slinging bullets with machine guns, lobbing howitzer shells the weight of five men, maneuvering fire-belching sea monsters displacing water measured in tons, slaughtering each other by the tens of thousands. From the opening shots, the little men with large teeth and bad eyesight shocked the world with their organized tenacity, and they did take Port Arthur, just as Shuzo had predicted and would go on to destroy the Russian fleet in the Tsushima Straits.

"And you, Colonel Kalama, I suppose you are for the Russians? Didn't you meet the Tsar's father and invite him to Hawai'i?"

Kalama laughed. "Yes, I did invite him to Hawai'i and I even met the young Nicholas. But I'm for the underdog. I wish we Hawaiians could have taken on the Americans and preserved our Kingdom."

"And what about Woody? Surely he for the Russians?"

"Davies's not sure. He hates the Russians but doesn't trust the Japanese. But don't worry, Shuzo. You've got a lot of support here. In fact, take a look at this." He pulled out a tightly folded copy of the *Hawaiian Gazette* and thumbed its pages until he found the article, "Japan the Civilizer," which argued that compared with Russia, Japan had better schools, religious freedom, the rule of law, enlightened prisons and guaranteed human rights. "Here," said Kalama, "let me read you the last lines. 'Dark, brutal, vengeful, a Middle Ages monstrosity in the fair domain of Europe, Russia stands for Cossack rule and nothing better. Modern, hopeful, progressive, a twentieth century influence in the affairs of Asia and the world, Japan stands for all that material civilization values and is as Christian in its Buddhism as Russia is pagan in its Christianity.'"

"Good," said Shuzo, "very good. Maybe America not so bad after all. Maybe we need to become better friends, help each other."

Kalama put his hand on Shuzo's shoulder. "We've been doing it already. Look at me. Retainer to the King, manager under Woodrow Davies, partner with the greatest Japanese businessman in Waialua. Everything is happening so fast. There won't be too many customers right now, but they're interested. I'll bring over three or four guests tonight, so get ready."

"Taste of death."

"Ha," he snickered, " 'āweoweo."

◆

Chiyo also supported the underdogs, but her *Uchinanchu* sensibilities made her cheer for the Chinese and Koreans. It didn't matter whether Russia or Japan won, in either case, the people lost. That's what had happened with Okinawa, why there was such hatred toward Japan. Okinawa too had been a proud kingdom, caught between Chinese and Japanese warlords until it was finally forced into the new Meiji nation. Okinawans became Japanese, but not by choice and only in theory. In Waialua, Chiyo was the rare Okinawan, but she was privileged and protected by Mako and Shuzo, who valued her for what she gave to them, not where she came from.

"I hope the Russians and Japanese kill each other on the battlefields until not a single soldier or sailor is left," she said. "Wouldn't that be wonderful for the people of China and Korea?"

"The way things are going," said Mako, "you might get your wish. But if there has to be a winner, who would you prefer?"

Chiyo thought for a moment. "I don't know."

"Oh, come on. It has to be Japan."

Shuzo walked into the kitchen and picked up on the conversation. "Is Chiyo for the Russians?"

"I'm for the people," she said. "And this war is terrible for those poor Chinese and Koreans."

"You're right," said Shuzo. "But it can't be helped and we have to make choices. To do our duty or not."

"Speaking of which," said Mako, "I've got to get over to the restaurant. We have some hotel guests coming and I have to see that the 'āweoweo are done right with red skin removed. Has to be authentic, you know." Mako finished his bottle of beer, grabbed his coat and started out. "Will you be over later for dinner?"

"As usual," said Shuzo.

Chiyo picked up her shamisen and started to play her favorite rice planting song. She sang it softly in Okinawan and while Shuzo could understand a few cognates, it was a foreign language to him. It was a field chant set to music and she drew out the syllables in rising and falling tones that put her back in the paddy, hunched over, seedlings in one hand, shoving them into the mud with the other, five seedlings planted left to right, then one step to the right, five more, step again, five and one, five and one. Her grandmother had been planting the row behind her and she started a song in her low rasping voice and no one came in on the refrain because it was her own composition, made up on the spot, sung to herself.

> *Five daughters and one son,*
> *Five daughters and one son,*
> *They sent him to China,*
> *And he never came back.*
> *Five daughters and one son,*
> *Five daughters and...*

Grandmother had stood up, feet spread firmly in the paddy, straightened her back and wiped the sweat from her face. One son? Chiyo had turned around and faced her grandmother. "Did you say one son? I had an uncle?"

"Get back to work," grandmother had said. And she never sang the song again.

228

"What's wrong, Chiyo? Are you crying?" Shuzo leaned on the kitchen table. She set her shamisen against the wall and folded her hands in her lap. She looked down, so different from the brash woman who had powdered Shuzo's nose at their bunks on the ship, telling him facts about fire and water. "You look tired," he said, standing up and walking behind her. He clasped her arms and helped her stand up. "Mako's busy," he said, "and we have a little time."

"Maybe we shouldn't," she said.

"Too tired?"

"It's not that. It's just…"

"Oh, it'll make you feel better. Always does."

"It's not right. I'm betraying him."

"And he's betraying his wife. Look, Chiyo, here in Hawai'i, we're far away from home. Distance changes everything. It's all right. Haven't you heard about the women leaving their husbands for other men? Everybody's doing it."

"That doesn't make it right."

"Don't make it complicated. It's just fire and water, that's all. Just lie on the bed and rest awhile. Think about our first time, remember?" He took her into his bedroom and returned to the kitchen.

Chiyo sat on the bed. So strange, this clever man who rescued me from the fields. He's so enterprising, so quick to turn problems into opportunities. So skilled with business and yet he's clumsy with women, uncertain and even blind, to Miki at least. He can't see that she adores him. He pays no attention to her, not the kind she craves. But that's what makes him such a challenge, to open his eyes and make him see. From the very first, even as he called us stinking pigs on the ship, he saw me, though Mako was more obvious about his feelings. Shuzo hides his fire, but why should he? Surely he's slept with Miki, but that night when we went out into the veranda while Mako had passed out, it was his first time. I could tell. It was as if he'd read a book or something, or, no, that's it, I remember, Mako said he had to explain it all to Shuzo. And on the ship, he wanted to know more from me.

I'm the only one he's ever had and he did it just to try it out, to see what it's like. And every time after that it's been the same, awkward, almost formal, as if there was an etiquette to it, as if he is supposed to like it. And yet he thinks he loves me, but making love is something else. Not like Mako. Umm, Mako. I wonder if Shuzo prefers men.

Shuzo opened the door and came back in. "Feeling better?" he asked and went back to the door to shut it. She held out her hand toward him and he took it like a handshake. She pulled him toward her and he sat on the bed. She guided his hand under her kimono, placing it on her breast. He pulled it away and stood up. "How stupid of me," he said, "I handled some fish and forgot to wash my hands. Don't move. I'll be right back." He rushed out to the kitchen and hurried back, wiping his hands on his shirt. He undressed and got into bed.

As she guided him, his motions were correct. He quickly tensed and then relaxed, dropping his head next to hers. He had once again proven himself to himself and Chiyo realized for the first time that his sighs had been more of relief than pleasure.

"Chi ... Chiyo," he said, clearing his throat, "you're the only woman I've ever loved."

She ran her fingers lightly down his back long after he fell asleep. She was wide awake and she held him, this would-be commander of men. He had announced his love, the only way he could make it known, but she didn't feel it as a love for her as a woman, but as an assurance he needed about himself. It was self-serving for the moment and could disappear as easily as he could declare it. "Now I understand," she whispered into his ear, deaf from sleep. His breathing was so deep and restful, far beyond dreaming. She shifted him to one side, turned to see his face and whispered as she smiled, "You're pretty good, Shuzo-san, pretty damn good, sleeping with a woman."

◆

The Japanese consulate officer returned to Waialua to serve

notices to several army reservists to report for duty. At his request, Shuzo went with him as his interpreter to see Mr. Goodale, who, much to their relief, sympathized with the official. He signed some papers releasing the men from their contracts and turned them over to the officer. "Teach those Russkies a good lesson," he said, as they shook hands.

"It's a good thing we made an example of that draft dodger," the official said, as they sat down in Restaurant Danger for lunch. "A bowl of moon-viewing *udon* noodles is fine for me," he said to the waitress, who looked slightly puzzled. "The kind with the egg cracked in it," he explained. Shuzo didn't order anything for himself.

"I'm planning a fundraising campaign," Shuzo told the officer. "On the first Sunday of every month, I'll have a patriotic rally instead of the usual stage performance and I'll ask each person to contribute a dollar a month for as long as the war lasts. I'll send the money to your office and you can transfer it to Japan. Why don't you come and give a speech?"

"I'm a terrible speaker. You'd be so much better. Tell you what. I'll send you the reports we receive and you can tell the story of our brave men. I'll get them to you by horse courier or the island steamer ... or both. When will the first rally be? I'd like to be there." The waitress brought his steaming bowl and he lifted a few noodles with his chopsticks to let them cool.

"I'm thinking of this Sunday," said Shuzo. "Do you really think we can win?"

The officer sucked the noodles in, barely chewed and swallowed. "So far, so good. But the cost is high. Terribly high."

◆

The House of Eternal Pleasure was packed, and men crowded against the walls. Shuzo had announced the patriotic rally in all of the camps and people came from as far away as Kahuku. They were eager to hear "the latest news based on official reports made available by the Japanese Consulate exclusively to the House of Eternal Pleasure." Chiyo led off with her usual rice planting song, Five Daughters and One Son. Shuzo and the officer waited in the wings.

"Isn't she singing in Okinawan?" the officer asked Shuzo.

"Right, it's Okinawan. No one understands what she's saying, but it's become a favorite among the men and they expect it at every opening. Look at them swaying, ready to plant rice." As Chiyo played the last notes, Shuzo walked onto the stage.

"Gentlemen — and I see some ladies in the back over there — welcome to our first patriotic rally. I know you are anxious for news from the front and I can give you more details than you can get in the newspapers. But first let me introduce, ah … ah … Manabe-san. He is the First Assistant to the Consul General and has given me exclusive access to their official reports. Manabe-san, please."

The officer came out looking embarrassed. He bowed, extended canned greetings on behalf of the Consul General and asked for everyone's cooperation. He turned to Shuzo, bowed and exited the stage.

Shuzo stood at attention, hands stiffly down his sides, an officer in charge. He looked at every face as if he were sending them into battle and he felt for them. They needed to know the meaning of this war, the reasons for sacrificing a dollar a month.

"You've all read the glowing reports in the newspapers, but I shall tell you the truth: we may lose. We've been deadlocked for several months, but the Russians have the advantage of the hills. They look down on our soldiers and pour bullets from machine guns like water, raining lead, mostly into the heads of our soldiers. Our men have been issued burlap bags, like the kind we use for shipping sugar, only they fill it with dirt and crawl up the barren hills, pushing the bags ahead of them, centimeters at a time, right into the wave of bullets, which tear into the burlap bags, *splat! splat! splat!*, just like that, until the bags are shredded into nothing and then the bullets hit their heads. But our brave men do not stop and they seek cover behind their fallen comrades, then break out and crawl to the next body. When they run out of bodies, they charge as far as they can, dodging the rolling grenades, trampling the barbed wire, that evil invention of twisted minds, and they get hit but they keep running until they fall, providing cover for the next man coming up. They lay themselves down like stepping stones and move up the hill, day after sleepless nights. When our men took Hill 174, which means it was 174 meters high, 16,000 of their comrades covered the hill like a bloody blanket. 16,000! In three days!"

Shuzo stopped for a drink of water and let the number sink in to draw out sadness, anger and guilt in their faces.

"Every one of us should be there in China, fighting with General Nogi, sailing with Admiral Togo. But we are here, safe in Hawai'i. A few of you will be going to the front, but most of us will be here. Whenever you find yourselves suffering in the cane fields, think of our soldiers crawling up the hills muddied with blood. So we must help them. And, oh, how little do we give compared to what they give, arms, legs, their lives. I call upon each and every one of you to give a dollar a month, more if you can. They are fighting for our nation, our families, for you, for me. Mako will pass around the donation box. If you don't have the money now, the box will always be at the entrance to the restaurant. And one more thing. No one wants to die, but everyone must serve. I want to thank all of you—and I'm sure Manabe-san joins me in this—for your cooperation in the recent search for the draft evader. He was a coward, a sissy, not a real man. He deserved his fate and had we captured him alive, he would have been shot. My friends, if we are brave and do our part, we can kick the Russians' asses. And that would be a lesson for the rest of the haoles, even here in Hawai'i." He paused and pointed toward the mill. "Right here on this plantation."

Shuzo clicked his heels, turned smartly and marched off the stage to the sounds of loud applause.

"Masterful, simply masterful," said the officer. "I wish I

could give talks like you. The details were so real, I could see the men on the hill. I've never heard it like that before. I'll tell the Consul General that we should send you to all of the plantations. Amazing, just amazing. And you brought it down to their level too, to this plantation. Just like you said." He pulled out a handkerchief and wiped his face.

Despite his disclaimer, the officer had his own verbal outpouring. But Shuzo was too high on his own words to have paid any attention to him and he didn't hear him say that, incidentally, his name was not Manabe.

◆

The news of the fall of Port Arthur reached Hawai'i on January 2, 1905. Already celebrating the New Year, the Japanese were frantic with joy and staged an emotional lantern parade in 'A'ala Park in Honolulu. In February and March, the Imperial Army routed the Russians in the Battle of Mukden, killing 90,000 of the enemy in two weeks and, having lost only 70,000 of their own, the military declared another glorious victory. In May, Admiral Togo annihilated two-thirds of the mighty Baltic Fleet in the Tsushima Strait and in September, the Russians traded battlefield defeats for peace.

The Japanese in Honolulu enshrined Admiral Togo as a god in their main Shinto shrine and vowed to name their sons Heihachiro after him. In a solemn ceremony at the Japan Institute, the Consul General conferred an Imperial award on Shuzo and other prominent supporters. In the garden reception after the formalities, the First Assistant to the Consul General — Takahashi was his name, not Manabe — introduced Shuzo to guests and recounted Shuzo's inspiring speech about burlap bags and stepping stones. A small brass band played military songs and red-dotted flags fluttered in the trade winds.

"Taga-san. Shuzo Taga. Remember me?" The older man wore a bowler hat, an expensive suit, shiny leather shoes. He looked vaguely familiar, but Shuzo couldn't place him until he spotted his gold watch chain. It was the fish agent from Shimonoseki.

"Fugu … fugu dealer," said Shuzo, trying to remember the man's name. "Did I ever know your name?"

"Probably not. You were just a young boy back then. But I remember how you forced your father and Kawa-san to supply me with fugu. They didn't want to do it, but you convinced them. I was so impressed with your determination. Do you remember that day? On the beach?"

"How can I forget? It was my first business deal. Are you … you…?"

"Watanabe's my name."

"Are you, Watanabe-san, still in the fish trade?"

"Fish products, seafood, really. I'm with the largest exporter of dried fish and seaweed in Shimonoseki. I hope to retire soon, but my company sent me here to set up a branch office. The market's good with so many Japanese here. We're looking at San Francisco too."

"Well, Watanabe-san," said Shuzo laughing, "you won't believe it, but I have my own fugu restaurant here."

"Really? Well, I'm not surprised, I guess. Not with your sharp business sense. Not with your experience with fugu. Where's your restaurant?"

"Out in Waialua, on the opposite side of the island from here. Why don't you come with me after this party is over? You can spend the night at my place."

"That'll be wonderful. You're right, I can hardly believe it. Well, well, so you have your own fugu restaurant. Your father must be proud of you."

They took the government road over the center of the island to Waialua. Shuzo pointed out the sights all along the way and stopped the carriage to allow his guest to stretch his legs and enjoy the views. The Americans were clearing the three lochs of Pearl Harbor to satisfy their need for a large base in the Pacific, especially since Japan had defeated Russia. Trade across the Pacific was developing rapidly, Watanabe's company being a case in point, and Hawai'i would surely become an international crossroads.

Shuzo told Watanabe about his business success and gave

all the credit to this land of opportunity, none to Miki. Watanabe knew his father well and though they no longer did business together, it was possible that they might meet upon the agent's return to Japan and Watanabe might say something about Miki if he knew about her. The chances were remote, but Shuzo could not bear the thought of his parents finding out. Everybody knew about Miki in Waialua, but no one besides Mako was from Iwakuni and besides, he had quit the evening trade. It was over, past and done with, best forgotten. Shuzo explained the details of his restaurant and theater, but of his whore he said nothing.

Watanabe was impressed by the vast stretches of the cane fields and the large number of plantations. As they headed up the central plateau between the Wai'anae Mountains and the Ko'olau Range, Shuzo pointed out the purple blue color of the distant forests and wondered how the shadow of the clouds on green leaves produced purple blue. What is the color of a shadow, anyway? At the crest of the plateau, they looked down on the sweeping Waialua coast dominated by Mt. Ka'ala and its deep ravines, into one of which, Shuzo explained, the draft evader, miserable coward, had fallen to his deserved death. As they descended the long, sloping terrain into the late afternoon sun, they discussed Japan's magnificent victory over Russia.

"Japan has entered the modern world of western countries," said Watanabe. "Don't you want to go back home and be a part of the adventure?"

"Home? In Iwakuni? But what would I do there?"

"There are lots of jobs, especially for one as capable as you."

"No," said Shuzo, "I like it here."

"Do you plan on staying forever?"

"Forever's a long time. I don't know. I haven't really thought about it. But I have time. I'll just see what happens."

Shuzo showed Watanabe the guest room in the back of the restaurant and told him to rest while he prepared a Hawaiian fugu dish for him. Miki was sitting in her kitchen chair and she watched Shuzo scoop a real fugu out of the holding tank and carefully slice it open. He removed the flesh without touching the liver and sliced it into tessa. He concentrated on his work, crucial not to be distracted and he did not see her smile.

"Why don't you go on back to the house, Miki. I have an important guest and want to be alone with him." She slipped out of the chair and left the kitchen.

Mariko Mahealani served them in a screened corner of the restaurant. She had a plumeria flower pinned over her ear and gave Watanabe a friendly smile every time she set a dish in front of him. "We don't have women like her in Japan," he said to Shuzo. "She makes me feel so relaxed."

"That's about right," said Shuzo, "for your age."

"And what about you at your age? What about marriage?"

"You keep asking me questions I never think about. Going home, getting married. I have plenty of time."

"Your parents must be anxious for you to go home and get married. I haven't seen them for a long time. I knew your father well. Saw him every time he made a delivery of fugu at Shimonoseki. Did he ever tell you about the man who survived death? No? This is a great story."

Watanabe gave a detailed account of the night when Sasaki ate an exquisitely poisoned piece of fugu, how everyone was certain that he had died, how he survived and went on to attack the Chinese envoy negotiating the end of the Sino-Japanese War. He survived the fugu all right, but his mind seems to have been poisoned. But what a night it was! So exciting! We hardly slept.

"What a great idea!" said Shuzo. "I should have an event like that right here in Restaurant Danger. I'll talk to Mako about this."

Mariko Mahealani came out with the tessa and set it in front of Watanabe. "A taste of death," she said, "just for you."

"Go on," said Shuzo, "take a bite. You're not afraid, are you?"

Watanabe took a piece and chewed it thoughtfully. "It's

good. Hard to tell the difference with Japanese fugu. Reminds me of the beach where Kawa-san lived." He took another piece. "Did you know, Shuzo, that Kawa-san died?"

"No, my parents never said anything to me."

"Came down with some kind of fever and passed away. I happened to be in Iwakuni on business and paid him a visit a couple of weeks, it turned out, before he died. He was troubled, very agitated and was glad to see me. He wanted to tell me something, but, well, you know Kawa-san, had a hard time expressing himself. When he finally got it out, he made me promise never to tell your father. But he didn't say I couldn't tell you. I'm sure you know he was very fond of you. He loved you like a son. Always carried your picture. I'm getting old myself and who knows how much longer I have and after I return to Japan, I may never see you again. So I will tell you what he said, but you must promise never to say anything to your father."

"I promise. Rarely talk to him anyway."

"Remember when I had to reduce the fugu orders in half and your father cut him off? Kawa-san was hurt and angry that your father kept on selling his fugu to me but prevented him from selling any of his own. He was mad at your father, felt betrayed and so he made a cut in the tiller of your father's boat from the underside. He said no one ever suspected him, that you all thought someone else had done it. He felt terribly guilty and he regretted it, especially after your father's boat was wrecked. He kept it a secret, but it bothered him more and more and he had to tell someone. I'm not sure it did any good though, telling me. He looked even more miserable after he confessed. Maybe that's what killed him. Shuzo, are you all right? You look white."

Shuzo stood up and walked outside. Kawa-san? Not Nozaki, who committed suicide because his son died because I reported him as a draft evader because I wanted revenge ... no, justice ... against Nozaki because I thought he had sawn the tiller? Perfectly reasonable, one thing leading to another in logical sequence, except that Nozaki didn't do it. Kawa-san?

Shuzo went back into the restaurant and sat across from Watanabe. "Are you all right?" Watanabe asked again. "Maybe I shouldn't have said anything. Please don't hold it against Kawa-san, even though he…"

"Don't worry, Watanabe-san. It's so good to see you. Those were the good old days, weren't they? Yes, that old man did treat me like a son and as far as what he did, well, it all turned out for the better. If it hadn't been for the boat accident, why, I wouldn't be here at all. And look at me now." Shuzo leaned back in his chair, spread his arms out and surveyed his restaurant. "Thank you, Kawa-san. Thank you."

But Nozaki?

CONFESSION

J EROME STEWART LEFT THE HONOLULU IRON WORKS AT FOUR
in the afternoon and walked past the clearing that used
to be the Kaumakapili Church. All of the debris from the
great fire five years earlier had been cleared and new
buildings outnumbered the empty lots. How quickly we
recover from disaster, he thought, remembering the charred
ruins of Chinatown. At the time, the task of cleaning and
rebuilding seemed impossible and yet, wheelbarrow by
wheelbarrow, the area had been cleaned, and board by board
was being rebuilt. The new Chinatown will quickly erase the
memory of the old and already the plague has passed. As
quickly as we recover, we forget.

So was it with his passion for the Pacific. Read in the
Idaho extremes of heat and cold, the exotic tales of tropical
paradise and the mystic East had worked their magic, and he
had arrived in Honolulu because the howling wolves and his
imagination gave him no other choice. Here he found his
dreams, warm lagoons, women tanned to friendly ease,
people as enigmatic as their languages, and yet—this is what
pleased him the most—familiarity made the exotic ordinary
on his terms. He had become equally comfortable with
Goodale, Kalama and Shuzo and he treasured their
friendships as gems of his island experience, something he
valued more than the gold in Idaho City. Everybody wants
the same wealth, comfort and happiness. Take away all the
superficial differences, expose the core and everyone is the
same. Jerome prided himself on his ability to dig right into

everyone's lode of common humanity. Everyone, that is, except Anna.

It frightened him to think of how he had imagined her at his side, the envy of his friends, the would-be mother of his children. He had been swept into her alien allure, but ever since that night when she had clawed at him, he knew she was possessed by something more powerful than her imagination, that he had been lucky to escape from this wreck of a woman whom he had come so close to taking for his wife. At first, he blamed her; for she was mad, but then he came to his clearest senses and realized that only someone suffering from self-delusion could have come as close as he had to falling for her. And what of his obsession with this place, the soft air, the mossy mountains, the strange people he had made familiar and friendly? This island was no different from Anna, possessed of a power to seduce those who let themselves be obsessed and he was frightened of losing his ability to see through his own fantasies. His brother had been right.

Damn Robert Louis Stevenson and Isabella Bird! Damn the Shoshoni wolves! But here I go again blaming someone else when the fault is mine. When I think of Peter and Idaho City, I know I do not belong here. The danger is that I should feel at ease in this place, comfortable, as I slip from my moorings, drifting on a course I've set without the slightest idea of where I'm going. I must get out, go back home, before it's too late.

Afraid of having second thoughts, Jerome immediately resigned his position at the Iron Works and booked passage on the next steamer to Seattle. He took the train around Ka'ena Point to Waialua to say goodbye to Kalama and Shuzo and to decline Mr. Goodale's generous offer of a job as head engineer of the Waialua Mill. And, of course, he had to see Anna for one last time to thank her for opening his eyes to his life and to see her ... just to see her.

◆

Miki was sitting in her chair in the kitchen watching Shuzo

prepare fugu. While he let the regular cook fix the 'āweoweo for the guests from the Haleiwa Hotel, he never let anyone else handle the fugu. Jerome entered the kitchen just as Shuzo finished and asked to see him alone.

"I'm going back to Idaho City," he said abruptly, as they sat down at an empty table. "It's a long story but I've come to the conclusion that I must go back to where I belong."

Shuzo wiped his hands on his apron and looked at Jerome's face, at once rugged and kind, and continued to wring his hands in his apron. Jerome's announcement felt like a personal rejection, going home being just an excuse for the real reason. He was afraid to ask but the word escaped anyway: "Why?"

"I've had the most amazing experience of my life here. Especially with you … and Anna. You've affected me so deeply and I cannot tell you how grateful I am. You've made me realize who I am and where I belong and I can't thank you enough for that."

"But you belong here," Shuzo argued, "with us … me. It's not hard to change your home. I'll never go back to Japan."

"Perhaps. But not for me. I just have to go home. But look, Shuzo, this is not the end of our friendship. I'll come back and visit and you'll do the same for me in Idaho City, won't you?"

"If I say yes, then it means you really leaving, but I guess I no have choice."

"No choice," said Jerome. "I take that as a promise."

"I promise."

"Thanks."

"*Oi!*" Shuzo called into the kitchen. "Beer!"

The cook brought out two bottles. Shuzo opened them and handed one to Jerome. "To you, Jerome, friend forever. I never forget you."

"To you, Shuzo, the most amazing entrepreneur."

"Whatever that is."

"It's good and you're the greatest."

They took long swigs, wiped their mouths and laughed like friends sharing a secret. Shuzo shook his head in wonder at the affection he felt for this tall, blond blacksmith and for one flashing moment, he wanted to ask Jerome to take him with him, but he quickly recovered his manners. Jerome tried to preserve the moment, maybe his last, of feeling no different than this stranger.

"I'd like to speak with Miki alone. Do you mind if we went back to the house?"

"Of course not," said Shuzo. "But how you going to speak with her when you don't know Japanese? You like me to interpret?"

"No, we managed in the past. At my house."

Jerome went into the kitchen and held out his hand to Miki. She took it and he led her out of the restaurant. They walked across the yard and she moved closer to him, holding his hand and he remembered the morning he had stopped at Fujita's house to say hello. They walked up the steps and Jerome held the front door open for her. She stepped in, took off her slippers and Jerome followed, removing his shoes. Miki opened the door to her bedroom, went in and he followed, leaving the door open behind him.

Miki sat on the bed and Jerome pulled up a chair for himself. She looked directly at him and he wondered what feelings might be coursing through her troubled mind. But she looked utterly at ease, serene with the memory, perhaps, of how he had carried her away from Fujita's house as the other girls watched with yearning. So hard to tell with Anna. She smiled at Jerome and he felt old feelings, which he now regarded as a mistake.

"Anna, I know you cannot understand me, but I shall speak freely anyway. Even if we shared the same language, I'm not sure I could explain what I feel for you, the effect you've had on me. But I am going home and I may never see you again, so I've come to say goodbye. At times like this, it's best to be brief. But believe me, Anna, I shall never forget you and you'll always have a special place in my heart. I will pray for you, for your ... recovery."

As he got up to leave, he pushed the chair back and its

legs scraped against the floor. Miki flinched, suddenly afraid. He had placed a chair against the door that night at his Makiki house and as she had pushed it open in the early morning to look for her cat, the chair had made the same scraping sound. Miki grasped her kimono at her neck and covered her heart with her other arm. She drew her legs up and curled as tightly as she could. He was going to cut her heart out and she pleaded with her eyes to be spared.

"Anna … what? Don't be afraid. I'm not going to hurt you."

She started to shiver and he reached out to lay a reassuring hand on her, but she recoiled and squirmed her way to the wall on the other side of her bed. She was too terrified to scream and she clutched her heart, afraid that he would take it home with him.

"Anna…" He moved slightly toward her, then stopped, knowing there was nothing he could do. He could feel her fear and he dropped to his knees and pressed his hands together, resting them on the edge of the bed. "Dear God, save this poor woman," he prayed and dropped his head into his hands, closed his eyes and felt the bed move as she made her way toward him. Let her attack me again, I deserve her punishment, for I have been wrong, so terribly wrong about everything in this place. He waited, then lifted his head and saw that Anna was gone.

◆

Shuzo drove his wagon from the restaurant toward the sugar mill and made his way through the Japanese camp with its vegetable gardens in the front and back yards, the stacked crates and boxes filled with old pots, used kerosene stoves, furniture, coils of wire, hinges, locks and anything else that might be useful someday, if not right away. They were hoarders saving things that might save them money, never throwing used items away, just in case. He passed into the Portuguese section with its houses less cluttered, cooing pigeons in wire mesh cages, squawking chickens, waddling ducks in mud holes and pig hunting dogs. It was late afternoon and the dominant aroma was of sweet bread baking in outdoor clay ovens.

Without shock absorbing springs between the axle and the wooden flatbed, the wagon clattered noisily. It was the same wagon he had Jerome purchase for him from the livery and Mako kept telling him that he should replace it with a nice trap or carriage. But Shuzo would never give up his wagon and he bounced on the riding bench, feeling the cushioning of the leaf springs under the seat. After Miki had suffered from the hard bench ride on their journey from Honolulu to Waialua, Jerome had offered to fabricate special springs and helped Shuzo install them. Actually, Shuzo did the helping, as he had never held a screwdriver before in all of his life and he happily followed Jerome's instructions. That's what he liked about Jerome, his easy command. He was the only person Shuzo would wish to serve in battle, to follow him anywhere, to do whatever he ordered, not because of rank, but because he was so intensely fond of him. "Hold the spring right there and I'll screw in my side, then yours," Jerome ordered. "No, no, like this, right here." They were lying on their backs under the riding bench and Jerome turned his body against Shuzo's and reached over to hold Shuzo's hands at the exact position for the spring. Jerome had a haole smell, musky, amiable, exotic and Shuzo wished they could lie together in the wagon forever. Trade the wagon in for a carriage? Never. Especially since Jerome had returned to the mainland. If only I had thought of asking him for a piece of his hair. Beautiful, blond hair.

He took the road to the old Halstead mill with its stone and cement smokestack still standing, abandoned after its owners went bankrupt from cane starving for irrigation. Goodale's genius was in his system of tunnels, ditches, reservoirs and small dams providing ample water thickening the cane with sweet juice. At the main intersection of the government road, Shuzo turned toward the Wai'anae Mountains and headed toward St. Michael's Church. From the top of a knoll, he saw the church against the foothills leading up to the deep cleavages of Mt. Ka'ala and he thought the pointed steeple looked like a hat, though the external buttresses reminded him of pictures of churches he had seen in books on Europe. He had been to the cemetery once before for the burial of a Japanese worker killed in a tunnel cave-in, but he had never been inside the sanctuary.

Shuzo stopped in front of the main entrance and walked through the open doors into the sanctuary kept cool by thick walls of blue stone and coral mortar. The Catholics build for an eternity, he thought, unlike the Buddhist temples made of wood easily ravaged by termites and dry rot, a strange term for a condition caused by excessive moisture. He unconsciously took off his hat as he walked slowly toward the altar and the cross with the man nailed to it. He stared at the scantily draped figure, mortally wounded, head bent to one side with the weight of a thorny crown. Was he dead? How different from the resplendent buddhas, erect, radiating golden rays of light, dressed in exquisite robes, hands freely forming sacred gestures of wisdom and eternal life. Buddhas do not suffer and die.

"Shuzo! What a surprise." Josephine came in from a side door carrying a bucket of water. She wore a work scarf over her head and a long waist apron around her dark blue dress.

"Ah, Josephine. Your neighbor told me I find you here. I went your house, but you not in."

"This is my cleaning day," she explained. "I used to come at night, but lately I've had things to do. So, what brings you here?

"I need your help with English problem. You see, Mr. Davies say the House of Eternal Pleasure sounds like whore … ah, excuse me, but maybe I shouldn't say such word in place like this."

"Go ahead, say it. You've already said it."

"Mr. Davies think House of Eternal Pleasure sound like whorehouse and asked me to say something more respectable. I told him I ask you for suggestions."

She set down her bucket. "Hmm, a respectable name for your theater. Let's see. The problem is with the word pleasure, so we've got to get rid of it. Eternal is an exaggeration and it might be good to be more, let's say, modest. And house. Is a theater a house? Come to think of it, playhouse is sometimes used for theaters. How about playhouse? And play means a drama performance as well as having fun."

"Perfect!" said Shuzo. "Playhouse. The Waialua Playhouse. Sound respectable?"

"I don't see why not. I like it and Mr. Davies should."

"Well, it will still be the House of Eternal Pleasure, Eiraku-za in Japanese, but in English for Davies's guests, it is the Waialua Playhouse. Thank you, Josephine. You always help."

"Glad to be of help." She stood waiting for him to say something else or leave, but he stood there, hat in hand, rehearsing words in his mind. "Is there anything else, Shuzo?"

"Your god," he said, "over there on cross, I heard he forgive people."

"Everyone is a sinner—do you know what that word means—everyone does things that are not right, and Jesus, over there on the cross, forgives sinners, but first you must confess your sins to the priest."

"The priest? But I don't know priest. How can I confess to stranger?"

"Shuzo, is something bothering you? Is that why you came here?"

"I come see you, tell you something, yes, bother me. I come see you because I know you, trust you."

"Why don't we sit down."

Shuzo told her the story from the beginning. "A fish agent had arranged for my father and his friend Kawa-san to provide fugu to the markets and restaurants in Shimonoseki, where my father met a lacquer dealer who helped him get into the wood business. As head of the Lumber Dealers Association in Iwakuni, Bunzo Nozaki ruined my father's business by sawing the tiller part way through from the underside, or that is what I thought at the time, causing him to wreck his boat in a storm. So, when Nozaki's son showed up in Waialua in order to escape the draft, I turned him in to the consulate authorities, not just because it was my duty, but to take revenge against Nozaki. But then, just a few days ago, the fish agent paid me a visit and told me that Kawa-san confessed to having sawn the tiller because he was angry at my father for cutting him out of the fugu arrangement when demand dropped. What is strange, Josephine, is that I the one who forced my father—he a weak man—to cut Kawa-san out. So now it turns out that Nozaki had not done it and I unknowingly took revenge on an innocent boy and by accident, though not exactly —he fell off a cliff—caused the death of his son. But here's the worst part. When the news of the boy's death reached Japan, Nozaki, who was head of the conscription board in my hometown, couldn't bear the shame of his son being exposed as a draft evader and so he killed himself. It's all so tragic, but they are both dead, they're all dead—Mrs. Nozaki died years ago—and nothing can be done to change that. Although I do not think I did anything wrong, you agree? I feel ... I feel, well not responsible because I wasn't, but I feel bad about ... about ... my mistake, though it wasn't really a mistake since I didn't know Kawa-san did it."

Josephine hid behind an impassive look. She was horrified by Shuzo's mistaken revenge and Nozaki's suicide but was relieved to learn that Yukio was now an orphan, eligible for adoption. She was also caught between their mutual ignorance: Yukio didn't know about his father's death and Shuzo didn't know that Yukio was alive. She needed time to sort through this mess, to figure out what she should do. She got up and walked to the alcove of the Holy Virgin and stood there with her eyes closed. It came to her quickly and she returned to Shuzo.

"What do you want me to do?" she asked him.

"Nothing, really. There nothing be done. It's over, right or wrong. Like I said, they all dead. It's just I respect your opinion and I like know what you think."

"You mean, you'd like me to say that everything is all right. Well, other than seeking revenge, you did nothing wrong."

"What that mean, other than seeking revenge? It sound like everything I did was wrong."

"Everything *went* wrong, whether you meant it or not. I don't know what you are responsible for, but you are at the center of this and it all revolves around you. What you did was wrong, seeking revenge. There, that's what I think."

Shuzo started to object, but she interrupted him, telling him she was not interested in arguing with him. He had asked for her opinion and she had given it to him. He was free to accept or reject it.

"Listen," she said, "the only advice I can give you is for you to listen to your heart. You can come up with all kinds of reasons to justify what you did, but the important point is this: what do you feel is right or wrong?"

Shuzo remained silent.

"And why did you come here in the first place?" she asked. "Your first question was about forgiveness."

"I thought you understand I do nothing wrong."

"I have to go," she said. "You can stay here if you like. I suggest you do. Talk to Mother Mary, over there in the alcove."

Shuzo looked at the shrouded lady, tall, slender, pretty mother of her wretched son nailed to the cross. They both looked so human, how can they be gods? "No," he replied, "I need get back. You like ride?" She went out to put her bucket away and met him at the wagon.

"You no lock doors?" he asked.

"It's a church." He helped her up into the wagon and slid over on the bench to make room for her. Josephine's weight tilted the seat in her favor. "Soft springs," she said.

"Special make by Jerome. For me."

"I heard Jerome went back to Idaho."

"He feel he had go home."

"I see. Home. Where is your home, Shuzo?"

"Everything used to be so clear, but now I not sure. I feel like I walking around in dark. I didn't want Jerome leave and now you tell me I did something wrong. Maybe I did. I don't know. If I did, maybe your god forgive me."

Josephine smiled. "It's not that simple, Shuzo. Forgiveness is not about what you *might* have done wrong. You have to be certain. Besides, in your case, Jesus will not be as helpful as someone else I know."

"No," he said. "I already told you. I don't know your priest and I no can talk like this to stranger."

Shuzo put the horse into a slow walk over the dirt road. They did not speak to each other, though to themselves they couldn't stop.

Who else can I talk to? Josephine doesn't seem to understand. I wish Jerome were here. He could help me. I miss Jerome. Maybe I'll talk to Chiyo. I wish Nozaki had been the one with the saw. But Kawa-san, I can't get over it. Kawa-san cut the tiller.

Josephine was lost in her unexpected discovery. An orphan, Yukio is an orphan. I feel bad for feeling so happy. I can go to Honolulu and file papers at the courthouse to adopt him legally. What Shuzo did was wrong, but he made Yukio an orphan. Maybe I'm being too hard on Shuzo. Maybe I should thank him and forgive him myself. But, no, it'd be better for Yukio to do that. Someday.

◆

From her chair in the wings, Miki watched Chiyo practice her shamisen on the stage in the empty dining room. She was trying to set one of the holehole bushi field songs to music. Her nostalgic tunes from the old country were nice, but the workers here were planting cane, not rice, and they needed to hear their own feelings about the plantation, not the paddies back home, in her songs. But their ditties were filled with resentment, and no matter how she tried it, she could not force their complaints into her lilting style.

> *I heard Hawai'i is paradise,*
> *But it looks more like hell.*
> *The manager's a devil,*
> *Demon foremen awful smell.*

Mako came in and grabbed the shamisen out of her hands. "You slut. Just heard a bunch of men talking about you sneaking around my back. I've been faithful, but you ... you... They mock me, saying that if only I had eyes on my ass, I could see what is going on behind my back. Damn it, who is it? Who're you sleeping with? How many? Doing it for free?" He raised the shamisen by its slender neck and smashed it on the floor. Chiyo lunged at him, driving him backwards and as he fell on his back he screamed in pain as the splintered neck of the shamisen stabbed his arm.

Shuzo ran in from the kitchen. "Mako!" He pulled a thick sliver of wood out of Mako's arm and pressed his hand over the wound. "What's going on?" He looked at the shattered shamisen and saw the implications for the theater. "What's wrong with you, Mako?" He took the dish cloth from the cook, ordered him back into the kitchen and wrapped the wound. Chiyo was furious and weeping. No one wanted to talk.

Except for Shuzo promising Chiyo a new shamisen, they never discussed the incident again. Shuzo didn't learn the reason for their fight. Although Mako later found out that the gossip mongers had fabricated their insinuations out of their own lascivious desires for the shamisen player, Chiyo said nothing. Mako was filled with regret over his outburst, admitted his loss of perspective and started to talk about it being time to go home to his wife and daughter in Japan. Chiyo moved to one of the lodging rooms and they managed to eat breakfast at separate times. Shuzo and Chiyo let Mako believe that he was mistaken about her infidelity and Mako felt used and unappreciated, working as hard as he did at the restaurant. Their secrets and resentments made it impossible for them to talk openly and resolve their differences and Miki watched, the only one who found it amusing.

◆

"Well," said the cat. "You've been having some excitement."
"Yes, it's like watching a play."

"Hilarious, isn't it?"

"Very funny. They've all gone mad."

"Even that Jerome," said the cat. "I couldn't believe it. He thinks there's something wrong with you and wanted to cut your heart out. He's lost his mind."

"It's a good thing he prayed by the bedside. His god helped me escape."

"And Mako. He's so different from what he used to be, so solid and stable. Now he's falling apart. Suspicious and angry. And what do you think about Chiyo?"

Miki was quiet.

"Well?" said the cat. "I can't wait forever."

"Something must be done about Chiyo."

"She's been sleeping with Shuzo."

"But she doesn't love him," said Miki. "She's in love with Mako."

"But now she's angry with him. He smashed her shamisen to bits. I think she's going to abandon Mako and go to Shuzo."

"No, she won't. And even if she did, Shuzo will not love her."

The cat grinned.

"Stop it! Why do you like to upset me?"

"It's not me," said the cat. "It's the truth."

Miki slammed her hands over her ears.

"Hah, Miki, don't you see? Shuzo doesn't love you anymore because you've become worthless, sitting around all day, doing nothing but watching." The cat broke into a singsong: "He doesn't love you, he doesn't love you…"

"Stop it! Stop it!"

The cat held up its paw and Miki started to cry.

"You stop it," said the cat. "So Shuzo doesn't love you anymore. So what? You know what you can do, don't you? You can get his heart back, easy, you know that, take it right back and hold it with your hands."

Miki wiped her eyes and nodded. Mad, they've all gone mad, but Shuzo is the only one who needs to be cured.

VIRGIN MOTHER

Dear Shuzo:

We are so grateful for the money you keep sending. I am well but have been worried about your father sitting around all day, thinking about too many things. While he has not been sick, he has not been well.

But all of that has changed. Two weeks ago, he took out his bowler hat, dressed in a suit and took the train to Yamaguchi. He would not tell me the reason for this sudden trip and he did not let me accompany him. He came back the following day and told me that he arranged your marriage to a girl, the daughter of a wealthy lacquer dealer named Yamada. You might not have met him, but he is the man who supplied your father with zelkova wood. Yamada-san and his wife came down to visit us and your father was like his old self, filled with energy, talking of the old days. We negotiated the details, which were very simple and on June 15, the Yamadas went to the Yamaguchi City office and crossed her off their family registry and we added her name to ours. It's official. You are married and her name is Hasumi.

She is an elegant girl, well educated, and trained in flower arrangement, tea ceremony and calligraphy. Excellent seamstress too. She dreams of traveling and is anxious to go to Hawai'i. She has studied English and can speak a little. Remember the Mizuta family? They live a few streets away from us toward the river. Their son is in Hawai'i and they concluded a marriage, but the girl changed her mind about going to Hawai'i. She threatened to kill herself. So they gave her a divorce and had to cross her name out of the family registry only a few weeks after entering it. But this will not happen with Hasumi. In fact, she is already living with us and will leave as soon as you make arrangements for her passage.

Your father made a good choice. Already I have grown fond of her and we talk and laugh about all sorts of things. Your father is happier too. We will miss her when she goes to Hawai'i.

I am enclosing a letter from her to you. Please write to her and welcome her as your wife.

Mother
◆

Dear Shuzo-sama:

The irises have passed their peak and the azaleas are starting to show their colors. It is getting hot here in Iwakuni and I dream of tropical breezes.

My name is Hasumi and I am your wife. I remember meeting your father when he visited our home on a business trip some years ago. At that time, your father said that you and I were the same age.

It is my deepest wish to be a good wife for you and to make you happy. I hope I can fulfill your expectations, especially since you are such a successful and wealthy man. Although we have never met, I believe we are a good match for our families.

I am excited about going to Hawai'i. I am reading all I can about the islands and about America too. I have so many questions, but I will wait until I get there to have them answered. I look forward to hearing from you about the arrangements for my trip.

I am enclosing a picture of myself. Your mother has shown me pictures of you and has told me so much about you. I feel as if I know you already. I hope you will like me and I ask that you receive me with kindness.

Hasumi

◆

Shuzo read the letters over again and stared at her picture. Her long hair dropped behind her shoulders, her brows were dark and thin, curving slightly over intelligent, innocent eyes. She held her finely shaped lips without a smile, but still looked happy and accepting. Her comment about reading books and his mother's remark about her fondness for travel made him think of her as worldly, even though she clearly had a privileged and protected upbringing. She seemed to have made up for her lack of experience with her education and a capacity for greater understanding. But could she deal with surly plantation workers, Eternal Pleasure, Danger, Mako's developing temper, Chiyo's loose manner and Miki? Miki and her wild antics? Shuzo could see Hasumi living at the Haleiwa Hotel, but not at Long Bridge. The only chance he saw of her fitting in was suggested by her long careless hair and her flower patterned yukata, an informal garment wisely chosen instead of a refined silk kimono. Had she worn cotton instead of silk to let him see that she was down-to-earth? Clever.

Shuzo thought of rejecting Hasumi, divorce being as simple to arrange as marriage. But his mother liked her so much and his father had awakened from his daytime slumber to arrange this gift, perhaps his last, for his only son. Shuzo could not reject Hasumi any more than he could tell his parents about Miki. In either case, they would die of disappointment. He would have to receive her and he had enough discipline to make himself do it, to override his disinterest and accept her as a token from his parents. He looked at her picture again and felt sorry for her and wondered if her education could accommodate his lack of love. Marriage is not about love anyway, but is a duty, for both of us, surely she understands that, and once we have children she can shower her love on them. That's what children are for.

◆

Dear Hasumi:

Thank you for your letter, which I received with the letter from my mother. You have made my parents very happy and I think we are a good match for our families. I will arrange for your ticket on a steamer to Hawai'i, but it will not be for some time. I am very busy right now and will have to build a house for you and the children. In the meantime, please take care of my parents. I thank you from the bottom of my heart.

Shuzo

He wrote an even shorter letter to his mother and enclosed both in an envelope. There, it's done. I have a wife. He went out to the paddock behind the house and hitched his horse to the wagon. As he crossed Long Bridge on the way to the post office, he heard the train whistle as it entered the rail bridge half a mile away toward the mouth of the river. He accepted his own challenge to race the train to the station, just for fun. Children, he thought. He snapped the reins and let out a shout.

◆

"Married?" said Mako, who was about to sit at the table for breakfast but kept on standing since Chiyo was already seated.

"A wife?" Chiyo got up to get herself another serving of miso soup.

Even Miki came out of her bedroom and Mako slowly eased himself into a chair. It had been several days since they all were together.

"Her name is Hasumi. I've never met her, but we're a good match and my parents are happy. She's been entered into the Taga family registry and she's living with my parents."

"When will she arrive?"

"Not for some time. I have to build a new house for them. You know, the children as well."

"Children?" said Chiyo and she started to laugh. "You, Shuzo, a father?"

"What's wrong with that? You don't think I can be a father?"

"Of course, you can be a father. All you have to do is…"

Mako grew sullen. He sipped his soup noisily but was not tasting anything. Father. He slammed his fist on the table, rattling the dishes, got up and walked out.

"What's wrong with him?" asked Shuzo, disappointed that their peace had shattered so quickly.

"Home. He wants to go home, but he wants to stay. He doesn't know what he wants." Chiyo wiped the spilled soup off the table and served Miki a steaming bowl.

"So what do you think, Miki?"

"Another woman in the house."

"Don't worry about that," said Shuzo. "She'll have her own place. Maybe by the paddock, close to the plum forest. Wouldn't it be fun to have children running around?"

"You're going to raise your family here?" asked Chiyo. "Do you ever think of going back home? Like Mako out there?"

"I feel for Mako. I suppose if I had a wife and daughter back there, I'd want to go home too. But Hasumi is coming here, to everything I've built here. What would I do if I went back to Iwakuni? And what about you, Chiyo, what about you and Okinawa?"

"I'll never go back. Life is so much better here because of you and Mako. You've done so much for me and I'm so grateful, even though Mako's angry with me."

"If you left," said Shuzo, lowering his voice, "I'd feel like Mako. I wouldn't know what to do."

Chiyo gave him a tense look, casting a side glance at Miki, trying to stare a message to Shuzo.

"Chiyo, when Hasumi comes, nothing will change between us. You know that, don't you?"

"Stop," she whispered. "Think of Miki."

"Oh, don't worry about Miki. Nothing will change between us too. I'll always take care of Miki. She's my treasure, the one who made everything possible. Right, Miki?"

Miki looked at Shuzo, then at Chiyo and tried to spot Mako somewhere out in the yard. "One more woman in the house," she said and got up and went back to her room.

"You really shouldn't talk about us in front of her," said Chiyo, resuming her normal voice. "She has deep feelings for you and you don't want to hurt her."

"Miki's beyond that, in her own world. As long as I take care of her, she doesn't care about anything, not even herself. Don't worry about Miki." He reached out and touched Chiyo's hand. "All of this talk about being a father. Look, I have some time this afternoon. Suppose we…"

"No. Not when Mako is feeling so upset. No. Not today." She got up and went to her room. Shuzo finished his breakfast and left for the restaurant.

Miki had left the door open and heard everything. She buried her head in the futon and giggled hysterically. They are so hilarious. That silly Shuzo. He doesn't know that Chiyo sleeps with him only out of gratitude for all he's done. She's just saying thank you, but he thinks gratitude is love. And Chiyo, what a funny woman! Can you imagine, she doesn't want to do it with Shuzo because Mako is upset? So, if Mako were happy, then would it be all right? If only Mako knew the power of his mood! When he's happy, they can make love. If sad, they can't. They're like puppets in his hands, only he doesn't know it. Wouldn't it be something if in the middle of their love making, Mako suddenly became sad! They're all so funny and all I have to do is watch. Can't wait till there is another woman in the house! So many women, but only I will have his heart.

◆

Josephine arrived in the late afternoon as usual at Uncle Hila's place. No one was at the hut. She threw fresh wood on the smoldering fire and wondered what they were preparing for dinner. Uncle Hila showed up with a box filled with wild bitter melons and Josephine helped him wash them in a bucket of water.

"The way is clear," she said to the old man. "I can adopt him because his parents are dead. He's an orphan."

"Both of them dead? Doesn't seem to care much for his Japan home anyway."

"Well, he didn't have a happy home life. His mother died years ago and his father was hard on him."

"Mine too," said Uncle Hila. "Always scolded me. Couldn't do anything right."

"Maybe that's why you two get along so well."

Yukio walked toward them with a small tin pail. The air was warm and humid and the sun was too low for the thatched overhang to shade what Uncle Hila called his patio. Yukio had helped him extend the overhang to twice the size of the hut itself and they did most of their living in the enlarged covered area. Yukio smiled when he saw Josephine and she wondered if Shuzo would recognize the young man, tanned, muscled, full beard and mustache.

"You need a haircut," she said.

He set the pail on the small wooden table. "Goat milk for you, Aunty."

"Thank you. My favorite." She turned to Uncle Hila. "Do you have scissors?"

Uncle Hila lifted the top of a hinged box, rummaged through it and pulled out a pair of scissors. He spread the blades and felt their edges with his leathery thumb. "Still sharp," he pronounced and handed them to Josephine.

Josephine moved a wooden stool into an open area and patted the seat, clicking the scissors as if she were warming up for an athletic event. Yukio sat down, the orange sunglow on his face and she started to untangle his long hair with her fingers. "Comb," she called out to Uncle Hila, but he swiveled both hands to indicate he had none. "A couple of wild men," she said, "in need of some civilization." Had it not been for the fading light, she would have prolonged the running of her fingers through his hair.

"Yukio, I need to talk with you about something important. Now, you know that everyone thinks you died in a fall in the mountains and your death was reported back to your family in Japan. You were identified in the newspapers as a draft dodger and your father ... well, your father, when he knew that everyone else knew, well, he ... I'm so sorry, but he took his own life."

Yukio sat still.

"Do you know what that means, taking your own life? He killed himself. I'm sorry to have to tell you this."

He straightened his back and reached up to stop her caressing. He stood up and walked toward what was left of the sun. Josephine retreated to Uncle Hila and explained everything to him. "Leave him alone," he said. "He'll come back when he's ready."

They watched, long after the darkness had swallowed him and Josephine wanted to go and get him, but Uncle Hila made her wait. He offered her strips of smoked pig — he never ate goat meat — and made some tea. "Tea?" Josephine asked. "I didn't know you drank tea."

"Started as a consideration for Yukio," he explained, "but it turns out that I like the clean taste better than muddy coffee." They watched and Uncle Hila served some stale biscuits.

"Where do you get your food out here? Not from the

cemetery, I hope." Uncle Hila winced and told her that he went to the village at least once a week. Maybe two or three times now.

They waited and stood up when they finally saw him emerge into the edge of the light from the kukui oil lantern and he walked straight into Josephine's arms. He was done with his crying, but she could not stop herself from starting.

"Oh, Yukio, I'm so sorry."

Uncle Hila got up, sniffling and walked out into the darkness, mumbling some excuse about having to piss. A goat bleated, then another, calling for the herder they could hear walking back to the hut.

"How would you feel," said Josephine after everyone had settled down with their cups of tea, "if I adopted you. Do you know what that means? Make you my own son."

"I no go back Japan," Yukio said, "no father, no mother."

"So, what if I adopted you as my son."

"Aunty, then you my mother?"

"Yes," she laughed. "Your Aunty Mother. Or Mother Aunty."

"What difference would it make?" asked Uncle Hila.

"All the difference in the world, for me. And for Yukio, it would mean that I could take him back into the village."

"Away from me?"

"You should come with us too," said Josephine. "You're getting old and you can't live out here in the wilds forever. I have plenty of room in my house for all of us — uncle, aunty, mother, son ... and nephew — all five of us."

Yukio turned to Uncle Hila. "What you think, Uncle? Good?"

"But what about my goats?"

"You can come out any time you like," said Josephine. "Even spend nights in this hut. You're not giving it up, you're adding another home. And Yukio will still help you, but he needs to do what God meant him to do."

"And what that?" asked Uncle Hila.

"Paint."

Yukio asked Uncle Hila again. "Uncle, what you say?"

"*E mālama 'ia kou makemake.*"

"All right," Yukio said to Josephine. "Let's do it."

◆

For the second time in his life, Shuzo walked into the Catholic church. Josephine was alone, waiting for him in the sanctuary. They greeted each other and sat in the front pew.

"Thank you for coming," she said. "I know you're busy, but I need to talk with you."

"I hope not about my mistake again," he said, remembering their earlier meeting before the news of his marriage to Hasumi made him unable to think of anything else. He wanted to tell her about his wife but gave her the chance to speak the reasons for her request to meet with him.

"I want you to meet someone." She signaled someone in the back of the church and Shuzo turned in his seat to look at the young man, vaguely familiar but too strange to recognize. It was hard enough to determine if he was Hawaiian or Japanese, but his eyes were Oriental.

"This is my *hānai* son, Kamaki Kaumaka, but you know him as Yukio Nozaki."

Shuzo opened his mouth and stared. He stood up, stepped forward for a confirming look, then backed away as he saw the ghost of Yukio emerging from behind the tangle of hair, the strong arms, the hard tan. "But you're dead," he blurted.

"Hardly," said Josephine, "as you can see for yourself. Now, I'm going to leave the two of you alone so you can speak in Japanese."

Yukio pointed toward the pew, inviting Shuzo to sit. Shuzo eased himself down, placing a guiding hand on the edge of the seat so that he could keep his eyes on Yukio, who sat down a respectable distance away.

"Taga-san, Aunty Josephine explained everything to me, how you sought revenge against my father, how you were mistaken in thinking that he had sawn the tiller, how my death was reported, how my father committed suicide in shame. Aunty told me everything, so you do not have to explain any of that to me. But you must be wondering how I survived, so allow me to tell you my story."

Shuzo listened to his narrative, laid out so clearly he had no questions. The young man told his story with ease, without emotion, though that is what it was all about. Shuzo was on the verge of tears, from embarrassment, remorse, admiration. How can this young man not feel any rancor, any urge for revenge? In the purity of Yukio's sentiment, Shuzo felt exposed and finally admitted to himself his responsibility for causing Nozaki's death out of a mistaken need for revenge. How stupid! Damn foolish! He resented the boy for making him admit his error, but the shock of seeing Yukio alive suddenly turned into euphoria, a tremendous relief that he had not compounded his mistake by driving the boy to his death. Thank goodness for Josephine! Shuzo looked around for Josephine, the virgin who had saved them both and saw her standing by Mary. He could no longer keep it all in.

"I've made a terrible mistake," Shuzo blurted, "and I ask for your forgiveness." He bent his head, fell on his hands and knees and wept, the first time that he could remember. Neither could he recall a time when he had asked to be pardoned.

"You did a terrible thing," Yukio said, "but it was a mistake. And I forgive you for whatever there is to forgive. But that terrible thing turned out good for me and I am glad that it all happened."

Good horse, bad horse, how can we tell? It's just as father had taught me. That old Chinese story keeps coming up. Over all those years. A terrible thing happens, but it turns out to be good and the reverse can happen as well. It doesn't always happen that way, but in this case it did. He is lucky and so am I. With Nozaki, it all began with Father's chance encounter with the lacquer dealer, who sold him scrap wood. One thing led to another and another until this moment and now Nozaki's son has a Hawaiian mother! Who would have thought! Shuzo placed both hands on his head. "It all seems like a fairy tale, except no one wrote the story you are living. But I'm glad you're all right, after all. What are you going to do?"

"I'm going to live with Aunty, help Uncle Hila. And paint. I want to do your portrait."

"The kind you hang on a wall? Of me?" He heard Josephine walking over to rejoin them. She had listened to them speaking in a language foreign to her, but she understood the entire exchange.

"I paint Taga-san," Yukio informed Josephine, who laughed at the literal meaning of his words again.

"Kamaki is a great painter," she said. "He can capture the inner essence of places, the deepest feelings of people. Are you sure you want to be revealed in form and color?"

The young artist had already drawn out a confession from him. No one had ever done that before. What other secrets might he expose? "Maybe," Shuzo said, smiling mischievously, "maybe he make me look better than I am."

"Kamaki's a magician. He can get right at you, just like that, or he can change you into a different person. He can make you laugh or cry."

Kamaki shook his head, denying his mother's boast. "I just try hard."

"You know," Shuzo said slowly in that scheming way he liked best, "what you need is a gallery and I know perfect place. I have plenty wall space in my restaurant and you can show your paintings there. If you want sell your pictures — and I not saying you should — but if you want, I arrange for you at the Haleiwa Hotel. Plantation workers no money to buy art, but visitors can."

"Always the businessman," Josephine said. "Do you ever stop?"

"No, never. In fact, I make deal with you, Yukio … ah, Kamaki. I pay you to make portrait."

"But I paint you for free."

"Yes, I understand. But I want you paint someone else, someone whose heart and soul I want see."

"Who is that?" asked Josephine.

"Miki."

"Who Miki?" asked Kamaki.

"That's it," said Shuzo. "I want you paint answer to that question."

"I see. She interesting but first I must know her, this Aunty Miki."

They all got in Shuzo's wagon and headed back to the village. Good horse, bad horse, thought Shuzo, as he flicked the reins. Isn't it funny the way how things work out? I felt horrible about what I had done, but now I feel so good. I will help Yukio get back into life, promote his art. But wait a minute. He stopped the wagon.

"Yukio, never shave off your mustache or beard. Never." Shuzo spoke in English so that Josephine could understand. Besides, Kamaki's English was not bad, Josephine being his teacher. "No one find out Yukio Nozaki alive, especially that fat officer from Consulate. From now on, you Kamaki Kaumaka. Yukio Nozaki dead. Understand? Dead."

"You don't have to preach to the choir," said Josephine, "but you probably haven't heard that expression. Samuél Smiles never used it, as I recall. But, yes, Shuzo, Kamaki understands. Yukio is dead. May his soul rest in peace forever."

Shuzo made a detour to Long Bridge and drove up to the house. He told his passengers to wait in the wagon and ran into the house. Josephine thought he was going to introduce Miki to Kamaki, but Shuzo came out alone, carrying a leather suitcase.

"My oils and brushes!" Kamaki said as he reached down to take his suitcase from Shuzo.

"Murakami from Consulate, lazy bum, no like take back to Honolulu. We clear out things from room you rent in Waialua and Murakami told me throw stuff away. I completely forgot. Got too busy."

"How fortunate," said Josephine. "It was meant."

Neither Shuzo nor Kamaki understood what she meant, but they didn't ask for an explanation.

"By the way," Shuzo said as he climbed back onto the wagon. "Did I tell you I married?" Josephine was fascinated to hear about the system of family registries and said she wished it could be as simple in modern Hawai'i. But on second thought, she admitted it was not that hard to adopt Kamaki since the only requirement of the court was his permission as an orphan over the age of fourteen.

"So, when your wife come?" Kamaki asked.

"Don't know," he replied, "but not right away. Lots of things to do first."

TASTE OF DEATH

F OR MONTHS, SHUZO TOLD THE SAME JOKE.
"I'm going to be a father."
"Oh, really? Who's the mother?"
"My wife."
"I didn't know you were married."
"Neither did I, until my mother told me!" At which point, Shuzo would laugh, leaving his hearer to figure out what was funny. If the hapless person made the mistake of asking to meet his wife, Shuzo had a follow-up line: "She's still in Japan!" No one thought any of it was funny and that is what amused Shuzo. Mako found his repetitions irritating and Chiyo wondered why Shuzo kept it up for so long, as if he had to make sure that everyone knew he was the kind of man who took a wife.

A semblance of normality returned, at least in that no one tried to avoid the others. They ate and worked together and did their best to accommodate. At dinner, Chiyo regularly served Mako more beer than usual to force him to retire early. She had trouble dealing with his shifting moods as he decided at one moment to go home to his wife in Japan, for sure, no doubt about it, only to swing to an equally adamant conviction to stay with Chiyo. If she supported his return, he accused her of trying to get rid him, and when she told him how much she wanted him to stay, he charged her with having a callous disregard of his family feelings. There was no point in swinging with him on his pendulum of indecision, so she took advantage of his low tolerance of alcohol and the ease it afforded to send him straight to bed.

"Poor Mako," said Chiyo, after Mako had gone off to his room. "What do you think he should do?"

Miki looked bored and went to her bedroom.

"I don't know," said Shuzo. "I can see both sides of his argument. I feel for him."

"You do know why he's all worked up about this, don't you?"

"It's because of Hasumi. Mako's already feeling it just thinking about my wife coming."

"When is she coming?"

"There's no hurry. We have lots of time."

"You know what's funny about your joke about Hasumi? You're scared about her coming and want her to stay in Japan."

"What? That makes no sense. I … I…"

"You're as bad as Mako, only he lets it out. You say you want Hasumi to come, hah, but you don't."

Why is everyone trying to get me to make confessions? Josephine and Kamaki forced me to admit I made a mistake with Nozaki and now Chiyo is trying to make me say that I don't want my wife to come. I want Hasumi to come. I want to have children. For my parents' sake, for the Taga family.

"Hasumi is my properly registered wife and is the only one who can give birth to my children. You know how I feel about you, but you cannot be their mother."

"What a thought! Having your children?" She made a sour face. "And when she comes, what happens to me?"

"I told you. Nothing. Everything will be the same."

"Oh, Shuzo, you're just like Mako. He thinks his wife and I can be good friends."

"Well, that's not how it'll be between you and Hasumi. She doesn't have to like you, or even get to know you. Everything will be the same because you're both different to me. And we'll keep it separate. Most times her, sometimes you."

Chiyo got up and went to the sink to do the dishes. Mako and Shuzo were caught between two women, but Shuzo had a plan for having both, while Mako was confused about which one to pick. So clever, that Shuzo.

He came up behind her and massaged her back. She continued with the dishes and let his hands please her, knowing that everything he touches turns into his favor. And Mako, Miki and I too have gained so much from his hands. Without him, I'd be out in the fields, hoeing weeds, digging ditches, carrying cane. He bought me a new shamisen the other day, went all the way to Honolulu just to get it, a gift to you, he said, for the enjoyment of the men, meaning our profits. So clever.

She wiped her hands on her apron, turned around to face him and led him to their couch on the veranda. She pushed him gently down on his back and unbuttoned his shirt.

Miki watched. *Oh my goodness*, they're breaking the rules. Mako went to bed upset, his problem unresolved. They're not supposed to do it when Mako is feeling troubled. They made that rule themselves and now they're breaking it. This is great! They're crazy! Completely! Miki ran to her bed and buried her face in her futon to muffle her laugh. If Mako's happy, they'll do it. If he's sad, they still do it! Poor Mako. Lost his power. They're no longer his puppets. But here's what's really funny. Chiyo loves only Mako, not Shuzo. Listen to her. She's noisy tonight, but she's just saying thank you, thank you, thank you. What a way to do it! So sexy, gratitude.

Miki laughed some more, got a hold of herself and went back to her slightly open door. She looked out and had to rub her eyes to confirm what she saw in the dim lantern light. Someone was standing off from their couch, watching them. This is too much! This is so weird! She hurried back to her bed and grabbed a pillow to muffle her delight. She went back to the door and peered out again.

They were quiet and the man was gone.

◆

Colonel Kalama looked at the account books and shook his head. He pulled out a booklet of Cheval de Sultan, Italian rolling papers given to him by Tsar Alexander III at his coronation, carefully removed a sheet and counted the remainder. Only eight left, but the need to think clearly about a critical matter justified the depletion of his precious collection by one sheet. He reached for a tin of tobacco, his own premium brand, grown in the hotel garden, dried in the barn and chopped by hand. Wild Hawaiian Tobacco. Wild referred to the uninvited tobacco growing sporadically along roadsides, although he knew it had to come from someplace, India or Mexico perhaps, but wild could also describe the native self he fancied being underneath his cultivated urbanity. Licking the edge of the paper after rolling it was his favorite part of the ritual, the one time a man could expose his tongue and perform a delicate maneuver in public. By the time he had arrived in Moscow, he had practiced and perfected his style, and the ladies at court had admired the handsome native's mastery of their western custom and had slyly gone up to him to request a hand roll, which, they whispered, they would smoke later, perhaps when they could be alone together. Wild. Those were the wild days. From his office over the curved portico of the hotel, Kalama looked at the ocean, flat as a lake that day and sucked on his cold cigarette to draw in its aroma, then lit it with a flexible Diamond match. He shook the flame out at arm's length to minimize the smell of burnt phosphorous and leaned back in his swivel chair. Tension was bad for thinking and he had to relax to allow fresh thoughts to arise and solve the persistent problem. Expenses were too high, the head cashier had said over and over and had presented a plan for terminating a gardener, two maids and a desk clerk in phase one, which would be followed by shutting off electrical service to the rooms after eleven o'clock, reducing the size of the massive lawn and eliminating complimentary afternoon tea. Kalama blew out smoke and rejected the cashier's proposal for saving money by cutting back on services, the essence of a fine hotel. There had to be a better way of balancing the books.

It was so simple, staring him in the face unseen until his wild tobacco smoke lifted the veil. He sat upright, pulled himself closer to the desk and laid his cigarette in the slot of a crystal ashtray, another gift of the Tsar, to free his hands for pencil and paper. The cashier had already determined occupancy at an average of forty-one persons per day for the sixty-guest hotel but had not calculated the break-even point. Kalama scribbled some quick numbers based on keeping all services intact and concluded that if he could raise occupancy to forty-eight persons, the books would balance. Anything above that was pure profit. All he needed was seven more daily guests and the way to accomplish that was to *increase* the hotel's attractions, not cut back on services. And for that, he went to see Shuzo.

The Taste of Death at Restaurant Danger had gained in popularity and the hotel staff reported that guests often talked about it as the high point of their stay. The suspicion of Japan's rising military power had been confirmed, but her victory over Russia transmuted that fear into respect and a necessity of acceptance. Like it or not, Japan was a world power and it was better to be her friend than enemy. Shuzo was openly touted as a Japanese chef, a master of an inscrutable Oriental art, and the hotel guests welcomed the opportunity for a firsthand experience of something authentic from the country of little yellow people working military and industrial miracles without sacrificing their ancient wisdom. Shuzo's work was guaranteed, but if by chance anyone died from the supposed fugu, Colonel Kalama would say seriously with a hint of condolence, that they would get a full refund back.

Shuzo added drama with demonstrations of the fugu's poison. Once the guests had settled down, he started his patter about the fish and passed around two dried specimens, one of normal size, the other its inflated version. When the spiny fish with its childlike eyes reached the inevitable woman who refused to handle it, Shuzo praised her caution, saying that those who had touched the spines were already infected with the residue poison—which caused whoever was holding it to drop it and the others to look worriedly at their hands. Those who had handled the puffer fish were alarmed by the tiny red spots on their palms and Shuzo let them sink into their fright for a few minutes before revealing the dots as pigments applied to the spine tips before the show. Their outburst of laughter was driven as much by relief as by the joke, and Shuzo made them solemnly swear not to tell anyone else about it, lest they spoil the effect. "Incredible," they would say cryptically to guests back at the hotel, "but you've got to experience it yourself," thereby preserving the joy of secret privilege.

The next demonstration had no trickery about it. Mariko Mahealani brought out a clear glass bowl, set it on a stand, then slipped her graceful hands off the bowl to reveal brightly colored fish swimming in the water. She exited with a gentle sway, then returned with a small vial and a toothpick. She handed the vial to Shuzo, who held it up for everyone to see the small amount of bile extracted from the liver of a fugu. "This," he said, "is the taste of death." He took the toothpick, dipped one end into the bile and stirred it in the fishbowl. One by one, the fish stopped swimming and sank to the bottom of the bowl. "What you have just seen," he said to the solemn group, "you may tell to your friends."

After serving miso soup, or corn chowder if they preferred, Mariko Mahealani brought out sliced fresh fruit, chicken cooked in coconut milk and taro leaves, baked bananas sprinkled with raw sugar straight from the mill and roasted sweet potatoes. The fugu was nearly a dessert, a final delicacy to top off the meal. Shuzo made Mariko Mahealani wait with the tray of small dishes of the cooked fish, while he explained the lineage of the recipe he used to add the liver bile with such miniscule exactitude it was safe. "You will detect a slightly bitter taste," he explained, "and that is the taste of death. But I should tell you from past experience that some people never taste it at all. It all depends on your moral character." He signaled Mariko Mahealani to serve the potions and everyone stared at the tiny plates, weighing the risks of the known poison with the chef's assurance of safety. They poked at it with their forks, sniffed it and started an exchange of nervous challenges. "If you go first, I'll follow you." "Go ahead, dear," wives would tell their husbands, "try it." And someone, usually a husband, would try it, chewing slowly in search of the bitter taste, which, after much trial and error, Shuzo approximated with the juice from crushed guava leaves added to the 'āweoweo.

The formula worked and guests returned satisfied with having been allowed into a sanctum opened exclusively for guests of the Haleiwa Hotel. This was not the usual passive entertainment for spectators but required an active commitment of nothing less than their lives. They had earned the right to taste death and treasured it as a badge of daring and personal trust in a Japanese chef, the one from the country that beat the Russians. We actually met him, spoke good English too. In fact, he served us personally. Remarkable man. Truly remarkable. Placed our lives in his hands. The taste? It can't be described. You'll have to try it for yourself. And, oh, that waitress; she was something else.

Kalama loved to listen to the guests talk about it and some went back again. But the occupancy level at the hotel stayed the same, hovering at an average of forty-one. Seven more, just seven more. Kalama needed something special and remembered Shuzo telling him about a man who had survived death.

"So, it was not just the bitter taste, but he actually died?" Kalama asked Shuzo for clarification.

"Well, I wasn't there," he explained, "my father was. But from what my father's friend told me, the guy stopped breathing and his heart stopped. But he got up again."

"That would be so spectacular. Do you think you could do it?"

"It just matter of finding right dosage. Of course, we need somebody try it out first. How about you? If you die, I give you your money back."

"Oh, so kind of you," Kalama said. "But seriously, think you could do it?"

"We need experiment on animal. Dog too small, horse too big. How about a goat?"

"Done!" said Kalama. "I'll get you a goat."

Dear Shuzo:

I cannot tell you how lucky I feel to have a daughter-in-law like Hasumi. It's quite rare. Most women I know have trouble with the wives of their sons. But Hasumi is like a dear friend, all the more remarkable and delightful for her being so much younger than I.

We were repairing some of my old kimonos one day and I told Hasumi of the women I knew who lamented their lack of skill to repair their old kimonos. She suggested we start a little business and already we have several customers and more inquiring. She has a good business sense, just like you, and I think both of you will make such a fine couple. She is anxious to join you in Hawai'i, but in the meantime, we are enjoying ourselves and I will truly miss her when she leaves.

Your father has fallen into his depression again and mopes around a lot. He worries all the time. Lately, he's been upset about a certain Miki. I don't know why he thinks this, but he's worried that some girl named Miki followed you to Hawai'i. He keeps mumbling things about Miki. I don't understand but he won't answer my questions. The only thing I know is that you have to take care of this Miki. Your father won't tell me anything and, frankly, I don't want to know anything about this. Just make her go away. I won't say anything about this to Hasumi.

I imagine that the house you are building for Hasumi must be nearing completion. For her sake, I hope it will be done soon. For my sake, well, you know how I feel.

Mother

That bastard Mako! He wrote the letter to Father after all. Well, he didn't write it, that illiterate fool. He got someone to write it for him, but it's his letter all the same. I thought we had an agreement. He was upset about finding Chiyo and me on the couch the other night, sneaked up, stood there watching and later threatened to let Hasumi know about Chiyo. He went so far as to say he'd let Father know all about Miki, about how I made my money pimping her. But who is he to talk like that? I told him I would write a letter to Shizuka and his daughter Yuki too and tell them what kind of husband and father he is. With an Okinawan woman at that. I reminded him that I didn't have to ask anyone to write for me. I pulled out a pen and paper right there in front of him and he backed down, knowing he was no better than I. And so we agreed to drop the matter, but he went back on his word and told Father about Miki. How else would he have known? And now Mother is upset, telling me that I have to "take care of this Miki." I hope Hasumi doesn't find out. Damn Mako! Blabber mouth.

Shuzo went to the restaurant and called Mako to meet him in one of the empty rooms. Mako didn't appear right away and Shuzo went back for him, telling him the matter was urgent. So was the preparation of the 'āweoweo for the guests from the Haleiwa Hotel, and Mako accused Shuzo of not caring about the restaurant. "I have to do all the dirty work around here," complained Mako. "Prepare the menu, buy the food, oversee the cooks, break up the fights and — bet you never thought of this — put up with Miki's staring. You act like the boss, but you've been spending less and less time with your business. Been running around too much with Josephine's son, that half-breed artist. If he were younger, I would've thought you were the father. Ha! What's it like to take Josephine to bed? If she happens to roll over on you, you'd be crushed to death."

"Shut up, Mako. If you were younger, I'd kick your ass. You're lucky to be an old man, lucky I have manners enough to respect the elderly. I'll be waiting in the room."

Mako entered the room and stood by the door. Shuzo told him to shut the door and take a seat. Mako didn't move. "Let's keep this short," he said. "I don't know about you, but I'm busy."

Shuzo held his mother's letter out in front of him. "My father found out about Miki and now they're asking about her. Why did you tell them about her?"

"I didn't. Never sent a letter."

"Liar. We agreed not to write letters about, well, our involvements here, but you went ahead and got somebody to write a letter for you about Miki."

"Why would I do that?"

"You're asking me? Ask yourself! Could it be, you want to get back at me because of Chiyo? I thought we settled that."

"I'm not that stupid. Think. If I sent a letter to your folks, you'd write one to Shizuka about me. You're thinking about that right now, I bet."

"Well, then, how did they find out about Miki?"

"Everybody here knows about Miki. Any one of hundreds of people could have written to them."

"People here know Miki but not my folks. They don't even know where I'm from."

"So how did your Father find out?" asked Mako, genuinely wanting to know.

"So you really didn't tell them?"

"Look, Shuzo, for the last time, no. Now I'm busy. You can believe me or not. What do I care. I'm sick and tired of this place. Of you and everyone else. You can have that slut Chiyo. I'm going back to Shizuka." Mako went back to the kitchen and Shuzo let him go.

Miki had moved from her chair and went into the hallway where she heard their argument. Why did Mako tell Shuzo's parents about me? Didn't he know that Shuzo wants to keep me a secret? What kind of a friend is he anyway? He's a weasel. Mako's not to be trusted. He's trying to destroy Shuzo, but I can't let him do that. Not before I get his heart back.

◆

276

Shuzo arranged for Kamaki to have lunch with Miki at the restaurant. After brief introductions, Shuzo left them alone. Kamaki had a small pad of paper and two pencils stuck in his thick hair over his ears. They sat across from each other and Miki couldn't take her eyes off Kamaki with his two pencils sticking out like the horns of some demon. He had come from Uncle Hila's and he smelled of animals and crushed flowers, a combination setting him apart from other men. His was not the simple smell of the field laborers, or Jerome, or Shuzo. Kamaki did not fit into anything she had known and she could not tell if he was cruel or kind, devious or honest, Japanese or Hawaiian. His thick beard and mustache formed a mask, but his lips were delicate and his eyes were like the two stars in the tip of the Scorpion's tail.

After lunch, they walked over to the house being built for Hasumi. The walls and roof were up and the carpenters were nailing battens over the butt seams of the one-by-twelve fir siding. Where they had finished, a painter brushed on a dark green, leaving the window trim for white. Miki watched the workers and Kamaki watched her. When he saw her lose interest, they walked toward the plum forest and followed the single trail leading to the river.

"Do you talk?" asked Kamaki. She didn't reply and he accepted her shyness, something he knew well himself. "Let me explain what I'm doing. I'm a painter and Taga-san has asked me to do a portrait of you. But in order to do that, I need to get to know you, to find out who you really are. Your face is very pretty, but I want to portray the real person inside you."

She stared at him. His Japanese is so smooth.

"I've got an idea," he said. "I'll do a quick sketch and show it to you. You can tell me if you think I've drawn an accurate picture of you. So sit down right here on this log and I'll sit over there."

Kamaki opened his pad and started sketching her features as he saw them, not trying to portray the character he had yet to discover. It was a flat drawing without shading, a bare outline of her face, falling strokes for her hair, long thin eyebrows, almond eyes, straight nose and lips that he could not get right. He looked at it, made a few additions and was satisfied with it as a starter. "Let's begin with this and you can tell me what to change." He sat next to her on the log and showed her the sketch.

Miki put a hand over her mouth and studied every line. Everything right, nothing to add or take away. He knows me perfectly. Incredible. She looked at him, trying to believe her good fortune. He's so rare, not even Shuzo knows me this well. And I like his smell, animal fur and crushed flowers. He knows me, like the cat. His eyes — how strange, just like the cat! The cat can look like stars or this painter, but it's the same cat. I can tell that this boy's heart was once cut out, but he's recovered and he's kind. He's not weird like the rest. And most of all, he's patient, pays attention to me. He knows me because he wants to know me. This cat is in love with me.

"It's beautiful," she said.

He pulled himself straight and looked at her. "So you do talk."

"Well, I like cats."

"I do too. But they are the hardest to paint. Goats are easy. They're hungry or sleepy, irritated or happy and always trusting. I've never seen a goat afraid. Angry, oh, they can get angry and fight, but never afraid. But cats are hard to figure out. Maybe I just haven't spent enough time with them."

"You're a cat."

Kamaki grinned.

"There!" she said. "Just like that."

"No one's called me a cat before."

Miki took the sketch from him, turned it over and raised it to her face like a mask.

"Looks just like you!" Kamaki said laughing.

She put the sketch down and was smiling, almost laughing. She turned the sketch over again and put it against his face.

"How do I look?" he asked, his voice slightly muffled by the paper.

"Like a cat," she said, removing herself from his face.

"So, do you think of yourself as a cat?" Finally, he thought, I'm getting beneath the surface.

"I like cats. I can tell them everything."

"Then tell me, Miss Cat, let's see ... who is your best friend?"

"You."

"Really? How about Taga-san?"

"He used to be my best friend, but now it's you."

"But you hardly know me. I can't be your best friend."

"Shuzo protects me and I trust him. But he doesn't love me. He loves Chiyo. And he's not a cat. But you, you're different."

"Different? How?"

"You love me."

Kamaki stood up. This was not what he wanted to find out about Miki. Like everyone else, he'd thought her strange, but what's this about both of them being loving cats? He had played along with her, but did not expect to become part of her delusion. He had to put an end to this right away, before it got out of hand, to make it absolutely clear that he was not in love with her. He sensed her fragility and he needed to tell her gently but in no uncertain terms. Kamaki sat down next to her again.

"Miki, you need to understand something. I don't love you. I..."

Miki put her hand over his mouth. So wise, so incredibly clever, saying you don't love me so that no one will ever find out. No need to tell me, Kamaki, I already know you love me. So sweet of you to say it that way to keep it a secret. I know it's not easy for a man to speak of love. You don't have to tell me what I already know.

She stood up and sat on his lap, cradled his neck with her arms and placed her head on his shoulder. Kamaki wanted to push her off, but he was swept by instincts. He didn't love her, but he couldn't resist a sudden urge to lie down with her, on her, to follow her directions. He'd never been alone with a girl before and Miki was taking the lead, pressing herself on him, caressing him, breathing in his ear, feeling him, masterfully. He knew it was wrong, but he was helpless against his own desire to take what she was giving.

It's just like the day Jerome carried me away from Fujita's house, only this forest is quiet and no one is watching, no girls hoping to take my place. I have him to myself and he will not betray me like Jerome did, wanting to cut out my heart. Shuzo used to love me, but now he wants Chiyo, but Kamaki, oh Kamaki, your smell is so different. You make me feel different. No one has made me feel this way. They all think I'm strange. The fools can't fool me. And now I know, for the very first time in my life, how it feels to be loved, truly loved, not just valued for business and it's so clear, so very clear that Shuzo never loved me, he's been using me, taking advantage of me, making money off me, not like Kamaki, who just wants to get to know me for who I am. So pure of heart, thank you, Kamaki, for opening my eyes. Why didn't I see it before? About the others, they're all like Jerome. They all want to cut out my heart! But not Kamaki. I'm drowning in you and if I'm not careful, I will throw all of my good sense away and do something I might regret. But I trust you and you'll do more than protect me. You're different because you love me. I love you. I'll do anything for you. The smell of crushed flowers hiding your love too precious to declare out loud. You're making me lose my mind.

Miki started to cry and Kamaki rocked her tenderly like a child. "Don't cry, Miki, don't cry. Everything will be all right." Her sobbing slowed, finally stopped and then she was very still.

◆

"Sumiko! Sumiko!"

Hasumi rushed into Gombei's room. "Mother's out shopping. Can I help you?"

"Tea. I'm so thirsty." It was nearly noon, but he was still lying on his futon.

Hasumi came back with a pot of tea and two cups. She poured a cup for Gombei and helped him sit up. She poured a cup for herself.

"When are you going to Hawai'i?" he asked. He had just passed his fifty-first birthday, but he looked and felt like a useless man waiting to die.

"I don't know. Soon, I hope."

"Hasumi, be careful of Miki."

"Miki? Who is Miki?"

"A little girl, well, a woman by now. She's a wandering soul, a free spirit and I'm afraid she followed Shuzo to Hawai'i."

"How do you know this, Father?"

Gombei drank his tea too quickly and coughed some of it out. Hasumi took out a small hand towel and wiped his mouth and the tatami mat. "My pillow, fix my pillow." She helped him find a comfortable position and he closed his eyes. Hasumi was determined to call the doctor, though his last examination had revealed nothing wrong, no physical reason for his weariness and melancholy. "He needs to have a positive view of life," the doctor had said as they were leaving. "I suggest a trip to a nice hot spring, or the seashore, or both." But Gombei refused to leave the house.

"Who is Miki?" Hasumi asked Sumiko when she returned.

"Did Father tell you?"

"Yes, but not much. Apparently, she followed Shuzo to Hawai'i. That's all he said. Do you know anything about her?"

"No more than you."

"I guess I'll find out when I go to Hawai'i."

Sumiko didn't want to hear any more about it and quickly went to her room to change. This Miki must have fallen for Shuzo and it sounds as if they are lovers. But it makes no sense. She looked in the mirror and hated herself for not telling Hasumi about Shuzo. Gombei doesn't know what he's talking about, he's confused and making things up about an affair between some girl and Shuzo. They can't be lovers, unless he's changed. From the time he started school, he never showed any interest in girls, even when his friends started to show off to attract their attention. Normal, at first, but as he grew older and became obsessed with soldiers, she knew — and how she hated to think of it—that he was like those samurai warriors who preferred their juniors. Of course, she had no proof and knew she could be mistaken, wished she was mistaken. Mothers think they know everything, but sometimes they're wrong. That's why she wouldn't say anything to Hasumi, why she was distressed about Gombei's mention of Miki. Now Hasumi is worried that Shuzo has a mistress, but he's not like that.

Sumiko changed her clothes and went to the kitchen. Hasumi was sitting at the table reading a book. "What are you reading?" she asked.

"*Treasure Island*. It's an English story and the translation just came out. It's so exciting. I wonder if there are pirates in Hawai'i."

"Hasumi, I want you to know something before you go. I'm pleased that you are fond of Shuzo, even if you've never met him, but Japanese husbands, they're not like American men, they don't show their feelings for their wives. So if Shuzo seems cold and distant, it's just normal. Marriage is a duty."

"I know that, Mother. I don't expect him to love me. Do you think he loves Miki?"

"No. I don't think there is a Miki. Gombei is just confused about a little girl he knew, and, well, you know how he gets depressed and worries about things that are not real. Miki lives only in his imagination. And besides, Shuzo has no interest in … well, never mind."

Hasumi looked puzzled but it was easier to agree than to figure it out herself, and surely Sumiko knew her husband and son better than anyone else. She smiled and said, "Mother, I think you'd like *Treasure Island*. I'll give you the book after I'm done and then we can talk about pirates."

◆

Kamaki told Shuzo he couldn't do Miki's portrait because he was still confused about her character. She had said she was a cat, but what did that mean? He couldn't just draw whiskers on her face. The other problem — and this he did not tell Shuzo — was his confusion about his own feelings for her. Shuzo suggested that he watch her dance on Sunday at the theater and join the rest of the men in trying to figure her out. He might even place a bet.

Chiyo was already on the stage when Kamaki arrived. The benches were already filled and Kamaki stood to one side so that he could watch the faces of the audience as well as Miki's dance. After *Five Daughters and One Son*, Miki walked out and stood in the middle of the stage and didn't move. Chiyo plucked three notes slowly, over and over.

Miki spread her arms straight out to her sides, flipped her palms skyward, then brought her stiff arms together in front of her and clapped three times, calling the Shinto gods to bless her marriage to Kamaki. She walked toward Chiyo and grasped a plate of matrimonial food, returned to the center and knelt on one knee, setting the plate reverentially on the floor. After repeating the offering three times, she offered a small cup to her new husband and he took it, holding it steadily in front of him as she poured sake into the cup from a porcelain bottle. He lifted it to his lips, his delicate lips and tipped his head back slowly. They reversed their roles, he pouring, she drinking and they exchanged cups three times. They pledged themselves to each other, promising to exist as the sun and moon, mountains and rivers, the fifty red oaks and the eight mulberry bushes. She let her new husband walk off the stage first, then she followed him into the wings. It was over and she and Kamaki were joined in the traditional wedding ceremony. Chiyo slowed her plucking and stopped.

Mako went into the audience to collect wagers and the men started their usual arguments. A bit boring, one complained, but another pointed out that an exciting performance was no easier to interpret. It didn't take long for several to suggest that it was a wedding ceremony, the triple exchange of drinking sake being fairly obvious and in no time everyone agreed. There were no alternatives given and they congratulated themselves on their consensus. Shuzo declared everyone a winner and splitting the pot meant that everyone got back what they had put in, minus, of course, the house's service fee. A few men grumbled about how it was no longer much fun and Shuzo wondered if modern dancing had run its course.

In the wings, Miki was radiant. Chiyo tried to get her to leave, but she wanted to sit alone. Shuzo went up to Kamaki and asked him if he had gained any insight. He shook his head. "A wedding ceremony?" he said. "What was that all about?"

"I think," said Chiyo, coming off the stage with her new shamisen in a cloth bag over her shoulder, "she was getting married to Shuzo."

"Don't be silly," said Shuzo. "I'm already married. I think she was playing Chiyo's part in getting married to Mako."

Miki covered her mouth to keep from laughing out loud. They were all wrong, telling each other their usual fantasies. Before I met Kamaki, Chiyo could have been right: I might have been dancing my marriage to Shuzo. But now I am Kamaki's wife and I can never marry anyone else. They have no idea what they're talking about, but that's good, because if they ever found out about us, they'd be jealous and who knows what they'd do to hurt us. It's a secret, a really big secret and Kamaki's not taking any chances, telling even me that he's not in love. Hah, we have them fooled. Completely. They know nothing, nothing whatsoever about Kamaki and me. Only the gods know and to them we pledged to love each other forever times three over.

THE CHOSEN MAN

I T ONLY TOOK ONE GOAT FOR SHUZO TO FIND THE RIGHT DOSAGE. Colonel Kalama never told Uncle Hila the real reason for purchasing the goat, the largest one he had, though he couldn't see any difference between sticking a knife into its heart or feeding it fugu poison. Shuzo started with a low dosage and when the goat didn't die, he waited a few days to let the poison clear out of its system before increasing the next dose. He kept careful notes of his measurements, noting the goat's reaction. At the lower levels, he thought he detected a bit of euphoria, but as he crept closer to the fatal point, the goat, a tough billy almost as heavy as a small man, stamped madly with irritation until the poison wore off and finally, with the dose increased by a drop, it convulsed and died of respiratory arrest. Shuzo drew a circle around the amount given previous to the last and determined that to be the point at which a man could survive death. "See here," he said triumphantly to Miki, who had watched it all, "I've found the exact amount." He kicked the goat gently, watched for signs of life, then realized he had no idea of how to get rid of the carcass.

"Ah, Kamaki, just in time!" Shuzo waved to Kamaki and called him over to the small yard behind the kitchen. Kamaki set down his box of paints, squinted against the sun and saw Miki. He hesitated, then noticed the dead goat still tied to a stake.

He ran over, leaving his paints on the side of the road. "What happened? Uncle Shuzo, what happened to the goat?"

Shuzo beamed. "It died in the service of science. I used it to find out just how much fugu poison to use."

"You poisoned it? Then no one can eat it. You killed it … for nothing?"

"Not, for nothing. To find out the right dosage for a man."

"But he was my favorite billy." Kamaki dropped to his knees and cradled the goat's head. Miki walked over to them, knelt and stroked the goat's back. Oh, Kamaki, don't cry. I would comfort you, hold you in my arms, but we can't let our secret out. Most of all, not to Shuzo.

"Oh, it's just a goat," said Shuzo. "Don't be silly."

"A waste, killing for nothing. You shouldn't have done it, Taga-san."

"Now wait a minute. Don't tell me what waste is. I paid Uncle Hila good money for it, for a good purpose. It was mine and I could do what I want with it. You wouldn't want me to experiment on a person, would you?"

"Lepo, oh, Lepo. I'm sorry. I should have been here." Kamaki placed his cheek against the goat's forehead and swayed gently.

"Well," said Shuzo. "If you love that shit bag so much, why don't you give it a decent burial?"

Miki jumped to her feet and stared at Shuzo. She ran back to the kitchen. Shit bag? Is that what he said? Where's that lye water? I'll wash his tongue. She looked in the closet where the cook kept his spices and chemicals and grabbed a bottle labeled Vitriol, a word she could not read, even if it had been written in Japanese. She nearly bumped into Shuzo stomping through the door and she unscrewed the cap and tried to tip the bottle into his mouth.

"What the…? Miki! What are you doing?" He grabbed her hand and took the bottle away from her and held it high and away as she kicked his shins. Kamaki ran toward them. "Stop it!" Shuzo shouted, pushing her away with one hand as he tried to control the uncapped bottle with the other. He stretched his arm as far as he could behind his back and overturned the bottle, right onto Kamaki's head. Kamaki screamed, slapped his open hands to his face and screamed again as his palms puddled the acid onto his face.

◆

"Open your eyes," said Josephine. "Can you see?"

Kamaki nodded.

"Good thing you had shut your eyes."

She dabbed the aloe stem on his burned forehead and cheeks, but his lips, once so fine, were too blistered to touch. Back then, it had been the scorching sun and now it was acid, again because of what Shuzo did. Josephine cursed him repeatedly in Hawaiian but told herself it was an accident. Shuzo didn't mean to do it. Besides, Miki had grabbed the bottle.

Miki retreated to a corner in the garden. Of course, Shuzo hadn't seen Kamaki rush over to help her, but that had not been the problem. No, that was not the reason for the accident. It was all Shuzo's fault arising from his callous disregard of Kamaki's love for his goat. He had mocked Kamaki for his tenderness, thought nothing of how much Kamaki cared for the goat and could not understand — that shallow bastard — how an animal was worthy of affection. He's the beast, caring only for money, but not for any living being with feelings, real feelings. Shuzo would mock us if he ever found out about our love. He'd laugh and say how silly! His contempt for love, worse than acid. But, oh, Kamaki's face! His beautiful face! If only I could be Aunty Josephine touching his face with aloe.

Shuzo visited to apologize and insisted on calling Kamaki his nephew. Besides paying for his medical treatments, inclusion into the Taga family had to have some kind of soothing effect, even though Josephine wondered how, in that case, she would be related to Shuzo.

"If he's my son and you're his uncle, then that makes you my brother. Right?"

"Not necessarily," replied Shuzo. "I could be…"

"Aha! Yes, yes, you could be his father's brother. A Nozaki!"

"Stop thinking like American," Shuzo said. "I just his uncle, you know, in the Hawai'i way."

But Josephine kept on laughing.

◆

"Well?" said the cat. "How much longer are you going to wait?"

"I'll take care of him. Soon."

"What happened? He wasn't always this way, not at first, when he loved you." "Money, that's the problem. He only loves money."

"So what are you going to do?

"I will have to…"

"No," said the cat. "You can't treat him like a goat. I thought you were going to make him love you again, you know, get his heart back."

"Of course, I will. What a funny way of speaking, getting his heart back. But first I have to make him lie very still."

"Think about it, Miki girl. Think very carefully about doing this."

Miki laughed. "I have already. Do you think I would do it without thinking about it? You silly cat!"

◆

Daring! Incredible!

See the Master of Life and Death
prepare the deadly puffer fish!
Watch the Chosen Man
eat and DIE and come back to LIFE again!

A special event exclusively at the Haleiwa Hotel

Don't Miss It!
Saturday, June 13, 7pm
Haleiwa Limited Express round trip fare: $2
Special hotel rates: $3 per night, $5.50 for two in the same room.
Details and reservations at the OR&L terminal in Iwilei.

"What do you think?" asked Colonel Kalama, waving the poster.

Shuzo held it at the edges and read it. "Look good, but what is Chosen Man?"

Colonel Kalama straightened his cuffs and posture. "During the Napoleonic Wars, the British Army selected the best soldiers from the regiments and formed an elite group of riflemen. Each platoon picked their outstanding soldier to be the Chosen Man, an honor signified by wearing a white arm band. I thought it appropriate for our purpose. Are you ready to be the Chosen Man?"

"Yes, especially since he's really going to be Mako."

"Mako? Too scared to do it yourself?"

"No, of course not. You see, if I do it, people will say I fake it. Best to have someone else. You know who be best? Woodrow Davies. Or how about you, Colonel?"

"Are you kidding? I'd never risk it."

"You see," said Shuzo, "you believe it could kill you. But if I ate it, would you believe it as real as it would be for yourself?"

"Hmm, I'm not sure I get it, but, hey, the real question is does Mako know it."

"Not yet, but I talk to him. You think people come?"

"They will," said Kalama. "Woodrow Davies himself is pushing the event. He passed out these flyers to all of his acquaintances and he has lots of them. He's going to try to get the Governor to come."

"Good. Make it worth the trouble."

Kalama looked troubled. "Shuzo, just one thing. Why are you doing this?"

"Why?" said Shuzo, puzzled by the question. "Hmm, why, well ... because I know how do it, because ... it spectacular, and because, well, because you my friend and I want to help fill up hotel." Shuzo put his hand on the Colonel's shoulder and squeezed twice.

◆

Fortunately, Vitriol was a diluted solution, and Kamaki's face healed with light scarring. He soon forgot about the acid accident, but he couldn't get Miki out of his mind and told Josephine about the sketching incident in the plum forest. More than her make-believe about being a cat, her declaration of his love worried him. He was puzzled by her modern dance about an ancient wedding ceremony and did not know what to make of her inventiveness, her expressive license. Dancing should be rooted in recognizable styles, a genre or tradition and Shuzo calling it modern was just a way of saying it resembled nothing familiar. Miki was wild but fragile, and Kamaki was afraid to insist again that he did not love her. There was no telling what she might do.

"Just stay away from her for a while," said Josephine.

"How long?"

"I don't know, but she'll get over it. May take a long or short time, but she'll get over it. I did. With Colonel Kalama and Father Marcel."

"The priest? You in love with priest?"

"Well, that's just it. It was all in my head and I pretended they loved me, but it was just a fantasy. Miki will wake up to it and it will all go away. It happens to every girl. Several times over. Falling out of love is as easy as falling into it."

"But I like going Long Bridge. Best place for sketching faces."

"Maybe you could do some landscapes for a change. How about the hotel, or, better yet, St. Michael's? You could spend some time helping Uncle Hila with the goats."

"Guess so, Aunty. I haven't done church yet, or cemetery."

◆

After three days of waiting for Kamaki to show up at the restaurant with his pad and pencils, Miki began to worry. He used to come almost every day; something must have happened. No one knows about our wedding, but maybe they found out. They must have figured it out and now they know my dance was about Kamaki and me. And they're jealous. They're so confused about themselves they don't know who loves whom. Especially Chiyo. She's all mixed up. But now our secret is out, shouldn't have done that dance, and now they see Kamaki and me, our love, so pure, so perfect and they envy us. They can't stand to see us so happy and they want to pull us down to their level. No, it's worse than that. They're out to get us, to destroy us. That's it. Oh, no. No! No! They couldn't have! They took Kamaki away from me! That's why he hasn't come! Shuzo doesn't want anyone to know what he did to Kamaki's face. They're hiding him. Aunty Josephine must be in on it too. I've got to find him, save him from them. Oh, Kamaki, I'll find you and then we'll run away and hide. They're out to destroy us. Oh, Kamaki! They're going to cut your heart out. Damn Shuzo! I'll take care of him and then go and find Kamaki.

◆

Shuzo asked Mako to meet him at Hasumi's House, where it would be clear that Shuzo was married and no longer interested in Chiyo. Mako agreed, not because he no longer saw Shuzo as a rival, but because he too wanted to leave Chiyo and go back to his wife. They met with common interests.

"Remember when we first met on the train?" Shuzo asked, offering Mako a cup of sake.

"I prevented you from eating your umbilical cord," said Mako. "Dried cuttlefish, that's what we ate and fugu too."

"I've learned so much from you, Mako, and I want us to part as friends."

"Yes, let's drink to that." They downed their cups and refilled for each other.

"Mako, would you be willing to eat fugu again. As the Chosen Man?"

"You mean in the big event?"

"Yes, the big event."

"I thought you were the Chosen Man? Everyone thinks so."

Shuzo explained the problem of having people believe

that nothing would be faked, that if he did it himself and died, it would be suicide, but if someone else died, it would be murder, a greater consequence with higher stakes, real seriousness, not just a game. "Now, it's perfectly safe," said Shuzo, "you know that. But if by chance something goes wrong, then I'd be arrested and even executed, so you see, we'd be in this together. Equal risk for two friends. My life tied in with yours. Would you do it, for me?"

"What the hell," said Mako. "My whole life here makes no sense, except that I made enough money to buy out my father's debt. And that, well, I should say it clearly, I could not have done without you. So, all right, for you, Shuzo, for all you've done for me. I'll be the Chosen Man."

◆

Though he wanted to see the Chosen Man eat the deadly fugu, Kamaki decided to stay away from Long Bridge and spend the night with Unlce Hila at his hut while Josephine attended the event. Josephine and Kamaki left the house together, he heading toward the mountains and she to the hotel, where she caught a ride in the carriage Colonel Kalama had arranged for transportation to Long Bridge. She arrived at Restaurant Danger around six o'clock and as she had had an early dinner to save on the cost—a dollar for the show, three dollars with dinner—she went to see the progress of Hasumi's House, as everyone had come to know it.

"It's almost done," said Shuzo walking up behind her.

"Why, Shuzo, you look so relaxed. Shouldn't you be getting ready?"

"My part easy. Mako and staff are busy, but they have everything ready in time."

"I hardly see you these days, you're so busy. I don't think I've congratulated you on your marriage."

"Thanks, Josephine. As you see, Hasumi House almost done."

"You're going to have a large family. Mako, Chiyo, Miki and now Hasumi."

"Well ... yes, that's right." He caught himself in time, remembering not to say anything about Mako's departure. Mako wanted to keep it a secret so that he could simply slip away by himself. "Where's Kamaki? He come tonight?"

"He had to help Uncle Hila, but I can tell him all about it. Shuzo, I don't mean to imply that anything is wrong, but is Miki all right?"

"Matter fact, haven't seen her for few days. But she here tonight. Saw her moment ago, sitting in kitchen chair. She so ... unpredictable and does many strange things, but I no worry. She take care herself. Sometime she just disappear for a while, but she always come back. Why you ask?"

"Oh, nothing. Just wondered. I hear so many stories about her but can't say I know her at all."

Shuzo pulled out his watch. "Guess I should go to restaurant. Come, I give you good seat."

"It's too early. I didn't buy a ticket for dinner."

"Never mind. You must try food. Special tonight. My treat for my teacher."

Shuzo found a seat for Josephine next to Woodrow Davies's table. Woodrow and his wife were already there, along with Mr. and Mrs. Goodale. Shuzo introduced Josephine to them and Woodrow rose to kiss her hand. "I'm sorry," he said to Shuzo, "Governor Carter couldn't make it tonight, but he's sending his senior assistant to represent him. Now, what was his name? Oh well, I'll remember it before he comes." He sat down and saw Mariko Mahealani carrying a tray of water glasses toward his table. "Good evening," he said to her, "nice of you to be serving us again." She smiled, but he did not see it, as he was already asking Goodale about the building of the new dam.

Consul General Matsubara arrived with his wife and a few members of his staff, including Murakami, the stout official who had handled the Yukio Nozaki case. Good thing Kamaki isn't coming, thought Shuzo, not that Murakami would recognize him, but better not to run the risk. Shuzo greeted them and showed them their table and suddenly thought of the possibility that they, surely having had the real thing in Japan, might not be fooled by the taste of 'āweoweo. Too late now.

Several waiters went about the room lighting the kerosene lamps. As the light outside faded, the wick flames took over and the room turned a smoky orange and everyone picked up a ruddy glow on their cheeks. This gathering was another accomplishment, and Shuzo looked at the crowd, the rich, the powerful, the ordinary. Whatever happened to Horisho? If only he could see my restaurant now. And what about Boss Morita? And to think, he expected me to work for him. It seems so long ago, another life, a time when none of this could have been anticipated. Look at everyone here. The leaders and workers of Hawai'i. In my restaurant. I wish Jerome were here. We could have worked something out. Mako was standing by the kitchen door, waving frantically and, when Shuzo finally noticed, he waved back and the waiters and waitresses streamed out of the kitchen, balancing wooden trays crammed with dishes.

Smoked duck, roast pig, barbecued mountain doves, stewed chicken, baked sweet potatoes and breadfruit, wild tomatoes, broiled shellfish, steamed eggplants, poi, Portuguese sweet bread, purple rice, fried bananas, coconut pudding, Spring soda and Restaurant Danger's homebrew of beer and sake. Everything was jammed onto the tables, everything but the fish. "My goodness," said Mrs. Goodale to Shuzo, who was sitting next to her, "I've never seen a spread like this."

Shuzo winked at Mr. Goodale, excused himself and went up on the stage and pulled his written speech out from his pocket. "Ladies and gentlemen, let me interrupt you for moment. I want to thank all of you for coming, especially the Governor's assistant, Mr. and Mrs. Davies, Mr. and Mrs. Goodale, Consul General Matsubara and his wife and staff. I want you enjoy your meal, but first I make announcement. Mr. Goodale?" Goodale got up and joined Shuzo on the stage. The waiters scurried about the room and extinguished the lamps. A few people murmured in the dark.

Goodale cleared his throat. "Ladies and gentlemen, I shall be brief. As God said at the dawn of creation, let there be light!"

Mako flipped a switch and the room exploded with light from electric bulbs dangling from the ceiling. Waves of *ooohs* and *aaaahs* crisscrossed the room as everyone looked up at Edison's miracle. "We finished the installation only a few days ago," said Goodale, "and I'm happy to announce that Mr. Taga is our first commercial customer for electricity generated at the mill. We have plans to run lines to other areas as well." Everyone burst into applause and cheers, and Woodrow Davies couldn't help but say in a loud voice that the Haleiwa Hotel already had lights from its in-house dynamo.

"And now," said Shuzo, as Goodale made his way back to the table, "the taste of death. You are being served the deadly puffer fish, fixed with its own poison just to give you a taste, but it is safe. At least, no one has died yet." A few people twittered. "After you finish your fish, we move to main attraction, something more than taste of death, but a demonstration of death itself. Please enjoy your puffer fish."

Mariko Mahealani led her team out with trays of the prepared fish. Shuzo stepped off the stage, then turned around and mounted it again. He looked at the Consul General's table and said in Japanese that Hawaii's fugu had a different taste from the ones in Japan. The Japanese guests nodded appreciatively.

Shuzo went to the back room where Mako was changing into a fresh, dark shirt. He held out his hands toward Shuzo, who buttoned his cuffs.

"Ready, Mako?"

"Ready."

"Well, let's give them some time to enjoy their meal. Did you have anything to eat yet?"

"Been too busy."

Shuzo went to the kitchen and came back with two plates heaped with food. He opened two bottles of beer and they clinked a toast to each other. Shuzo was still in a reflective mood and he wanted to tell Mako how much he loved him, to reminisce about their past. Mako—father, brother, friend, partner—Shuzo had never been involved with anyone as intensely as he had with Mako. "Mako..." he said, but he couldn't bring himself to speak his feelings. Even with his most intimate friend, he retained a reserve, a mutual respect that allowed them to recover from their quarrels. Shuzo tried not to think of Mako's departure in two days on a ship to Yokohama. First, Jerome and now Mako. Maybe I could persuade him to stay, but that would be unkind to his wife and daughter. Mako's such a good man. What will I do without him?

Shuzo grabbed Mako's shoulder and reassured him. "Mako ... Mako, everything will be all right about the fugu. Trust me." Mako smiled and looked happy about his last act, certain that there couldn't be an alternative to everything being all right. "I'm ready," he said, wiping his mouth with a small hand towel, "let's go."

Miki slid off her chair and rushed up to Shuzo.

"Not now, Miki, I've got to get on stage with Mako." He leaned toward her and whispered, "He's the Chosen Man, you know, the one to eat the fugu."

"But, no, wait..." she managed, but Shuzo pushed her aside.

The two men walked out onto the stage. Shuzo called Colonel Kalama up to explain the meaning of the Chosen Man and Shuzo translated for the benefit of his Japanese guests. Kalama attached the white arm band to Mako's arm. Miki ran onto the stage and tried to tear off the arm band. What? What's going on? Isn't she the crazy dancer? Is this part of the show? Some laughed nervously, most were puzzled. Shuzo snatched the arm band out of Miki's hand and tossed it to Kalama.

"You see," said Shuzo, as he held Miki by her arms and started toward the wings, "she's worried that the Chosen Man will die." People looked at each other.

Kalama beamed. So clever, that Shuzo. It's all a set-up.

He'll do anything to make it look authentic. "You may be surprised to see Mako Toki as the Chosen Man," said the Colonel, "but tonight we will witness not just the culinary skill of the Master of Life and Death, not just the courage of the Chosen Man, but the remarkable friendship of these two men right here before me — well, as soon as Shuzo comes back — trusting their lives to each other. Ladies and gentlemen, I ask you: what could be more noble?" The audience broke into a hard applause and Kalama returned to his seat. Shuzo did not return to the stage.

Mako bowed to the crowd and everyone, the haoles included, returned his bow. He sat on the floor behind a low table. The room was hushed, except for sporadic coughing. The entire kitchen staff was lined along one wall. Mako closed his eyes in meditation. Mariko Mahealani disappeared into the kitchen, opening the door and allowing the sound of a hissing kettle to escape. She returned with a tray holding a dish of cooked fugu, a vial of the poison and a medicine dropper. Shuzo walked quickly back to the stage and pinched the vial between his thumb and index finger and held it up for everyone to see. Mariko Mahealani brought out a fishbowl with three mullet fingerlings and set it on a stand, and Shuzo, using exaggerated motions of a stage magician, squeezed some poison into the bowl with a medicine dropper and the fish plummeted lifeless to the bottom. He dipped the dropper back into the vial, sucked up more poison and gestured dismay — ah, too much — and squeezed some back, checking the level until he had the right amount. He held the dropper up against one of the electric lights and scrutinized its contents like a scientist using the latest technology, then squirted all of it on the fugu. Mako kept his eyes closed and Shuzo stepped to the side.

Useless daring, his mother Sumiko had said, of interest only to men. Kawa-san had taught them how to clean the deadly fish, there on the beach where they ate their fugu without an audience, so long ago. Kawa-san had sawn the tiller, angry at Gombei for cutting him out of their fugu partnership, only he didn't know that it was Shuzo who had forced his father into that decision. Until the fish agent told him the truth about the tiller, Shuzo had thought Nozaki was the culprit. I acted too hastily on what I thought I knew but really didn't. But that was long ago and tonight, I know exactly what I'm doing and Mako will go down to the door of death and come back—like what's his name? Sasaki—though he will not be a pretty sight. Daring, for sure, but hardly useless. Look at the crowd it brought out tonight. If only Father and Mother could see me now. This distinguished gathering, waiting to see this great thing I've done. Now it's up to you, Mako. Open your eyes and eat.

Mako opened his eyes and ate. He sat quietly, closed his eyes again and chewed slowly. Guests in the back of the room stood up to get a better view. Fifteen minutes passed and Shuzo wondered if he had put in enough.

"*Argh!*" He grabbed his throat and jumped to his feet. Shuzo was startled—this was the point at which he should have felt tingling and rubbed his hands together. Mako fell on his knees and whacked the floor with his open hands. Shuzo started forward to help him but stopped himself from showing any worry. Mako yelled again, eliciting small screams and gasps from the crowd. He grabbed his throat and started choking himself, spun around and kicked the fishbowl over, sending the dead fish sliding to the feet of those closest to the stage. "*Argh!*"

"Mako!" Shuzo rushed up and tried to pull his hands away from his throat. "Mako!" Several men hurried on stage to help Shuzo and together they wrestled Mako down to the floor, turned him on his stomach and pinned his hands away from his body so that he could breathe and retch. The audience fell into a disarray of not knowing what to do, watch or turn away, leave or stay. Mako heaved violently—pig, shellfish, sweet potatoes—everything and the fugu. Mariko Mahealani kept wiping it all up frantically. He continued to heave on his emptied stomach, writhing against the hold of the men and suddenly stopped as Mariko Mahealani screamed at the sight of blood trickling from his mouth and his eyes bulging wide open. The crowd stood still, immobilized by the same horrible thought and women started crying.

The men let go of his hands and legs and moved away from the body slowly, turning their palms up with shrugs to demonstrate their innocence. Chiyo broke free from her horror and threw herself across his back, sobbing uncontrollably. "Mako, Mako, wake up." Shuzo knelt by his head, placed a hand over Mako's eyes and wiped the blood from his mouth. "Mako, Mako." Chiyo wailed and sobbed uncontrollably.

Suddenly Shuzo looked up at the ceiling and pressed his fingertips more securely on Mako's temple. Chiyo sat up straight, looked at Shuzo, dropped her head sideways on his back again and listened.

"He's breathing," she said, just as Shuzo felt a pulse.

The men helped Shuzo turn Mako over on his back and Chiyo pressed down on his chest rhythmically, pressing air out, letting it in, until Mako coughed and opened his eyes. The men shouted and the women screamed, crying even harder. Mako asked for water and Shuzo collapsed.

"My God!" said Woodrow Davies. "This is nuts. I've never seen anything like it!"

Everyone started talking at once, repeating their declarations, trying to find different words to say the same thing. Incredible! Amazing! What a relief! Shuzo picked himself up slowly and several men helped Mako get up on his feet. He took a few wobbly steps, breathed deeply and everyone broke into wild applause. Colonel Kalama held up Mako's white banded arm. "I present to you," he shouted, "the Chosen Man!" Everyone cheered, the men stamped their feet and the rocking jubilance set the electric bulbs dancing at the end of their double twisted cords.

Mako was exhausted and had to be carried back to the house. Chiyo helped him undress, wiped his body down, put on a clean yukata and put him to bed. She sat at the kitchen table, sobbing between cups of tea and waited for Shuzo to return. It was past midnight when he finally came back and fell into a chair, ran both hands over his head. He began to shake and cry, still trying to get over his fear and relief. Chiyo ran her hand up and down his back.

"What happened?" she asked. "I didn't know Mako was the Chosen Man."

"I don't know," he said, rubbing his chin. "It wasn't supposed to be like that."

"Did you make a…"

"No! I didn't. It was the right amount. Everybody saw it."

"Let's not do this again. Ever."

"I don't understand. I didn't do anything wrong."

"Well, it turned out all right. Don't blame yourself. But this was enough." She poured more tea.

"That Mako," he said, "scared me to death."

"That Shuzo," she said, "*you* scared me to death."

They managed a quiet laugh signaling the end of their analysis. Chiyo finished her tea and walked off to her bedroom. Shuzo sat thinking of nothing. He dozed, too tired to get up and go to bed. That Mako. That…

Mako's death was a thrilling illusion. You see, I knew the right dosage and he only seemed to be dead. That's the whole point. You see, this thing fails if you don't think he's dead and it also fails if he doesn't get up again. Get it?

"Shuzo, wake up!" Shuzo opened his eyes and saw Chiyo, tears streaming. She was shaking him. "Wake up."

"What? Chiyo?"

She waited a moment to be sure he was awake, then sank slowly to her knees and buried her face in his lap. Her voice was muffled, but he heard her clearly.

"Mako's dead."

SPLIT FLOWERS

K AMAKI TRIED TO COMPOSE THE WHOLE NORTH SHORE onto a single sheet of paper. The Mokulē'ia coastline would go into the left third, the mill and the village in the center and the Kawailoa coast and highlands into the remaining space on the right. The foothills where he stood on the upslope from Uncle Hila's hut would sweep from the bottom into the central landscape, the distant shoreline and white caps at the top. The descending vista swept a plane away from him, but the painter had to compress it all into a vertical piece of paper. It was the painter's paradox of creating depth on a flat surface through tricks of color and perspective.

He started his sketch, but erased more than he kept, tentative squiggles, straights and curves resembling nothing of the fullness before him. Faces were so much easier, once he determined character, and therein was another paradox — abstract feelings were easier to portray than the concrete world around him. But the paradox was an illusion, the real problem was scale and size, not the tangibility of things. The up-close brevity of still life was a temptation, flowers and fruit ready to wither and rot, instead of the endless expanses of the living land and sea.

And yet distance stilled the panorama into a nature devoid of people, at least none that could be seen. The only sign of human activity was the smoke from the stack of the Waialua Mill, but the houses in the camps were like boxes fixed in the landscape. Buried in the silent scene were thousands of people, all within the frame of his vision and he was looking at them even if he could not see them. He had to think of the landscape as a face, had to find its character, the personality of all the people who together made it their place. Aunty was always trying to describe what was special about Waialua and she said it was its culture, whatever that meant.

And so he drew the mill, larger in proportion and shaded in more smoke than the thin wisp he could see. That was on the left. In the center, he outlined Restaurant Danger and the House of Eternal Pleasure, again outsized and Long Bridge leading to the Haleiwa Hotel on the edge of what was left on the right. Though he could not actually see Aunty Josephine's house, he knew where it was and he drew it in, large and lovely. In the rest of the in-between spaces, he placed tiny houses, splotches for trees, the other bridges, the ocean with whitecap dots and the sugar cane, miles and miles of smudged green. There, he had rendered the character of the landscape by selective exaggeration, Waialua, Kamaki's place.

And what about Miki? Taga-san still wanted her portrait. He leafed backward through his pad and found the loose sheet of the drawing he had made of her in the plum forest. A cat? A cat who thinks I love her? What am I to make of that? She thought the drawing was beautiful and she does have a pretty face. Maybe I could round the tops and bottoms of her eyes, drawing the lines to points at the sides, like that, there. The slight distortion frightened him, her eyes out of proportion, her face a feline transmutation and he slipped the drawing back into his pad and was frustrated by how she slipped away from every line he made to inscribe her soul.

◆

On the day Mako was supposed to have boarded a ship for Yokohama, his funeral was held. There were no Buddhist priests in Waialua and the one at the Aiea Plantation had another funeral to perform. One of the workers had had a few years of training in a temple back in Japan and though he had not been ordained, he knew some sutras by heart and could chant invocations for the journey to the other world. No one understood the meaning of his scriptural recitations and even he could not explain what he was saying, let alone be confident that he had chanted correctly. Sectarian affiliation did not matter on the plantation because most people had no idea what sect they belonged to and Sensei, as he was called, performed the same service for everyone. A sandalwood rosary, which he had made himself, a small hand bell fashioned from a brass pipe, and a narrow band of brocade draped around his neck signified his holiness. Though in his mid-twenties, Sensei still looked like a teenager, but once he began his ancient chanting, he embodied a thousand years.

Hundreds of mourners jammed into the yard behind Restaurant Danger. They stood with their heads bowed as Sensei intoned the strange sounds made familiar by too many funerals. He sat on a folding chair in front of Mako's plain wooden coffin, tapped his hand bell to punctuate his chant, a long, run-on sentence with commas for breathing and only one period at the very end. Wisps of smoke rose from a small bowl on a stand and he broke thin sticks of incense after lighting them in a votive candle and dropped them into the well-ashed bowl. Except for the incense and scriptures, everything was homemade and makeshift, the coffin, the rosary, the censor, the priest himself.

After the short service, they loaded the coffin onto Shuzo's wagon. Chiyo and Sensei sat on either side of the coffin and Shuzo took the reins. He kept the horse to a slow walk, allowing the crowd to follow on foot, and the long procession marched through the cane fields on the shortest route to St. Michael's integrated cemetery. Colonel Kalama, Josephine and Father Marcel were waiting at the church and joined Shuzo and Chiyo next to the freshly dug grave in the Japanese Buddhist section. Four of Mako's cooks lowered his coffin on ropes slung underneath and Sensei repeated his chanting. Father Marcel prayed quietly in Latin, another language beautifully intoned but not for ordinary understanding.

Kamaki and Uncle Hila watched from a nearby cane field.

Mako would stay in Waialua after all, another permanent resident in the cemetery, where the inhabitants of different ancestries and their discordant religions rested in harmony. Kamaki bowed his head to all of them, remembering the food he had stolen from them and thanked them all for their generosity. He wanted to join the gathering, but didn't want to run into Miki, even though he could not see her. "Goodbye, Uncle Mako," he said quietly. "After Miki, I wanted to paint you next."

◆

"Mr. Taga, please come with us." Sheriff Moses Brown and one of his constables approached Shuzo as he stepped out of the kitchen. Both were large Hawaiian men with wrestler arms filling out the short sleeves of their starched khaki shirts. Their wide leather belts wrestled with their waists, though the Sheriff showed his greater age in his softer girth. Their silver octagonal badges glimmered in the unlit room and they carried their visored caps in their hands. Shuzo had just talked with the cooks about the menu for lunch and had scrutinized them to see who would be best to succeed Mako as manager.

"What this about?" he asked.

"We're investigating the puffer fish death, and you'll have to come with us to Honolulu for questioning."

"But I not do anything wrong."

"We're not saying you did," said Sheriff Brown. "We just want to get the facts. We're not putting you under arrest. Not yet."

"Why not we talk right here?"

Sheriff Brown looked at his partner. "It's not the way we do it."

The constable took Shuzo by his arm and led him out to the waiting carriage. The entire kitchen staff watched quietly, then chattered excitedly among themselves and word soon spread that Shuzo Taga had been arrested for the murder of Mako Toki.

◆

Colonel Kalama called Woodrow Davies on his new telephone line to tell him about Shuzo's arrest. "This contraption is amazing," he told Davies. "You sound as if you're right here in the room." Kalama asked Davies to do something to secure Shuzo's release and reminded him that the Chosen Man event was designed to boost occupancy at his hotel. "We benefited from it," he said, "and we bear some kind of responsibility. Remember we promoted it heavily."

"Some kind of responsibility?" said Davies. "Maybe but nothing illegal."

"Of course not. But still…"

"Did you know Emma Louise passed out for a moment? She was horrified by the whole spectacle."

"That's why it was such a hit."

"James, I was fascinated myself, but Emma Louise said it was cruel. She has a point, I guess. If it's wrong to torture animals, she said, then it's worse to do it to men. She wants me to get the legislature to pass a law outlawing the consumption of puffer fish."

"But, Woody…"

"I know, James, you don't have to remind me about the hotel, but Emma Louise feels strongly about this one and I'll be damned to oppose her. Besides, she does have a point. I'll admit to that."

"So what about Shuzo?"

Davies chuckled. "Oh, don't worry about him, he'll be released. I needed information from him to draft the bill and I asked the Sheriff to do the interrogation. But you know Brown, he certainly likes that shiny badge of his."

◆

Josephine and Kamaki boarded the train bound for Kahuku. As the train pulled out of Waialua Station, Kamaki opened a map of O'ahu to chart their journey and was struck by how straight the coastlines were from Ka'ena Point to Waialua and from Waialua to Kahuku Point. Their village was at the pivotal ends of the two lines, which spread apart like a Japanese fan from point to point. The rest of the island's shorelines undulated in gentle curves or jagged erosions of land into the sea. The line from Waialua to Kahuku Point did have one indentation at the halfway spot in and around Waimea Bay. Kamaki looked out the window and could only see straight tracks ahead, rising up a gentle slope and disappearing over the top, a gain in elevation not shown on his flat map.

The train was half full and Josephine told Kamaki to move to a window seat on the left side of the car. The train dropped in speed as it started up the slope and as it reached the top a hundred feet above the sea, it made a sharp right turn onto a narrow ledge cut into the side of the cliff and the bay below came into view so suddenly in a deep emerald and blue, Kamaki let out a little cry. The engineer slowed the train to a crawl and everyone marveled at the sight of the wide beach of ivory sand far below, a gigantic mound of black lava jutting out of the water like a beached whale, its surface worn smooth by massive swells crashing around it and hitting the beach as walls of water flattening out on the sand all the way to the bottom of the cliff. After lingering as slowly as it could without stopping, the train rolled downhill into the bottom curve of the bay, where it crossed a bridge over the Waimea River and stopped to let off passengers eager for the thrill of standing as close as they dared to the foaming edges of the water flooding the beach and racing back into the ocean as a deadly undertow. Josephine and Kamaki got off and joined the few Hawaiians who went the other way on the path along the river to the settlement in the valley.

Since the valley was a conduit connecting mountain and ocean, it was perfect for habitation. The wild forests were tamed by generations of knowledge and were at once a garden, orchard, meat market and pharmacy. The ocean was a locker of fish, eels, shellfish, lobster, octopus, crabs and a wide selection of seaweed, all available according to wind and tide, season and skill. A steep, winding trail led to a high bluff affording a vista of the valley, the bay, all the way out to Ka'ena Point, nearly the entire North Shore coastline. No one remembered its exact origins, except to say that ancients had built a *heiau*, a shrine of descending earthen terraces outlined in long fences of stacked rock. In the days before the missionary religion, it had been a place for rituals, another kind of conduit connecting people with the gods. Though no one performed sacred rites at the heiau anymore, the spreading view of ocean, land and sky colored by the sun was exhilarating, and as panoramic as was the sight by day, it was on dark nights that one could see the farthest. A thousand stars shimmered just overhead in patterns that made people spread their arms far out and tell stories of pigs and sharks, wily and wise, of old men guiding canoes over epic distances by looking at stars charted in memory, of gods acting like men or women as they pleased. No Gothic cathedral trying to pass off a painted ceiling as heaven could come as close to the real thing at Waimea: a cosmic shrine made of earth and sky.

"Eh, Josie, *pehea'oe*? It's been so long. *Hele mai, hele mai.* Thank you for coming."

"So good to be back," replied Josephine. "It's been a long time."

A slender Hawaiian woman in her fifties like Josephine walked toward them and pressed her cheek against her old friend's face and did the same to Kamaki. She held him at arm's length to see him better, then pulled him into her warm embrace.

"So, this is Kamaki," she said to him and then to her. "Your new son."

"Kamaki," said Josephine, "this is Mele Pa. We went to school together. A long time ago." He smiled.

"I'm so glad you came."

"Well, I wouldn't have ignored your invitation," said Josephine. "It's not every day that your mother turns ninety."

"Other than having a little trouble walking, she's in good health. She's waiting for you." Mele Pa picked up the folds of her plain cotton muumuu and warned her guests to watch for mud puddles. Her hair was woven into a single braid, thick black streaked with gray. She led them to the first house at the head of the valley, an old, sturdy home posted the usual three feet off the ground, walled with planks and battens, roofed with corrugated iron, rusted, of course.

"This brings back such memories," said Josephine, as she stood on the steps. "I used to spend my summer vacations here with Mele Pa. We had so much fun. She was the ringleader. Knows every rock, kukui tree and ti leaf in the valley."

A white-haired woman was sitting in the tidy living room, reading the *Hawaiian Gazette*. She looked up and brushed the sleeve of her calico dress of patterned leaves in green and red. "Do I hear my Josephine?" she said, pushing her eyeglasses up her nose. "My long-lost Josephine?"

"Happy Birthday, Mrs. Akana." Josephine held the old woman's shoulders and gave her a kiss on the cheek. "You're looking well."

"You mean for an old woman of ninety."

"No, no, really. I hope to look as well when I turn seventy. What's your secret?"

"She's standing over there," she said with a nudging motion toward Mele Pa. "Never married, to take care of me." Mele Pa waved her hand, dismissing her mother's homage. "And," Mrs. Akana added, "no drinking or fooling around. Rev. John made sure of that at the seminary."

"Well, I never married too, but I want you to meet my hānai son, Kamaki."

Mrs. Akana stretched out both arms. Kamaki greeted her in Hawaiian, leaned down and received the woman's acceptance.

"He speaks so well! Where did you find him?"

Mele Pa winced and raised her eyes at Josephine. "Ma, it's not like Josephine just happened to find him like a stray cat or something."

"Well," said Kamaki, speaking before Josephine had a chance, "actually happened like that."

"It's a long story," said Josephine, "and I'll tell you about it. But first, my present." She handed a wrapped package to Mrs. Akana, who took it with her bony hands wrinkled with papery skin. She untied the string carefully, opened the cardboard box and pulled out a shawl. "Oh, it's so beautiful!" She ran her hands over the red and yellow knitting. "What's it made of?"

"Australian wool," said Josephine. "I knitted it myself, in the colors of a royal cape."

Mrs. Akana held one corner against her cheek. "It feels so good. Thank you, Josephine." She tried to put it on and Josephine helped spread it around her shoulders. "Do you remember, Josephine, when you almost drowned in the river out there?"

"I'll never forget."

"Good thing Papa was close by. He jumped in and grabbed you. The water was shallow, but you had panicked, and Mele Pa, screaming her useless head off."

"I was so scared," Mele Pa said. "It was all my fault."

"Papa carried both of you back here to the house. Both of you were shaking, more afraid than cold, and I wrapped you together in a wool blanket. It's still in there." She pointed to a wooden chest. "Mele Pa, would you take it out?"

The blanket was gray and thin, like old military issue of the kind rolled up on top of soldiers' knapsacks. She took it from Mele Pa and held it out. "I want you to have it."

"Oh, no," said Josephine. "It's ... a family treasure, I'm sure. Mele Pa should have it." Mele Pa winced again and shook her head.

"I'm not giving it to you, Josephine. It's for Kamaki."

Kamaki looked puzzled, uncertain about the significance of the gift. An old army blanket? That had once wrapped Josephine and Mele Pa? "Thank you," he said and looked at Mele Pa, who shrugged her shoulders.

"Time to eat," said Mrs. Akana.

"We have lots of leftovers from the party last night. The neighbors threw a big party for her birthday." Mele Pa went into the kitchen and Josephine followed to help. Mrs. Akana asked Kamaki to tell her about being found like a lost cat by Josephine.

"You'll have to tell me about that," said Mele Pa, unwrapping a dish. "I don't think I heard the full story. And speaking of finding someone, didn't you tell me that Kamaki is Japanese?"

Josephine put her finger over her lips. "Yes," she whispered, "and I'll explain to you later why we don't want to talk about that."

"Oh, sorry." She leaned closer to Josephine and lowered her voice. "So ... he speaks Japanese, right?" Josephine nodded. "Well, we need his help. Remember Loki, the guy we used to make fun of because of his lisp? He lives further in the valley and was out fishing at Kawailoa and he found this girl. Very pretty Japanese girl. She was sitting in the sand, talking to herself. Looked like she'd been crying. Definitely lost. Loki brought her back and his wife is caring for her. They're going to take her to the Japanese camp, but now that Kamaki is here, maybe he can talk with her."

"Do you know her name?"

"We wouldn't know it even if she said it. Don't know one Japanese word from another."

"I don't know," said Josephine. "It might not be good for Kamaki to talk to her."

"Oh, come on, Josie. You're always so cautious. Trying to keep him away from girls? I'll go get her and she can join us. No harm, right? Bet she's starving to speak with another ..." she lowered her voice, "Japanese." Just as she used to take off running and then yell back a challenge to race, Mele Pa wiped her hands and dashed out the kitchen door.

"Wait!" Josephine shouted, but Mele Pa showed only her back.

◆

Dear Shizuka,

By now you have surely received official notice of Mako's death. I was told by an official from the Honolulu Consulate that they listed the cause as an unknown illness. It came as a shock to all of us and I feel that I should explain some things.

Mako missed you and Yuki very much. He was always talking about you and always wanted to go home. I know you had agreed not to exchange letters and now as I look back on it, I should have been a better friend and offered to write his messages to you. He might have felt awkward about having to tell me his private feelings about you, feelings he couldn't tell you if he had been back at home. I am so sorry that you have spent years living without a word from him. I am writing now to tell you that despite his silence, he missed you very much.

In fact, Mako had made arrangements to go home. I was the only one he told about this, as he wanted to leave quietly and quickly. He had bought a ticket for a ship leaving Honolulu just a few days after he died. All he wanted was to be with you and Yuki. We had a big party for him and after that he went back to the house. Later that night, he died peacefully in his sleep. We could not understand why he died and even a doctor could not explain it. I am sure he was dreaming of you and Yuki.

He is buried in a beautiful cemetery at the foot of the tallest mountain on O'ahu. I have ordered a large headstone for his grave. Mako was my best friend and I miss him very much. We did so many things together. He was more than a brother to me.

Please send me your bank account number and I will transfer Mako's savings. Mako had enough to buy off his father's debt. I will add to that amount enough money for you and Yuki to come to Hawai'i for a visit. I am sure you want to visit his grave.

Please accept my deepest sympathy.
Shuzo Taga

◆

Even though he had never seen a picture of her, Shuzo had a definite image of Shizuka. Her favorite color was red, she was smart and liked to write poetry. He imagined her with long hair tied behind her back, her dark, thin brows over intelligent eyes. For several days after he mailed the letter to her, he added more details to his imagination, her devotion, hard work, pure spirit and she became so clear in his mind that he felt certain he must have seen her photo, though he could not remember Mako having one. As Shuzo imagined himself greeting Shizuka and Yuki at Honolulu Harbor and showing them around Waialua, he wondered if they would understand Mako's transformation from a simple farmer into the moody manager of Restaurant Danger and the House of Eternal Pleasure, working and living and sleeping with Chiyo, though he would never tell them that, and Shuzo wished he could retrieve his letter and cross out his invitation for them to visit.

◆

Mele Pa walked up the path holding Miki's hand. Josephine had suggested to Kamaki that he leave, but he thought it would be better to face her and work things out. It's too early, Josephine warned, she has to work it out herself and she hasn't had enough time. But it could go on for a long, long time, Kamaki replied, and he couldn't hide from her much longer. Josephine remained unconvinced by the time Mele Pa entered the yard and Mrs. Akana, happy with her royal shawl, had no idea what they had meant about "him" and "her."

Miki took off her sandals, stepped in the doorway and stopped. She stared at the apparition of her husband standing in the parlor and dropped to her knees. "Are you all right?" Mrs. Akana asked. "She only understands Japanese," Mele Pa explained. "Then ask her in Japanese if she's all right," said Mrs. Akana, not knowing that Kamaki had already done so.

"I think," said Josephine, "we'd better leave the two of

them alone. Don't we have more leftovers to fix?" Mrs. Akana said she would not be bothering the young couple by remaining in the parlor and Josephine promised to tell Mele Pa what was going on between Kamaki and the girl as they went into the kitchen.

"Are you all right?" Kamaki asked again, as he helped Miki to a couch. She wiped her eyes with her sleeves, looked at Kamaki and started crying again.

"Get her a towel from the bathroom," said Mrs. Akana.

Kamaki came back with a towel, handed it to Miki and sat next to her. She said nothing and Mrs. Akana, discomforted by the silence, gave Kamaki a look as if to ask if something was wrong with him. What's that English saying? Kamaki wondered. The one about a cat getting somebody's tongue? I hope Mrs. Akana doesn't say it. Not that Miki would understand, but I don't want the subject of cats to come up again.

"I was so worried," Miki finally said. "You stopped coming to the restaurant. I thought something had happened to you. Did they catch you?"

"I, ah, got busy with my painting and had no time to go to the restaurant. I stayed away … from it all."

"They sent Mako after you, to hurt you."

"What? Mako? No, not that I know of. Did you know that Mako … ah … passed away?"

"I saw the funeral procession. That's when I knew you must be safe, but I didn't know where you were. I tried to get rid of Shuzo, but Mako ate the fish."

"Get rid of? What do you mean?"

"Oh, you know, like what he did to your goat."

Is she saying what I think she's saying? Can't be. She may be crazy, but surely not like that. But, then, now hold it, wait a minute. She didn't get rid of Shuzo, but Mako ate her fish? No, it can't be. No way. Should I tell Aunty? "Ah, Miki, tell me, how did you get here?"

"After Mako ate the fugu, I wanted to get far away, just like you, away from them all. A fisherman found me on the beach while I was looking for you, and his family has been taking care of me. They're so kind. Oh, I'm so happy you're alive." She ran her hand up and down his thigh.

"Excuse me," Mrs. Akana said, pushing her eyeglasses up her nose, "but please, not in my house."

"Ma," said Mele Pa, coming out of the kitchen. "Ma, why don't you come into the kitchen? We need your help." Josephine stood in the doorway as Mele Pa helped her mother up and said to Kamaki in Hawaiian, "Be strong, my Naupaka."

"What did she say to you?" Miki asked when they were alone.

Kamaki told her the story of the naupaka flowers, half by the ocean, the other half in the mountains, lovers forbidden to be together, though they felt as one.

Miki was quiet and kept looking at the kitchen. That woman, she understands us exactly. Naupaka. Kamaki is safe now since Mako is gone. But Shuzo is still alive. It was supposed to be him, lying still in his bed, where I could get his heart back. But with Mako gone, he and Chiyo have each other and maybe they'll leave us alone. Or maybe not. If they find out we're married, they're going to get jealous again, so we've got to keep it a secret. Naupaka. As long as we pretend we're not married, pretend we're not even in love, they won't be upset. They're so envious of us. But we'll be naupaka, Kamaki in the mountains, me at the ocean, forever separated, forever in love. They won't even suspect. This is how I'll protect him. I'm ready to go back now. Ready to sit and watch again, just to see my husband once in a while will make me happy. Naupaka.

Miki lifted her hand off Kamaki's thigh and felt secure. No one would know as long as they remained separated. Naupaka. Kamaki saw the ease in her face, her pretty face, a girl, nothing more and the time was right to tell her again, to make her understand.

"Miki," he said, "please don't get upset and try to understand. But I must tell you that I do not love you."

Miki smiled. My silly Naupaka! Of course, I'm not upset.

It's you I worried about. People can tell when you're in love, but now I see you know how to hide it, even from me. We're safe.

CLEVER BASTARD

ON THE EVE OF SHUZO'S DEPARTURE FROM JAPAN TO Hawai'i, the reserve lieutenant in charge of the Army Youth League chapter in Iwakuni had presented a certificate of merit to Shuzo for having the highest score in tests about uniforms, ranks, military awards and discipline. The League was a civilian training program for potential officers and rewarded its best students with prizes and promises of a glorious military career. The lieutenant also had presented him with a gift, a small box wrapped in red paper. "Take this to Hawai'i with you and use it for your benefit," he had said, "and when you return, you'll be ready to join the army and become an officer." Shuzo had no idea what the thin rubber membranes were, rounded at one end and open on the other and until he met Mako on the *America Maru*, he thought they were specialty balloons, though they were not that easy to blow up.

The Japanese military issued rubber sheaths to every soldier and sailor and doubled the allotment to those going abroad. Venereal disease had become a major problem and the condoms were essential to keeping fighting men healthy and sated. Unlike the *kawagata* made of thin leather, the new condoms were soft and washable—until the rubber deteriorated—and like so much of the military equipment of the time, they represented the latest western technology imported from England and France. Soldiers valued their rations of rubbers more than medals and were forbidden to give them to fellow civilians, whose duty it was to produce as many children as possible.

Shuzo had little use for them in Hawai'i and gave them to Miki for her protection and to safeguard his lucrative source of income. They worked better than the engineer's cotton pads. Shuzo told her to be sure to get them back after each man's use and wash them out for as long as they lasted. As his wealth grew, he sent donations back home to the League and informed the lieutenant that the condoms helped make his financial support possible. Without asking for an explanation, the lieutenant periodically sent new shipments, and Miki, well supplied, never got pregnant. She was diligent and demure and was never afflicted by wild passions distracting her from proper preparation. She was a professional.

But Chiyo was not and she left it to Mako to remember the condoms Shuzo had given him. Shuzo disregarded them himself, believing that his lack of frequency lowered the odds to nothing, since conception, as Mako had experienced it, was really a thin matter of chance enhanced by repetition. Mako and his wife had never used contraceptive methods, and for all those years, the result had been but one child.

"I'm pregnant," Chiyo told Shuzo when he returned to Long Bridge after Sherriff Brown had released him from custody. Shuzo had been deeply embarrassed by the investigation into Mako's death and wanted nothing more than to be left alone. Without a manager, the cooks had serious arguments among themselves over petty issues and had it not been for Mariko Mahealani's skillful intervention, the restaurant might have completely shut down. Colonel Kalama no longer brought over guests and even the plantation workers, believing their own spiraling rumors, began to stay away. Mariko Mahealani's lovely presence was the only reason why a few continued to eat at the restaurant, but expenses exceeded revenues. The theater was dead and Miki had disappeared. Only a short while earlier, Shuzo had hosted the most powerful figures in society, and now everyone stayed away from Long Bridge and its dangers and pleasures. Shuzo could not wrap his mind around the sudden ruin of his miracle and while he heard Chiyo say something, her words were muffled in the din of his anxiety. Good horse, bad horse.

"I'm pregnant," Chiyo said again. They were sitting alone at the kitchen table. "Did you hear what I said?"

"It's all over," Shuzo said, looking at Restaurant Danger. "Our business is gone, Mako is dead and Miki is missing." He stirred his tea with a chopstick. "How did it come to this so quickly? It's over. I'm ruined."

"Did you hear what I said?"

"What?" said Shuzo. "I heard you, you're pregnant."

"What are we going to do about it?"

"We? It's your child, I mean, Mako's too. But I'll help you, of course, in whatever way you want. How do you want to handle it?"

"I want an abortion."

"There's nobody here who can do that. You'll have to go to Honolulu. I can try to make arrangements."

"Don't you care about the child?"

"Me? Why should I?"

"I think it's yours."

"That's a pile of shit! You and Mako ... all the time."

"But you never bothered to be cautious. And besides, I could tell. I know exactly when it happened."

"Liar. You're just trying to make me responsible because Mako's gone. Nobody can tell. It's a matter of chance. You're making it up."

"You're the father, I tell you, it's your child."

Shuzo shuddered. Things were bad enough and now this. Hasumi's house was ready, but she couldn't come until he could regain his footing. A minor delay, he hoped, a little setback, but he'd make the restaurant thrive again. He wanted Hasumi to see his success, his bloated bank account, and he planned on sending her enough money for a first-class cabin. Waialua was a plantation village, but it did have a fancy hotel, easy train access to Honolulu, and Hasumi would live as well as the Goodales, maybe better. Shuzo had contacts with people

318

of significance and once he revived his business, his next objective was to have children, descendants for the Taga family, well bred, educated, socially respected, raised by a sophisticated wife. There was no place for a bastard child, none whatsoever, especially one that was not even his, forced on him by a desperate, lying woman, once a friend, now a spoiler.

"Okinawan bitch! After all I've done for you. Take back your filthy lie or get the hell outta here!"

Chiyo got up, went to the kitchen and came back with a mango and a knife. She sat down and started peeling the skin in one long, unbroken strand. So deliberate, so contemptuous, a challenge he could not ignore, but as he got up, she said in a calm voice, "Sit down, Shuzo, and let me help you stop fooling yourself."

He slammed his hand on the table. "Don't ... you ... ever ... tell me what to do! You're the one who's trying to fool me. But I'm not falling for it. I know who I am and I'm no damn father of that ... that..."

"Okinawan pig? Excuse me, I mean, half Okinawan pig."

Shuzo reached across the table and whacked her across the cheek with his open hand. Her head snapped to one side and she held it there. She put the mango down on the table but held onto the knife. Shuzo stood up, grabbed the teapot and threw it against a wall. He reached out to take hold of her shoulder, but she held the knife up.

"Go ahead, cut me. You don't have the nerve."

"I wouldn't muck this place up with your filthy blood," she said. "But if you lay your hand on me again..." She put the knife down on the table and wiped her hands on her apron. She sneered. "What a mess is right. Here I am, pregnant, fucked by a fairy." She walked out.

Shuzo stood with his mouth open. There's no end to her wicked lies. Why is she turning against me? Where is all of this coming from? Why did she call me a fairy?

◆

For the next few days, Shuzo did not see Chiyo and he didn't care. Over and over, the same refrain ran through his mind. It always happened, never failed. You do somebody a favor and they shit on you in return. I did so much for her because of Mako, bought out her contract, gave her work, let her live with us, even gave my love to her and she turns around and calls me names, tells dirty lies. I should have known better than to trust an Okinawan bitch. I guess I was fooled by her, but not anymore. When Shuzo finally checked her room, he found it cleaned out and empty. Chiyo must have gone to Honolulu and if she knew what was good for her, she'd never come back, not to my house. Stinking pig. Well, at least she's getting rid of the child and I can concentrate on rebuilding my business. Hasumi will be coming soon. Chiyo—what a liar. Where the hell is Miki?

◆

Shuzo had learned to disregard rumors about himself and did not bother to set them straight. Several men from the irrigation gang said he kept his fabulous wealth buried somewhere in the plum forest and they actually went there to look for signs of freshly dug earth. Then there was the story about the fortune he had lost by investing in the failed Keihin Bank. He was, alternately, a heartless miser and a generous benefactor. Shuzo paid no attention to the tales of his rise and fall, but when he heard someone say they had heard another man say he saw Shuzo empty an entire vial of poison on the fugu fed to Mako, he tried to track the story to its source, but stopped when he overheard one of his own cooks say that his failure, no, even his attempt to find a culprit would prove the story to be true. Best to ignore all rumors, Shuzo concluded, whether it was about him or not, since by nature they were untrue and impossible to control. Open rumors were innocent though no less false and the ones passed on secretly in a small community, where confidentiality was frequently invoked but seldom practiced, just had to be tolerated. The easiest way of handling falsehoods was to ignore them.

It's a secret, a customer told Shuzo as he was paying his bill at the nearly empty restaurant, but there's going to be a sugar strike of Japanese workers at every plantation on the island — just the Japanese, no one else, not the Filipinos or the Portuguese and that's why you should keep your mouth shut. Of course, said Shuzo, smiling, while he counted the man's change.

◆

Mr. Goodale heard the same rumor and called Shuzo to his office. Goodale had been at the Sugar Planters' Association meeting a week earlier and had supported the unanimous vote to reject a Japanese demand for pay equal to what the Puerto Ricans and Portuguese were getting, twenty-one dollars a month instead of eighteen. The Japanese had organized the Higher Wages Association with representatives from all of the plantations on the island and were capable of calling a general strike. While the threat was unprecedented, the planters knew of the deep division within the Japanese community between radicals willing to confront the plantations and conservatives bent on conciliation. The Japanese language newspapers were evenly split and the planters counted on this rift and refused to negotiate.

"Is it true," Goodale asked Shuzo, "this thing about a strike?"

"I never trust rumors," replied Shuzo.

"But is it true?"

"If you hear the same rumor enough times, I suppose it might be true. Everyone's talking about it. That's all I can say about it."

"On our side too. At our meeting yesterday, all of the managers were talking about it. But no one's sure. We hear the Japanese are divided over this."

"That, for sure, is true. But what'll you do if there's a strike?"

"Same as everyone else," said Goodale. "Evict the workers from plantation housing and hope they come around as soon as possible. We're hanging together on this one and not raising your, I mean, their wages, period. It's not really a matter of money but of principle. We're not going to be pushed around by some loudmouth agitators like that Matsugoro Sato. We're keeping an eye on him. The sooner he understands our resolve, the better it'll be for everyone."

"Maybe I can help."

"That's what I was hoping you'd say. I trust you, Mr. Taga, you know that, don't you?"

◆

The Japanese workers at Aiea Plantation were the first to strike. Waipahu, Kahuku and Wai'anae followed quickly, as did 'Ewa and Waialua. Evicted from company housing, thousands of workers swarmed into Honolulu, where sympathizers put them up in homes and backyard tents. Workers from the outer islands sent money and food to the Higher Wages Association, which paid no attention to the proclamation issued by the Japanese Consul General calling for the strikers to go back to work and settle their grievances with the cooperative and respectful spirit inherent to the Japanese nation. He urged reconciliation and peace, even after the Planters' Association issued their own resolution never to increase wages for a race of workers lacking in ambition, responsibility and a willingness to do a fair and full day of work. They were by nature loafers and didn't deserve pay equal to the hard-working others.

Shuzo told Goodale to hold off on the housing evictions and asked a circuit riding Buddhist priest to talk to the workers. Eager to demonstrate a practical application of his faith in the compassionate Buddha, the priest was nervous but delighted with the chance to address the largest assembly he had ever faced. He got up on an overturned crate, chanted a mantra, sucked in his breath noisily between his teeth and started on a sermon to the men and women gathered in an empty lot in the Japanese camp.

"Do not forget the compassion of the Buddha. Why is the

Buddha compassionate? Because he knows we are weak and cannot attain enlightenment by ourselves. We cannot even do what is morally right. How many of you are perfect? Step forward if you are. Who has pure karma? Step forward if you do. Do you always do what is right? Of course not. Not even me and I am a priest. I am not a saint. Far from it! Are you a saint? You there, young man, yes, you, hold your head up and tell me you're perfect. Well? So you see, we must confront the truth about ourselves, we are weak human beings, no one here is a buddha. And that is why we put our faith in the Buddha, the Perfect One, the Enlightened One, the Compassionate One who made a vow to save us because we do not have the power to save ourselves. But we fool ourselves into thinking that we can make ourselves better, that we can change wrong into right. If we could do that, we don't need the Buddha. Do you understand what I'm saying? *We do not have the power to save ourselves.* Do you understand? We cannot improve our lives by taking matters into our own hands. Trust the Buddha."

He stopped, finally, and asked several persons individually if they trusted the Buddha to take care of them. Each person nodded. The priest waited and allowed the lesson to sink in. Trust the Buddha? Yes. Take matters into your own hands. No.

"Now, then, go back to work." The priest pressed his hands together and bowed and everyone responded with the same gesture. "*Na-man-da, na-man-da, na-man-da.*" He sucked in his breath. "*Na-man-da, na-man-da, na-man-da.*" He rubbed his rosary between his hands and stepped down. Shuzo took his place.

"My friends, you've heard the good priest. There is no point in taking matters into our own hands and trying to change what is beyond our power to change. Do not make the mistake of the workers on the other plantations. They have been thrown out of their homes. No roof over their head, no job, no pay. But here in Waialua, no one has been evicted. Goodale-san is not like the other managers. He is taking care of everyone. Trust him. Trust the Buddha. Go back to your homes, be grateful for your blessings and tomorrow, go back to work."

A young man stepped out of the crowd and faced Shuzo. Matsugoro Sato had heard enough of surrender. "Traitor," he said. "Whose side are you on, theirs or ours? You're not a plantation worker, so why are you sticking your butt into our business?" He took off his thick glasses and wiped the lenses with the loose ends of his shirt. He put his glasses back on and pointed a finger at Shuzo, then swung it like a rifle to the priest. "Look at them. They don't know what it's like to cut cane, dig ditches, feel the sting of the luna's whip. They want us to go back to work. You know why? Because they make their money off our backs. Blood suckers, that's what these two are. How dare you talk to us like this."

The priest dropped his eyes to the ground and fingered the beads of his lotus seed rosary. Matsugoro was a man who took matters into his own callused hands, which he never pressed together in deference to other men, no matter what their status, or to the Buddha. A graduate of his prefectural middle school, he could have gone on to one of the new universities in Tokyo, but family poverty forced him to Hawai'i, the heavenly country, where anyone could become rich. Poverty was also the reason for his membership in the newly formed Japanese Socialist Party and his experience with capitalists in Hawai'i strengthened his belief in Karl Marx, the only man worthy of reverence. Goodale and Shuzo exploited workers, and the priest, faking it as a holy man, was a drug dealer passing out opiates to the people.

"Don't let them fool you," Matsugoro said, "they have the upper hand over us and the only weapon we have is to go on strike. How else can we improve our wages?" The men nodded their heads and murmured.

Shuzo was still standing on the overturned crate and he held out his hand to quiet the men. "Matsugoro is right. A strike is a powerful weapon, the only one you have. It would be good if it always worked, but it doesn't. You can go on strike, sure, but what Matsugoro did not say is that the plantation has more money than you do and can outlast you in any strike."

"Not if we stay united together," Matsugoro interjected.

"For how long? A month? Two? Three?" Shuzo looked at a man in the front row and asked him, "How many months can you last without pay?"

Matsugoro went up to the man and put his hand on his shoulder. "If we stay united, we can help each other and force the plantation to give in."

"Never," said Shuzo, "they will never raise your wages because of a strike."

"You don't know that," Matsugoro countered.

"Yes, I do. The plantation has enough money to raise your wages and it might be persuaded, but not by a strike. It's not a question of money, but a matter of principle, not to give in to agitators like you."

"See, there!" said Matsugoro, pointing his finger at Shuzo again. "Taga-san, how can you be so sure of this?"

"Mr. Goodale told me."

Matsugoro stiffened his outstretched arm, paralyzed by Shuzo's frank and sudden confession of his collaboration with the enemy. Matsugoro stood there, trying to figure out how to respond to his opponent, who had just admitted what Matsugoro had been planning to force out into the open and expose. He couldn't believe that Shuzo would reveal his cooperation with the manager. "Mr. Goodale told you?"

"That's right, directly to my face. And that is why I'm telling you not to continue this strike, for your own sake, since it'll never get what you want."

Mynah birds squabbled among themselves in a mango tree. Complain, complain, that's all they did. They had their persuasions too and they stopped, as if they'd arrived at a settlement, temporary, for sure. "He's right," someone said quietly, "Taga-san's right." Matsugoro was ready to retort, but Shuzo continued.

"Don't strike, I tell you, go back to work. If you should

be so foolish as to stay on strike, remember that you'll be evicted, and the Higher Wages Association in town can no longer feed and house any more strikers. They've reached their capacity. Now, I've persuaded Mr. Goodale to let you stay in your homes for a little longer, but if you refuse to work, he'll throw you out." Shuzo paused, as everyone wondered how he could so blatantly be on Goodale's side and yet stand in their midst. "And if he does throw you out," Shuzo continued, "then I will house as many of you as can sleep on the floor of my restaurant and I'll feed all of you, for free."

"You'll what?" Matsugoro was totally baffled and tried to make sense of how the management stooge could help the strikers. But the men were not confused. Shuzo's offer convinced them that he was on their side, that his talk with Goodale was to find out the truth, that he was giving them a choice to be foolish or realistic. The sobered crowd dispersed slowly despite Matsugoro's attempt to recapture their attention and the priest stood by, astonished at the shifting sentiments and summoned just enough courage to urge them again, though not very audibly, to trust the Buddha.

◆

By the time Mr. Goodale arrived in his office the next day, the morning shifts were already at work at the mill and in the fields. Shuzo was waiting for him and Goodale ushered him in, inviting Shuzo to enter first.

"You continue to amaze me," Goodale said. "How'd you do it this time?"

"With your help. I told them you'd never give in and they believed me. They're not fools."

"I'm grateful, Mr. Taga. We're the only plantation back at work."

"For the moment, at least. Matsugoro Sato is not done yet, so don't be surprised if they change their minds and go back on strike. If they do, evict them immediately."

"Are you sure? I held off the last time and it worked."

"Throw them out and I'll take them in and if that doesn't make any sense to you, then you'll just have to trust me."

"All right, Mr. Taga. But you're right, it doesn't make sense. I'll trust you again on this one and I hope it's not a mistake."

◆

It took Matsugoro Sato a week to change their minds. They knew the consequences and were ready for it. Goodale evicted them immediately. Although the Higher Wages Association couldn't take them in, they resumed their strike on Shuzo's promise, which he kept, and they packed themselves into the restaurant, the rooms in the back, Hasumi's house, the parlor and veranda of his home by the plum forest. The rest pitched tents in the yard and they dug latrines in the back of the horse paddock. Shuzo served them meals in shifts, and Long Bridge —home of the wealthiest Japanese capitalist—was the headquarters, camp and staging ground for the strikers. Matsugoro was not at ease and he distrusted Shuzo's motives, but he could not discern any disadvantage and, besides, he had no choice. The strike dragged on for a month, then two and they heard reports from Honolulu about the dwindling supplies of food and money, but Shuzo cared for them as usual. Workers helped in the kitchen, served in the dining room, made repairs and small improvements, brought in vegetables from gardens planted in available spaces and delivered fish and seaweed. Restaurant Danger had never been busier, there being no better price than free, and impromptu singing contests and skits packed the House of Eternal Pleasure.

"How long are you willing to do this?" asked Matsugoro.

"For as long as it takes," replied Shuzo.

"Don't get me wrong, Taga-san, I grateful for what you're doing. But why are you doing this?"

"We're all Japanese, aren't we?" Shuzo excused himself to confer with Mariko Mahealani.

At the beginning of the third month, everyone knew it would not last much longer. The resources of the Higher

Wages Association were nearly depleted and rumors predicted a week or two at most. The Association leaders decided to hold out as long as possible, to jack up plantation losses, to show them the workers' willingness to sacrifice for justice. Shuzo went to see Matsugoro and told him to call off the strike at Waialua.

"I can't break from the Association," said Matsugoro. "We've got to stick together. It's a matter of principle."

"Of course," said Shuzo, "but think of the men. Let's face it, it's over and the sooner they get back to work, the less they lose."

Some of workers had already left for other jobs, others had broken rank and returned to the plantation payroll. Matsugoro was caught in his own contest between principle and practicality, and Shuzo sensed his vulnerability.

"You once accused me of making money off the workers' backs and you're now using the same backs to carry your empty principles. Don't exploit them for your purpose; call off the strike."

Matsugoro took off his glasses and wiped its lenses with a cotton hand towel and Shuzo knew to leave him alone. He turned to go, but Matsugoro stopped him. "I'm calling a meeting tonight," he said, "and I want you to be there."

They met in the empty lot with the mango tree, the public square of the Japanese camp. They tied lamps to cords attached to branches, just as they did for gambling or drinking or a late-night party. There was no wind to scatter the smoke, black with unburned carbon, heavy with the smell of kerosene. Matsugoro got on a box and announced what everyone already knew: the strike was over. No one argued with the decision to end their strike before the Association declared it over. The men turned to each other and expressed relief and their willingness to return to the same unjust wages. Better than nothing.

"Before you all go home tonight," said Matsugoro, "we should express our appreciation to Shuzo Taga for his generous support of our cause." The crowd broke into applause, almost as if it were a moment of victory, and a lone voice from the shadowy edge of the crowd shouted, "Taga-san, *banzai*!" Everyone raised both arms straight into the air and yelled out, "*Banzai! Banzai! Banzai!*"

Shuzo bowed in acknowledgment and for a fleeting moment, imagined himself at Port Arthur with General Nogi.

◆

It took the Higher Wages Association two weeks to follow Waialua's lead and the agitators spoke constantly about the matter of principle. The Planters' Association celebrated their victory, though they admitted their losses were heavy, but the cost, the members reminded themselves repeatedly, was worth the preservation of their principle. To put that principle further into actual practice, they sought and received a court order for the arrest of the leaders of the strike as dangerous disrupters of public order. Sheriff Brown arrived in Waialua with the constable wagon and arrested Matsugoro Sato. As he was led into the wagon, his glasses fell to the ground and though he asked for them back, the Sheriff drove him off without them.

◆

"My goodness," said William Goodale, as Shuzo entered his office, "we had the shortest strike of all. The other managers asked me how I did it and I told them it was because of you, how you supported the strike and then ended it. It made no sense to them, of course and I suppose I'm just as puzzled."

"I could have pushed for an earlier end, but I wanted to stretch out my support."

"But why put off what was going to happen anyway?"

"The longer I feed and house them, the greater their obligation and gratitude to me. They cheer me as their hero. And Matsugoro listen to me when I tell him end the strike."

"I must say I feel grateful to you as well, but I won't cheer you as my hero."

Shuzo laughed. "Of course not. But the short strike save you money?"

Goodale thought for a moment about the wisdom of a reply and then admitted, "A fair amount, yes, it did."

"Then you consider do me a favor? Two, in fact."

"It depends on what you want," said Goodale.

"First, I like you promise to raise their wages soon."

Goodale looked relieved. "Oh yes, that's easy. As I said before, the issue was never money. We just didn't want to be pressured by a bunch of radicals. My bookkeeper is already working on it. It'll be on our terms, of course. And your other request?"

"Use your influence and have Matsugoro Sato release without charges."

"Well, now, that I can't do. He's a troublemaker and must be taught a lesson."

"Of course," said Shuzo, "but prison not the way to do it. If you throw him into jail, he become a hero."

"You mean a martyr. Well, I see your point."

"If you want teach him lesson, on your terms, as you say, then promote him and pay him more. He make a good supervisor. The men respect him. Make him grateful to you and if you treat him well, he feel obligate and if you're lucky, he start to feel … what the word, you know when somebody owe you plenty but no can repay?"

"Indebted," said Goodale.

"Is that it? Then that's what you want, if you know what I mean."

"Oh, you Japanese…" said Goodale.

"Samuel Smiles talk about it."

Goodale didn't recognize the name and didn't care to ask. "I guess if it works for you, it'll work for me. All right, I'll see what I can do about Sato. Anything else you want?"

"That it." Shuzo got up to leave.

Goodale walked him to the door. "I do appreciate what you've done," he said, holding out his hand. They shook hands, unlikely partners closing a deal. "You clever bastard," Goodale said in farewell, and Shuzo took it as a compliment.

BABY SHUZO

T ENGOKU, *HEAVENLY COUNTRY.* FOR THE REST OF THE SIXTH year of the twentieth century, the world, by some miracle, was mostly at peace. Japan and America recognized each other's colonial claims in Korea and the Philippines, and the other major powers found no reason to be waging war, at least for the moment. Steamships flying a wide array of colors crowded into Honolulu Harbor, and the city pushed itself further into valleys, higher onto ridges with roads, houses, utility poles and water lines. In Waialua, the plantation opened new fields, a patchwork of swaying green and red dirt crisscrossed by roads and ditches, numbered or named, and wages went up, though not in proportion to the rise in production. Still, the laborers benefited, as did Goodale, from Shuzo's skill in balancing the manager's paternalism with the workers' sense of obligation, and both sides called him Boss, though Shuzo preferred something less reminiscent of thugs. After consulting Josephine, he suggested the title of Mediator, but no one adopted the word, and Josephine herself confessed later that it was three syllables too long.

The resurgent popularity of the restaurant during the strike proved to Shuzo that he could get along quite well without Mako and Chiyo. Mariko Mahealani took over as manager with ease and added to the menu dishes made from recipes collected from customers. Shuzo was relieved when Miki returned to live at the house, resumed her watching at the restaurant and, unbeknownst to him, quietly delighted in keeping her secret.

"Where's Miki?" Shuzo asked one morning, noticing her empty chair.

"She'll be here soon," replied Mariko Mahealani. "To stare at Kamaki, if he comes. She's so funny. She pretends like nothing's happening, but it's so obvious that she's madly in love with him."

◆

Miki was the first to spot the bundle. She had been out in the yard early in the morning, long before the first cooks arrived. She loved the cool air at dawn, the dew soaking her slippered feet. Kamaki was an early riser as well and she imagined them to be the only two people awake in Waialua. If he were at Uncle Hila's, he would be feeding and milking the goats and watching the changing colors creep over the mountain. As she passed the back entrance to the kitchen, she saw the blanket move and heard short, soft cries.

The baby's eyes were closed and it yawned from hunger. One hand was free, five miniature fingers, pink and perfect. She picked up the baby and it started to cry, demanding to be fed. Miki walked quickly to the house and nestled the baby safely on the couch and went into the kitchen to find something to feed it. She found a bowl of leftover poi, mixed a little sugar and lots of goat milk into it and went back to the veranda. The baby was complaining loudly, such a strong voice for a tiny creature, and Miki dipped her fingertip into the liquid and lightly touched its open mouth. The baby sucked on her finger and Miki smiled, amused by its tickling gums.

Awakened by the crying, Shuzo came out of his bedroom. Only when he walked out into the veranda did he see Miki kneeling by the couch, finger feeding the baby.

"What's going on?" he asked and Miki looked back at him, surprised that he should have to ask. "Whose baby is that?"

Miki shrugged. "Found it by the kitchen."

Shuzo saw a corner of a piece of paper sticking out from a fold in the blanket and pulled it out.

Birth Certificate
Territory of Hawai'i
Name of Mother: *Chiyo Taira*   Name of Father: *Shuzo Taga*
Race: *Okinawan*   Race: *Japanese*
Name of Child: *Shuzo*

The vital information was written in a florid hand and the certificate was signed by the attending physician and sealed by the director of the Board of Health.

"Bitch. She's really out to get me. Look at this, Miki. Can you believe it? Chiyo claims I'm the father of her child. She's nuts. She's even named it Shuzo. The nerve."

"Baby Shuzo," said Miki. She picked it up and stroked its silky black hair. "Baby Shuzo."

"Don't say that. That's not his name."

Miki wondered why he was contradicting himself. Didn't he just say the baby's name was Shuzo? And he was reading from the birth certificate. Shuzo reached for the baby, but Miki held it tighter and turned away from him.

"It's not your child," Shuzo said. "Give it to me."

"Is it yours?"

"Damn it, give it to me. We've got to send it back."

"Where?"

"Somewhere, anywhere. Maybe an orphanage if we can't find Chiyo. It's hers. And Mako's."

"She doesn't want it," said Miki. "I'll take it."

"And if people ask if the child is yours?

"It's mine. I'm the mother. Like Aunty Josephine."

"Like Josephine," said Shuzo slowly. "Like Josephine. Hmm, Miki, I think you've just solved my problem. So you'd adopt this orphan baby, whom you found and nobody knows who the parents are. And really, we don't know. It could be anybody's baby and this birth certificate is full of lies anyway. It's no good." Shuzo crumpled the birth certificate and threw it in the trash box. "I'll ask Josephine about raising babies. I'm sure she knows more about them than we do."

Miki pressed her face close to the child's. "Baby Shuzo."

"Stop saying that. We've got to find a different name before Hasumi comes."

◆

Josephine smiled and said something in Hawaiian when Shuzo asked her to help with caring for the baby. She brought over suckling bottles with rubber teats, hand-me-downs from one of the women at St. Michael's, and Kamaki came over with fresh goat's milk every day. Watching Kamaki help Miki with the milk and bottles made her feel like a grandmother and Miki never seemed so normal. A wife and mother, if only in name.

◆

"I can't believe how smoothly things are going," said the cat.

"I've never been happier," said Miki.

"Did you ever think it would turn out this way?"

"No," said Miki. "It was a mess, everyone acting so crazy. I had to make it better."

"You're right. Ever since Mako died, things have been going smoothly."

"Shuzo shouldn't have ordered Mako to go after Kamaki," said Miki.

"Well, Mako never caught him and Shuzo got distracted by the strike and getting ready for Hasumi."

Miki clipped a small barrette on her hair and adjusted its position.

"All set?" said the cat. "Ready for work?"

"Maybe I should take this off," said Miki, removing the barrette. "Don't want people to think I'm making myself pretty for Kamaki."

"Got to keep it a secret," said the cat. "Like what you did to Mako."

"Oh, no one will find out. Unless you blab about it."

"I'm always on your side. You know that."

"I was very careful," said Miki. "Everyone in the kitchen had gone out to watch the electric lights go on, so no one saw me squeeze two livers on the fugu. But it was supposed to have been for Shuzo. I thought he was going to be the Chosen Man."

"So how will you get his heart back?"

"I took his baby and he likes me now."

"So smooth, Miki, you're so smooth. Just like how everything is going now."

"It'll get better once Hasumi arrives."

"Oh?"

"Think of it. Mako's dead, Chiyo is gone and Shuzo will have Hasumi. No one left to be jealous of Kamaki and me. We can stop being naupaka and live together like a normal husband and wife. And we'll have our own children."

"Hmm," said the cat, starting to purr. "What about Baby Shuzo?"

"I'll give it to Hasumi."

"But you told Shuzo you'd keep it as your own."

"Look, be reasonable. Put yourself in Hasumi's place. If you came to Long Bridge and found out your husband is living in a house with a woman who has a baby, who'd you think's the father?"

"Oh, I get it. She'd think you're Shuzo's lover."

"And she'd hate me. I don't need that. I'd tell her the truth about Shuzo and Chiyo. She'll be upset, but what's she going to do? Abandon her husband's child. Besides, it's only right. Baby Shuzo belongs to them. Chiyo doesn't want the child."

"You know Shuzo will deny being the father."

"He'll try. But I'll give Hasumi this." Miki opened up the crumpled birth certificate. Signed and sealed. "And she will do her duty."

"Oh, Miki," laughed the cat. "You're so smooth!"

"Tengoku," said Miki. "Hawai'i is truly Tengoku."

HEAVENLY COUNTRY

Sumiko cried at the Iwakuni station and Gombei steadied himself with his cane. Hasumi put her hand on his shoulder, then turned to give Sumiko a hug. The embrace would have seemed strange, especially in public, had it not been for the long dress Hasumi wore, buttoned in front over her breasts, cinched at the waist and flowing over her hips down to her ankles. Her long arms were elegantly sleeved, cuffed at the wrists with a flair of lace. Sumiko didn't care what other people might think. Hasumi could have been in a kimono, but she was a modern woman heading out into the modern world. "Please," she said, "take good care of yourself. I will miss you so much."

"Thank you for everything you've done for me, Mother. I'll write as often as I can. Take care of Father. And don't worry about us."

Sumiko nodded with her sobs and wiped her nose with her handkerchief, the one Hasumi had given her, embroidered with tiny roses.

"All aboard!"

Hasumi picked up her leather hand case. Two larger suitcases and a trunk had been loaded by a porter into the baggage section. She dabbed her eyes with her fingertips and made a long, low and formal bow. It was more than Sumiko could bear and she turned away as Hasumi stepped onto the train. Gombei hurried up to her and caught her by the shoulder. She turned and saw his worry.

"Miki," he said. "Be careful. You see, at Bungo Bridge…"

"No, no, Father, you do not have to talk about the past. Mother explained it all so please don't worry about it. Everything will be all right. Take good care of Mother … and yourself. Sayonara, Father."

Hasumi let go of the handhold, placed both hands in front of her, and made a deep bow.

◆

"Are you getting off in Hawai'i or going on to San Francisco?"

Hasumi turned around and was surprised to see a young American woman asking her destination in flawless Japanese. Her auburn hair was thick, falling in curly strands in the wind blowing over the deck of the *S. S. Siberia*, the largest luxury liner in the service of the Pacific Mail Steamship Company. Hasumi tightened the scarf around her head and felt the top button of her blouse to make sure it had not been undone by the stiff breeze.

"Oh," she managed to say. "Hawai'i. I'm going to Hawai'i."

"Visiting family, perhaps?"

"Ah, well, yes."

"Excuse me for intruding, but my name is Elaine, Elaine Waterhouse. I'm going to Hawai'i as well."

"How nice," Hasumi said. "Your Japanese is excellent."

"Thank you. I grew up in Tokyo. My parents are missionaries at the Mitaka church. I'll be teaching at the Damien School in Honolulu and I'm worried about keeping up my Japanese. I hope you don't mind my intrusion."

"Not at all. My name is Hasumi Taga. I'm joining my husband in Hawai'i. Maybe we could exchange language lessons. Not that you need it, your Japanese is better than mine. But I want to learn English as quickly as I can."

"Wonderful! Let's do it. Shall we start with dinner tonight? I'm traveling alone and it would be nice."

"Good. I'll meet you at the dining room entrance at, say, seven o'clock."

Back in her private cabin, Hasumi thought of writing to Sumiko, but she was too excited to settle her thoughts on paper. The first day out of Yokohama and already she had an American friend. This is how it'll be in Hawai'i, new friends, new places, new languages. Oh Shuzo, I'll do everything to be a good wife. I'm so lucky to be married to you. How many women can have this kind of adventure, going to my own Treasure Island, but without the pirates. Already I feel so fortunate, you've worked so hard to give me this. I can't imagine what it must have been like, traveling in steerage, working long hours in the cane fields, saving your money, not drinking or gambling it away, until you had enough for a restaurant. And a theater too! Music, dancing, plays! We'll dress up for performances and I'll place my hand in your arm and we'll walk from our new house to have dinner at our restaurant and stay on for the stage performance. I know a Kabuki group in Yamaguchi and maybe we can arrange for them to come. What'll you do with the old house, with no one in it? Maybe we can rent it out, add to our income. But you're already so rich, so well-known. Mother said you know the governor, the police, important business leaders. I'll learn English quickly, from Elaine and others, I'm sure. Mother said your English is excellent. Wouldn't it be fun for both of us to speak English to each other, to our children? Let's have a large family. Father will be so happy about that. We'll name our first son after you. Baby Shuzo.

Hasumi glanced at the silver clock her father had given her as a going away present. Enough time for a nap, if she could relax enough to sleep and then get ready for dinner with Elaine.

Tengoku. Now I understand why they call Hawai'i the heavenly country.

 George Tanabe earned a Ph.D. in Japanese religions (esp. Buddhism) from Columbia University and taught in the Department of Religion at the University of Hawai'i. His academic books have been published by university presses at Harvard, Princeton, Columbia and Hawai'i. For promoting cultural understanding between Japan and the United States, he was awarded the Japanese Foreign Minister's Award in 2007 and the Imperial Order of the Rising Sun in 2012. Since his retirement in 2006, he has written four novels.

tanabebooks.com

Made in the USA
Columbia, SC
17 September 2024

42459204R00209